Prince of Israel

Prince of Israel

A NOVEL ON BAR-KOKBA'S UPRISING AGAINST ROME

by Elias Gilner

They were swifter than eagles,
They were stronger than lions.
—II Samuel 1:23

EXPOSITION PRESS • NEW YORK

FIRST EDITION

Copyright, 1952, by Elias Gilner
Published by the Exposition Press Inc.
386 Fourth Avenue, New York 16, N. Y.
Designed by Morry M. Gropper
Manufactured in the United States of America
Consolidated Book Producers, Inc.
Library of Congress catalog card number: 52-11665
475

To Violet, the girl who stood with me under a canopy on a sunlit roof against the background of the hills of Jerusalem, and who has since stood by me through thick and thin, mostly thin.

The Triumph of Bar-Kokba's Cause

Jerusalem is the only city in the world that has the word "peace" woven into its name. Peace was the cherished dream of the city's founder, King David. In naming his capital the City of Peace he expressed the innermost yearning of the soul of Israel, his people. That was three thousand years ago. Since then, in freedom and in exile, Israel has striven for peace steadfastly but futilely, and suffered for it immeasurably.

Besides being emblematic of peace, Jerusalem, during the centuries of Jewish rule, became the symbol of the whole of Israel, the land as well as the people. For in that city resided Israel's moral essence, its spirit, its soul, its heart, the lofty imponderables which made the Israelites different from the heathen and exposed them to rancor, fury and insatiable hate. The whole of the Land of Israel might be under the heel of the conqueror, but if Jerusalem still held out, Israel was intact. To go to the Holy City was to "go up," to rise (laalot). One went there for his spiritual uplift; to discard the gross, the sinful, the unseemly; to become worthy of communion with his Maker.

It is for that reason that the city was always defended by its rightful owners with such fierce courage and unprecedented devotion. As the first mayor of modern Jerusalem, I was privileged to administer the city before and during the baleful siege of five years ago, and I saw that courage displayed equally by soldier and civilian, housewife and nurse. In the history of sieges, there is little comparable to the perseverance and gallantry I then witnessed, unless it be the feats of heroism and endurance of Bar-Kokba's war against Rome, so movingly and forcefully depicted in *Prince of Israel* by my old friend Elias Gilner.

The emblem of modern Jerusalem adopted by the Municipal Council, under my chairmanship, perpetuates the established tradition of the city. The Lion of Judah stands guard on the city walls against the background of the Wailing Wall, and this symbol of self-defense is encircled by an olive branch.

I am glad *Prince of Israel* has been written. After reading it one understands better the significance of Israel's eternal struggle, the inevitability of Bar-Kokba's rebellion and the unavoidability of the eventual triumph of his cause, the cause of freedom. One also understands better why brave men, whoever and wherever they may be, die for freedom.

After reading Mr. Gilner's book one also comes to realize that no fight for a great cause is ever really lost, that somewhere along the milestones of eternity it comes marching in victorious. One thousand, eight hundred and thirteen years after Bar-Kokba and his stalwarts laid down their lives, their cause triumphed through the emergence of the State of Israel and the rise of the new Jerusalem.

DANIEL AUSTER

Contents

Reflections on the Threshold

This is the story of a war for freedom and national independence; of an epic struggle between two religious philosophies, two ways of life—that of Judea six decades after the destruction of the Jerusalem Temple and pagan Rome under Emperor Hadrian. It is the story of an oppressed people, who, no longer able to endure the crushing weight of the conqueror, challenged his terrifying might and rose, scantily armed, hastily organized, woefully outnumbered. Moved by faith and the will to live, the rebels defeated the oppressor and attained a brief period of freedom.

This is also the story of two courageous men: Shemon* Bar-Kokba, the leader of the physical war, and Rabbi Akiba ben-Joseph, the spiritual head of his people.

This story was conceived and written in the bleak days of World War Two and was partly rewritten as the State of Israel was re-emerging.

What impelled the author to write it was the striking resemblance of the drama enacted eighteen centuries ago and the events of the last decade. Somehow he felt that the final curtain of the drama had not yet come down and humanity could still write a just and happy ending to many acts of stark tragedy.

The causes of the struggle then and now were strikingly similar. The bearers of an enlightened and ethical way of life were fighting the code and the bearers of brute force, enslavement for gain and disregard of other men's human rights. The society of imperial Rome, which thrived on conquest and slave labor, approved and perpetuated by pseudogods, of which the emperors were the most vicious, could not tolerate the existence of a people that introduced the *Sabbath,* a weekly day of rest; the *Shemita,* the liberation of slaves every seventh year; the *Jubilee,* the law against the concentration of wealth which required that every fiftieth year immovable property acquired for gainful purposes be returned to the original owners. Above all, Hadrian's society could not permit the existence of a people that advocated

---

* Shemon (*She-món*) is the original, Hebrew form of the name Simon.

the tenet of treating—loving—one's neighbor as oneself. The empire could not exist without violating its neighbors' rights and seizing their territories.

Some eighteen hundred years later Hitler set out to annihilate Jewry for identical reasons. While he was destroying the Jews as a people other forces strove to prevent Jewry from re-establishing itself as a nation in its ancient homeland. The combined strength of the hostile forces appeared to be more powerful than those of Hadrian's Rome. But they failed. Jewry lives, the State of Israel is here, and Jerusalem, the capital of King David, is shaking off her age-old shackles, striving to fulfill her destiny as symbolized by her name.

The freedom of Jerusalem and Judea under Bar-Kokba was short-lived. Only two years of definite independence are indicated by ancient coins. The State of Israel is well into its fifth year, growing stronger and showing every promise of a long and impressive life. Why did Bar-Kokba's victories end in defeat and why will the State of Israel survive?

Bar-Kokba failed because Rome dominated the major part of the then known world and the little state stood against Rome's might alone and friendless. Even the Jews who lived in various parts of Hadrian's empire could do nothing to help their brothers in the Land of Israel for fear of being accused of treason. Only at the beginning of the uprising did the Jews of Alexandria and Rome attempt to help.

The State of Israel will survive because the world, however imperfect it is, however far it still is from the Law of God as interpreted by Isaiah, is no longer a world of unbridled marauders. There is a concord of nations, among whom Israel has numerous friends, including the most powerful of them all—the United States of America. There are loving and helpful brothers in many friendly countries. And important non-Jewish religious leaders see in the re-emergence of Israel the fulfillment or the beginning of the fulfillment of a divine prophecy.

And so, to the anguished query of Shemon's widow, as she went into exile: "Will redemption ever come?" one may venture to answer solemnly: "Redemption will come."   E. G.

Part One

The Limit of Endurance

Chapter One

A spring, hidden from the road below by jutting rocks, cascaded gently above the cavern. Evening shadows were rapidly engulfing the purple mists over the Hills of Ephraim and the Galilean range, farther north. Low over the sea, several miles to the west, a sweep of blood-tinted gold was the day's last challenge to the approaching night.

Shemon leaped from the cooling water to the cave where his clothes lay. He shook the drops from his thick bronze locks and reddish beard, straightened his powerful body, swung his arms up and down and jumped about for a while. Then he donned a pair of ankle-length pants, a tunic and a fringed ritual vest, girded his waist with a sash and, attaching to it a short Roman sword, stepped into the cavern. Leaving his robe and sandals in a niche, he went toward a dim light filtering through the gloom.

The lighted section of the cave was large and high, ventilated through inconspicuous holes at the other end. Here, where, during the anti-Trajan uprising, rebels had assembled to plot against Rome, lived Daniel ben-Ezer, Shemon's uncle. In a carpeted area illuminated by a menorah were a low table and a bed of skins, where old Ben-Ezer lay. Dried figs, unleavened bread, medicinal herbs and a parchment scroll cluttered the table, and an earthen water jar and cups stood on a wooden form beside the bed.

"Peace be with you," Shemon greeted cheerfully. "I'm a day late but I bear good tidings."

The old man stirred and muttered unintelligibly; his usual affectionate response was missing. Shemon hastened to the old rebel's bedside. This man meant more than an uncle to him. He was savior and hero, father and priest, mentor and friend; one who had taught him stoicism and perseverance, love of freedom, contempt of pain, and above all, the Law of God in a world governed by primitive passions and deified beasts.

Daniel ben-Ezer's eyes were closed. Strands of thin white

hair, straggling from beneath his skull cap, fell across his high forehead. His earlocks and gray beard were tangled and he breathed with difficulty. Shemon touched his uncle's brow. It was alarmingly hot. He felt bewildered and helpless. "Can I do anything for my uncle?" he called with deep anxiety.

Daniel opened his eyes. With an effort he shook his head and whispered, "Drink."

Shemon brought water, applied a wet cloth to his uncle's head and waited.

After an interval Ben-Ezer spoke feebly: "I'm on my way, son. My work, blessed be Jehovah, is done. I've saved you for Israel." He paused for breath. "You've begun the great work, but the road is long and hard. Do not walk it alone. Scorn not a wise guide—Rabbi Akiba. Read the scroll. Go to Bnai Brak. . . ." The old man, gasping for breath, stopped. Shemon gave him more water. After a while Ben-Ezer resumed: "Bury me nearby. Tell no one where my grave is, so foes won't desecrate it. Come closer."

Shemon bent over the bloodless, emaciated face. The dying man attempted to raise his right hand in benediction but succeeded only in moving a few trembling fingers. "May the Lord bless you and keep you, Shemon, my brother's son. May you be the liberator of your people."

He was shaken by a spasm of violent coughing, which suddenly ceased. Shemon grasped his uncle's hand, but there was no response. The end of Daniel's journey had come. A fugitive from Roman persecution for his part in the anti-Trajan insurrection fifteen years before, he had lived and died a recluse, true to his faith and purpose.

In the morning Shemon cleansed his uncle's body as prescribed by law, shrouded him in the white ceremonial robe which had lain in a cedar chest, buried him some distance away from the cavern and built a small pyramid of boulders over the grave. Then he returned to the cave and rent his garments as a mourner would for his parent.

There was a void in his heart. In the shadow of his loss

values seemed to fall and events shrank in significance. Shemon's perilous exploit of the day before, which had loomed large in his mind and was to have cheered his uncle, had now receded into the background.

As he lay brooding, memories came trooping over the span which linked the present with the fatal night in Ludd fifteen years before.

Shemon was then ten years old. His father was a wealthy, highly respected woolgrower and communal leader; his mother was known for her beauty and hospitality. Both came of distinguished lineage, and the family lived in a spacious, well-ordered house. They had belonged to that school of thought which advocated mingling with enlightened pagans and copying the names and dress of the Greco-Romans, and such of their ways as were not incompatible with the fundamentals of Judaism. They had believed that to remove external barriers meant to pave the way to sympathetic understanding. Thus, little Shemon's father, Elisha, had been known as Artemion; his older brother Daniel, as Julianus; and Shemon himself, as Romulus. The boy had been taught not only the lore and customs of Israel, but also the languages, manners and sports of the foreign rulers. The greed and rapacity of the last years of Trajan's regime had jolted these Israelites out of their delusion, however, sending most of them back to the language and ways of their own people and throwing many of them into open rebellion.

Then the fateful night came. That evening Shemon went to bed as usual, with the blessings and kisses of his mother. In the afternoon his father had gone somewhere in great haste; his mother seemed upset, and Uncle Daniel, a widower who lived with them, was nowhere to be seen. Toward evening excited men, hiding things under their robes, had gathered in the street. There were shouts: "Quietus is coming! . . . Fight the Moor!"

In the middle of the night Shemon was awakened by a frightful din. In the street men were shouting and running, hoofs clattered on the cobblestones and a red glow tinged the sky. In the adjacent room his younger brother and sister were crying for their mother: *"Imma!"* From the ground floor rose his father's voice, breathless and hoarse, and the house was shaking from a terrific pounding.

Shemon sat frightened, unable to move. Then a pointed, glittering object came crashing through the window and embedded itself in the door. He was about to yell when a dreadful scream—to him, sharper than a dagger—cut through him. His mother! He ran for the door. A burning torch, hurtling through the broken pane, fell on his bed. In horror he rushed out of the room. He looked about him in bewilderment, for tongues of flame were leaping from many places—worst of all, from the closed door of the children's room. They were no longer crying. Suddenly his uncle appeared at the burning door. He wrapped his cloak about his head and attempted to dash through the flames. But he failed.

Shemon had barely managed to catch his breath, when he found himself in his uncle's powerful arms. In an instant he was downstairs, in the rear end of the house. A pull, and a trap door opened. Before going down into the murk of the cellar Shemon caught a glimpse of his father, battling helmeted men in the front doorway, and of his mother, sprawling nearby on the floor. He began to sob but Uncle Daniel quieted him. A few seconds later another trap door was lifted and they were out in a dark lane. Uncle paused and looked back at the burning house, a bundle on his back, Shemon in his arms.

They came to a palm grove where a camel was tethered. Shemon remembered being robed in a large, ill-fitting garment and lifted onto the back of the camel. The ride was fantastic. They hurried through villages where men in long blankets made queer motions but said not a word. They passed people on donkeys; hid in the woods. At night they traveled over narrow paths in high mountains. They stayed in some villages where strangers asked questions and threw ashes on their heads while women wailed. After some days and nights they reached a friendly hamlet, Kozib by name—Kozib above Acca, in Galilee. Here, after being taken to a bathhouse and a synagogue, they were given food and a shed to live in. Uncle Daniel said it was a good place to stay, for escape was possible by land or sea. So they stayed there for two years.

Daniel ben-Ezer was a learned man. Though never ordained, he had the erudition of a rabbi. As a former advocate of a closer understanding with the Romans, he knew Greek and Latin, which had also been advantageous in his foreign-trade establishment. Shortly after settling in Kozib he took Shemon into his arms and told him that he would teach him the Law as well as more of the tongues of Israel's foes. Shemon must be prepared to serve his people well, for the Lord assuredly had chosen him for a mission. Was he not the only member of his family to be spared? Shemon would come to understand in the years ahead. Meanwhile, every day the boy was to rehearse in his heart: *Revere God, love Israel, hate Edom*. He, Daniel, had vowed to hate Edom to his last breath.

Within the limitations of his circumstances Daniel proceeded to put his program into effect. Save on the days when he sailed with fishermen into the open sea and the neighbors looked after the boy, Daniel devoted his time to Shemon. Besides tutoring him, he played games with him and whenever he could spare a drachma from his meagre earnings, he bought little gifts. Shemon loved his uncle for his strength, gruff affection, contagious laughter at games and patience. In their two years at Kozib, Shemon never saw Daniel ill-tempered except once, when Eliezer of Modin, an uncle on Shemon's maternal side, visited them. On that occasion the two men argued about some mysterious treasure.

They lived in the house of Ada, a widow, and her fishermen sons.

As Shemon looked back on his life in Kozib, he saw himself as a restless, curious, pugnacious boy, and strangely enough, somewhat of a dreamer. In the early months of his sojourn there, when his uncle's injunctions were strict and Ada's eye vigilant, he stuck to the shed, orchard and yard and divided his time among his studies, moping over the loss of his family and longing for Daniel's return. But later, when his uncle and Ada became less exacting, he began, in his guardian's absence, to slip away.

At first his excursions were limited to the villa of Sagbion, the local Croesus and head archon, and to the public buildings— the council house, the synagogue and the bathhouse. Sagbion's two-story mansion, with its colonnades, garden and massive wall, brought memories of his own home in Ludd. Lost in a trance, Shemon would often stand before the mansion, oblivious of time, gazing with dim, nostalgic eyes. The bathhouse, on the other hand, was a source of amusement, a laundry of human beings. It was fun to see big men emerging with water still dripping from their beards and earlocks; or women with flushed faces hurrying away from the other side of the building as they pulled their kerchiefs over their wet hair and knotted them under their chins. The council house presented little of interest, as children were barred on the rare occasions when the elders conferred or a rabbi sat in judgment. But the synagogue, which served as a schoolhouse, was a place of great attraction. Here the boys rehearsed beautiful prayers, chanted psalms and portions of the Law and, at given periods, played games. Here, too, Shemon could hear the familiar yet ever stirring tales about David and Solomon, Gideon and Samson, the Hasmoneans and Hannah and her seven sons, and other stories about Judea's and Israel's heroism in the wars against the Syrian Greeks and Rome. The synagogue was most fascinating at sundown, when a chance red glow tinted the somber, vaulted ceiling or the tablet of the Ten Commandments above the holy ark, as shadows below rested upon the wooden benches and the swaying, whispering, sighing worshippers. The mystery of the God for whom his uncle and so many other good men and women had sacrificed and endured deepened, but He became more acceptable. The God who, surrounded by seraphim and angels, sat in Heaven, the Seventh Heaven, on a glittering throne of gold and precious stones, was terribly, terribly far; but the God who mingled with the shadows, listened to the sighs of His children and cast an awe-inspiring glow on His commandments, a celestial glow that everyone could see, was near and almost real.

The public buildings at the southern end of the settlement stood off the highway which led to the Galilean Hills and Sepphoris, Tiberias and Jotapata—wonderful cities about whose struggles, triumphs, downfalls and recoveries Uncle Daniel had much to tell. At the other end of Kozib there was a well and, some distance away, a fishpond. These, too, claimed Shemon's interest. It was absorbing to watch the filled pails and vats come up from the mysterious depths of the pits, or to gape at women with rolled-up skirts laundering clothes, or to see a young mother offer her breast to her baby's eager mouth. What brought water into the depths of the earth and milk into a woman's breast was a source of wonderment. No less fascinating was the teeming life in the kingdom of fish, where a variety of specimens darted about like boys at play.

Between Kozib and the sea there rolled stadia and stadia of dunes. Eventually Shemon succumbed to their lure. Gripped by fear and excitement, he went roaming through the heavy, scorching sand, sinking ankle-deep into it and losing sight of human habitations as well as the sea, his ultimate goal. Upon reaching it he was amply rewarded. He found there majesty and wilderness; a quiet which was alive; a solitude which was peopled with nonhuman presences; the sun in the thrall of the deep; leagues of rolling, dipping, leaping yet never-escaping fire; seaweed stretching farther than the eye could see; fish writhing in the surf; lizards darting about or basking in the sun's blinding glare; sea gulls preying over the flaming waters, and occasionally a jackal or a fox skulking in the distance. God's creations, God's wonders. Freedom and power and beauty. And no fear—he liked that best. When he grew up he would be very powerful and fear no one. Not even the Edomites, with their two-edged swords. Not even their centurions. Was he not already the strongest of all his playmates?

Not infrequently he lay on the shore speculating about his future, thinking of the things his uncle expected him to do when he grew up, and wondering how he could do them.

Uppermost in his thoughts were the people of Kozib and their troubles. The men, grim, strong, black-bearded and black-robed, smelled of the soil or of fish, spoke little and sang rarely. Only on the Sabbath, at the noon and evening meals, did they chant songs about their wives, their children, Sabbath the Queen and the glory of the Lord—cheerful words with mournful tunes. The women, neat and comely in their Sabbath attire, served the modest meals, fed the young brood, gazed admiringly at their men and chanted with them. They were olive-skinned, cherry-eyed, tall and lean, these women of Kozib, and their faces seemed veiled in shadows. They knew little rest. They washed and scrubbed and baked and spun; they tended the orchards, bore and reared children and mended their men's clothing and fishing nets. But few could boast of knowing no want or fear, for the Roman soldier and the tax collector were ever upon them. Yet on the Sabbath they were able to smile and chant. The periodic descent of tax collectors and soldiers upon Kozib was at times the subject of altercations and fights between Shemon and the other boys. He would speak harshly of the big black-bearded men for their failure to drive the robbers out. The youngsters stood up for their fathers. They would unite against Shemon, scratch him, tear his tunic, knock him down. But he never fled. It was some of them who, bleeding and crying, ran to their mothers.

Such was Shemon's life when Trajan died and his mantle passed to Hadrian. Lucius Quietus, the Moor, was executed for treason and Tinneus Rufus was given the Moor's office, the procuratorship of Judea. The political atmosphere cleared slightly. Plundering in the guise of taxing temporarily ceased. The harshest edicts were suspended; life and property were treated with more respect; an old, grievous Greco-Judean dispute was settled equitably, and rumors persisted that the "good emperor" had promised to restore the Temple in Jerusalem.

The easing of Judea's bonds, however, affected Daniel and his ward but little. No amnesty had been granted to rebels. The eyes of the law were as searching and keen as ever, and eventually Kozib came within their focus. Forewarned, uncle and nephew fled into the Galilean hills. Their kinsman, Pappus, who had been sentenced to the gallows, had his sentence commuted to servitude through the influence of powerful Egyptian friends, who subsequently manumitted him and brought him to Alexandria.

Trying years followed. The pair lived in caves, in rag-and-skin tents and in the open, depending on the season. They subsisted on carobs, dates and pomegranates, and occasionally on catches of Lake Kinnereth fish. Once in a while Daniel secured food from neighboring villages. Few denied him help, for some had heard of his past and others regarded him as a godly man. But whenever he attempted to talk sedition, ears were deaf. At times uncle and ward crossed the lake to Sussita and Kfar Haroob in Transjordan. In Kfar Haroob, a fortified village once razed by the Romans, Shemon struck up a friendship with two brothers, Asher and Noah, youngsters slightly older than he. They were orphans, carpenter's apprentices, and their knowledge of the Law was scant. What brought them and Shemon together was their uncommon physical strength and a similarity in their pasts. The parents of the brothers, too, had been killed by the Romans. Shemon grew particularly fond of Asher, the older, a lad in his fifteenth year who resembled him in his directness and intrepidity.

Every day except the Sabbath uncle and nephew devoted hours to reading a variety of parchments and to conversations in foreign tongues. The rest of the time Shemon was free to roam the hills and even to hunt, a sport not encouraged by the rabbis. In his encounters with animals and reptiles Shemon became quick, resourceful and hard, and skillful with the knife and bow. At the age of fourteen he was as tall as his uncle, a man of imposing stature; a year later, two fists taller.

When Shemon announced that he would go down to the coast to work and learn the ways of Edom, Daniel did not object. He had prepared his nephew for the test. It was agreed that Shemon would go to Acca; if he failed there, he was to try Caesarea and Apollonia. Daniel would move to the nearest hills to maintain contact.

Shemon spent four years in harbors and Roman forts. He worked as a porter, stableboy and smith's apprentice. He cleaned equipment and ran errands for officers and men and, gaining their confidence, was permitted to ride idle horses and to participate in games and minor contests. He did not stay in one spot too long and used his early childhood name, Romulus, which his coppery hair and straight nose made plausible. He became expert in the habits, sports and warcraft of his overlords, and a devil in horsemanship. A wrestling match with a legionary at the Emmaus citadel in Judea concluded this phase of his adventures. The soldier suffered a broken neck and failed to rise from the mat. Shemon deemed it imprudent to wait for Roman justice. He stole a cavalry horse and rejoined his uncle, who promptly dispatched him to Andreas, a kinsman in Alexandria. Andreas, a banker and exporter who made periodic trips abroad, took Shemon to Rome and placed him with influential coreligionists in the Subura district, on the left bank of the Tiber. For three years Shemon divided his time between the Roman War School on the nearby Campus Martius, the hall of gymnastics called the Plethrium and the Suburesian house of study maintained by the Israelites of the district.

Upon returning to his uncle in the Samarian Hills, Shemon found that the situation in the country had again deteriorated. Hadrian, firm on his throne, was too preoccupied with fashioning his juridical and military codes, with the construction of lavish baths and temples, with his cultural hobbies and, later, with his homosexual indulgences to pay any particular attention to his remote Judean province. The expected annual revenue flowed in; no disorders were reported; no additional troops were required. So there the matter ended. Rufus was discharging his duties well.

But Rufus, after more than a decade in office, became despotic and grasping. Under spurious pretexts he burdened the impoverished country with more and more levies, principally for his own coffers. Those unable to pay were robbed of their livestock or were forced to mortgage their groves or vineyards and eventually lost them. Local officials became corrupt and overbearing; women feared to leave their villages; starving men took to crime and the highways became unsafe. Resentment and despair were again taking hold, and though the memory of Quietus' savagery lingered, ears were no longer deaf to seditious utterances.

Since Shemon's return from Rome his only diversion had been Leveah, a lioness he had reared from cubhood. He had trained her to let him ride her, and had dreamt that some day he would come storming into Rufus' palace mounted on her back. His disappointment was bitter when one morning he had found her cage broken and empty.

His search for her was futile. Weeks later he learned that a Roman patrol had killed a lioness. For a time he brooded over his loss, but Daniel's gentle chiding restored Shemon's equilibrium.

One day uncle and nephew stood in the sun's glare on a ledge above their cavern. The aging man looked up with pride at his nephew and said, "Now you are as I wanted you to be: good to behold, mighty of limb and well instructed for war and for peace. What will you do?"

"Will my uncle let me think?"

"That I will."

Shemon took his time. In the solitude of the unpeopled hills he lay staring for hours at the untarnished blue sky, hatching schemes. Ideas bright with promise would flash in his mind and as rapidly fade. To wage a successful war one needed men, arms and supplies and, for the initial steps, treasure. Should these be obtained through brigandage, or was there another way?

"If I had money," he said to his uncle, "I would go up to Kfar Haroob, speak with Asher and Noah and gather about us men who hate Edom as I do and who fear nothing. These I would teach to ride and fight. Then we would lay our plans."

Daniel's eyes twinkled. "You shall have the money," he said mysteriously. "Kfar Haroob," he added, "is a good beginning. From there we can go to Galilee, where the misery is great and people will listen with open ears; and Syria, where there are horses, will be close."

"True," Shemon agreed, "but where will the money come from?"

"Bide your time," Daniel replied noncommittally.

The next day he went up to the Judean Hills near Modin and, on returning, produced a surprising amount in gold coins.

It would have been a simple matter to find brigands among the paupers and roughnecks of Galilee. But old Daniel exhorted Shemon to select his men with care. "They will be the kernel of Israel's fighting hosts," he said, "and they must find favor in the eyes of God and man." So Shemon, after a successful beginning at Kfar Haroob, went from village to village choosing young patriots who, like himself, had suffered bitterly at the hands of Rome and whose motives and loyalty were above suspicion. Of these, Asher of Kfar Haroob, Itamar of Kfar Hanan, and Nadav of Caesarea had chopped off their left thumbs as a test of courage; before long this became the standard test of the band.

The Thumbless Riders, or the Thumbless—that was what Shemon's big-boned, rough-riding men finally came to be called—appeared first in Transjordan, along the shores of Lake Kinnereth; then they turned up in the environs of Mount Canaan in Galilee and, later, on the Syrian frontier. They raided heathen caravans and small patrols inside Syria, in quest of horses, food and arms. No Roman was safe in the vicinity of Kfar Haroob; and if one strayed up the hill which harbored the village on its wooded crest, he never returned. "The two brothers again," the villagers would whisper among themselves, and some would add, "Nothing good will come of it." But official inquiries found the natives sphinx-faced and uncommunicative.

Gradually Shemon extended his field of operations to Lower Galilee and Samaria. At Bnai Brak in Judea students from Rabbi Akiba's academy established surreptitious contact with Shemon, and an insurrectionary brotherhood, called *Heruth o Mavet,* abbreviated to *Heromav,* was formed among them.

In other parts of the country groups of potential rebels sprang up spontaneously and sought guidance and arms from the Thumbless. These were mere harbingers of growing unrest, but old Daniel saw in them unmistakable signs of the impending storm. In the past he had had his own secret contacts and had not infrequently disappeared for days. Of late, however, he was obliged to confine himself to his cave and its immediate vicinity. Fever and inexplicable pains harassed the once-powerful man and his health failed rapidly. Shemon prayed that Providence might spare his beloved uncle long enough to see his people's triumph. Alas! that did not come to pass.

Chapter Two

Shemon shook off his grief and read the scroll at which he had scarcely more than glanced the preceding day. It directed him to look for a will. He found it in the cedarwood chest among Daniel's scant belongings. The parchment contained an amazing revelation, likely to add strength and impetus to the liberation movement. It unveiled the mystery of the almost forgotten disagreement between his two uncles and shed new light on Rabbi Akiba's personality. Hitherto the rabbi had been to Shemon an object of reverence, the symbol of the spirit of his people. It had been difficult to visualize him in a role not associated with spiritual leadership. Now a touch of earthliness had been added to his personality. It became possible to think of him in terms of rebellion, to see him as a revolutionary figure swaying the masses to insurrection even as he inspired them to the ways of God.

Shemon settled down to memorize the contents of the parchment. Then he buried it. It was too precious a document to risk carrying on a hazardous journey. Tinneus Rufus, the Procurator of Judea, could ill afford to permit a considerable material loss and a stinging blow to his prestige to go unpunished. Not when herds of cattle and more than a century of horses had been driven off, and legionaries had been beaten and trussed up, under the very walls of Caesarea. Unheard-of effrontery! By now, the search for the perpetrators undoubtedly was on in full cry.

Shemon spent another night in the cave. At dawn he climbed to the top of the hill, where, in the ruins of a village destroyed by Titus, he was to meet Nadav.

The multicolored patterns of daybreak were giving way to a golden haze which spread slowly from the hills to the sea. The plain, the pastures, the city walls, the fortress and palace on the mound and then Caesarea itself were emerging. Here was the bastion of Israel's mortal enemy, the seat of the Roman procurator nicknamed Tyrannus.

As the haze cleared, the capital, extending for four miles along the Mediterranean coast, came into view. From where he stood

Shemon could see the small Judean quarter, with its unadorned dwellings, in the southern part of the city, and the adjoining markets and the port. Long jetties lay like thin shadows amid the frigates, Arabian dhows, Roman galleys and smaller craft dotting the harbor. Far in the north, on an artificial mound paved with white marble, the citadel and the palace glistened in the early sun. Below the mound the large districts of the heathens—Greek, Syrian, Italian and Sidonian—were easily discernible by their temples and the stadium. Some day soon, God willing, these temples of idolatry and licentiousness would lie charred and desolate, even as this once-thriving village.

A mounted patrol came out of the northern gate and took the road to Acca. Another patrol cut across the plain and cantered south. Shemon smiled. It pleased him that the Romans had not been so vigilant the other day.

He heard footsteps and turned. Nadav's young brother, a lanky, swarthy, fiery-eyed lad of fourteen, was making his way through the ruins; "Peace," he said timidly.

"Peace. What brings you here, Ovadya?"

"Nadav sent me. I'm coming from the Cave of Vengeance. I went there last night to bring Shemon greetings from my brother Raphael."

"Why did not Nadav come?"

"I told him that many soldiers were on the roads, and he said it was best for him to stay with the others. He asks Shemon to hurry to the gorge."

Shemon frowned. "And what did Raphael want?"

"He asked me to tell Shemon: 'The iron came.'"

Shemon brightened up. "Good. Tell him Nadav will be in the smithy tomorrow. No new tidings in Caesarea?"

Ovadya looked up apologetically at Shemon, shifted his weight to one foot, and removing the sandal from the other foot and shaking the dust and gravel out of it, spoke. "Soldiers were in the Judean quarter yesterday. They beat people, broke into homes. They wanted a big man—a Hercules they called him. He had a shorn round red beard, they said, and eyes like glowing copper. Coppery hair, too. He might be dressed as an Edomite soldier, they said, and again he might not. He stole cattle and horses, they said."

Shemon's eyes twinkled. "Did they find him?" Ovadya laughed a little sheepishly. Shemon asked earnestly, "Did anybody tell the big man's name?"

The lad shook his head vigorously. "Few know it, and the others wouldn't tell if they knew."

Shemon tousled the lad's curly hair. "Good boy! Helping Raphael much?"

"With everything. Soon I'll know how to make daggers all by myself."

"Very good. We'll need many of them." Again Shemon ruffled Ovadya's black hair. "Will you see Rabbi Uziel for me?"

"I will."

"Ask him to say a prayer for the soul of Daniel ben-Ezer."

"Shemon's uncle?" the boy stammered, and his eyes grew large and a little frightened. Shemon nodded sadly.

"Edomites?"

"No, fever. I buried him yesterday."

There was a long pause. Then Ovadya muttered, "Soldiers are everywhere. Best to go through the hills and caves."

Shemon grinned, pinched the lad's cheek and sent him on his way.

In less than two hours Shemon reached a wooded section of the hills where a wall of boulders concealed an entrance to the Cave of Vengeance. From there a system of hide-outs and underground passages extended for miles north and south. The uninitiated rarely discovered more than the outer caves of the system—small lairlike holes. Tradition had it that a whole maniple of legionaries had, during the anti-Trajan uprising, tracelessly disappeared in these caverns—hence the name Cave of Vengeance.

Shemon entered a catacomb-like tunnel that diverged suddenly into other corridors. After a time he reached a spacious division where the prize of his recently acquired booty, a thoroughbred mare apparently from the procurator's stables, was munching at a manger to which she was tethered. Nearby there was a channel whose water came through a small archway at the bottom of the external wall. A few paces away a sturdy door opened onto a gorge. Shemon patted the horse and stepped outside.

The gorge was a forbidding spot, gloomy, oppressive, mysterious. Immense cliffs turreted over a sinuous brook. High above, on each side of the stream, granite promontories jutted forth and almost met in space. A narrow strip of sunlit blue, far as a dream, peeped through the projections. It would hardly occur to those who would venture to approach the tips of these ledges that the abyss below could serve as a hide-out for human beings or that it might be linked with brighter vistas. Yet some furlongs away the gorge widened into a ravine where hills were ablaze with light and color; with poppies, marigolds and anemones against a background of deep green.

Shemon placed his forefingers in his mouth and whistled. The sound, beating against the cliffs, reverberated in countless echoes and an eagle's cry responded from above.

Presently Nadav and Itamar appeared, carrying a slaughtered sheep, bread, olives and herbs. They built a fire, placed the meat on spits to broil and, washing their hands in the brook, squatted with Shemon around the fire.

Nadav, a larger replica of Ovadya, was a willowy young man in his mid-twenties, bronzed, muscular and scar-faced, a Roman saber-cut running across the lower part of his left cheek and a good half of his neck. He wore a dark sleeveless tunic girded with rope, from which a large dagger was suspended. His only other articles of clothing were a loincloth and sandals. The previous day, he reported, Roman patrols had come close to the ridge which, to the Thumbless, was the border line of their fastness. It was necessary to stand ready to defend it, for the cattle had not been securely hidden and half the horses were not yet distributed.

Shemon was satisfied. They talked about various matters and at the end of the meal Shemon apprised them of his intention to set out for Bnai Brak. Nadav protested that it was still too dangerous.

"I am going," Shemon said resolutely. "There are unbeaten paths unknown to the Edomites. Of course there are hazards. Whatever we do is hazardous. What did you hack a thumb off for, to worry about me like old women? I must see the rabbi now. We cannot go on with a few hundred men forever. Ours must be a people's war. Men like Rabbi Akiba could do in days what we alone couldn't do in years. Forty-eight thousand students have sat at his feet and he is like a prince to them."

"The princes of the Torah fight not with the sword," exclaimed Itamar, jumping to his feet, "and Akiba is too old to use one even if he wished."

He stared at Shemon with unflinching coal-black eyes set in a strong, weather-beaten face. He, too, had a distinctive mark—an ear had been slashed off by a Roman punitive expedition. This had been the fate of all the males of a rebellious village in which he had lived when a mere lad of twelve. Garbed like Nadav, his brawn all but bursting through his tunic, he was strong and mercurial, and looked a bit sinister when aroused.

"In a holy war the Word is as important as the sword," Shemon persisted, "but Akiba's disciples *will* fight with the sword. Shall we forget the Heromavs? Are they not Akiba's disciples? Take Elon, the son of Gad; or Joel, the son of Gedalia. Are they not as good as the best of the Thumbless?" Shemon rose.

Nadav did likewise. "You've decided," he muttered wistfully. "I wish I could go with you."

"I, too," Itamar said softly, and his face mellowed surprisingly. "If evil there be on your way, let it befall me."

Shemon, prizing their loyalty, embraced them warmly. "No evil will befall me. Evil fears me," he jested. "And now, Nadav, concerning the iron in your brother's smithy: Tyrannus wants more swords. Raphael can make good ones and defective ones. Let half of them be defective. Rufus won't take them and Raphael can remake them for us. If there is a loss we'll look after it later."

"I will speak with him."

"Also, see Rabbi Uziel. We want the names of wronged villagers. Where cattle was taken by the Edomites, we will give it back." Nadav nodded. "And you, Itamar, look after the camp.

Keep scouts far out in the hills. The enemy must never surprise us."

When they were gone Shemon went into the cave to fondle his mare. "You're a beauty. Legs and eyes like an *ayalah*—gazelle. That is what I will call you—Ayalah. We will do great things, Ayalah. We will ride fast and far. But not yet. Now the Edomites would know you and catch me. So we must wait."

He replenished the manger and gave the animal a parting stroke. Then he tucked the skirts of his cloak into his sash, picked up the staff, flung a small bag of food over his shoulder and proceeded along the brook toward a gully. Here steplike depressions, wrought by torrential rains, led halfway up a hill. Shemon scaled it and reached a plateau, above which a dome-shaped crest rolled toward further heights.

He untucked his cloak, secured his sword and headed south. It would have been simpler to descend into the Plain of Sharon, follow the coast to Apollonia and swing southeast toward Ludd. But that was the route which Roman patrols were most likely to be scouring in search of him.

Chapter Three

Clinging to the outer fringe of the Har Hamelek mountain range, Shemon passed uneventfully many of the thousand villages scattered on its slopes and crests and, turning slightly westward, found himself within two stadia of Zofith. There he planned to spend the night with his friend Elon ben-Gad.

The sun, still aglow with a merciless fire, hung low over the sea. Shemon had expected to make better progress but was impeded by the heat, which time and again compelled him to detour in quest of water. For the end of the month of Nisan, when the atmosphere is mellow and the perfumes and hues of spring are at their best, this was a bad day. It was one of those days known as *hamishim* or *hamseen*—meaning "fifty"—when the withering breath of the desert hung in the air, eating its way into the eyes and throats of man and beast, sucking shallow streams dry, killing tender plants and flowers and scorching fresh green grass a lifeless brown. Fifty times a year, it was said, Ashmodai, the Angel of Evil, who was condemned to roam the arid desert wastes forever, came close to the Negev and blew his fiery breath upon the Promised Land. But Jehovah, in His wisdom and compassion for the living, drove him away before nightfall and brought a refreshing breeze from the heights of Lebanon. Not infrequently, when the ways of mortals were righteous, the Holy One would keep the Despoiler away from the frontiers of the land until the advent of the cold spell. Then the curse of Ashmodai proved a blessing, for his fury would often convert a winter day into springtime.

From his point of vantage Shemon saw Zofith, with its vineyards, citrus groves and low, flat-roofed buildings, parapeted in places, sprawling upward. He could see the coast on the west, the mountains of Samaria to the northeast, and more dimly, the lowlands of Judea to the south.

He slackened his pace and threw the flaps of his white headdress back from his face. For the present the danger appeared to have passed. The woodland beside the path was still and the town looked quiet and peaceful. Between him and the highway far below there were other paths, the nearest of which was obscured by trees and wild bushes.

Suddenly he heard a noise in the underbrush and a burly Roman soldier, armed with sword and spear, emerged. From his look of amazement, he had not expected to find anyone on the road, and for a few seconds he stared at Shemon speechlessly. Then he recovered himself and, pointing his spear, ordered Shemon to halt. He came forward slowly, scrutinizing the unexpected wayfarer as he approached. "Who are you?" he demanded.

"I'm a peaceful man of the soil," said Shemon quietly.

The Roman eyed him suspiciously. "The glow in your eyes, and the way you speak . . . you are no peasant." He raised his voice. "Who *are* you?" The spearpoint moved closer to Shemon's chest. "Your name?"

Shemon smiled. "What's in a name," he said evasively, "if you believe not the man?"

A glint of recognition came into the Roman's eyes, then panic. Shemon's smile had become a mocking grin.

"Raise your hands," the legionary commanded, but there was a tremor of fear in his voice. Shemon stared at him derisively without moving. Then the soldier shouted, "Up, up with them, or I'll pierce your swinish heart!"

From far below voices and the fitful barking of a dog were heard. Apparently they belonged to members of the Roman's patrol and his face brightened. "Ahoo-hoo-hoo! Ahoo-hoo-hoo!" he called, and for a moment he relaxed his guard.

Instantly Shemon grasped the spear. The soldier clung to it desperately and managed to rip Shemon's cloak and cut his face. But his struggle was futile. Shemon wrenched away the spear with such violence that it broke in half. The Roman attempted to unsheath his sword, but two fist blows to the head sent him sprawling and he lay still. From below, the Romans were calling and whistling for their dogs. There was no time to lose. Shemon tucked in his robe and raced for Zofith.

To his gratification, the outskirts of the town were deserted. Striding rapidly through a dusty, cactus-lined road, he turned into a lane hedged with vineyards and entered a familiar gate.

A cherry-eyed, olive-skinned maidservant glanced at him from a distance and swiftly ran to her young mistress. "There's a giant in the yard," she announced breathlessly.

"An Israelite?"

"I know not," said the maid.

Meredya, Joel's cousin, daughter of the local head archon, hurried out. Shemon had drawn water from the well and was drinking it from a wooden vat, his back toward the girls. Raam, the sheepdog, straining at the kennel chain, was barking lustily.

"He *is* a giant," whispered Meredya, and came forward, her maidservant keeping a few paces behind. "Quiet, Raam!" she called and the barking subsided.

Shemon turned quickly and put down the vat.

"Shemon!" gasped Meredya. "What brings you here? There's blood on your face."

"A scratch. It's nothing," he muttered, and paused in astonishment. It was hard to reconcile the awkward thirteen-year-old fledgeling he had last seen some four years back, with this lovely specimen of womanhood. She sensed his surprise and was covertly pleased with it.

"Meredya . . . you are Meredya, are you not? It's hard to believe—how you have changed!"

"For the worse?" she asked roguishly.

"Oh, no, no!" he protested. "Quite the contrary."

He was a bit confused but she took no further advantage of the fact. His lacerated face troubled her. "The blood . . ." she said again.

"The blood is nothing," he shrugged, taking command of himself. "The danger is elsewhere."

"Where?"

"I would rather not upset you. May I not speak with your father?"

"He is at the council house."

"I will speak to you, then, for time is precious." He came close to her and said quietly, "Edomites will be upon me soon. I must hide."

"Edomites were looking for one like you when the sun was high," she replied.

"And . . .?" His eyes were upon her, glowing, eager, disturbing.

"No one knew you." She looked away, trying to decide what to do. "Zarooba," she called to the maidservant. The girl hastened over. "Prepare food and drink for our guest and say nothing to anyone. On your life, Zarooba! Do you hear?"

"On my life!" muttered the maid, looking up at Shemon somewhat fearfully. "On my life!" she repeated, and ran into an outbuilding which served as a kitchen.

"She is as faithful as a dog," remarked Meredya, and instantly her thoughts were elsewhere. She had an urgent and risky problem to solve—finding a hiding-place for him. There was the cellar of the house, the barn, the grain shed, the threshing floor and the orchard. Which should it be?

"Come," she said. He followed her silently into the orchard as she walked toward a bower. She pushed away the floor mat and opened a trap door. "This is our wine cellar," she said. "Be careful as you go down." She pointed at the wooden steps disappearing into the murk. "I think you will be safe for the present."

She turned to go but looked back with a heart-warming smile. "I shall return soon."

"Wait," he said. "There is something to be done at once. The Edomites have a dog or dogs, which will assuredly bring them here. That must not be."

"What would you have me do?"

"Is there, perchance, ground mustard in your house?"

"There is much of it."

"Be blessed. Let a trustworthy runner take as much of the powder as you can spare to the north end of the hillside road, and there let him spread handfuls of it upon the road and upon some of the byways, your own lane among them. That will throw the hounds off the scent."

"It will be as you say. And now, go down quick and pull the door shut." She pushed the mat into its former position and ran back.

Shemon descended the steep steps carefully and sat down on the last one. An impenetrable blackness encompassed him. The odor was sour, musty and sepulchral. It took some time before he began to discern shapes—barrels, shelves, wineskins, cruses, boxes. Slowly he realized that a faint suggestion of light and air was seeping in from an invisible source. He rose cautiously and, stooping, went forward, feeling his way with his outstretched hands and counting his steps. The count was thirty-six when he touched the opposite wall. The width measured fifteen steps from wall to shelves, and three more for the shelves, which, like the walls, were white. Some cellars had concealed passages beneath them and to meet any eventuality Shemon decided to investigate. Tapping the earthen floor foot by foot, he found it solid until he reached the shelves. By now he was able to see objects at close range; some of the lower shelves were empty. An examination of these yielded the secret; one of them, responding to pressure, swung inward and came back of its own accord. The opening was large enough for a man to get through.

He returned to the wooden steps and listened. There was no sound. He was anxious and hungry, time crept slowly and his confinement was becoming irksome. Yielding to impatience, he went up the steps and pushed the trap door open. He could see nothing, for the mat obstructed his view. But in the yard, or perhaps where it bordered on the orchard, he could hear heavy footfalls and a mild hubbub dominated by gruff voices. Edomites! Quickly he pulled the door shut and went down again.

He did not know how long he had waited, and must have been dozing, when a dull, measured tramping, up and down, up and down, shook him from his inertia. He stood up, tense and alert. The tramping lingered and then died away. He kept standing, wondering. Despite the coolness of the cellar he was beginning to feel the lack of air. Or perhaps it was his uneasiness. Before long he heard lighter steps; then came a pause. Again he grew tense. The trap door opened, a faint light gleamed, air wafted in and a voice—a young woman's voice, rich and gentle, cautious and sweet—called, "Shemon!"

Never before had any one spoken his name with such tenderness. Not his uncle. Not even his mother, long, long ago. Or was this an illusion?

The voice called again, "Shemon!"

"Meredya!"

"I am bringing you food."

A dim, smoky light was held by an invisible hand. A shapely foot in a sandal appeared, followed by a wide, pleated skirt and the flicker of an ankle. Then came softly curving hips, a slim waist, a trayful of food in long-fingered hands, a slender neck on well molded shoulders and, at last, the heart-warming smile which had fascinated him.

Meredya handed him the tray before reaching the last step. "Forgive me for keeping you waiting and hungry," she said, adjusting her silken kerchief and pushing back an unruly curl. "The Edomites came before Zarooba could bring you the food. But the mustard was spread in time." She smiled merrily and her white teeth flashed.

"Who did it?" he asked, and deposited the tray on a square four-legged bench which he had not noticed in the dark.

"Thy humble maidservant, Meredya." She bowed playfully, but instantly paid for her levity, for she lost her footing and tumbled forward.

He caught her and held her in his arms. "Hurt?" he asked

gently, but there was also a hint of amusement in his voice.

She shook her head, but dared not lift her face, for it was flushed with embarrassment. He let her go.

"Forgive me again," she muttered, fixing her hair and kerchief and avoiding his gaze. When their eyes met, the two burst into laughter.

"Not so loud," Zarooba's voice admonished from above. "Has Meredya forgotten that an Edomite is still about?"

"Zarooba is right; this is no time for lightheartedness," said Meredya, putting a cautioning finger to her lips. "But there is no danger. Father has been wining the Edomite and he is heavy with drink. Besides, we are out of earshot." She paused, and for a while they stood gazing at each other in silence.

"Shall I bring down the light?" asked Zarooba.

They woke from their trance. "When we go," Meredya replied. She turned to him. "You must eat. Wait, let me wash the blood off your cheek first." She took a piece of saturated cloth from a bowl of lotion on the tray and dabbed the clotted blood off his face. "Clean," she smiled up at him. "Now eat."

"Is there a greater blessing than a comely woman, brave and sweet in her ways?"

She flashed a grateful glance at him and removed the lotion from the tray.

"Eat, eat," she murmured, and pushed the bench toward him.

He squatted, scanned the food and rubbed his hands with pleasure. "Baked fish, cheese, olives, bread, goat's milk."

For a while he ate without speaking while she told him how the legionaries—more than a score of them—had been put off the trail by the mustard, so that the bloodhounds, useless, had been taken away; and how the Romans, threatening and cursing, had then gone searching from lane to lane, from yard to yard. "From what they said, I gathered that one of their number had been found on the road, badly hurt and unconscious."

"Not dead?" he asked.

"No. Later, Edomites came up under a centurion and threatened to impose a heavy fine. Guards are everywhere and they are still searching."

"What is the centurion's name?"

"Caunus."

"Caunus?" Shemon swallowed his mouthful quickly and looked up at her, somewhat alarmed. "I know the rogue. He hates us but loves our women. Beware of him."

She lowered her long-lashed eyelids and promptly raised them again. "You are right," she said. "The Edomite stared at me wickedly. He asked me whether I had a husband."

"A bride-snatcher!" Shemon savagely popped an olive into his mouth. "Beware of him," he warned again, "and let all virgins beware of him." Presently he declared, "I mean to see Elon ben-Gad tonight."

"Verily?" she asked in amazement. "Do you wish to give yourself into the hands of the Edomites?"

"I must have a word with Elon and be on my way."

"You will be on your way to the hangman if you venture into the streets now," she said.

Shemon reflected. "Where does the cellar beneath lead to?"

"How do you know it leads anywhere?"

"I found out—and Elon once told me about an underground passage in Zofith which is connected with houses. Is this perhaps the passage?"

She hesitated. "Take no offense, Shemon. Your question is for Father to answer. If the pagan is overcome with wine, I will ask Father to come."

He thanked her and rose. She picked up the tray but he took it from her, brought it up to Zarooba and came down again.

"Your cloak," she said, "needs mending. I will take it with me and mend it quickly."

He handed the garment to her. "A maiden of all virtues," he said, regarding her admiringly.

She gave him a puzzling smile and gathered up her skirts. On reaching the surface she laughed. "A maiden of all virtues am I," she scoffed, "and among them deceit. I can now keep your cloak, brave one, until it is safe for you to go." Calling to Zarooba, "Take the light down to Shemon," she ran off.

"A wicked little imp!" he thought. He was about to pursue her, but the maidservant was already on her way down and his ascent was blocked.

The girl handed him the lamp, a triple-nozzled earthen oil vessel with lighted wicks. "My mistress will surely be back," she said confidently, her glittering pupils dancing with mirth. "She has her ways with those she favors." She concluded, "I will keep watch."

The night was well advanced when Abner descended into the cellar, carrying the mended cloak. The two men greeted each other warmly. Shemon had not seen Joel's uncle for four years and found him looking a little older. There was a profusion of silvery strands in his fine black beard; there were deeper lines under his eyes and on his high forehead; and the keen, electric eyes were dimmer. But the hovering shadows of age seemed to enhance his dignity as he stood studying Shemon with paternal benevolence.

Shemon had had no occasion to see Abner often and what he knew about him came chiefly from Joel, who, like Shemon, had lost his father early and had been brought up by his uncle. Joel's parents, however, had died a natural death and Abner ostensibly had no reason to fear the Roman authorities. He had come to Zofith some ten years back, had taken possession of his brother's house, vineyards and herds and had looked after his orphaned nephew. Before long he had multiplied the inheritance which he shared with Joel, had gained the confidence of the community and had become one of its distinguished trustees and leaders. For the last three years he had served Zofith as its head archon, or parnas—president of the community. During this decade his two older daughters had married and gone with their husbands to live out of town. The community had come to know him as a Levite by descent and a man of learning, rectitude and good judgment in practical affairs—but also, on rare occasions, as a man of explosive temperament. He was known to have arrived from the vicinity of Ein Gedi in Southern Judea. Beyond that his history was vague. His position restrained him from expressing his attitude toward the policies of the government, but privately he was known to be an adherent of Rabbi Akiba.

"It is past the tenth hour," Abner said. "The drunken Edomite has been taken away by his comrades and most of them are gone. Patrols remain. The house of Elon ben-Gad is guarded."

Shemon knitted his brows. "Only his?"

Abner nodded.

"Why?" asked Shemon, visibly annoyed.

"He is known to have spoken against the procurator," the older man replied, "and Caunus no doubt thought—and rightly so—that if the wanted culprit were in Zofith, he would come to Elon."

"So that's how it is." Shemon paced up and down for a while. "Is Caunus still about?"

"No, he's gone."

"I will see Elon, guard or no guard," Shemon decided. "Will my lord tell me how far this underground passage goes? I already know how to enter it." He explained how he had come by the secret.

"I will," Abner agreed, "but not before we have confided in each other a little more." He placed his hands on Shemon's shoulders and said gravely, "Son of Artemion! I was a friend of your brave father, may he rest in peace, and of your whole lamented family. My name was not Abner when yours was Romulus. Come into the house with me. Let us converse. May it not be that there is a reason why the Lord brings us together again?"

Abner's house was a spacious two-story structure built of large stone blocks. It stood amid palm trees, and its entrance and grated windows, for reasons of security, faced the yard. A few stone steps led to a stout wooden door, reinforced with iron bands, which opened directly into a large hall, the principal room of the dwelling. The ceiling was high and unadorned; the floor, of black and white slabs, was carpeted. Rugs covered part of the whitewashed walls, and a door led into internal rooms and the upper story. A bronze oil lamp, with curving, snakelike spouts holding lighted wicks, stood on a square table supported by a single three-pronged base. Other articles of furniture included an olivewood chest, a mirror, square benches, cushions and tiny tables. In a land impoverished by wars and burdensome levies Abner's home bespoke affluence.

The host motioned Shemon to the table and sat facing him. Abner was a fluent speaker with a deep, pleasant voice. At intervals he paused to weigh his words; at such times he bit his mustache or rubbed lightly the tip of his longish, straight nose.

His tale unfolded rapidly: He had participated in the ill-fated uprising against Trajan and, with others, was in Ludd on the fateful night of defeat. He managed to escape and lived for a time in the Desert of Tekoa and Ein Gedi. His possessions, like those of other rebels, had been confiscated and the years in Southern Judea were hard. He lost his wife and had to look after three daughters, the youngest an infant, after fleeing from Ludd. His name, blessed be the Lord, was not as renowned, his part in the rebellion not so pronounced and his description not as familiar, as that of Julianus, which made it possible for him, on his brother's death, to come to Zofith as "Abner." He never relinquished the hope of rebelling against Edom, but was scarcely able to go beyond hoping. The trustees of the community feared the sword of Edom no less than the Almighty Himself— might he, Abner, be forgiven for these words—and would rather risk the wrath of the Lord than the displeasure of their over- lords. Those who had "bread to eat and a garment to wear" worked too hard to think about their oppressors; and the peasants, burdened with levies, fines, mortgages and fears of losing the roofs over their heads, if not their very lives, saw the knife at their throats too often to hazard the thought of grasping it. It was good to hear of the deeds of the Thumbless, but what was a band of stouthearted men against the might of a wanton empire which held its heel on the throat of the world? He, Abner, alas, already knew the worth of such bands. Never- theless, some three years back, when Elon, sensing rather than learning from Joel the manner of man he, Abner, had been, came to talk of the Heromavs, his ears were open, though his heart was heavy with misgivings. Preparations were necessary and the least he, Abner, could do was to agree to the digging of a tunnel which would connect his orchard with Elon's and which later might be connected with others. It had taken almost three years to dig it, for only men counted as trustworthy could work at it. It had also been agreed that the tunnel would be used only in times of compelling urgency. Was Shemon's need to see Elon compelling? And another question: Did he, Shemon, *know* something which would draw a defeated dreamer of the past closer to the dreamers of today?

Shemon listened to his host with intense interest, slowly sipping the wine he had been offered and comparing in his mind the steadfastness of his late uncle with the vacillation of the man before him. Perhaps, Shemon reflected, it was unjust to make the comparison, for the circumstances in which the two had found themselves after the rebellion were incomparable. Yet he could not banish the thought that had his uncle returned to normal living—efforts to ransom him had been made—he would have plotted against Rome none the less. Abner was no Daniel. But there was nothing in his face to indicate lack of will. It was the face of a courageous man. Not every rock could stand unshaken against buffeting storms.

Abner was waiting. It was time for Shemon to speak. "I am a man of action, my lord," Shemon said slowly. "Whatever I decide to do must be done now—else why decide? If in my judgment—I do not spurn the judgment of others before deciding —a matter is important, it is *the* most important matter, although tomorrow there may be a more important one. Do I know what will come tomorrow?" He paused to allow his host to comment, but Abner said nothing. Shemon continued, "I am on my way to Bnai Brak. There are tidings the old sage will want to hear. There is advice only Akiba can give. There are questions I will be called upon to answer. Some of the answers I bring from others; some I know; one must come from Elon."

"But what of the peril that threatens you if you go now? Cannot Elon's answer wait?"

"Whatever I do is perilous—perilous to me, to my friends, to my enemies. That is the road I have chosen. If I avoid one peril today, may there not be another tomorrow? Wherefore postpone?"

Abner thought: *This young man's mind is as clear as his eyes and as strong as his body. He will not falter. The young will follow him; perhaps the old, too.*

"The secret is yours," Abner said at last. "Walk to the end of the tunnel and you will reach a wall of eight boards. The fourth will open. Go forward. At the other end you will find a ladder that will take you to a cellar like mine, and from there into a booth in Elon's orchard. Remember, Edomites guard the house and horsemen make the rounds."

Shemon thanked him and rose.

Abner took him into the yard and hushed the growling Raam. "Our house is always open to you," he said, "day or night."

"More than one matter will bring me back here," Shemon replied, bowing. "And how can I forget the kindness of my lord's virtuous daughter? Will he thank her for me?"

A cloaked feminine form rose from a bench in the bower and came to the entrance to meet Shemon. Her kerchief all but covered her face, and in the starlight it was only by the brilliance of her eyes that he recognized her.

"Meredya!"

She put a finger to her lips. "Not so loud," she whispered, a little out of breath. "I had to talk to you, though Father would be angry if he found me here. It wasn't meet to leave you as I did before. Please do not think ill of me."

"Ill of you? How come you to say it? Ill of you! I shall never stop being grateful." He was groping for words. Her kerchief had slipped back from her wavy black hair; her neck gleamed above the silk of her cloak; her face, uplifted, was pallid; her soft, full lips were lightly parted by a smile, and the look in her eyes was warm and rousing. To him, who had rarely associated with women of her class, she was at once baffling and alluring. "You are very comely, Meredya," he blurted out. "Rachel could not have been comelier."

The warmth in her eyes flashed into pleasure, evanesced into moods he could not read. "I have not come to seek praise from your lips," she said, "or to be a stumbling block in your path. I have come to tell you that the girls of Zofith, like the young men, will follow you unto death when your call comes."

His puzzlement deepened. What had these brave, selfless words to do with the intimate mysteries which sparkled and faded in the shadows of her long lashes? Should these not go with whispers and gentle touches and words like pungent perfumes that quickened the blood and kindled the imagination like *The Song of Songs?* "How will the girls help?" he asked.

"They will spin and weave and cook, tend the wounded, carry messages. They will hearten the fighters, shame the cowards."

It was good to know all this about the daughters of Zofith, but there was something at the moment that mattered more. He laid his hands on her soft shoulders. "And love their men?"

Gently she removed his hands. "I must go now. Father may look for me."

"I may not see you for a long time. May we not sit for a while?"

She shook her head sweetly. "If we sit, you may forget Elon and I my father. Good night." She pulled up her kerchief but tarried and lifted the mat. "I almost forgot. There is a torch and a flint on the bench below."

"Thank you." He hastened to open the trap door. "Peace be with you," he said, descending.

"May angels guard your path," she murmured.

Chapter Four

Extinguishing his torch, Shemon emerged into a bower similar to the one at Abner's house, and then into Elon's extensive garden, famed throughout the Har Hamelek region for its apples, grapes and vegetables. The house and outbuildings, including clay hovels for hired hands, lay a good furlong off, and the unpaved paths were narrow, uneven and dark. Shemon proceeded cautiously, thinking now of the Roman guards ahead, now of his friend. Elon had come by his possessions as the sole survivor of Gad's four sons, of whom two had been devoured by the bubonic plague and one by the anti-Trajan revolt. Gad, a devout and peaceful man, had died brokenhearted. Elon's only sister, Elisheba, had found favor with a wealthy Alexandrian merchant, Shilo, and had settled with him in the great Egyptian metropolis. Elon had been taught by his late mother, even as Shemon had been by his uncle, to hate the Roman oppressor. In Rabbi Akiba's academy, where Elon had studied, he had found a surprising number of like-minded youths whose hatred for Rome had grown with the years. He had come upon Shemon in the hills, and impressed by his strength and purpose, had aligned himself with him and had taken Joel into his confidence, and the student brotherhood Heruth o Mavet sworn to a freedom-or-death struggle with Edom, had eventuated. "Heromav," compounded from the first syllables of Heruth o Mavet, had become its popular name.

When the shape of Elon's two-story dwelling house, partly hidden by cycads, became discernible, Shemon paused. In a shed in the invisible courtyard a rooster was crowing, jackals were howling behind the cactus fence on the left and, close by on the right, sentries were marching up and down either outside the stone wall or at the entrance to the house. Shemon decided to try the rear of the building and to signal first. When the wail of the jackals seemed particularly near, he cupped his hands and laughed like a hyena three times. He heard the startled sentries halt and utter obscenities.

When they resumed their tramping, Shemon went stealing forward and soon came to an external stairway which connected Elon's bedroom, on the upper floor, with the rear door below. He stepped behind a tree and waited. Presently a tall figure tiptoed down the stairway and paused. Shemon whistled lightly. Elon responded and the two friends, still cautious, met in a silent embrace. Shemon whispered an explanation and was taken into the house.

Structurally the main room differed but little from that in Abner's house, and the furnishings, except for design and colors, were also similar. The flame of the single wick of a small bronze lamp on the highest table flickered feebly.

Elon had been away to Egypt for some months and Shemon was glad to see his friend hale and happy. The tan of his face had deepened, his coal-black eyes shone brighter and his black beard was neatly trimmed and shorter than ever before. He had a generous mouth, an aquiline nose and a straight, well-shaped forehead. At the moment he wore a skull cap, perched perilously high on the thick, slightly disheveled black mass of his hair; a long, loose white garment, and sandals.

Elon discarded his robe and, bare to his loins, stretched his athletic body on the carpeted floor, his head against the cushions. A small dagger rested between his linen breeches and his bronzed skin. He invited his friend to join him on the floor, but Shemon preferred to pace up and down.

Shemon gave Elon a brief account of his recent adventures and plans for the future. "Rabbi Akiba," he said, "will surely ask me how strong we are. I should like to tell him the truth, and so we must count heads. How many men will Zofith give us if we strike?"

Elon sat up and folded his long legs beneath him. "It depends on *when* we strike."

"I don't know yet. Perhaps by the end of the summer, in Ab; or after the holy days, late in Tishri, before the rains. Events will show."

Elon reflected. "Right now I can count on one hundred and forty men. They can fight, but not all of them have weapons. By Tishri we may have twice as many, and at least another hundred from neighboring villages."

"Let us say four hundred, then."

"Yes." Elon rose. "Besides men, it will take much treasure, which won't be easy to get. But the old wizard is a master-mind at such matters."

"I've heard. There's little that Akiba has not learned in his travels. But for the time being we must look to ourselves for men *and* treasure." Shemon smiled significantly.

Elon understood. His eyes kindled with mirth and he laid his hands on his friend's shoulders. "A hint? To me? I have long since put aside for our cause a full talent in gold."

Shemon took Elon into his powerful arms and pressed him close. "Five thousand seven hundred gold shekels—princely! And truly worthy of you."

"Is it not a paltry price to pay for liberation?" Elon asked, beaming happily.

"If only our truly wealthy brothers thought so," Shemon muttered. He stopped abruptly, made a few steps toward the door and listened. "Do I hear footsteps?"

Elon pricked up his ears and a smile spread over his face. "Perhaps you do."

"It can't be an Edomite—the steps are too light, and they seem to come from above. Who is it?"

"Who indeed?" Elon laughed. "Can't you surmise? It is now almost two moons since I sent you word."

Shemon eyed his friend blankly. "I received no word from you which would explain midnight footfalls in your house."

Elon chuckled, for even as Shemon was speaking a feminine figure slipped into the room.

"I believe him," said a soft voice.

Shemon turned abruptly. He found himself looking down at a slender girl, almost hidden in a night cloak which reached to her sandaled feet. Rebellious strands of sunset-brown hair escaped from beneath a sea-blue kerchief, and a captivating smile played on her lips. Her large dark-gray eyes, from which, clearly, sleep had just been washed, twinkled with humor. She could scarcely have passed her eighteenth birthday.

"Tamar, my wife!" Elon announced triumphantly, putting his arm around her shoulders. "And this is Shemon." He allowed the effect to sink in.

"He who can ride a lioness and uproot trees?" she murmured with simulated awe.

"He and no other," affirmed Elon.

She came closer to Shemon and said earnestly, "Elon thinks you are the bravest man in the world."

Elon embraced her. "I brought her from Alexandria. Belongs

to the Shilo family. They took *my* sister *to* Egypt; I took *their* sister *from* Egypt. What do you say?"

Shemon, still nonplussed, looked from one to the other and finally muttered felicitations.

"In the morning, when the sons of Edom are gone, I'll fetch wine of the oldest vintage and we'll toast each other," said Elon.

"No wine can make my heart warmer or my good wishes deeper," Shemon responded quietly. "I shall drink to both of you some other time. I must go now."

Their pleas and admonitions were to no avail. He embraced his friend, bowed to his young wife and slipped out into the night.

Chapter Five

Dawn was slowly tinting the horizon as Shemon reached the dusty road below the Bnai Brak mound. A weird grayness lay on the fences of broken stone, on the citrus trees behind them and on scattered date palms hanging over hovels of burnt clay. Sparrows squabbled in the foliage, and bats, disturbed by the oncoming light, zigzagged for cover. In the distant orchards, extending south as far as Ludd, the barking of dogs mingled with the receding yowls of foxes; and from an adjacent dirt road, running west from the Judean plain, came the dingdong of camel bells— a caravan was bound for the port of Joppa.

Shemon went up a narrow path to the top of the mound, where a stretch of open dunes was skirted by fig groves. A lean man of about thirty, wearing a long, black robe and an embroidered skull cap, appeared. He had an ascetic face, a thin, tapering nose and a beard that was tufty at the sides, thick and pointed at the chin. He was advancing slowly, deep in thought, his eyes on the ground, his hands folded behind him. Shemon said, "Good morning," and the man, somewhat startled, stopped. His keen, strangely disturbing eyes were filled with intense surprise. "Good morning," he replied, "and who may the mighty stranger be?"

"My name is Shemon, the son of Elisha."

"Simeon is mine; I am the son of Johai, and they call me Bar-Johai. What brings you here?"

"I come to pay homage to the great master." Bar-Johai scanned Shemon from headdress to sandals. "Not to sit at his feet, I am sure."

"What makes you say that?"

"There is too much strength and fire in your visage for a seeker of learning; and where there's strength and fire, there is violence."

Shemon regarded Simeon with respectful interest. "But what if the strength controls the fire?"

"Then a hero is born, for it is said: 'He is a hero who masters his passions.' "

"I need not ask whether you are a disciple of Rabbi Akiba," said Shemon.

"You have asked and answered."

"I would like to see the master."

Bar-Johai smiled. "Not before I know who you are and what you seek."

"Will you direct me to Joel, son of Gedaliah of Zofith?"

"That I will."

Shemon glanced at him gratefully and they proceeded. Despite the early hour, voices hummed in the tents and booths scattered in clearings among the fig trees. Now and then students in prayer shawls and phylacteries hurried toward a lawn, in the center of which a curtained ark, facing east, stood on a railed platform and worshipers chanted the morning prayer.

"You will find Joel here," Bar-Johai said, and left. Joel caught sight of his friend and went running toward him. They embraced with unreserved affection and plied each other with inquiries. Then Joel said, "I have much to tell you."

"So have I. But seeing the rabbi is uppermost in my mind."

"The master cannot see you before evening. So you will wash and eat and hear what you should know before seeing him."

Joel, the son of Gedaliah, was a man in his early twenties, well on his way toward ordainment as a rabbi. Externally he bore a strong resemblance to his uncle, Abner—the same fine physique, the same impressive facial characteristics, unmarred by age and its vicissitudes. There was one marked difference: Abner's eyes were shaped evenly, while Joel's were uneven. When he raised his black eyebrows one eye became elongated, the other round. One was electric, keen and somewhat hard; the other, dreamy and a little sad. One, Joel jested, he had inherited from his father, a purposeful and determined man; the other, from his mother, a pensive and retiring woman. In times of tranquillity Joel was drawn to the complex, abstract and placid; in times of unrest, to the direct, concrete and turbulent. Shemon's influence and circumstances more often brought the fighter in Joel to the fore. At times, however, the dreamer and budding rabbi in him arose to challenge the fighter. But it was a feeble and futile challenge.

After breakfast the two friends came to the solitude of Joel's tent, where they discarded their robes and relaxed on long straw mats. After a silence Joel said quietly, "The rabbi saw the emperor."

Shemon, electrified, sat up. "When and where?" he demanded.

"At Alexandria. He returned yesterday."

"And the tidings?" Shemon asked eagerly.

"Few know anything with certainty. The rumors are all bad. Some say Hadrian went back on his promise to restore the Temple; others have it that temples of idolatry will be built instead."

Shemon leaped to his feet. "Blood will flow!"

Joel sat up and smiled sadly. "It is further rumored that there will be new prohibitions. I do not know what they are. Rabbi Akiba has invited dignitaries in Israel to confer with him today. We may know later."

"Therefore I cannot see him?"

"You will see him soon enough."

Shemon, flushed, threw himself on the mat and folded his hands beneath his head. "War may burst upon us before we want it. It must not be! We must prepare." He came to his feet again and put on his robe. "Come, Joel, I cannot rest. Let me speak with our Heromavs. Let me see what the secret smithies are doing."

"You will be pleased with what you see," Joel responded as he rose.

On their way Shemon learned that Rabbi Akiba had become an advocate of sports, provided they were limited in purpose to improving the body and not elevated into the rituals of a cult; that the Heromav Brotherhood was becoming an impressive force among the students; that two underground smithies in the village of Bnai Brak were producing weapons day and night; that the procurator's wife, Ruffina, had presented the sage with a gift of several horses of pure Arabian stock, which he had willingly loaned to the Heromav for training. "Like your Thumbless, we have races," said Joel, "and for the strongest, tree-pulling contests once in a while. We had one yesterday, and two out of twenty-seven won."

"Who are they?"

"Ben-Dov and Amitai. You can see them tonight, when the Brotherhood will receive them as full members. I will take you to the gathering."

"I will go with you, but I must see the rabbi first."

"You will see him, as you say, Shemon."

Chapter Six

For many hours that day Rabbi Akiba had been closeted with other men of learning and wisdom in Israel. Among those who had been seen entering the dean's mansion were Rabbi Johanan the Cobbler, a saintly man who mended shoes despite his great store of knowledge; Rabbi Jose ben-Halafta, a tanner who, as was prescribed for men of this humble calling, lived outside the town limits of Sepphoris, and did so contentedly although he was an outstanding teacher and scribe; Rabbi Judah ben-Baba, an eminent scholar and patriot who not only taught the Law without compensation—an established practice—but taught it anywhere—in a cave, in a barn, in the fields. Rabbi Johanan ben-Torta, known for his acerbity, was among the new arrivals, who also included some bankers and merchants.

The afternoon was well advanced when criers announced that Akiba would speak on the lawn. Immediately students began to stream toward it and before long the lawn where the services had been held that morning was densely packed with an impatiently waiting crowd. Soon the measured staff beats of the dean's chief attendant and disciple, Joshua Hagarsi, heralded his master's coming. Wearing a prayer shawl over his fur-trimmed black robe, and phylacteries on his brow, under a fur-trimmed black turban, the old man, a picture of majesty, paced gravely some distance behind, followed by an impressive retinue. Hagarsi stepped aside and the rabbi ascended the platform while his colleagues and followers lined up directly below. There were whispers: "Where is Johanan ben-Torta? . . . Where is Jose ben-Halafta?" "Probably a disagreement," someone conjectured.

Joel and Shemon were in the front row of the assembly. For lack of room, all the benches had been removed and men sat or squatted on the ground, leaned against trees or straddled branches.

Rabbi Akiba began solemnly: "My teachers and disciples! Black clouds are again rising over our holy land. We have already endured much. Our material welfare has suffered; the peace of our dead has been disturbed and the purity of our women defiled. Now a dagger is thrust at the heart of our faith." A rumble of indignation passed through the audience. "Until my visit to Alexandria," Akiba continued, "we had been hoping that the Roman Caesar Aelis Hadrian, who, upon the death of Trajan, his predecessor, promised us to restore our holy Temple in our holy capital, Jerusalem, would keep his promise. Now we know. A temple will indeed be built on the holy site. But it will not be dedicated to the King of Kings, blessed be He, but to Jupiter, one of Rome's abominations."

There was an outburst of wrath. It was with difficulty that Rabbi Akiba subdued it. "Yes, a temple to Jupiter in Jerusalem, henceforth to be known as Aelia Capitolina. A temple to deify the name of a mortal. That we cannot accept. A mortal, even if he be a king and as powerful as Aelis Hadrian, is but the child and servant of God, as we all are, and never His equal. Vain and presumptuous is the man, however highly placed, who dares to set himself up as an equal of the Almighty.

"We had been aware of the danger. Last winter, after our visit to Hadrian at Alexandria, a glimmer of hope remained. But about three weeks ago, I learned that Hadrian had been to Antioch to see the marble and cedarwood that were to be shipped for the erection of his temple. With a small delegation I again went to Alexandria. Hadrian received us. And this is what he said: He would grant us Roman citizenship and treat us like Romans, but we must become like them—eat what they eat, worship their gods, abandon our holy Sabbath and the rite of circumcision. We pleaded, but our pleas were in vain. He was sending his instructions to Rufus, he said, and returning to Rome. These instructions, my teachers and disciples, mean new laws, under which we shall no longer be able to live as Israelites."

Pandemonium broke loose. Students leaped to their feet, stamping, shaking their fists and shouting, "Death to the oppressors! . . . Shame! . . . Cut the throats of the swine! . . . If we can't live as Israelites, let's die fighting as Israelites! . . . Give us arms!"

Seeing that Rabbi Akiba was unable to proceed, Shemon rushed to the steps of the platform. "Silence!" he bellowed. "Silence! If you act like a herd, you will die like a herd. If you listen to your leaders, there is hope for you."

His stature, his voice and his eyes caused the uproar to subside. The rabbi cast a surprised glance at the unfamiliar man and resumed his address.

"I have seen greater indignation than yours, but also the wanton cruelties that followed in its wake. I am in my eighty-second year. In my days our holy Temple was destroyed by Titus; in my days the heroes of Masada died to a man by their own hands; in my days, barely seventeen years ago, rebellion against Edomite oppression swept many lands beside our own. Great was the heroism, long and persistent the struggle. But in the end our towns were sacked and the flower of our people slaughtered. What is the lesson? We were divided and we were not ready. So the Almighty frowned upon us and the enemy laughed at us. That must not happen again. Even as our Lord is One, so must we be one. Meanwhile we shall seek to avert the

danger in other ways. The word of the law is one matter, and
the word of its executor another. Let us pray to the Almighty
and let me try to see Tinneus Rufus."

Scattered shouts—"The tyrant! . . . The thief! . . . The
robber! . . . The assassin!"—interrupted Akiba, but he continued: "Whatever he may be, he rules this land and I propose
to see him. Nothing will be left undone before the sword is
unsheathed. Speak up, those who disagree." His voice rose to a
powerful pitch and hung in the air.

There was silence.

Rabbi Akiba turned slowly, parted the curtain of the ark
and lifted his arms heavenward. "God of Abraham, Isaac and
Jacob!" he chanted, and the sorrow of martyred generations was
in his voice. "Thou hast delivered us from the servitude of
Egypt, from the captivity of Nebuchadnezzar, from the yoke
and indignities of Antiochus Epiphanes. Thou wilt also deliver
us from these pernicious designs. For we alone among the peoples,
with all our faults and transgressions—we alone, O merciful God
in Heaven, worship Thee, uphold Thy holy commandments
with all our hearts, with all our souls, with all our might, and
will die, if need be, for the sanctification of Thy Name and
Thy holy Torah."

He came close to the railing, his eyes moist and his hands
trembling. But his voice rang out clear and powerful: *"Adonai
Hoo Haëlohim*—Our Lord, He is God!" Seven times, as in the
days of the Temple, when the high priest stood before the Holy
of Holies on the Day of Atonement. *"Adonai Hoo Haëlohim!"*

The audience responded as one, *"Adonai Hoo Haëlohim!"*
Seven times, each time with growing fervor, each time with more
defiance, each time with sterner determination, until the leaves
on the branches trembled and the birds winged off in terror.

Chapter Seven

That evening hundreds of students sought to join the
Heromav Brotherhood. Young men who abhorred the thought of

bloodshed were eager to learn the art of war. Hadrian threatened the heritage of Israel. To them that heritage was a superior way of living based on a divine code of ethics, too lofty and exacting for other peoples to accept. With it and through it man was sublime; without it, mere clay. To defend it with one's life was a high privilege.

All was quiet about the old dean's mansion. The guards, appropriately instructed, promptly admitted the visitors into the moonlit garden.

A broad, graveled lane led to the house. On the right, paths ran through rows of date trees, carobs and cypresses; on the left, trellised bowers stood amid beds of roses and lilies of Sharon. Jasmine shrubs lined the flower beds along the fence, and their perfume blended with the sweetness of the roses and the delicate scent of the lilies. Directly in front of the building, in a circle paved with smooth white stone slabs, a large urn rose from a waterless fountain. Star-shaped purple-gray cactus flowers brimmed in profusion in the urn. Broad steps led to a large open terrace, where a double row of marble columns supported the upper structure.

Shemon paused in amazement. "A veritable palace."

"Yes," said Joel. "Rabbi Akiba's late wife, Rachel, built it. It was, as she used to say, a dwelling befitting the majesty of the Torah and its great interpreter."

"Was she so rich?"

"Very rich; that is, after inheriting her father's wealth."

"Who was her father?"

"Kalba Sabua. Surely you must have heard the name. For years he was counted among the wealthiest men in the country, and he was as niggardly as he was rich. His caravans carried wool and wines and oil to foreign parts. But he was best known as the father of Rachel. It was she who sensed the greatness of Rabbi Akiba and married him against her father's will when Akiba was a mere illiterate shepherd-plowman. She was disowned by her father, suffered much but helped Akiba rise to greatness. Eventually Kalba Sabua sought her forgiveness. Her triumph was complete."

There should be, Shemon reflected, a Rachel for every man, who sets himself a high purpose in life. Could Meredya be the one for him? She was brave and beautiful. There was witchery in her smile. *"Thy lips are like a thread of scarlet and thy mouth is comely,"* he quoted to himself from *The Song of Songs.*

Hagarsi came down the steps to meet them. "The master will see you," he said. "Follow me."

Through an ironclad cedarwood door, opening from a terrace, they entered a waiting room. There Joel pulled over a cushioned footstool while Joshua drew aside a sky-blue curtain and admitted Shemon into Rabbi Akiba's presence.

The sage came toward him, smiling genially, his hand outstretched in welcome. His dark eyes, which had glowed with unusual intensity when he was speaking that afternoon, were now lucid and friendly. The magnificent robe and turban had been replaced by a simple, loose-fitting tunic and a black skull cap that was too small for his large, bald head.

Despite his age and informality, his bearing was erect, his gait firm and his tall, broad-boned frame suggestive of latent strength. His shoulders were almost as high as Shemon's as the two men clasped hands. It was Akiba's drawn, deeply incised face, the shriveling skin about his beaked nose, and the snow-white beard fanning out across his chest which disclosed his years. But the effect was tempered by the searching brightness of his eyes, lodged beneath heavy eyebrows that were not completely gray.

"May the visitor be blessed," said the rabbi warmly, scanning the young man, about whom he had heard a good deal. "So you are Shemon, the son of Artemion of Ludd and Rebecca of Modin . . . Artemion, who later became "Elisha." You are as I have seen you in my mind. You have your mother's coloring and your father's bulk—a good specimen."

"Thank you, Rabbi."

"And I have heard with sorrow of the passing of your father's brother, Daniel. May his memory be blessed."

Shemon inclined his head, and after a few beats of suspense, said quietly, "Uncle Daniel was hunted by Rufus unto death.

The murder of my family by Quietus was not enough for Rufus. I won't forget."

"We all remember," muttered Akiba. "Where are his remains?"

"Under a heap of stones by the cave in which he lived. Such was his will."

"May the righteous Judge be blessed," Akiba murmured piously. "What brings you to me?"

"Things to come, Rabbi, and uncle's will."

"Sit down."

They pulled over divans and sat facing each other.

Shemon rubbed his beard and glanced about him as he sought words for an appropriate beginning. The room was huge and high, carpeted and tapestried, illuminated by a seven-branched silver menorah. The furnishings consisted of a pulpit draped in blue, an olivewood closet and chests, small round tables with inlaid tops, shelves for parchments and tablets, upholstered stools, small divans and cushions.

"We have been preparing for a day which must come," Shemon began at last, "and from what the rabbi said this afternoon, the day seems to be upon us sooner than we expected."

Akiba looked at him penetratingly. "The day is not upon us yet and we must do nothing to hasten it. To be well prepared for battle is to have half the battle won."

"I'm in full agreement with the rabbi," Shemon said, "but will it be easy to restrain the people?"

"It may not be, but we must try—which is why I want to see Rufus."

"The rabbi's wisdom is far greater than mine, but I would not trust the treacherous dog."

"Dogs are won over with meat."

"He will take the meat and bite the hand that feeds him," said Shemon.

"He may, but not immediately."

"Perhaps not immediately," Shemon conceded.

"And time is what is wanted."

There was a pause, and then Shemon said, "But the day will come sooner or later. The Thumbless and the Heromav alone cannot drive the oppressor from the land. The people must rise up from Dan to Beersheba. There is no king, no high priest and no Sanhedrin to give the word. But, thank God, there is a Rabbi Akiba ben-Joseph."

"I am a teacher, not a marshal of hosts."

"Moses was both, Rabbi."

"There was only one Moses, my son." The sage regarded the young man searchingly. "And even he led Israel into the wilderness, not out of it. Young Joshua was the one to bring his people into the Promised Land." For a while Akiba stared into space. "Perhaps I should have said," he seemed to murmur to himself, "that Moses led Israel out of the wilderness of fear, disorder and mental confusion, onto the paths of order and law, but Joshua led them out of the wilderness itself." A faint smile kindled his eyes as he again turned to Shemon. "I will help, with the guidance of the Holy One, blessed be He, in many ways in what is bound to come, but the hosts will be led by a young man, and his name is Shemon."

Shemon looked down, and stared at the floor for a long time. Then he said quietly, "Will the people follow one as young as I?"

"I believe they will," Akiba responded slowly, "though not immediately and not with unanimity. There are good reasons why they should," he continued, smoothing and gathering up his beard. "By your father you come from the House of David, by your mother—I wonder whether you know it—from the Hasmoneans of Modin. Your house has been all but uprooted by the hand of Edom, and you have stood without fear against the enemy these several years. But there are important men in Israel who are much exercised over the murders of Edomites by the brothers of Kfar Haroob, and over the escapades of your band."

"Can we please everybody in all we do? Won't these important men be displeased even more when war begins in earnest?"

"I presume so," muttered Akiba. "If it is difficult to find oneness of mind in a single family, how much more difficult must it be to have oneness of mind in the House of Israel. And now," he added, "what of your Uncle Daniel's will?"

"He bade me share with the rabbi a great secret of which I had known nothing until his passing, and which, now, after hearing of my descent from the Hasmoneans, I understand better."

"What is it?"

"A treasure in gold, hidden away before the destruction of the Temple."

The sage sat up, grave and eager.

"It is," continued Shemon, "in two caves, one near Modin and one south of Jerusalem. I can take the rabbi there or set the details down in writing. But the gold may be used for only one of two purposes: to destroy the destroyers of the Temple or to restore the Temple itself."

"How much is there?"

"At least five hundred talents in gold."

"A great fortune," Akiba murmured, "almost tenfold one hundred and fifty thousand gold shekels. It can provide much in war and peace."

"We shall not have God's Temple in peace," Shemon said forcefully.

"For war," Akiba sighed, "even this amount will not suffice. We cannot expect a short and easy struggle. Rome is powerful and obdurate. We need a fleet, thousands of horses and countless weapons if we are to win."

"Will the rabbi help us to get them?"

"I will," Akiba responded cautiously, "through others."

"And what," Shemon asked, "is the rabbi's will concerning the treasure?"

Akiba reflected. "It would be wise," he said slowly, "to bring it closer to Bnai Brak and place it in reliable hands."

"Shall I write out the details?"

"No. You will give them to Nitsa of Ludd, the wealthiest grain merchant there and the keeper of our chest. He will go with you. I sense your misgivings, Shemon, but in his company you will not be molested. His grain-carrying caravans frequent the roads and his gifts to the Edomites are generous. In his hands our funds will be safe and used prudently."

"Can it be done quickly?"

"There will be no delay. I expect Nitsa here in the morning and there is no reason why, tomorrow night, the Almighty willing, you should not attend to this matter. Have you a dwelling place here?"

"Joel ben-Gedaliah's tent."

"He is a fine young man. If you wish the comfort of a house, I have ample room for you here."

Shemon's eyes twinkled. "I dwell in caves, Rabbi; a tent is a place of great comfort to me."

"At your age," replied Akiba, "I would have made the same choice."

Shemon rose. "Shall I come in the morning?" he asked.

"I will send Joshua for you." The old man rose. "And, yes, should I forget to mention this to you tomorrow—I may set out for Caesarea in the forenoon—do you come back here from Ludd the next day. You won't find me here but Joel or one of my own men will introduce you to Zevulun, a wizard in ships and a great mariner. You can trust him. Lay plans with him."

Akiba took Shemon by the arm and went with him toward the silken curtain. "You have made no mention of your late mother's brother, Reb Eliezer of Modin."

"Uncle Eliezer has no interest in a nephew like me," said Shemon, not without irony. "He is too virtuous, too much the man of peace."

Rabbi Akiba smiled with his eyes alone. "Pay him your respects," he counseled quietly. "Do not be quick to judge. He is a man of learning and, like yourself, a scion of a princely house. A time is nearing when destiny will bring you together."

Shemon found it difficult to warm up to an uncle who had manifested no interest in the fate of his sister's son through all these hard years; and who had appeared, long ago, only once, to argue over a treasure which, it now became clear, had been in the right hands. In deference to the sage, however, Shemon agreed to call on Eliezer.

In a state of elation, Shemon set out with Joel for the induction ceremony. At last he had conferred with the man whose name was wreathed in legend, and he had found him to be an ally. In a few hours the cause which he, Shemon, and his uncle had fostered for years had leaped forward with a mighty bound. He had suddenly discovered that it was to be the business not only of bands of desperate youths, aided by a mature patriot here and there, but also of the most distinguished leader of the people, a leader who counted his adherents in the tens of thousands. Now their forces would join, grow, and strike.

Shemon was holding forth in this vein when they came upon Bar-Johai.

"Where are you going?" he asked.

"To swear in two Heromavs," said Joel.

"One of those self-torture rites again?" The young mystic frowned. "I do not like it. Self-inflicted cruelty is against the spirit of our people."

"The future leaders of our army must be tested," Shemon retorted. "There must be no weaklings among them."

"There should be other ways of testing them," persisted Bar-Johai.

"Forgive us, Simeon," Joel interposed. "We are in a hurry."

Joel asked Shemon not to misjudge Bar-Johai, who hated Edom no less than they. The son of a wealthy Galilean, Simeon had often supported the brotherhood with generous gifts and at times with a useful thought. But he abhorred blood in any form. "Why should an Israelite," he argued, "shed his own blood, when a son of Edom will sooner or later do it much better?"

The two passed through Bnai Brak and reached a structure fashioned somewhat like a house of worship. It stood in the shadow of palm trees. Guards were silhouetted on the turreted roof and men were waiting on the steps.

Inside, between rows of wooden benches, several hundred bearded, white-robed young men stood holding aloft torches fixed on dagger points. They were facing a platform on which there was an ark, a table and a menorah, and in front of which there stood Ben-Dov, Amitai and the officiating Levites, all in white. Amitai was a dusky giant, as tall as Shemon, and Ben-Dov was of the Elon ben-Gad type.

Shemon and Joel robed themselves in white and mounted the platform. The doors were locked and Joel spoke: "Ben-Dov and

Amitai, you are about to be admitted into the Heromav Brotherhood. Whoever takes our oath will live to see the redemption of
Judah and Israel or find salvation in death. He cannot renounce
the oath. No earthly power can absolve him. You, Ben-Dov and
Amitai, have proven yourselves to be stouthearted sons of our
people. Now your courage will be tested once more. Each of
you will cut the letter *yud,* the first letter of His holy Name,
blessed be He, in his left forearm and seal his oath with his
blood." He paused. "You are still free to withdraw. Will you go
with us?"

In the tense stillness the voice of each fell clear and determined: "I will go with you. . . . I will go with you."

"David, King of Israel, lives and endures!" Joel uttered
solemnly.

"David, King of Israel, lives and endures!" responded the
assembly.

An officer handed the inductees two small, sharp daggers.
A Levite blew a ram's horn. The doors of the ark were opened.
A priest read the oath, spread upon a parchment in large, bold
characters: "I, the undersigned, solemnly swear to dedicate my
wealth and my life to God and the liberation of Judah and
Israel from Rome. I enter the holy Brotherhood of Heromav,
which stands for freedom or death. I shall do whatever is required of me. I shall obey the orders of the commanders of the
brotherhood or forfeit my life. Not until the last Edomite is slain
or driven from our holy land will I be absolved from this solemn
oath, which I sign with my hand and seal with my blood."

The two signed in grim silence and each of them, rolling up
his sleeve, tight-lipped and pretending to disdain his pain,
carved with one sharp stroke the *yud* in his skin. But there was
no mistaking the excruciating pain. Their faces were moist and
pale as they impressed their blood upon the parchment.

Promptly the Levites applied a lotion and bandages to the
bleeding arms. A trumpet blared and the assembled, shaking their
torches, shouted, "Long live the stalwarts of Judah! *Heruth o
mavet!*"

The doors of the ark were closed. The leaders embraced the
inductees, and these embraced each other.

Shemon, facing the new members said, "You and all of us

here are now limbs of one body, which, with God's help, will grow powerful enough to strangle the monster of Edom. We are sworn to freedom or death. It shall be freedom."

"Freedom! Freedom!" thundered the Heromavs.

The oldest Levite present, holding his torch high, chanted a psalm and the assembly repeated each verse:

Thy right hand shall be equal to all Thine enemies:
Thy right hand shall overtake those that hate Thee:
Thou shalt make them as a fiery furnace in the time of Thine
    anger;
The Lord shall swallow them in His wrath,
And the fire shall devour them.
Their fruit shalt Thou destroy from the earth,
And their seed from among the children of men,
For they intended evil against Thee.
They imagined a device, wherewith they shall not prevail,
For Thou shalt make them turn their back,
Thou shalt make ready with Thy bowstrings against the face
    of them.
Be Thou exalted, O Lord, in Thy strength!
So we will sing and praise Thy power.

With each verse the chant gathered force and volume, inspiring the chanters, inflaming their blood and imaginations, giving substance to their dreams. Shemon chanted with them. Watching their faces, flushed with faith and ecstasy in the leaping lights of their torches, he, too, became inspired and transported. For him, too, the ephemeral became real.

The walls of the building seemed to recede, part and disappear. A scarlet sun over a raging battlefield came into view. Rabbi Akiba stood on a mountain and, like Moses in the Sinai Desert, held his arms extended to Heaven. And Shemon, heading a cyclonic army of avengers, was routing the enemy.

There was little sleep that night for Shemon and Joel. For many hours they lay arguing, planning and weaving fantastic schemes.

Chapter Eight

Canopus, Dedius and Valentinus, cohort commanders of the Roman garrison at Caesarea, stood purple-faced, erect and silent as Tinneus Rufus stormed up and down his cabinet in the citadel. Their left hands hung motionless at the hems of their pleated skirts, their right hands lay on their sword handles, and their chests heaved agitatedly under their breastplates. They fumed impotently at the ruthless, unjustified abuse which gushed from Rufus' thick, sensual lips. Was it their fault, they thought bitterly, that Caunus, the cavalry commander, had had an ass of a centurion in one of his companies who had sent an even stupider ass of a legionary to look after a century of grazing horses? And was it their fault if the fool had been tricked by some bandit into a race for a wager and had gotten himself trussed up while the mounts had been stolen from under his nose? Why should they be berated like some stinking, fishmongering barbarians for Caunus' shortcomings? But there was the procurator, raving like a lunatic and reviling them as though they had surrendered Rome.

Such were their thoughts but they dared not utter a sound. The procurator's word was law in this land, and to challenge it was dangerous folly. Even complaints to the imperial legate at Antioch would avail them little beyond further trouble. Rufus, strong in the emperor's favor, was sure to be upheld. Something dark and sinister bound the procurator with Hadrian; something dating back fifteen years to Trajan's sudden death at Selinus; something which had linked Trajan's wife, Plotina, with Hadrian. Rumor had it that Rufus—a captain in the *Equites Singulares,* the emperor's personal bodyguard, at the time of his death—knew the details surrounding it but would not speak. He was reported to know the circumstances of Plotina's unheralded journey from Antioch to Selinus; of the emperor's— and, some asserted, Plotina's—urgent summons to Hadrian, then Imperial Legate of Syria, to join them; and of the old Caesar's sudden paralytic stroke. Rufus, as captain of Trajan's bodyguard, had not excelled in any particular manner. He was one of a number; a mediocre officer of strong physique, clever with the sword and good in the saddle. That was all. And that was certainly the minimum to be expected of a captain in Trajan's bodyguard. Yet after his emperor's death Rufus had risen from rank to rank with astounding swiftness and, upon Lucius Quietus' execution, had glided into the high office of procurator with incredible ease, receiving a beautiful young wife to boot. So what was there for the three commanders to do but to wait with sizzling impatience for the puffed-up pighead to spend his fury?

Eventually the storm showed signs of abating. Tinneus Rufus stopped and, fixing his small gray-blue eyes on them, barked, "Where is that idiot Caunus?"

"Out looking for the bandits, Your Excellency," replied Valentinus, a powerful man of Germanic appearance.

" 'Out looking for the bandits'!" mimicked Rufus vitriolically. "Much good will his zeal do now! For three days he discovers no trace of the animals or the thieves, and he is still looking for them. A Roman cavalry officer! A leaping frog could do better. Shame! One hundred horses, and one thoroughbred from my stable, taken from under his very nose! The whole thing is so disgraceful, so unbelievably insolent, that I—er—that I—lose—" Words failed him. His rage had overwhelmed him again and he was choking with it. His puffed face was red, his jowls trembled and beads of perspiration glistened on his bulbous nose and narrow though straight forehead beneath the fringe of his chocolate-colored wig. He was a massive, bullnecked, well-knit, somewhat paunchy man in his late forties. A loose tunic, fastened by a silver belt, covered his fleshy body down to his knees; his feet were sandaled; a gold chain supporting the Order of the Roman Empire dangled from his neck, and a short Roman sword hung from his belt. His choking turned into a fit of coughing, his face grew livid and his eyes, welling with tears, all but popped from their sockets.

That, the officers knew, spelled the end of today's choleric eruption. Mixing some wine with water, Rufus swallowed a few sips, strode over to one of the grated windows and stared down into the inner court at a magnificent statue of Hadrian, towering over a fountain.

Upon returning to his subordinates he was calm, and only lingering red splotches on his cheeks testified to his fit. "Sit down," he murmured, and motioned them to a couch.

They relaxed. One could almost hear them sigh with relief as they sat opposite his ornate olivewood table. He sank into a cushioned seat at the table and played with his chain and medal for a while as he reflected before speaking. "Whoever got away with a century of horses and a herd of cattle from under our very noses, and then hid them tracelessly, is a clever and dangerous bandit. If we can't find the animals, we must find him."

"That, Your Excellency," ventured Valentinus cautiously, "may prove a drawn-out business; the natives don't talk easily."

Rufus glared at him. "Bribe them," he said sternly, "and ask our tax collectors to single out the traitorous scoundrels you need."

Valentinus caught his breath but held his ground. "When the Israelites are in an angry mood," he persisted, "the tax collectors can't come near the villages."

"Take the tax collectors with you! Protect them!" shouted the governor. "Do I have to tell a Roman commander what to do under such circumstances?"

Valentinus bowed his head in silence.

Encountering no further opposition, Rufus lapsed into an attitude of simulated boredom. Short grunts, puncturing his speech, impaired the patrician pose. "I'll make them pay dearly for their insolence if they don't talk; and if they do, they'll pay less, but they'll pay. What I must know is: Who is the thief, and what did he want the horses for? He can't sell them or give them away in the country. No native is allowed to own horses without our permission. Every horse is accounted for. The bandit can either sell them outside the country or use them for mischief. If he sells them in Syria or Egypt, I don't care. Fines on the natives will bring several times the value of the horses. But if he wants the horses for mischief, I must know what kind of mischief. Understand? If, for instance, he aims at highway robbery, we'll know how to handle the situation soon enough. If his aim is rebellion, he must be nailed to the cross. Understand?"

"Yes, Your Excellency," muttered Valentinus.

Canopus, a big-boned, black-eyed, corpulent Italian of peasant stock, cleared his throat and said huskily, "The hard way is the surest way, Excellency; and the sooner, the better."

Dedius, a typical Roman patrician, much younger than his colleagues, glanced impassively at Canopus and suppressed a yawn.

The procurator livened up. "You're right, Canopus, but a certain procedure must be followed." He now again addressed himself to all of them. "Begin by squeezing a little money out of the barbarians. My secretary, Ovidius, will give you the names of two hundred villages north of here and two hundred villages south and southeast. Fine them as you see fit, and take your payment in gold, in silver and in kind until you've collected five times the cost of the animals. Put down resistance without pity, but be more lenient with their elders and rabbis."

He grinned meaningfully and Canopus and Valentinus responded with understanding smirks. Dedius retained his aloofness, which annoyed the procurator. He would have liked to take this young man to task. There was unspoken disdain in his manner. But he was giving no tangible offense and had powerful connections in Rome and Alexandria.

The officers shifted in their seats. The procurator sounded a gong. Ovidius, Rufus' personal secretary and adviser, a tall, suave, thin-lipped, bald-headed Roman of forty, with a perpetual cynical glint in his eyes, entered, nodded to the officers and raised his eyebrows.

"Ovidius," said Rufus tartly, "we are fining four hundred villages north and south of here for the robbery. See that the captains get the details." Ovidius bowed. "Also, prepare a transfer order for Caunus. We are sending him to Apollonia. Inform the Apollonian centurion—er—what's his name?"

"Gordius."

"That's right—Gordius. Instruct Gordius to report to Caesarea by the end of the week to assume charge of a cohort of cavalry."

The officers exchanged significant glances. Ovidius bowed again, ushered the officers into the next room and returned to his chief.

"What is it, Ovidius?"

"Rabbi Uziel is waiting below."

"What does he want?"

"He came to advise us that Rabbi Akiba would arrive at Caesarea before sunset today and would like to be received by Your Excellency tomorrow morning."

"I see."

The two exchanged meaningful glances and laughed.

"Quite interesting. The old devil never comes empty-handed."

"Oughtn't we perhaps to delay the punitive expedition?" suggested Ovidius cautiously.

"No, no. Let them start. Bargaining with Akiba will be more effective when the villages are yelping."

"There will be casualties, Your Excellency; probably quite a few. Again dead Israelites. We have been having too many dead ones of late. The dead yield no revenue."

"Sometimes they do—but that's not the point. I don't think there'll be any trouble to speak of. The barbarians are too cowed and they have nothing to fight with. We must frighten them and get some money. That's all the expedition means."

"As you say, Excellency. And Akiba?"

"I'll see him."

"Very well."

"Any communications?"

"Two. Both under His Divine Majesty's seals."

"Why didn't you tell me? Bring them in, bring them in. Turn the officers over to your assistant and bring the epistles at once."

Ovidius hurried away. Rufus poured himself some wine and enjoyed the drink with the relish of an epicurean. Ovidius returned with two sealed parchments.

"Open them."

The secretary broke the seals and unrolled the thinner scroll.

"What does it say?"

"His Divine Majesty, accompanied by four legions, is leaving Alexandria for Rome. He sends greetings to Your Excellency and hopes that his new decree will cause no undue trouble."

"New decree? What new decree?"

"This must be it," said Ovidius, unrolling the bulkier parchment.

"Read, read."

"To His Excellency the Procurator of Judea, Tinneus Rufus: Greetings from—"

"Omit that," interrupted Rufus impatiently. "Come straight to the important part." He rose and peeped over his secretary's shoulder at the parchment.

Ovidius fumbled for a moment before finding the essential portion. "Here it is," he said at last.

"Proceed."

Ovidius began to read:

"I have come to the conclusion that it would be to the best interests of the empire and Judea to introduce some fundamental changes in the laws governing this restless colony so as to make them conform to the general imperial code, on the one hand, and, on the other, to give Judeans the privilege of Roman citizenship, and the blessings under Jupiter which such citizenship entails. As long as we suffer the Judeans to continue their indulgence in the unrestricted worship of a nonexistent Deity, in whose name the gods of the empire, its institutions and the supreme prerogatives of the imperial Caesars are blasphemed and disparaged, and as long as the Judeans continue to mutilate the bodies of their males, a mutilation which is barbarous and against our fundamental belief in the veneration and preservation of the human body in its natural beauty, there can be no friendship between the Judean colony and Rome and there will be no lasting peace in Judea. The enforcement of this new policy may arouse the opposition—temporary, I am certain—of the more fanatical and obstinate elements among the Judeans. These, for the ultimate good of the majority, will have to be dealt with firmly.

"Accordingly I, Aelis Hadrian, *Caesar et Imperator* of Rome and all its vassal states, dependencies and colonies, hereby confirm a previous decree to the effect that a temple of Jupiter, fashioned after a similar edifice in Rome, be erected forthwith on the site of Herod's Temple in Jerusalem, and that a second temple and theater, dedicated to our goddess Venus, be erected on the site of the tomb of the Galilean, the executed imposter king of the outlawed Christian sect. Jerusalem shall henceforth take the name Aelia Capitolina. You, Tinneus Rufus, the Procurator of Judea, are hereby authorized to make the requisite appropriations and to use such building materials as have been and will be brought to Jerusalem for the purpose.

"You are, moreover, authorized and ordered to enact decrees tending to implement, in the territory under your jurisdiction, the spirit and the letter of this epistle, and to designate such punishment for violations thereof as you may see fit. However, the punishment for the mutilation of bodies and for acts of vandalism against Roman temples and deities shall be death."

"By Jupiter!" exclaimed Rufus as Ovidius concluded the last formal sentences of the message. "What a document! What implications!"

"And what possibilities!" chuckled the secretary.

"And, ho! ho! what possibilities!" echoed the procurator, slapping Ovidius on the back.

He stamped up and down the room and dropped into his seat at the table. "Possibilities, Ovidius, but also difficulties," he observed as an afterthought. "From what I know of the Judean devils, it may be easier to exact fines and taxes from them than to make them turn from their mysterious God and His Laws."

"You are right, Procurator."

"We must build the temples. The fools will whine but we'll silence them. The antimutilation law is worse. It means interference with their rite of circumcision. Why these idiots persist in paining their infants I will never understand."

"We must face it, Your Excellency. The instructions are clear. They say 'authorized and ordered.' That leaves us no choice in the matter."

"No, not in the matter of circumcision. But the punishment for teaching the Judeans' Law is not specific. The epistle is too wordy. I would have put the whole of it in two or three sentences: 'No teaching of your Law, no worship of your invisible God, no circumcision. Accept our temples and the pleasures that go with them. In short, here is your choice: Become good Romans and be happy, or sulk and die.'"

Ovidius laughed. "A blunt but apt summary, Your Excellency.

But His Divine Majesty prefers to explain his orders and to show why he is right."

"That's his philosophic bent. Futile. What's the use of telling a man you are going to kill him for his own benefit? It takes too long to tell and is not convincing."

"The epistle does not say that, Excellency. It says a few may be killed for the benefit of the many, if they don't obey."

"I know, I know," muttered Rufus deprecatingly. "I like to call things by their right names without serving them in poetic sauce. Reread that portion which refers to worship."

"You mean the reference to blasphemy?"

"Right."

"As long as we suffer the Judeans—"

"No, a little further down."

"—to continue their indulgence in the unrestricted worship of a nonexistent Deity—"

"That's it. *Unrestricted* worship. There is a loophole there for permitting some kind of worship, Ovidius. We'll have to think that out and see what it'll be worth to Akiba. Probably that's what brings him here. The old devil must have found out about the document already."

"Dangerous old man. Sharp," said the secretary.

"That he is, but tractable. Let me see that parchment. I want to examine it carefully."

Ovidius handed the parchment to his chief. "And the expedition? Are the captains to go out?" he asked.

"Yes, yes, by all means," Rufus insisted. "But cut the number of villages and tell the commanders to report tomorrow at sunset. Wait, you told me recently that the Christians were becoming active again in Galilee. Instruct Canopus to go after them and get some good slaves for the Gaza mart next week. Nicholas Padulos will advance us the money for them as soon as they are brought here. Canopus can take four days. And, yes, see that this is kept confidential. Not even Lady Ruffina is to know. That's all."

Ovidius bowed and left, grinning cynically. There was money in the information if he allowed it to leak out to Judith, Lady Ruffina's favorite seamstress, or even to Rabbi Uziel.

Chapter Nine

On the eve of Rabbi Akiba's audience with the procurator, Israelite notables of Caesarea were summoned by Rabbi Uziel to his house, and after the evening meal they gathered about the Bnai Brak dean to confer with him.

Rabbi Uziel, a dignified, pallid, middle-aged man with an iron-gray beard and deep, melancholy eyes, bowed to Rabbi Akiba reverently and then to the entire assembly, and in flowery words introduced the sage.

The old leader rose. For some seconds he stood silent and immobile, his large, bony hand on his beard, his eyes fixed but unseeing. Then he swayed a little, his fingers sank into his beard and he spoke:

"My teachers, rabbis and disciples, this is an hour of impending evil for Israel. Sixty-two years ago Titus destroyed the seat of God and the capital of His people. He slew myriads of holy warriors and men, women and children. He carried off countless thousands into slavery. It was said that he had made war not against the Almighty, but against the people who had defied the supremacy of Edom. The subjection imposed by Titus, cruel and hateful as it was, did not seem to be directed at the soul of Israel. Perhaps *that* was beyond his comprehension. The fact remains, however, that Titus allowed Johanan ben-Zakkai to establish an academy at Jabneh and to continue spreading the light of the Law. Not so Hadrian. He aims to destroy our soul and to obliterate from the earth the very name of Almighty God. Hadrian is against our exclusiveness. He wants to batter down the moral walls that protect it. He even pretends to bestow a favor on us. It is a 'favor' which may drive us into the deepest and darkest pit in our history as a people. We are asked to exchange the holiness of the spirit, the loftiness of man as God's chosen handiwork, for the pleasures of the body and the free play of the animal wantonness in him. The eradication of the spirit of Israel is the eradication of Israel."

He paused to adjust his skull cap and let his penetrating gaze fall upon every one within its orbit.

"I am come here to try to avert the evil design. It has not yet been decreed. Our purpose is to stay the decree, to gain time. It is said: 'Repentance, supplication and charity overcome the wicked designs of potentates.' We must therefore fast tomorrow and give freely, each man according to his means. The tyrant in Rufus wavers at the sight of gold. Abstinence and treasure will melt into surrender the tyrant's wavering heart."

Slowly he eased himself into his seat. Immediately Rabbi Uziel rose to support Akiba's plea. Others did likewise.

But Ezra Harrar, a graying, stocky, pink-faced man, robed in silk, with a scented beard curled in the old Assyrian fashion, took issue. He was a man of wealth, an elder in the community, and spoke with overbearing authority. He held that the Israelites themselves were in a measure responsible for the evil visited upon them, for they tolerated in their midst men who aroused the ire of the rulers by robbing soldiers of their garb and weapons, by assaulting tax collectors and by daring to make off with herds of cattle and war horses belonging to the authorities. "As late as this afternoon," he exclaimed indignantly, "I, as punishment for the impudent robbery, had to pay five hundred gold drachmas. I and other men of substance were threatened with further fines if we failed to reveal the name of the bandit leader. How can we? So, whether we pay or we do not pay, we are the victims."

Simeon bar-Johai, who, with Hagarsi, had accompanied Rabbi Akiba on this mission, and whose age demanded that he hold his peace among his elders, broke the established rule of etiquette. "Does the esteemed parnas hold," he asked with biting irony, "that we, the people of Israel, invited the Edomites to invade our land and, upon their arrival, looted their property? Or was it they who, like beasts of the forest, came down upon us and tore at our flesh? Why should our men, who risk their heads to reclaim part of the spoils, be reviled by their own brothers?"

Ezra's pink deepened into crimson. "The young man, who has not yet been admitted into the rabbinate," he retorted, glaring at Bar-Johai, "will do well to remember that our land could not have been overrun without the will of the Almighty, and that seditious acts have brought us nothing save misery and destruction."

"Were it not for the arrogance of those who place themselves high above the people and the disunity they are causing," Bar-Johai snapped back, "the Almighty would not have suffered the invader to defile our holy soil." Then, although he had not had his full say, he stopped at a gesture from Akiba.

Rabbi Uziel, fearing that the disagreement would defeat the purpose of the gathering, was quick to rise with an impassioned plea for unity. One after another the notables rose to support him and to extol Akiba's virtues. Ezra, isolated, accepted his defeat, murmuring, "One must follow the majority." Then the meeting broke up in a spirit of amity and heralds went out to proclaim the local fast.

Later, Judith the seamstress brought word that Ruffina wished to see the dean at Judith's house early the following morning.

The fast had been decreed to begin at dawn, and the populace, awakened by cries and the blasts of a ram's horn, flocked to places of worship. The streets of the Judean quarter of Caesarea lay still and deserted when, later that morning, Akiba, escorted by Hagarsi, arrived at Judith's home.

Judith was a shapely, vivacious, raven-haired young widow with flashing black eyes, a small nose, a somewhat voluptuous mouth and an alluring, worldly-wise smile. Her husband had died under the wheels of a chariot in the second year of their marriage, some two summers before, and the accident, which had involved a Roman of high standing and his wife, eventually, by way of compensation, had brought Judith into Ruffina's favor. She now lived with her father, Noah, an old widower of a retiring disposition, in a modest flat-roofed stone dwelling, one of many standing in small courts and orchards, fenced off by cactus hedges from a quiet lane. The interior of the house, whose kitchen was in the rear, consisted of two whitewashed rooms, to which a third, with a special entrance from the court, had recently been added. It had been built for the comfort of Judith's eminent clientele and as her own workshop. Apart from her equipment and materials, the extra room included a mirror, a screen, an ornate vanity cabinet and other furnishings designed to keep her patronesses satisfied. Of the original two rooms, one, which served many purposes by day and as Judith's bedroom at night, was large and somber, devoid of tapestries and ornaments, but spotlessly clean. Its stone floor was bare and its furniture consisted of a table, an ottoman, a clothes chest, square wooden forms and low stools. That morning, in anticipation of Ruffina's visit, a small divan had been brought in.

Akiba said a few kindly words to Noah, whose eyes welled with tears at the great honor. He bowed himself out of the room as Hagarsi stepped outside to watch.

The fast imposed abstinence from all avoidable pleasures and Akiba pulled over a low stool. Judith, wearing a dark embroidered dress over long pantalets, watched the sage with glowing eyes and answered his questions concisely. He gathered from her that Dedius, the cohort commander, who had vague leanings toward Judaism and a sympathetic curiosity about Christianity, had seen Ruffina and apprised her of her husband's designs. Judith was unable to tell the rabbi much beyond what Ovidius had seen fit to disclose to Rabbi Uziel.

A sound came from behind the curtained door leading to the special room. "Ruffina," murmured Judith apologetically, and she hastened out.

In a few minutes a dainty hand and braceleted wrist parted the curtain, and the procurator's wife slipped in, smiling, exquisitely feminine. As she came toward Akiba, she lifted her belt-clasped stola, which fell in bright, ample folds from her supple waist to her gilded sandals. Her hair, a mass of auburn ringlets, was held in check by a diadem, and her greenish-blue eyes sparkled with genuine animation. The stately octogenarian rose to greet her. Wearing sackcloth over his customary attire, he presented an incongruous contrast to her glamor.

"*Shalom*—Peace," she greeted him, and extended her hand.

He bowed and touched her fingers. "Lady Ruffina is Rome at its best."

"No young patrician could be more gallant," she responded, frankly pleased. "But why the sackcloth? Am I a thing to be mourned?"

"No, my lady. The sackcloth is to avert the danger of our falling into the grip of Rome at its worst."

She laughed and slipped into the comfort of the divan as he reclaimed his stool. "Why not sit beside me?" she asked.

"It is gracious of Lady Ruffina. I should like nothing better but I must forego the pleasure. We are fasting today, and even to behold beauty such as yours is an indulgence."

"You and your rigid rules," she chaffed. "Absurd."

"Rigid rules of behavior, dear lady," he said wistfully, "mean the dominance of man over animal, sublimity over baseness, spirit over flesh. This is our essence, differing from the essence of Rome."

"And what, pray, is the essence of Rome?" she asked earnestly.

"Greed and unbridled passions, deified and sanctified by law," he said sternly.

The hard words stung, but she smiled. "Passions are the joy of life," she said captivatingly. "Why should they be condemned?"

"Can the destruction of the life of one person for the lust of the other be regarded as the joy of life?"

"The attraction of sex is life and the source of life," she parried.

"The source of life is above us, my lady, and within us is merely an extinguishable spark."

She struggled to hold her ground. "That spark, nevertheless, is what makes for the continuity of life."

"So far we encourage it. But there we stop. There we build a fence. Beyond it is lust. In its wild race for satisfaction lust meets or deals out death. At times it is violent death; at times, slow and imperceptible." He fixed his intense gaze upon her and she looked down.

"I often think the rabbi is right," she said slowly, toying with her bracelets. "But then I ask, 'Why, if Akiba is right, does Jerusalem lie in ashes while Rome flourishes?' "

"Because Jerusalem failed to become all it had set out to be, and Rome was and is what Jerusalem did not wish to be."

"Will the rabbi make that clear to me?"

"The essence of Judaism is this: Curb your desires and share what you can. The essence of Rome is: Satisfy your desires and seize what you can. If King Solomon had not breached our moral code, and his descendants, emulating his vices without possessing his virtues, had not widened the gap, neither Babylon nor Rome would have been able to conquer Israel's physical citadels."

"Why not?"

"Because there would have been unity between God and man, and between man and man. No army of sinners would have been able to conquer such a fortress. But once there was a gap in the moral citadel, the Holy One, blessed be He, departed from it and the forces of evil could have their way. That is why Rome flourishes for the present."

"I find it hard to disagree, remembering what brings us together again," she said after a pause.

Akiba nodded sorrowfully. "It is sad that we meet only under such circumstances. Again Rome adds new injuries, and again I come to resort to gold and to appeal to a heart of gold."

"I wonder whether either will justify the rabbi's expectations."

He glanced at her apprehensively.

"The procurator is still avid for gold," she explained, seeing his concern, "and will take it. But can he be expected to defy the will of his Caesar?"

"No. But with Lady Ruffina's gracious intercession, can he not be expected to give his Caesar's will a mild interpretation?"

"He has hardened, dear Rabbi, and is no longer as tractable as he used to be. He indulges in excesses and, above all, in his concubines." She laughed—it was a hard and bitter laugh. "He hasn't too much time for me and doesn't seek my advice as often as before."

Akiba shook his head in unbelief and said, "Green grass grows everywhere and is pleasant to behold, but does it ravish the eye like a flower of the Garden of Eden? King Solomon had countless wives, but did he not dedicate *The Song of Songs* to Shulamith?"

She leaned forward, laid her soft, warm hand on his large, bony one and said impulsively, "I know of no one as gallant as you, my Rabbi, and no one as appealing to the heart of a woman. You know how to glorify what you choose and the one you choose—one God, one purpose, one woman."

He withdrew his hand gently. "One God above all. He stands alone and apart. But His greatest gift to man is a woman comely in appearance and in deeds."

"Does not the rabbi think that the mystery of love is part of the greater mystery of God?"

"Love is the handiwork of the Almighty, and is mysterious only insofar as all His handiwork is mysterious. But the result of this mystery is man, the highest form of God's art. Can man's art compare with that of the Almighty? No. Yet the men of Rome presume to say yes. With the tiny particle of divine power in them they create lifeless images of themselves and of inferior creatures; and these images, they make believe, possess the whole of the power that created them, the creators of the images. Ridiculous and loathsome!"

Ruffina reflected. "There is truth in your words, and I begin to understand the enormity of the crime of murder. If a statue, made by man, is precious, how much more precious is man?"

"Truly so, my dear lady. You are on the right path."

"It is good to know that I am. The thought of Him has taken hold of me. But the severe demands of your Law frighten me."

"Do not think of them now. The hour set by the procurator is approaching. May I not speak—?"

"You may," she interrupted with a disarming smile, "but bear with me for a little while." She paused and lowered her eyelids, and when she raised them, her eyes were soft and solemn. "I feel," she said, "like one whose feet are caught in a net when he is about to swim."

"To swim with us? Now? Would it not be like swimming to one's death?" he said gruffly.

"I could face it," she replied quietly, gazing at her ornate sandals. "I long to come closer to the One who is everywhere but whom I cannot see. A change," she continued hesitantly, "has come over me, dear Rabbi. I find pleasure in helping others. And I've begun to loathe the arena. I had a horrible dream. A lion was tearing a naked slave apart, and the spectators, among them my husband, were tiger-headed beasts, leaping in their seats and roaring with laughter. Suddenly a man of majestic appearance took me by the hand and led me into a sunlit garden. Won't you, dear Rabbi, interpret . . . ?"

"Not now, dear lady," Akiba pleaded, "not now. If you are beginning to see the light, you can serve God and us best by being what you are and staying where you are."

His lack of responsiveness nettled her. "Speak," she ordered curtly, but instantly she regretted it and smiled apologetically. "I will do all I can, my friend. Speak."

"Is it true that the procurator has already sent out punitive expeditions?"

"It is. Bad news about heavy fines and executions will be brought to Rufus in your presence to exact more money from you. But the order to punish four hundred villages has been stayed."

"Four hundred! Merciful God!"

"A hunt of Christians for the slave mart has been ordered. Canopus is in command and Upper Galilee is the region. The Greek, Padulos, the old scoundrel, will advance money in anticipation of profits."

Akiba bowed his head in grief. Ruffina continued, "And a reward of five thousand gold drachmas for the head of the brigand will be announced today—twice that amount if the man is brought in alive. Rufus is seeking a victim for the great spectacle and there could be no one better than the culprit."

"Does Rufus know who the man is?"

"No. Fortunately, Rufus has never heard Judith's praise of a giant named Shemon. If he had, he would have suspected no one else."

"Your discretion is more praiseworthy than Judith's ardor."

Ruffina smiled. "Are not all causes served by both ardor and discretion? And are they not both valuable?"

Rabbi Akiba accepted the friendly rebuff. "Your wisdom is equal to your charm. How can the procurator resist the power of such a combination?"

"I shall speak to him on my return and will try to see you while you are there. But I must find a pretext."

"Will not the old pretext do?"

She contracted her eyebrows. "Oh, I recall. A gift for me, delivered through him."

"Yes."

"But I desire no gifts."

"You desired no gift five years ago."

"This time I shall return it, whatever it may be."

He bowed his head appreciatively. She rose and he came slowly to his feet. The contrast between her glamorous beauty and his somber majesty, as they stood close to each other, was strikingly pronounced. It was more than a mere physical contrast. Here, too, Rome seemed to stand against Jerusalem. But it was a restless, yielding, alluring and groping Rome; a Rome seeking to surrender in order to conquer, and being conquered instead.

Ruffina looked up at Akiba and her eyes were earnest and serene. "I regret that your ritual laws deprive me of the pleasure of entertaining you at the palace. I should have liked to invite you."

"Thank you, gracious Ruffina. No food or wine can be as pleasurable as your company."

She smiled her appreciation but felt a vague sense of defeat. She did not quite know why. Something was missing. Some indefinable barrier had to be removed. She was willing to go a long, long way for this grand, unfathomable old man. Yet he elbowed her away. Why? And why did it matter? And was it he or what he personified that mattered? These questions rose nebulously in her mind as she extended her hand to him. He took it, held it and then lifted his arms over her head in silent benediction. Solemnly she bade him *shalom* and called Judith.

Chapter Ten

The procession moved through verdant, sunlit avenues where costly dwellings stood in gardens behind high walls above the road. The narrow, tortuous alleys and sudden dead ends of the Judean quarter had been left behind; the general mart and storage district, which, boisterous and malodorous, ran the width of the city to a quay of caravanserais, inns and jetties, had also been transversed. Now one could see the entire column of the marchers as it proceeded slowly and jerkily along the clean, far-flung roads paved with brown slabs.

First came a muscular, barefoot, shaggy individual carrying a big drum. Behind him marched three signalers holding rams' horns. After an interval of several yards some two score ash-covered young men in sackcloth paced to the slow rhythm of a repetitive, plaintive chant and an occasional boom of the drum. Shutting their eyes in mystical ecstasy, three of them intoned a prayer while the rest responded in unison:

We beseech Thee, Adonai: help us;
We beseech Thee, Adonai: save us from perfidy;
We beseech Thee, Adonai: foil the designs of Satan;
We beseech Thee, Adonai: respond on the day of our supplication.

After a second interval a pack horse, laden with two heavy bags, ambled apathetically, flanked by two tall serfs of Ezra Harrar's household. Each carried a cushion of black velvet upon which lay precious gifts—a pair of armlets of chased gold studded with rubies, for Lady Ruffina, and a gold-hilted sword in a golden scabbard, for the procurator. A short distance away Joshua Hagarsi, a long rod in his right hand, walked with his head high, as befitted the attendant of an illustrious scholar. Several paces behind came Akiba, tense and solemn, slightly in advance of a semicircle of elders and disciples, that included Rabbi Uziel, Ezra Harrar and Bar Johai. Then came another unit of ash-covered, barefoot men dressed in sackcloth, with Nadav in the center; trudging mournfully, they beat their chests in the traditional manner of suppliants and took up the chant of the first group as it fell silent. Under their mourners' raiment a keen observer could discover fearless faces, strong bodies and thumbless left hands. Knives were concealed beneath their rags. A mob of cheerless men and women of various ages and stations in life closed the procession.

Onlookers, predominantly Syrian Greeks and old Roman reservists, lined the road. Egyptian, Ethiopian and Moabite slaves watched from roofs and walls, and now and then the master or mistress of a mansion glanced down in amusement from a lofty window or portico. Nondescript ragamuffins, whistling, taunting and mimicking the fanatics, skipped along.

As the column moved into the marble-paved streets of the exclusive district where temples intermingled with the palatial homes of patricians, an escort of Roman cavalry arrived and flanked the marchers. As they rode along, the horsemen sneered at the grotesque, incomprehensible barbarians.

The battlements of the Caesarean citadel, several furlongs distant, came into view. The procession had now entered an avenue of heathen temples. Some of them, resplendent with precious marble and glittering ornaments, gazed down upon the road from artificial mounds. Others stood in groves of old cypresses, and only their domes or ornate cornices were visible from the road. One, a Syrian shrine, was completely exposed to view. Through the wide open portals of the building, against a background of black marble, a huge white figure of Astarte, goddess of fecundity, stood out in striking relief, earthly, voluptuous, enticing. Her lips were parted in a seductive smile; her breasts thrust forward; her waist was thin above her full hips. Two lotuses in her upraised hands reached above her gorgeous feather crown, while a python, curling from her left shoulder over her bare torso, pointed its head toward her left thigh. She was an image at once fascinating and repelling, the embodiment of lewdness and shameless temptation. The marchers quickened their pace, the more pious whispering, "Loathe and banish her, loathe and banish her, for she is abomination."

At last they reached the reservoir-shaped citadel, which towered above a deep moat paved with jagged stones. In front of a large iron gate a primitive drawbridge hung over the moat.

The ragged Levites sounded their horns; a Roman bugler in a turret responded. The massive gate was opened, the bridge lowered. The cavalrymen blocked the procession and directed all who preceded the gift-bearers to retire to the rear. A centurion then invited the old master and his entourage to enter, while the bulk of the marchers remained outside, kept at a distance from the moat by the Roman horsemen.

The delegation was requested to wait in an assembly hall, where a bronze eagle, behind a solitary table, faced rows of benches in the center and statuettes of Caesars along the white-washed walls. From where Akiba sat, he could see the tremendous court encircled by barracks. Two archways led to the inner courts, one housing the offices of state. Akiba knew that beyond the first lay a large training field; beyond the second, Rufus' magnificent residence, a good imitation of the Domitian Palace in Rome. While the training field was enclosed within the citadel walls, the palace stood outside. A fenced-off garden, with a secret underground corridor, connected it with the fort. The archways could shut off the inner courts by means of iron doors at each end and a solid block of stone, four feet thick, that could be lowered from the top between the doors. In the center of the outer court, between spouting fountains, two gigantic statues of Jupiter, king of men and deities, and Juno, goddess of power and patroness of riches, were ensconced on huge thrones mounted on pedestals of Parian marble.

The old sage gazed at these symbols of wealth and domination, and his thoughts were melancholy. By bringing more gold to the servant and worshiper of these idols, did he not in fact fortify their stand against God and indirectly transgress the most important commandment?

They were kept waiting for hours. Rufus, whose ego in the matter of the herds rankled more from humbled pride than because of the loss sustained, had found another outlet for his vindictiveness—humiliation of the Israelite leadership. So Akiba was kept waiting. It was not until late in the afternoon that a centurion invited the delegation to follow him into the inner court. In the anteroom to Rufus' atrium the centurion again requested them to wait.

The afternoon was well advanced when the old sage, Harrar and the gift-bearers were ushered in by the centurion. Akiba, unsmiling and erect, entered first and said stiffly, "Peace and greetings to His Excellency, the Roman Procurator of Judea."

There was unspoken reproof in his deliberate lack of animation. Ezra Harrar, however, bowed low. The two gift-bearing attendants waited by the door in awed immobility.

Rufus narrowed his small eyes, divined the mood of his callers and, without inviting them to sit, muttered with faint derision, "What can I do for the elders of Judea?"

"Before making our plea," Akiba responded, "and so that the serfs are not kept on their feet too long"—there was a perceptible touch of sarcasm in this phrase, which deepened in the next—"we wish, as a token of our esteem for His Excellency and for the Lady Ruffina, to offer these small gifts. . . ."

Harrar motioned to the attendants and they hastened over. He handed the ornate sword to Rufus, who balanced it in his hand and examined it with pleasure. Harrar said, "May we pray His Excellency to accept it for the glory of Rome, and may it never be used against Israel."

Rufus grinned dubiously and placed the sword on the table.

Akiba then handed him the velvet cushion with the gem-studded armlets. "May I ask His Excellency to send this modest gift to the most gracious lady in the land, from an admiring and grateful population?"

"Thank you," said Rufus coldly. He placed the cushion on the table and sounded the gong. Ovidius stalked in. "See that this is delivered to Lady Ruffina," Rufus said. Ovidius nodded, took the cushion and left the room. Harrar dismissed his serfs.

"You may perhaps find it more comfortable to sit," suggested Rufus with a mocking grin.

Harrar simulated laughter. Akiba, still taut and morose, pulled over a small couch. Harrar did likewise.

Akiba spoke. "We are fasting today."

"Why?" inquired the procurator with feigned surprise.

"Because my people and we, their messengers, are invoking the aid of the Almighty in preventing the issuance of a decree which will bring Judea much harm and Rome little good."

"The Romans and the Romans alone know what is good for Rome."

"Heaven knows best, Your Excellency."

"We've discussed this before, Rabbi. Assuming that Heaven does know best, does the rabbi pretend to speak for it?"

"I speak for my people. Rome's interference with our laws and customs will add neither to the power of Rome nor to her revenue," Akiba paused, "nor yet to the fortune of her Judean governor."

Rufus was quick to grasp the hint. "Since the rabbi is already aware of the intended decree, he assuredly knows that it is the wish of my emperor. Can I be expected to defy his wish?"

"No. But is it not the duty of a governor, most familiar with the land and the people he governs, to draw his emperor's attention to the possibility of a grievous error?"

"Would not an emperor as great as His Divine Majesty," retorted Rufus, "who himself has but recently visited these parts, consider interference by his subordinates presumptuous? And what makes the rabbi think that I disagree with my emperor? He does not mean to harm your people; he means to improve their lot. Romanization is not a punishment; it is a privilege. It is the emperor's wish that your people enjoy the benefits of a better life, that they stop their grumbling and sullenness. They will receive theaters and baths and games and many glorious temples for the one in ruins. . . ."

"His Excellency will remember," Akiba interrupted with unconcealed displeasure, "that this, too, has been discussed before."

Rufus eyed his old opponent in amazement. Did not the man realize the difference in their stations? Was this man not a petitioner, come to seek the favor of his overlord? Confoundedly strange people, these Judeans! Should he regard the interruption as insolent or as another peculiarity of an unpredictable barbarian? He laughed. "From the manner of the rabbi's speaking, one could gather that it is the rabbi who controls life and death in this country, and not I."

"Life and death are in the hands of the Almighty," said Akiba dryly.

The procurator narrowed his eyes. "If so, what brings the rabbi to me?"

Harrar looked alarmed. "We came to assure Your Excellency," he said hurriedly, "that our people is loyal. The community had nothing to do with the unpleasant incident and is not responsible for it. Nevertheless, reasonable compensation for losses will be paid. We shall use our influence to prevent the recurrence of such incidents. We petition Your Excellency not to deal harshly with the community."

"How soon can you produce the culprits, Harrar? And who are they?"

Ezra was taken aback. "I—I don't know," he stammered.

"Indeed?" the procurator sneered. "One for all and all for one. And what purpose do your speeches serve? All of you are guilty; you are willful and persistent in your folly, and only hard blows will bring you to reason."

Harrar was flabbergasted at this unexpected turn. Akiba flushed with anger. Suddenly he commanded, "Leave His Excellency and me alone."

Bewildered, Harrar looked at Akiba, then at Rufus, then again at the old master; both, for different reasons, waited in stern silence. He bowed and left the room.

Rufus dropped his official manner. "Why did you send him away, Akiba?"

"Because you and I, with only the Almighty as our witness, can be frank with each other. We have been frank with each other before."

"Speak."

"Two bags of gold—three times as much as last time—are waiting for you in the outer court."

"What do you want?" Rufus asked dryly.

"Time. Time to use influence in Rome. Maybe you, too, can add a little to this influence."

"Do not count on me."

"But you will stay the decree?"

Ovidius entered.

"What is it, Ovidius?" asked the procurator.

"Valentinus is reporting. And yes, some villagers from the nearby hills have joined the mob waiting outside the citadel and caused a disturbance. A horseman's leg was scratched and a few of them were mauled a little. It was necessary to disperse the mob. Arrests were made."

"The idiots! Show Valentinus in."

The huge officer lumbered into the room and saluted.

"Report, Valentinus."

"Collected from ten villages, Your Excellency. Six paid without trouble. Two surrendered half their livestock. Two resisted and it was necessary to crucify three men."

"Too bad."

"Shall we continue tomorrow?"

"Rest your men tonight and report for instructions in the morning."

Valentinus saluted and retired. The procurator glanced at Akiba. The sage was staring at the floor. His face was calm but his long fingers twitched.

"The incidents are regrettable," said Rufus sanctimoniously.

Akiba fixed a gaze of blistering contempt on the Roman. "Your ruse is too obvious, Rufus. We could have struck our bargain without bloodshed."

"Don't preach to me. As you see, I can easily collect more than your bagfuls of gold."

"And have the country up in arms again?"

"Is this a threat?" Rufus demanded belligerently.

"No, a possibility," said Akiba without flinching. "You know how such rebellions end."

"I know. But do not Roman lives count?"

"War is our business." The Roman reflected for a moment. "Akiba, I will take what you offer now and will expect as much in a week."

"That will be hard. What do you promise in return?"

"The expeditions against the villages will be suspended. The decree against worship, teaching and circumcision will be delayed, but you must waste no time. Put your influence in Rome to work at once."

"And the building of the temples?"

"That I can't stop."

"There will be disturbances."

"They will be crushed," snapped the Roman, glaring at Akiba. "And the brigand must be handed over to me."

The old sage leaned forward and, fixing a scorching stare on Rufus, uttered slowly, "Brigands are out of my reach."

The implication was clear and it made the Roman uncomfortable. "I shall return to the subject when the balance of the gold is delivered," he murmured.

"I must ask you to wait for it until the next moon."

"I'll wait."

"And will you leave the Christians alone, too? There can be no greater sin than to enslave free men."

"The Christians are none of your business and I forbid you to preach to me."

The procurator stood up, summoned Ovidius and directed him to accept the gold.

As Akiba rose to go, Ruffina entered through a hidden door. She obviously had not bothered to change her clothes, for she wore a house chiton, over which she had thrown a light blue palla.

Her husband made no effort to conceal his annoyance at her unexpected visit. "You!" he said, smiling wryly.

"Yes, dear," she said, her greenish eyes twinkling mischievously, and came forward to extend her hand to Akiba. "Greetings, dear Rabbi. It was wrong of you, Rufus, to hide from me the visit of such a distinguished friend. Your gift is charming, Rabbi. It is good of you to remember a Roman ruler's wife."

She took her husband's arm, and leaning against it, looked up at him with a gently mocking smile. "Am I intruding?"

"No, darling," he muttered sullenly. "Our business is finished. Rabbi Akiba was taking leave."

"I hope you've done nothing to hurt our friend."

"How could I, my dear?" he asked ironically.

"Can one be sure of a Roman governor," she replied coquettishly, "who shows so little reverence for the Israelite God?"

"How can I revere a God I can't see, my dear?"

She laughed. "And the rabbi finds it equally difficult to revere one he *can* see."

"When he is a handmade one, gracious lady," murmured Akiba. "But we are drifting toward our old dispute again. I'd better take my leave."

"Please, Rufus, ask the rabbi not to hurry away."

"She is irresistible, Rabbi. It would be a pleasure if you

stayed for a while. I did mean to ask a few questions which are not unrelated to the subject of our previous conversation."

The old sage bowed to both. "I'm grateful for the honor, but my friends are waiting and it is almost time for the sunset prayers."

"Please, Rabbi, let him ask the questions," Ruffina pleaded, relinquishing her husband's arm.

He answered her with smiling eyes, "How can I refuse you, gracious lady?"

Rufus motioned to Akiba to resume his seat, allowed his wife to take his, and pulled over a divan for himself. "I have heard it said that your invisible God is jealous of our visible gods, which, as you assert, are nonexistent. If your God is as great as you say He is, why should He be jealous of nonexistent rivals?"

Akiba's eyes flashed with amusement and became enigmatic as he uttered with deliberate unconcern, "I dreamed last night of two dogs named Rufus and Ruffina."

A flush of anger suffused the procurator's face and Ruffina gasped.

"Where is the connection, Rabbi?" choked the procurator, "and why couldn't the dogs be given other names?"

Akiba chuckled. "Now, see for yourself. If I jestingly bestow —and I beg your pardon—upon two nonexistent dogs such illustrious names, you take offense. Yet you are only a procurator, not a deity. Shall the Holy One, the King of Kings, blessed be He, not be offended when blocks of wood or marble are called by His Name?"

Ruffina laughed aloud while Rufus smiled sheepishly. But the setback did not discourage the procurator from pressing a second question: "Circumcision, which to us is an act of mutilation, and which, as you know, our emperor intends to prohibit, is to you a holy rite. Why is it so important?"

"It is a token of the covenant between us and the Almighty, and it is an improvement of God's raw creation."

"What!" exclaimed the Roman in mock horror. "Do you, insignificant mortals that you claim to be, presume to improve your great God's creation?"

Ruffina grew tense with interest.

"Are not the ears of grain God's creation?" countered Akiba, utterly unperturbed.

"Yes," agreed the procurator, wonderingly.

"And do we not turn them into loaves of bread?"

"Ah!" sighed Ruffina in unconcealed admiration, and applauded.

Her husband rose abruptly. Akiba was up on his feet at the same time. "The time for prayers is really here," he said. "The sun will set soon."

Touching his heart and brow, he bowed to Ruffina and, still holding his hand against his forehead, to the procurator.

"If you were not a stubborn Israelite," muttered Rufus as he took the old master to the door, "you could hold a seat in the Roman senate."

Akiba smiled noncommittally, provoking Rufus to take a parting fling at his opponent. "Tell me," he challenged, "if your God is omnipotent, why does He not destroy our idols?"

"If you worshiped only your own handiwork, He might do so. But you also worship His great masterpieces: the sun, the moon, the planets. Should He destroy the world?"

Akiba left the procurator irate and thwarted. He turned his face to his waiting wife. "Do you not think, my dear," he said acidly, "that your gloating over this old man's cleverness is a little too pronounced?"

"You must admit he is a great artist in his field," she parried, "and why should a Roman lady hide her admiration for an unusual display of art?"

"That 'art' happens to challenge all that Rome stands for and what your husband, the emperor's Procurator of Judea, is expected to uphold and enforce."

She yawned. "Don't be too pompous with me, dear. I am quite familiar with your high rank and I bask in its glory. I also know what Rome stands for." She picked up the gold-hilted sword from the table and played with it meaningfully. "If we take what we want and kill whom we want, can we not at least allow our victims to *say* what they want?"

Rufus lost his patience. "Speech is war," he shouted, "and the father of war! Let this man and others like him talk without restraint and they will destroy our empire. You may admire his art. But I tell you I will tear his tongue out! Even as he talked I said to myself, 'Rufus, you must tear this man's tongue out.' Our Emperor is right. What is exasperating about these people is their ability to make you feel wrong. Yes, I'll tear their tongues out!" He began pacing up and down the room.

Her face hardened and her eyes grew cold and dark green. "You've driven a bargain with them," she said, "have you not? You have taken their gold!"

He stopped abruptly. "How do you know?"

She shrugged. "Who does not?"

"And what if I have taken their gold? They brought it to me. I rule here! It would have been mine sooner or later."

"Have you no code of honor, my dear?"

"Pooh!" he laughed. "Honor! Are they Romans? They are worms! Worms with exasperating habits and blistering tongues."

She rose indignantly. Her palla fell to the floor, exposing her bare shoulders. "I warn you, Rufus, for your sake and the sake of Rome! If you let madness rule you, madness will rise to overpower you. Do not try the patience of these people too much. We have all but wiped them out three times but they still produce their Akibas and are dangerously alive! Perhaps there *is* an invisible God!"

She flung the sword on the table, and with her abrupt motion her chiton slipped from her shoulder, exposing part of her softly swelling breast.

He caught his breath. "So you, too, are falling under the senseless spell," he said weakly, and came closer. "Am I to allow them to snatch my beautiful wife from me?" He came still closer. The scent and beauty of her skin aroused him; his thoughts were losing coherence. "Darling," he said huskily, "why should we quarrel? You are so beautiful."

"I'll have nothing to do with you," she said, moving away, "unless you behave honorably and keep your promise to Akiba."

"How do you know what I promised?" Again he came closer and attempted to put his arms about her.

"I know." She adjusted her chiton and bent to pick up her palla. He tried to seize her, but she wriggled away, and again her chiton slid off her shoulder.

"Will you keep your promise to Akiba?" she repeated.

"I will," he whispered hoarsely.

That night, as Akiba, his disciples and adherents were break-ing the fast at Rabbi Uziel's, Judith brought an appropriate warning from her mistress along with the gem-studded armlets.

It was the judgment of the gathering that powerful core-ligionists in Alexandria must at once be influenced to reach leading senators in Rome and, if possible, the court itself; that the most suitable emissary was Johai of Tiberias, Simeon's father; that the son be requested to induce his aging parent to undertake the mission, and, if need be, that he accompany his father to Alexandria. The next morning Akiba set out for Bnai Brak and Simeon bar-Johai left for Tiberias.

Chapter Eleven

As indicated in Daniel's will, the treasure had been found in secluded, well-concealed spots in the Judean Mountains, south-east of Modin and south of Jerusalem, and a caravan of pack horses and donkeys, led by Shemon and Nitsa, was now taking the precious cargo to Ludd. The most dangerous point on their journey, Jerusalem, where the Tenth Roman Legion was quartered, had been left behind without mishap, and the heavily laden caravan was slowly climbing the tortuous highway in the heart of the hills.

Shemon and Nitsa, a slight, quicksilvery man with a large, impressive head, a tapering nose, keen, dark eyes and a silver-streaked black beard, rode on stout horses noted for endurance rather than speed. Directly behind, on a large donkey, was Nitsa's chief overseer, Abiezer, a black-bearded, resolute man with a prodigious nose and long legs. A few paces away ten husky men with staffs in their hands strode beside the animals, and Asaph, a young Betarian with a daredevil face and formidable shoulders, closed the rear. Excepting Nitsa, garbed in a costly robe and turban, they all wore hooded camel's-hair cloaks, under which long two-edged daggers were comfortably hidden.

Shemon was pleased with these men, who, like their master, were given to little talk and pursued their hazardous task fearlessly and confidently. They were Judeans, but there were many men like them among the hillmen of Galilee, the plainsmen of Sharon, and the fishermen of the seacoast and the banks of Lake Kinnereth. They propounded no laws, sat not at the feet of the great, did not engage in casuistry, enjoyed few of the pleasures of this world and expected little in the world to come. Yet, like their forbears, they carried in their hearts an unquenchable thirst for freedom and, like them, too, would be among the first to die for it if the call came. If they did not know why their fathers had failed, they would have to be told; they would have to be taught how to succeed. They would have to be taught warcraft, the art of being one and acting as one. There was likely to be a race against time, but they would learn quickly—they had good minds. Was not Akiba one of them? Conversely, why should one like the old, learned Eliezer, a descendant of the house of liberators, the Hasmoneans, be aloof, cold and discouraging? Was he, Shemon, perhaps unjust to his uncle? Was the image created in his childhood perhaps a distorted image? It would have been good to find him at home that morning when Shemon had risked seeing him at Modin, but unfortunately the old man had been away.

"If all goes well," said Nitsa, "we shall, God willing, reach Ludd before daybreak."

Shemon glanced at the sky. The moon was gone and clouds driven by a light westerly breeze were drifting in from the sea.

"It seems that the spring *yalkosh* is coming. It is not enough of a rain to keep the guards off the roads," he observed.

Nitsa looked up. "No," he agreed, "it will be a drizzle if it comes. But Shemon need have no misgivings about the guards."

Again silence fell. Their road now lay between rugged mountain walls that rose steeply above the highway; further on, still higher terraces, slopes and wooded crests towered darkly over the gaping ravines. The beasts were slackening their pace in the steady uphill climb and the drivers urged them on with a gentle word, a cluck of the tongue and at times with a prod of the staff. Occasionally Abiezer turned to his men to make a brusque remark.

Shemon's thoughts drifted to the man beside him. A remarkable person, this Nitsa. How many men in his position would risk their heads in such an adventure? Not one he could bring to mind. Those he knew would not go out of the way to ward off the evil, but would rather rely on their treasure to keep the evil away if it came to their doorsteps. Nitsa was an exception.

A light drizzle had come and gone and the small caravan was still plying its way in the Judean Hills when Shemon threw back his head, pricked up his ears and muttered, "Men are coming."

"I hear nothing," said Nitsa. He turned to his overseer. "Do you hear anything, Abiezer?"

"Nothing, my lord, save foxes in the distance and an owl in yonder tree."

"Men are climbing up a path from the left," asserted Shemon and halted his horse.

Nitsa stopped the caravan but could not conceal his amazement. "The Emmaus citadel," he said, "is a distance away to the left and men may be coming, but I still hear no footfalls."

"My lord will hear them soon," Shemon insisted, and pulling up his hood, buried his face in it.

Nitsa rose in his stirrups and peered at the mountainside on the left. "Shemon was right," he muttered in astonishment. "Men are coming. I see a light moving up and a glint of helmets." He turned to Abiezer. "Assuredly the Emmaus road watch."

"Assuredly, my lord," agreed Abiezer.

"Undo your wineskin bag," said Nitsa.

Abiezer did and Nitsa motioned to the caravan to proceed. Soon six cloaked and helmeted legionaries appeared and, waving a lantern, blocked the highway. Nitsa and Abiezer spurred on their horses and the caravan stopped.

Slowly Shemon rode down the line of drivers, halting at each one of them and muttering, "We'll cut their throats if they molest us."

And each one of them responded with a nod and a gleam in his eyes.

Meanwhile, up the road, where master and servant were negotiating with the patrol, there was no sign of hostility. A laugh and another laugh indicated that all was well, and this became a certainty when Abiezer was seen handing out the wineskins.

Nitsa's possessions on the outskirts of Ludd amounted to a little private domain. Here mills, silos, storehouses, stalls, workmen's huts, wells, a smithy, a bathhouse and a synagogue lay within a spiked ten-foot wall with four iron gates. One of them opened onto the Joppa-Jerusalem highway and faced the large plain extending through Ramat Lechi to the Judean Hills; another served the northern traffic; the third linked his yard with Ludd proper, and the fourth led to his private garden and residence.

When the caravan reached its destination the place, despite the early hour, was humming with life. Camels, pack asses and oxcarts were arriving, departing or waiting to be loaded or unloaded; porters ran to and fro; shaggy rustics crowded about the mules; drivers with vats and buckets jostled, cursed and jested at the well, and a group of merchants was discussing prices on their way to the synagogue.

When the gold had been deposited in Nitsa's underground vault, Shemon was prevailed upon by his host to rest for a few hours before proceeding to Bnai Brak. Nitsa's house was a commodious two-story structure with a cellar and an attic. But he had a large family. Solicitous of Shemon's comfort, Nitsa therefore suggested that he stay at his private hostel, built to accommodate friends. It was still dark when they stepped into the garden, wet with morning dew. At the entrance to the hostel, which adjoined the main building, two men were talking softly.

"If it is not Zevulun!" Nitsa exclaimed, but not too loudly.

The shorter of the two men turned. "It is he," he said in a gruff, husky voice.

The taller man also turned, and Shemon recognized Joel. "I am surprised indeed," Shemon said. "What brings you here?"

"Word from Itamar, and your mare Ayalah, which he brought to Bnai Brak for you."

"Is she still there?"

"No, she is here and has been taken to the stable."

Shemon paused to reflect. "Odd," he mused, knitting his brows. "It must be important if Itamar ventured to bring Ayalah. Did he go back?"

"Yes," said Joel.

Nitsa interrupted to introduce Shemon to Zevulun, a middle-statured, thickset man in Egyptian garb, and invited them into the hostel. They threw down some cushions and settled comfortably on the carpeted floor while Nitsa summoned a servant and ordered food. Briefly, Joel relayed Itamar's message:

Soldiers on foot and on horseback swarmed over the country-side, questioning villagers and wayfarers, searching, extorting money and humiliating women. In Geidera and Afra, where resistance had been attempted, some men had been flogged to death and some houses had been burned. Late in the afternoon word had spread that Rabbi Akiba was in Caesarea. Victims, a number of them tattered and bleeding, had come to the capital. The sight of them had sent the waiting Israelites into a frenzy and Rufus' horsemen had attacked them. Many had been injured and killed.

In the discussion that followed, Nitsa counseled waiting for Akiba's return. Shemon agreed to refrain from precipitate action; but he held that an early uprising was imminent, and that nothing was as important, therefore, as the training of men. Hence he urged Joel to return to Bnai Brak forthwith. Joel did so after they had washed, prayed and eaten. Presently Shemon and Zevulun were left alone.

Slowly the mariner removed his white turban and flowing white robe and placed them carefully beside him, and as slowly produced a skull cap, which he clapped upon his closely cropped head. The Roman tunic and kilt in which he now remained amused Shemon, and Zevulun, catching the other's mood, grinned. "A seafarer," he said, "finds it convenient to be an Edomite among Edomites and an Egyptian among Egyptians—without, that is—but always an Israelite within."

Shemon made no comment but regarded with interest the man whom Akiba had praised. He studied the powerful limbs and neck; the shoulders that were too broad for his height: the leathery skin; the small, needle-pointed black eyes under shaggy eyebrows; the fleshy nose, and the clipped beard of carob-fruit brown.

The other was scanning Shemon with equal interest. *Not a man to trifle with,* Shemon decided.

"Now that we know each other," said Zevulun with his characteristic husky gruffness, "let us talk."

"Let us," agreed Shemon, and came straight to the point. "It would help us on land if we could strike at them from the sea."

"It is not impossible," the mariner responded after a pause. "How soon will you strike?"

"As soon as we have enough men, arms, horses and food."

"These, and ships, too, will take much gold."

"There will be gold," Shemon said convincingly.

The needle points of Zevulun's eyes rested on Shemon for a while. "Horses, nevertheless, will be hard to get and still harder to transport in large numbers," he said. "How many horses do you need for striking?"

"Three thousand would be a good beginning; we have only three hundred now."

Zevulun shook his head gravely. "Hard. It will take a long time."

Shemon refused to be discouraged. He proceeded to question Zevulun and established the fact that three large galleys and twenty small boats would be available at the beginning; that they were part of a commercial fleet owned by an Israelite who had old accounts to settle with Rome, but whose name would not be revealed for the present; that shipments of supplies would commence as soon as this Israelite, a resident of Alexandria, gave his consent; and that Zevulun would return to Egypt without delay. They also agreed on landing and meeting places.

Their arrangements completed, they both felt that a great stride toward their common goal had been made and that they had been united by inseparable bonds springing from mutual trust and singleness of purpose. They rose, beaming with friendship, clasped hands and, guided by impulse, embraced each other.

Chapter Twelve

Well fed, and spurred on by Shemon's affectionate coaxing, Ayalah trotted jauntily in the hills paralleling the coastal plains. Far away, isles of gold shimmered in the unruffled blue of the sea and hawks darted from dizzy heights at invisible prey. Shemon watched the distant road below, the underbrush above it, and the donkey trails that now and then cut across his path, but there were few patrols in sight; the hunt had obviously abated. Pleased, he fondled his mare. "Good going, Ayalah. It seems that no evil will befall us today; the Edomites are resting. Like the stinging insects of the marshes, they are heavy with blood."

When he reached the southern outskirts of Zofith an ungovernable urge to see Meredya possessed him. His emotion, a great restless eagerness mingled with a peculiar fear, was unlike anything he had ever felt before. Reasoning against it proved futile.

To avoid undue attention Shemon swung to the narrow path skirting the town and rimming its sloping pastures. Close to its northern end, he recognized the lane where Abner's homestead was located and dismounted at the familiar gate.

From the yard, on the other side of the house, came excited feminine voices. His unexpected visit might prove unwelcome. Yet his instinct urged him on. To call attention to himself he deliberately allowed the wooden gate to bang, but no one appeared to hear. Since the chattering continued, he tethered his horse and proceeded into the yard.

In front of the house a group of arguing and gesticulating girls was clustered about Meredya, slightly taller than the rest, who manifestly was trying to drive some point home. Facing the other way, she failed to see him.

Discreetly he paused some distance away. The girls who noticed him stopped talking and gaped. He heard Meredya's voice. "I tell you again," she was saying, "there is nothing to fear. He is not an Edomite, just a scoundrel, and no one will care. He received what he deserved, and there the matter ends."

Suddenly becoming aware of the strange stillness and the frozen stares about her, she turned. Her eyes distended with frightened surprise and the color rushed into her cheeks. She swung round to face him but did not come toward him. There was a strange weakness in her knees and the blood kept mounting into her face.

He smiled and advanced awkwardly. Her confusion was communicating itself to him and the curious staring of the girls added to his discomfort. The few yards that divided him from Meredya seemed a long distance. "I was passing by," he muttered, "and thought I would come in to see your father."

She caught her breath. "He went to a neighboring village," she replied, "and will not return before sunset."

"A pity," he said. "I will have to see him some other time. I have only a few minutes to spare."

"It is a pity." Meredya's restraint was disappearing and giving way to an eager friendliness. "You must have come a long way and are probably hungry or thirsty."

She was lovely in the starlight and she is lovely in the sunlight, even in a work dress, he thought. *How good it would be to take anything from her hands—if only those other girls did not gape!* Aloud he said, "No, thank you, Meredya. There are mountain springs on the way. I will come some other time."

He bowed, swung round abruptly and strode away. As he was turning the corner the girls began to giggle. He heard hurried footsteps behind him. Mortified with himself and the girls, he kept going without looking back.

As he reached his horse, Meredya caught up with him. "You must not be angry," she pleaded, flushed and a little out of breath. "The girls meant no offense. Please forgive me for them."

His chagrin was melting as snow under a warm sun, and irresistible impulses were stirring within him. He took her hands. "It is I who must ask for forgiveness. I came without warning."

What he was saying did not matter to her. It was his voice, his gaze, his touch—they were terribly disturbing. A little frightened, she withdrew her hands. Then she laughed. "I am glad you have come, Shemon. If Father were here I would ask you to stay. But you must allow me to give you a drink." Ever so lightly she touched his arm. "Please wait."

She ran off. His mortification had disappeared. He was now glad he had followed his impulse. Akiba's Rachel could not have been more pleasing to the eye, more captivating in her ways. He patted his mare. "And what sayest thou, Ayalah?"

Meredya returned with a jarful of diluted grape syrup. Immediately behind, Zarooba carried water for the horse. "This is cool," Meredya said, pouring out a cupful of the syrup. "We keep it in the cellar."

He gulped it down. Despite his restraining hand, she refilled the cup. This time he sipped the juice with relish. The maid went off with the empty pail. On the other side of the house the girls became vociferous again.

"What's wrong?" Shemon asked.

"Nothing important," she smiled.

"But the girls are aroused and you spoke of a 'scoundrel.'"

"So you heard me." She became serious. "He is unworthy of your thoughts."

"But he is in yours. Who may he be?"

"A tax collector's assistant; by his looks, a Phoenician." She hesitated.

"What did he do?"

"This morning he came to a neighbor across the lane to collect taxes. There was no one at home but the daughter, a good, modest virgin. The man seized her, and when she cried out, I unchained Raam and ran to her aid. There was no one else about." Her eyes twinkled. "He found no favor in Raam's eyes."

"Who does?" he smiled. "Then what happened?"

"Raam told him not to molest the daughters of Israel," she said mirthfully. "He tore his robe and partook of his softer spots before the man's master came to lead him off."

"And wherefore are the girls aroused now?"

"They fear the collector will return with Edomites and they say that the girl and I should hide. But I say there is nothing to fear. The collector will not complain about a few bites at a

Phoenician's seat when the taxes are duly paid. Undeserved punishment of people punishes the collector, too, for it brings the payment of taxes down."

"Perhaps I ought to tarry for a while?" Shemon asked.

"The two are gone, Shemon; and will they return, knowing the temper of the people? Also, word has been sent to Elon and our Heromavs will surely watch."

He thanked her for the drink and began to fumble with Ayalah's reins, searching for a pretext to prolong the pleasure of these precious moments. Perils and conflict and hate and a thousand forms of human viciousness would wait for him wherever he went. But would such sweetness and charm and warmth wait? He mounted, and as he glanced at her he caught a glimpse of his own emotion in her eyes. She quickly averted them. From the other side of the house the girls were calling her.

"I must go," he said slowly. "I will come again one evening when your father is home."

"The doors of our house will always be wide open for you," she replied quietly. He saluted and pulled at the reins.

Some distance out of Zofith, Shemon caught sight of a strange procession on the coastal highway; it consisted of riders, most of them on donkeys, followed by a crowd of people on foot.

He halted to watch. They could not be Romans, for that was not their marching style; nor slaves in transfer, because that was not their formation; nor traders, for there were no laden animals. A pilgrimage? At this time of the year? Where to? What for? The procession was some twenty furlongs outside Caesarea, heading south. Upon further reflection it occurred to him that this might be Akiba's party returning to Bnai Brak. In that case he must see Akiba without delay.

He guided Ayalah down the mountainside and stopped to wait in the shade of a cluster of carob trees above the highway. The procession was approaching. His surmise had been correct. Despite the pall of dust, he could now discern Akiba on horseback, flanked by his bodyguards, and immediately behind them on donkeys, Joshua Hagarsi and several unfamiliar individuals. Scores of gesticulating men trudged in the rear. The old master, erect in the saddle, held his head down, oblivious to his surroundings.

Shemon hid most of his face in the flaps of his headdress and descended to the road. He waited for the van of the procession to pass and unobtrusively rode up to one of the bodyguards. "I am Shemon," he said under his breath. "Move forward; show no surprise. Take the other guard with you."

The man cast one astounded look at the unexpected speaker, recognized him and obeyed, beckoning to his friend to follow him. Joshua, too, recognized Shemon, but prudently refrained from exhibiting his discovery. Shemon studied Akiba's careworn face for a while and, seeing that his presence went unnoticed, said softly, "I beg the rabbi's pardon. This is Shemon."

Akiba started. "Peace be with you. I've been thinking of you."

"The Lord must have heard the rabbi's thoughts, for here I am."

"It is propitious. Coming from Ludd?"

"Yes, my Rabbi."

"Everything in order? No mishaps?"

"Everything in order and all is well."

"May His Name be blessed. Have you seen Zevulun?"

"Yes, my Rabbi. Zevulun is a tower of strength."

"I am glad you are pleased, Shemon. What is he willing to do?"

"Everything. But he will speak to his wealthy master first."

"That is how it should be." Akiba paused. "And now, so as not to keep you on the highway too long," he said solicitously, "I will give you the tidings."

Briefly the sage described the events at Caesarea and declared sorrowfully that although the edict would be delayed, the procurator would undoubtedly break faith. "Nevertheless," he admonished, "we must exercise the utmost restraint, on the one hand, and prepare, prepare, prepare, on the other. Time will serve us well. Meanwhile I expect that the worthy Johai of Tiberias and his son will seek out their influential friends in Alexandria. Maybe they will find a way to the Caesar's heart."

"The idolator has no heart," Shemon said gruffly.

"He who creates men also created the hearts of men," the rabbi replied solemnly.

"And shall nothing be done about the new murders and plunderings?" Shemon queried bitterly.

"Nothing now," Akiba responded gloomily.

"I will bring to my men the rabbi's words," Shemon said reluctantly, "but we are reaching the limit of our endurance."

"You look after your men, Shemon. The limit of endurance will be set by Heaven."

Shemon bade the rabbi *Shalom* and took to the hills.

Akiba glanced after him and muttered a benediction.

Chapter Thirteen

Returning to the Cave of Vengeance, Shemon found that there had been no mishaps, that his instructions had been carried out and that arms would shortly arrive from Raphael's smithy. Itamar, as had been arranged early that morning, had changed his horse at the cave and had gone to Upper Galilee and Kfar Haroob for more volunteers.

Shemon, who was in the gorge talking to his headmen, muttered something about being satisfied. He had had little sleep since his departure for Bnai Brak, and now that his mind had been relieved from immediate anxiety, he suddenly felt extremely fatigued and an almost paralyzing drowsiness came upon him. He meant to ask for food but only blinked and, sinking to the ground, slept.

He awoke some hours later. Issachar, a lanky, taciturn young man with a misshapen nose that had been broken by a legionary, small, fanatical eyes, and a sparse beard sprouting mainly from beneath his chin, had made a fire by the brook and was broiling lamb. Shemon washed and they broke bread. They were at the end of their meal when Nadav appeared. His large black eyes were aglow with excitement and perspiration was dripping from his face.

"Hungry?" inquired Shemon.

"No," Nadav replied sullenly. "How can one eat when friends are dying?"

"I heard the evil tidings from Rabbi Akiba," Shemon muttered. "But those who strike at the evil must eat for strength."

"You could not have heard all of the evil, Shemon. Hear you what my brother has to say." He stepped toward the cave door and called, "Come out, Ovadya!"

Ovadya, flushed, grimy and out of breath, staggered into the gorge. He was overwrought and could not speak.

"Tell them," Nadav said impatiently.

The gawky youth sniffled, wiped his face with the sleeve of his dusty garment and took another step forward. His lips quivered and in the glow of the sputtering fire his eyes gleamed with anguish. "They beat him, they whipped him, and now they are crucifying him!" he gasped.

Shemon came to his feet. "Whom are they crucifying?"

"My friend . . . Shmaya." The lad was shaking with sobs, and his speech was blurred and broken, but few words were required to tell his tale.

When the men from Geidera had come and the Israelites, still waiting for Akiba at the citadel gates, had protested against the maltreatment of their brethren, the Roman horsemen had attacked them with sticks and spears. Shmaya, infuriated by a blow, had caught a Roman's leg and sunk his teeth into it. Was one to die for biting a dog? "Save him," Ovadya pleaded. "Please save him. Shmaya is only fifteen. He is my friend."

Shemon stood still, his heart in conflict with his mind. Issachar came closer, and with the others, watched him tensely. "Your distress is hard to bear," Shemon said blankly, "but we are not ready."

"Not ready, not ready, not ready!" exploded Ovadya, his adolescent voice cracking but vibrant with passion. "When is 'ready'? After everybody is dead? We have horses and arms. Why can we not bear down upon our enemies now? Is Shemon, the giant, afraid?"

Shemon could not be angry with the lad. Who better than he understood the lad's anguish and impotent rage? And who could find it harder than he not to reveal his emotions, not to succumb to the clamoring impulses of his heart? Slowly he came over to Ovadya and took the boy's shaking body into his arms.

"Some day soon," he said, "God will give you the answer. It is much harder to fight one's feelings than one's enemy. Shmaya is lost, whatever we do. Is it not better to kill multitudes of Edomites and drive them from the land a little later than to kill a few of them now and be driven out ourselves?"

There was no reply. Ovadya, pressing his face against Shemon's chest, continued to sob. Shemon caressed the lad gently until his spasms subsided.

"Now, freshen up at the brook, Ovadya," he said presently, "and you too, Nadav, and fortify yourselves with food. Let us gather up our hurts even as thunderclouds gather before the rain, and when the time is ripe, let the storm break with might and fury."

The brothers washed and took places by the fire, where chunks of lamb still sizzled on the spits. And as they ate, Shemon told them as much about his meeting with Nitsa and Zevulun as would hearten them. Then they felt better and he assigned tasks to them. Nadav, in a beggar's disguise, was to spy on jetties, barracks, markets and inns in order to learn about the coming and going of troops and boats and caravans. Ovadya was to return to his brother Raphael's smithy to forge more and more weapons. And every evening he was to ask Judith the seamstress whether or not she had word to send.

Some weeks later Zevulun came and Issachar showed him to his chief's tent in the gorge. Shemon was delighted to see the mariner and welcomed him with food and wine.

"I bring you good tidings from my master," said Zevulun. "Most of his boats and half of his fortune are at our command." He paused to relish Shemon's unconcealed pleasure; then he continued, "And this, too, you may now know. My master is none other than your kinsman who, with your father and uncle, tried seventeen years ago to do what you are trying to do now, and who was saved from the noose of the wicked Moor only by the grace of the Almighty."

"Pappus!" exclaimed Shemon.

"He and no other!" said the mariner, his leathery face crinkling with delight and his pin-point eyes brightening. "And he bids me tell you that your other kinsmen and a good many more Alexandrian Israelites of substance have met and will meet again with Johai and his son; they will spare no gold to the end that where Artemion, Julianus and Pappus failed, Shemon shall, with God's help, prevail."

"No man could have brought me better tidings," Shemon said gratefully.

There was an air of pleasant suspense, each waiting for the other to speak. Then Zevulun became his gruff self again. "I bring you less pleasing tidings, too," he began, and Shemon pricked up his ears. "Yesterday I anchored one of Pappus' ships off Joppa shoals." Slowly and circumspectly he proceeded to unfold a tale to which Shemon listened with unbroken fascination:

The ship was still at anchor, unloaded, waiting for his, Zevulun's, return. Her cargo included two large statues of naked goddesses and many smaller images for Hadrian's temple in Jerusalem. It was said that the site of the holy Temple would be cleared and plowed in preparation for the laying of the new foundation.

Now what was he, Zevulun, to do? Send the images ashore and let them be taken to Jerusalem? Or destroy them? If they went to Jerusalem, the people might rise up in arms too soon. If the abominations were destroyed aboard the ship, the consequences for him and his crew would be grave.

"If your men are good divers," suggested Shemon, "let there be a mishap on the way from ship to shore, with no harm to your men."

"A good thought," agreed Zevulun upon reflection. "We can unload the images into the small boats at dusk, and on their way to shore there will be a collision. The images will break; some of the boatmen will seem to drown. But they are excellent swimmers and we need have no misgivings. They will be saved after dark."

"So be it," said Shemon.

The two conspirators laughed and drank to success.

Later they went out and Shemon took Zevulun to the gully and up to a point sixty feet below the summit of a hill two thousand feet high. Shemon led Zevulun into a dark tunnel winding into a shorter but broader one and came out behind a huge boulder on a promontory. Here, ringed by a chain of hill crests, in a bowl-shaped space, hundreds of men were pitching tents, digging trenches and erecting sheds. On each of the surrounding hills, directly above the camp in preparation, more men were digging and sentries were standing on guard. Zevulun rubbed his clipped beard in astonishment. "Hidden from the enemy, and a good spot to strike from— northward, southward and at the coast," he muttered.

"This is our first large camp," said Shemon. "We call it the Bowl."

"And what are the men on those hill crests doing?" asked the mariner.

"Digging deep pits."

"What for?"

A mischievous twinkle came into Shemon's coppery eyes. "Snares," he said. "Later, walls will be built in front of them." Zevulun appeared unenlightened.

"In each of those hills," Shemon explained, "there will be deep pits descending into passages like those through which we've just now come. The mouth of the pit on each hill will be closed by wooden covers, on which soil will be spread. Long ropes will be fastened to hooks in the boards. If the enemy should take the wall and reach this far, the rope will be pulled, the trap will open and the enemy will go hurtling sixty feet down, to where we will be waiting."

Zevulun gave Shemon a resounding slap on the back and they both roared with laughter.

Chapter Fourteen

After Zevulun's departure an ungovernable desire to see Meredya possessed Shemon. He was in good spirits and no longer hunted intensely, and there was no reason why he should not go. His intentions regarding Abner's daughter had not crystalized—and he was reluctant to permit them to crystalize, fearful that at this juncture a wife might prove a handicap. Nevertheless, he was seven years past eighteen—a man's age for marrying, according to the sages—and here was a daughter in Israel, possessed of beauty, courage and good sense, whose image had taken irresistible hold of him. It was best to yield to the ungovernable urge and leave the rest to fate.

In the afternoon, when the heat of the day was declining, Shemon saddled his mare, donned a colorful robe and turban and set out for Zofith. It was dark when Ayalah ambled into town. The tree-lined central avenue was unlighted, dusty, and at first glance, deserted. But as he proceeded, he encountered at long intervals small groups of promenading men. The air was charged with the scent of flowers and ripening fruit, mingled with the odor of manure and burning refuse. Knots of people chatted quietly in front of their vineyards and orchards, where the contours of square, flat-roofed dwellings were discernible in the dark. Here and there palm trees rose high above them. Some of the promenaders paused to scan the unfamiliar horseman but, upon being greeted in their own tongue, resumed their stroll. However, the lone late rider became the subject of their conversations. Their interest was particularly aroused by his thoroughbred Arabian horse, the kind which an Israelite was rarely permitted to own.

Shemon decided to have a word with Elon before calling on Meredya, and so went to the southeastern end of the town. He passed the council house, the bathhouse and the synagogue, where a few diligent students were still chanting a portion of the Torah. The market place, a circular clearing with a few wooden stands and much animal leavings, was now completely deserted.

Tamar had gone to bed and it was easy to talk. Shemon acquainted Elon briefly with the events of the last few weeks; he was glad to learn in turn that the local ranks of the Heromavs were growing. Most of the strollers on the central avenue were, Elon assured his friend, "watchers in the night." Shemon took leave.

At Abner's gate he dismounted. His arrival, as Ayalah

clumped after him into the darkness of the courtyard, caused a commotion dominated by Zarooba's exclamations and Raam's stentorian barks.

A timeworn, nearsighted servant, whom Shemon had not noticed before, came panting from the garden, cudgel in hand. "What may your wish be?" he demanded hoarsely, his voice shaking as much from his own bravado as at the sight of the huge man and the horse.

"Not so loud, Methuselah," Shemon said good-naturedly, going farther into the courtyard. "All I want is to see your master."

"The master is away," said the old man grumpily. "And who may you be?"

"Who is it?" came Meredya's rich voice from the dimness of the doorway.

A wave of warmth swept through Shemon and caught his breath for an instant. He had not realized that a voice could have such an effect. "This is Shemon, Meredya," he replied a bit tremulously.

He heard a queer little gasp, and after a pause: "In a moment." Then she called to the dog, "Quiet, Raam! This is a friend." The canine growled his doubts and subsided. Zarooba, who had apparently intended to unchain the dog, dashed, scantily clad, from the kennel into a shed.

Ahab, the aged servant, lowered his cudgel and asked respectfully, "Shall I take the horse to the stable?"

"No, give her a drink and tie her to a tree." Shemon slipped a coin into Ahab's hand. The old man mumbled his gratitude and took Ayalah to the well.

Meredya reappeared in the doorway, ran for a space and stopped within several feet of Shemon. She was breathing unsteadily and her eyes were brilliant with excitement. "Father is not home," she said.

"Again!" He smiled uncertainly. "And will he be gone long?"

"I know not. He is at a meeting of the elders."

"Always meeting with the elders," Shemon murmured, but there was no trace of dissatisfaction in his voice. He came nearer and they stood gazing at each other. The already-familiar silken kerchief covered her shoulders and accentuated the gleaming whiteness of her neck. He came still closer. "Truly, it is to see *you* that I came."

His breath was warm and his eyes burned with an intensity that she felt like a torch. She did not avert her gaze, which was steady. But the rise and fall of her shawl betrayed her agitation. "I know," she whispered. "I was hoping. . . ."

He took her soft hands and held them in his large, hard ones. After a feeble effort to withdraw hers, she let them stay.

"I meant to speak to your father," he began, and broke off. "Let us walk in the garden," he offered.

She wavered. "Just a little," she said. "Father may come at any moment."

"Let him come."

"You know what fathers think of seemliness."

He released her hands. But in the garden, under the hood of an ancient carob that shut out the starlight, Shemon stopped and grasped her arms. "I've been thinking of you all these weeks," he said. She waited. "I know of no better or comelier maiden that a man could wish to be his wife." There was a slightly perceptible tremor in her arms but still she said nothing. "Have I a right to ask such a maiden to marry me?"

"Why not?" she inquired softly. There was a tinge of disappointment in her voice.

"I have picked a dangerous road for myself and can offer a wife nothing but heartaches and anguish."

"That a maiden and her father must decide; her joys may outweigh her sorrows."

"There will be war, Meredya. You may find yourself without a husband."

She shrank from him and said scornfully, "Is that your faith in yourself and in God?"

A little disconcerted, he replied gently, "It is not lack of faith, Meredya; it is concern for you. I said to myself, *I will not blind her with words like myrrh. Shemon's bride must know that she is taking the sting with the sweetness.*"

"She would be a fool if she knew it not. What can a virgin now expect from marriage except hope? Can she know the future? Any day, under Edom, may become a long night. But with a man like you," her voice sank to a whisper, "any night has starlight and hope; hope not for me alone, but for all of us."

He drew her close. Her kerchief slipped off her shoulders. His arms clasped her with an ardor that hurt. She threw her head back.

"Say yes."

His voice was low and thick, but to her the two little words rang out like bells. "Yes," she whispered.

He bent his face down to hers, held her as one holds something precious and fragile and kissed her.

"Meredya!" That was Abner calling from the yard.

"Father!" she murmured, nestling to Shemon. He kissed her again.

"Come, my lovely bride," he said, and led her to Abner.

The wedding was set for a fortnight after the harvest festival, which was but a little more than one week off.

Shemon glowed with unbounded happiness and faith as Ayalah carried him back to the caves. To him his first great success augured well for the future.

Chapter Fifteen

Zevulun succeeded; the goddesses which were to beautify Hadrian's temple in Jerusalem lay smashed on the bottom of the Joppa harbor. The plotters were gleeful; the procurator, enraged. No one could be held responsible. Everything pointed to the genuineness of the accident. There was no loss of Roman life. Only natives suffered—four boatmen appeared to have been drowned. Yet somehow Rufus sensed a plot. It was strange that the boatmen's bodies had not been recovered or washed up by the tide. Just as strange was the fact that the mishap had played into the hands of the confounded Israelites; Hadrian's construction timetable had been upset.

Hence, instructions were issued to the Joppa commander to set the port spies in motion for clues. By way of advance retribution if conspiracy could be established, or to provoke inflammatory incidents according to plan if it could not, Rufus allowed the hint to be circulated that a little "sport" at the expense of the natives would be in order. The "hint" was received with favor. It broke the drab monotony of life in the inactive Roman garrisons and brought the soldiers "souvenirs" and extra food and money. At the same time the rumblings of the dormant Judean volcano became more pronounced.

Despite the rising tension in the country, Meredya prepared for her nuptials. One of her married sisters, Nehama, a dark, buxom woman in her late twenties, came down from Cabul in Galilee to help. Abner made a special trip to the Shukpatris mart to buy silks, linen and oils. Joel and other close kinsmen were notified, and hands were hired to accelerate the harvesting.

There were many questions to be settled, foremost among them the place of residence for the couple. Zofith would expose Shemon to the danger of easy detection. Upper Galilee, where he had some safe retreats, was too far for the bride and would interfere with his schemes. Ein Gedi, where Hemda, Meredya's second sister, lived, was too far south in Judea. Shemon's plans required a central location whence his forces could strike with facility north, south, seaward and across the Jordan. The caves in the Hills of Ephraim answered the purpose, and the hazards to a woman notwithstanding, it was decided to build a special hut on a hill overlooking the Bowl. Abner suggested that Eliezer of Modin, Shemon's nearest of kin, act the part of his parent at the wedding. Shemon agreed.

Immediately after the harvest festival Shemon, accompanied by Issachar, took a hurried trip to Modin. They reached the Mount of Interment, the resting place of the Hasmoneans, toward evening. At the foot of the mountain, which rolled upward above Modin, a stream lapped its way toward the heart of the Judean Hills. Directly opposite, some distance away, there was a somewhat lower hill, and on its summit stood a Roman post.

Shemon felt that it was best not to disturb his aged uncle at night and encamped with Issachar in a secluded spot, where they built a fire and ate. On his previous trip Shemon had not been able to spare the time to visit the tomb of his ancestors, which he had never seen. Now that the whole night was before him, he decided to go and asked Issachar to look after the horses.

Shemon turned east. The young moon, emerging from behind small clouds, dimly and fitfully illuminated the hard, uneven terrain dotted with clumps of wild vegetation, loose stones and projecting boulders. He reached his destination soon. In the shadow of slender palms a magnificent colonnaded multidomed structure stood in a time-ravaged stone enclosure. Around it, as far as the eye could see, the mountain was barren and uninhabited. Close to the entrance the ground was parched and fissured.

Shemon approached the iron gate and stepped inside. Suddenly a shriveled old man, who had been squatting unobserved beneath a palm tree, rose with the aid of a heavy staff and, grunting, confronted the newcomer. Stouthearted as Shemon was, he recoiled. Bent, hollow-cheeked, beak-nosed and white, his sunken lips shut and moving ruminatingly, the man had a spectral appearance. And the imperturbability with which he regarded the strange giant strengthened this impression. "What do you want?" he mumbled.

Shemon, speechless, stared at the old man.

"What do you want?" he repeated, striking the ground with his staff. His voice was hoarse, jerky, choleric.

"I've come to see the tombs," Shemon said.

"At this hour? Who are you?"

The moon emerged for an instant; Shemon caught a human glint in the old man's eyes; his voice, too, sounded steadier.

"I am Shemon, the son of Elisha."

"Never heard of you."

"The nephew of Eliezer of Modin."

"Ah!" drawled the old man, and a note of respect tinged his voice. "A strange hour this is for seeing the holy place."

"And who may you be?" inquired Shemon.

"I am Athniel, the watchman; I've been watching here since the destruction of our holy Temple. The last glory of Israel am I watching."

"Who feeds you? Where do you live?"

"I live where I watch, and I eat what the Lord sends. These trees bear dates and good men sometimes remember me."

"And you've been doing this for sixty-two years?" asked Shemon somewhat incredulously.

"Yes, almost all my life. I was seventeen when I came here."

"And what do you do when the rains come?"

"I put up a stout booth for the Feast of Tabernacles and it lasts me through the winter."

"Why have you dedicated your life to these graves?"

"You may not understand, my son."

"Please tell me."

"I saw our Temple burned and the bravest of the brave slain. In the glare of fire, over heaps of corpses, through rows of tall crosses on which dying men groaned, I escaped. I ran westward. I ran and ran until I fell. The next day I ran again until I fell again, exhausted—it was at this gate. Prostrate, I wept and called to the Almighty. . . . Then I heard a voice. 'Athniel,' the Voice said, 'arise, cleanse thyself and return to this spot. Return to this spot and watch over the glory of Israel. Guard it; guard it long and patiently. One day, in thy presence, the new hope of Israel will rise from this sepulcher.' "

A chill ran down Shemon's spine. Could it be that this old man *was* something different from what he appeared to be? Was it possible that unearthly beings in earthly guise still appeared among the mortals? He dismissed the thought. "So you are waiting and watching," he said mechanically.

"Watching and waiting, my son."

Shemon came close to the marble pillars, on which weapons and boats of the Maccabean wars were modeled in bas-relief, and peered into the murky depths of the mausoleum. "May I go in?"

"You may, if you do not fear to be lost in the dark."

"I do not."

The watchman ordered Shemon to remove his sandals and

opened the gate. Some distance away a solitary yellowish light flickered beneath a stone pyramid. The dim contours of six similar pyramids were discernible to the left of the first. The light was too feeble to be detected from outside.

"Mattathias, his wife and their five sons," Athniel said reverently.

"It is Judah's tomb that I would like to see," said Shemon.

"The sepulcher is below, in the cave," the old man responded hollowly, "and there is no light there."

"Then, if you will tell me how, I will make my way in the dark to it and offer a prayer."

Athniel took Shemon to the mouth of the cavern. "There are twenty paces to the first grave," he said, "and they are twenty paces apart. The fourth is Judah's."

Shemon entered. A thick, misty blackness wrapped him like a blanket. He groped his way slowly forward. At the count of eighty he stopped. He extended his hands to the right and then to the left—nothing but empty space. He bent down, and his hands touched the cold marble of a tablet. Shivering, he moved his fingers and felt the letters of the epitaph. They were close, crowded and unintelligible in the upper rows. But in the center of the slab there were several segregated, prominent symbols. They Spelled: Y E H U D A—the liberator! It really mattered little what the other words said. The name alone spoke most eloquently. A proud and valiant Israelite! A man who had smashed armies literally fifteen times the strength of his desperate band! A man who, even as his noble old father, had remained simple and unpretentious in his death, as he had been in his life. Here were ancestors worthy of emulation! Why could not their feat against the Greeks be, with the aid of the Almighty, repeated against Edom? Was there a man today to measure up to the task? Shemon asked himself. If the measure were courage, did not he, Shemon, possess it? If it were love for his people, could it be deeper than his? If it were hate for the enemy, could his hate be surpassed? If it were the cup of Israel's sorrow, was it not full to overflowing? And was not the blood in his veins their blood?

Shaking with emotion, he prostrated himself on the cold stone floor, buried his face in his arms and prayed: "Lord of the universe, make me worthy of giving my people freedom. In the presence of these immortal shadows I beseech Thee: Help! Help me drive the enemy from our land and wash away the shame of his oppression! Help me restore peace and happiness to my people and dignity to Thy Name. And you, great shadows, unforgettable ancestors, intercede in our behalf. See that we are granted wisdom, strength and unflagging faith."

With bated breath, still quivering with emotion, he lay there waiting for a voice or omen of divine recognition. But none came. He rose and, weighed down by doubt, groped his way out.

In the open air he felt better. As he was strapping on his sandals, old Athniel approached, bowed, held out a coin box and mumbled, "I have heard. The time has come. New hope rises from the sepulcher. May it live." He sighed. "I can now die in peace." He paused and shook the box. "Charity saves from death," he chanted.

Once more Shemon felt as though he were in the presence of a specter. Who was this queer, tottering old man? What power put such strange words into his mouth?

Shemon dropped a silver coin into the box and ran, stumbling, to rejoin Issachar.

At dawn Shemon crossed the little stream and, striding over a path curving through silent orchards, reached the boundary of his uncle's possessions.

Eliezer's old garden was heavy with the scent of flowers and of ripe or ripening fruit. Green figs, still moist with dew, glistened in the early morning glow. Brown-red henna shrubs mingled with mustard, mint, sage and cinnamon. An alley of sycamores led to a somber structure with a front portico.

The chant of morning prayer kept Shemon from entering. Congregational devotions implied the presence of at least nine strangers who, with his uncle, would constitute the prescribed *minyan* (quorum) of ten. For obvious reasons he did not care to meet them. It was clear, at any rate, that at least nine Modin residents held Eliezer in sufficient esteem to join him at dawn for a community service.

Shemon went to the rear of the house, drew water from an

irrigation well, washed, murmured his prayers and settled down to wait for the worshipers to depart. When he could no longer hear their voices he returned to the house. His uncle, waited on by his grizzled housekeeper, was breakfasting on the portico.

The old man raised his eyes, which were sheltered by heavy white eyebrows. The colossus was faintly familiar. He had not seen Shemon since his boyhood.

"This," muttered the housekeeper, "is the man who sought my Master's presence some time ago."

"My nephew Shemon?" Eliezer's voice, hollow and somewhat cracked, registered guarded surprise.

"It is he indeed."

"Sit down. You've certainly grown." He paused. "Prayed?" he asked. Shemon nodded. "Join me. Here is milk, cheese, honey. Here are bread cakes." For a while they ate in silence; then Eliezer said, "Surely it is something important that brings you here if, after all these years, you came to see me twice."

"It is," said Shemon. Eliezer smoothed his long white beard and waited, studying his nephew. His eyes of fading brown were still keen and penetrating.

"I had only one reason for coming the first time," said Shemon. "I have two reasons today." Eliezer's stare was cold, fixed, discomfiting; the stare of a domineering man, confident of his own righteousness. "On my first visit I came to seek my uncle's support for our cause—"

"What cause?" Eliezer interrupted.

"Liberation."

Eliezer frowned. "Dangerous nonsense."

"Dangerous, but not nonsense," Shemon retorted with dignity.

Uncle regarded nephew critically. "I see that in your thoughts and manners you take after your father and his brother of blessed memory," he said with a touch of irony. "They, too, imagined they were stronger than Edom; they, too, had no respect for the counsel of age and wisdom."

"I have not come to quarrel with my uncle," said Shemon, subduing his anger. "I've come to find out whether my uncle would aid the cause of our people in whatever manner may seem best in his eyes. Neither Father nor his brother, may their souls rest in Paradise, thought they were stronger than Edom; nor do I. What I do believe is that the justice of our cause is stronger and—with God's help—must prevail sooner or later."

"That justice will prevail in the end, I agree. But the time must be ripe and we must be worthy; then Heaven will give us an unmistakable sign. Until then whatever we do against Edom will come to plague us. I was not swayed by the folly of blind passion before; I will not be now." Eliezer bent forward and said in a somewhat kindlier tone, "You're young and not without wits, Shemon. You can rebuild your father's house or stay with me and be an honor to our family." His voice dropped to a soft undertone. "I am old and alone in the world." He made a sweeping gesture. "All this will be yours. Why do you not take the path of patience and peace?"

"Are we allowed to take the path of patience and peace even when we choose it?" challenged Shemon.

"Why not? Am I not an example of one who has made this choice?"

"Uncle may be. But how long will it last?"

"I don't understand."

"Has not Uncle heard of Hadrian's decree, which Tyrannus is holding back for a large bribe?"

"No."

"Our people in Galilee and Lower Judea have been troubled about it since Passover."

"I stay away from public affairs, and my counted friends are men of peace like myself. What would this decree threaten?"

"Everything, Uncle, everything. It aims to eradicate the Holy One's Name from the face of the earth. It would prohibit the observance of the Sabbath, prayer, instruction of the Torah and even circumcision."

At last Eliezer's placidity was broken. "Unbelievable!" he said with feeling. "May the Merciful One protect us from such evil."

"It is the truth, Uncle. Should the evil come, we will either have to live as Edomite slaves or fight to live as free Israelites."

"Or die as Israelites," Eliezer said glumly.

"Should that be our destiny, I would accept it."

"I know you would," the old man said after a long and heavy silence. "But I shall say and do nothing to encourage you, Shemon. He who prevented Israel's destruction many times before, will prevent it again. I can wait."

The answer was decisive. Shemon no longer felt impelled to broach the subject of his wedding to this man. There was little in common between them. Their kinship was a mere accident.

Shemon made as if to leave, but Eliezer manifestly did not altogether dislike his rash nephew. "You have not given me the second reason for your coming," he said a little less frigidly.

"It is personal," Shemon replied reluctantly, "and I do not feel that I have the right to impose."

"Whatever your opinions, I am your mother's brother."

Shemon wavered. "It is that I am getting married. I meant to ask you—"

For the first time the old man's face brightened. "Ah! Ah! That's what you should have told me first. The passion of matrimony is a brake to the passion of rebellion. May you wed in a happy hour. Who is the virgin?"

"Meredya, daughter of Abner, the head archon of Zofith."

"Zofith? Is it the hamlet on a hill off the plain of Sharon?"

"It is, Uncle."

"I had occasion to be there some years ago. I can remember no Abner. What was his father's name?"

"Jacob. He is Abner ben-Jacob." The inquisition began to irk Shemon, but he continued. "He took over his brother Gedaliah's homestead. He formerly lived in Ludd."

Eliezer wrinkled his brow. "Ludd, Ludd—let us see. Abner ben-Jacob. A tall, dark man. Was he not your father's friend?"

"Indeed he was."

Instantly Eliezer froze. "Another rebel," he muttered acidly. "Dangerous and impudent. With a venomous tongue."

Shemon's ire was rising, but he kept it in check. "That was a long time ago, Uncle. Abner is the head of his town council now."

"You're courting trouble, my nephew," Eliezer said, shaking his finger admonishingly. "I knew this Abner well. I advise you to think twice before—"

"I have done my thinking, Uncle," Shemon interrupted sharply. "Abner is a good man and there are few to match his daughter. It behooves my uncle to be a little charitable. One may be wrong in uncle's eyes and still be right in the eyes of God and other men, as is shown by the judgment of the people of Zofith. Besides, it is me that uncle is hurting. I have no parents. I am alone. Uncle is my only kin in our land. I have come to invite him."

"Sorry, sorry, nephew. You have chosen your wife; you have chosen your path, and you must walk it alone. No one else is responsible. As one makes his bed, so he sleeps."

Shemon had had his fill. Choking with anger, he muttered, "Peace," and strode away.

Chapter Sixteen

Like any young girl in Israel, Meredya had been looking forward to a wedding preceded by ceremonial gift-bearing processions marching to the sound of songs and cymbals, and followed by seven days of happy revelry—the Week of Seven Blessings. But it was not in the stars for her. Since the destruction of the Temple rejoicing had been curtailed, and the prevailing situation made even greater curtailment imperative. And so the festivities had to be confined to the wedding night. The groom's gift, a headband and bracelets of antique gold coins, a family heirloom salvaged by Daniel ben-Ezer, was brought by Elon, who had agreed to substitute for Shemon's nearest of kin. He alone knew of his friend's galling experience with his uncle and confided to Abner only as much of the episode as was essential. Rabbi Akiba had been invited and had accepted. It was even hoped that he would perform the wedding ceremony; but two days before the event, due to an urgent call from Galilee, he sent his apologies. With these, Joshua brought a pair of magnificent earrings for the bride.

The wedding was set for the twenty-first day of the month of Sivan. Everyone of consequence in Zofith and all local

Heromavs were invited. Of Shemon's personal lieutenants, only Itamar, Nadav and Issachar could be spared from their duties for a day; Joel naturally came as cousin and friend, burdened though he was with the military training of the academy students.

Nehama, assisted by hired hands, took charge of the cooking and baking on the wedding day, while Tamar decorated the premises. Egg-shaped oil lamps were suspended from colored ropes fastened to poles. The gates, the well, and the entrance to the main building were hung with white and blue bunting. Long, low tables were set up in the garden, and rugs spread in the yard. A canopy of palm leaves and fresh flowers, supported by long rods, was placed in the center of the yard. The shepherd dog was taken to the back of the outbuildings. Abner himself supervised the slaughter of the sheep, which took place late that afternoon. An abundant supply of wine was prepared. All day long, small alms were handed out to local and transient beggars. Hemda, Meredya's oldest sister, who had arrived from Ein Gedi the night before, concentrated on the bride's toilet, while Shemon cooled his heels at Elon's, waiting impatiently for the sun to set.

An air of mild excitement mingled with eager expectancy prevailed all that day in Zofith. It was withheld from Shemon that during the last fortnight unsuccessful attempts to abduct Zofith girls had been made by Roman soldiers. It was even rumored that one evening Caunus himself had come to Abner to seek Meredya's hand. As Caunus had seen it, it was a great honor that he, Commander of Apollonia, was prepared to bestow upon a simple native girl. Abner's indignant refusal had been as stinging as it was incomprehensible. True or not, such were the rumors and Elon, again without Shemon's knowledge, and contrary to custom, directed two score of his best men to bring hidden arms to the wedding.

Evening came at last. Abner's courtyard was crowded with people in their Sabbath finery. Middle-aged men stood in knots discussing politics, taxation and crops or delighting in Talmudic casuistry. Women gossiped and cheered the absent bride at intervals with shrill rhythmic outbursts of praise, accompanied by clapping. The younger element talked earnestly of things to come or engaged in good-natured banter.

A whisper passed from mouth to mouth: "The bridegroom is coming." The young men lighted their torches and swiftly assumed positions on each side of the route from the entrance up to the canopy. Drums and cymbals struck up. All talk ceased. Shemon entered, accompanied by Elon and Joel. Erect as a palm tree, he walked with measured gait to the canopy. No sooner did he stop than the bride, flanked by her father and Hemda, emerged from the doorway. Meredya, in white and heavily veiled, stepped gracefully over the flowers which two rows of bridesmaids in white scattered in her path.

The ceremony of sanctification was performed with much dignity. Yair ben-Habib, the honorary chief elder, a thin, frail man with a gray goatee and nervously blinking eyes, delivered an address. Abner blessed the newlyweds in moving words. There was a whirlwind of congratulations and the guests were invited to the garden. After the banquet they filed back into the yard and made ready for the dance.

First came the bride. Discarding the veil and donning the coin headband and bracelets, her husband's gifts, she moved to the center of a circle of men and women. A big drum boomed a slow, rhythmical prelude. The crowd began to clap in unison. A shepherd's pipe joined in. For a while Meredya swayed like a baby about to brave its first steps. Next, with captivating charm, always keeping time with the rhythm of the music and clapping, she moved forward with hesitant steps, her arms spread winglike for balance. The tempo of her pace and motions increased gradually as her pantomime took her audience through the various stages of a girl's growth. It became wild, gawky and amusing before growing delicately seductive, and culminated in a dizzy whirl that sent the onlookers into a vociferous burst of enthusiasm, accompanied by a shower of coins and small gifts thrown in tribute at her feet.

Exhausted but happy, she came to the side of her admiring husband. But as he began to whisper tender words into her ear, he was whisked to the center of the circle by Elon and members of the younger set, who clamored for a solo dance. For once in

his life Shemon, to the amusement of the crowd, appeared helpless, looking about appealingly and muttering words of excuse.

But at the height of his discomfiture the instigator of the
trouble came to Shemon's rescue. Elon called for silence. "Do
you remember, Shemon, how at one of our first meetings you
described an Edomite dagger dance and how we tried it in our
own way?

"Yes," admitted Shemon weakly.

"Do you remember how, each time you pretended to stab
your enemy, you muttered, 'Thus Adonai, shall perish all Your
foes'?"

"Yes," confirmed Shemon meekly.

"If you dance the dance with me, we will excuse you from
any other dancing, will we not, friends?" Elon looked about him
with a provocative grin.

Shemon realized that there was no escape. The ordeal had
to be faced. Marrying obviously had its bitter side. Off came
Elon's mantle. Shemon removed his, threw it to Joel and unsheathed his dagger. Cymbals clashed a signal. The two men
sprang to their positions. The crowd, unfamiliar with the rhythm
of the new dance, began to clap hesitantly.

Suddenly old Ahab, who had not relaxed his vigilance even
on this festive night, staggered into the yard, blood trickling
from his mouth, and gasped, "Save yourselves! Edomites!"

But it was too late. Roman soldiers, yelling and brandishing
swords, were trooping into the courtyard. Like stampeding cattle
they bore down the old servant, and trampling over him, shoved
aside some women paralyzed with fright, and halted within a
few yards of the main body of the guests. Panic-stricken men
and women, shouting, shrieking and calling to the Almighty
for help, ran pell-mell, jostling, stumbling, falling and leaping
over each other.

Shemon's powerful voice brought them to their senses and
they herded together behind the younger men. In front of these
Shemon and Elon, their daggers still in their hands, stood facing
the intruders. Meredya and the diminutive Tamar clung to their
husbands' arms. Between them stood Joel, still holding his
friends' mantles. Shemon's three lieutenants formed a semi-

circle behind their commander and his bride, and most of Elon's chosen men elbowed their way to the line behind. "Do nothing until I order it," Shemon directed as the pandemonium subsided.

The Roman headman, a burly, freckled, straw-haired fellow, sheathed his sword, advanced a little and, scowling, announced, "We won't harm you if you do as you're told."

Only Shemon, Elon, Tamar and Abner understood, but they said nothing. Abner, who, after the meal, had gone with the elders into the house for a quiet chat, was now in his doorway, in the rear of the soldiers. He stood there, dark, oaklike, smoldering with unspoken hate.

"Why the silence?" the headman demanded. "Does no one understand me?" There was no response. The Roman was losing his patience. "Does not one of you dogs understand me?" he roared.

Strangely enough, Tamar spoke up. "I do."

The Roman appraised her with knowing eyes and grinned. "Good, very good. Will you translate my words to these barbarians?"

"If I am to translate, there will be no abuse," said Tamar with quiet but firm dignity.

The soldier laughed. "What a wench!" He smacked his lips and made a salacious gesture. His men guffawed. He again turned to Tamar. "Tell them this: We come in the name of the Commander of Apollonia, Justus Caunus." She translated. He continued: "Under the rule of *Jus Primae Noctis,* established by Procurator Quietus, our noble commander demands that the bride be given him for tonight, and he promises upon his Roman honor, to restore her in the morning, safe and sound."

In mute terror Tamar looked up at her husband, who averted his eyes. Shemon, who had apparently determined what to do, patted his bride and whispered, "No matter what I say or do, trust in me, beloved."

Meredya gave him a quick, reassuring smile.

The Roman leered at Tamar. "No answer, little girl? Frightened?"

Elon interposed. "I will translate."

"So you, too, understand me, you son of a pig. Wherefore did you not speak up before?" Elon's reply was a stare of hate and the headman did not pursue the question. "Translate," he said. "And also tell them that every one of us—we are thirty-two men here—will pick a girl for himself for tonight. If there is no rumpus, we will deliver them in good condition in the morning."

Tamar covered her eyes. A quivering lip betrayed Elon's emotions. He glanced at Shemon—a mute call for guidance. But none came beyond a muttered "Translate." It was baffling and humiliating, but Elon trusted in his friend's judgment.

While seeking a way of intimating to Shemon the presence of armed Heromavs, Elon spoke. "People of Zofith," he said with feigned calm, "the scoundrels demand the bride for the Apollonian commander for the night and each of them desires a maiden—"

A collective moan, in which shock, indignation and terror merged, cut Elon short. Sobs broke out.

Shemon looked at Meredya. There were no signs of fear in her face. Quite the opposite; her eyes were dry and fierce. She seized her husband's hand. "Give me that dagger!"

"Steady, darling. Have faith in me."

At the same time Abner brushed past the elders into the house, seized an axe and, hiding it under his robe, dashed back into the yard.

Meanwhile Ben-Habib had made his way through the soldiers' ranks and was pleading in a Latin-Greek jargon with the headman: "Please do not do this to us," he was saying shakily. "Don't inflict this unspeakable shame upon us. What have we done to deserve it? We will give you money; we will give you wine. Go to the other end of the village. There is a bawdy inn there, and harlots for your lust. Please do not defile our women."

"We don't want those hags, you goat," laughed the headman, seizing the elder by the beard. "Do you hear? We don't want your stinking money, either. We want these appetizing wenches. Now be quick about it—tell them." He pulled Ben-Habib down to his knees. "Tell them!"

"Please, please," sobbed the old man, "don't do this wicked

thing. Name your price. You will get it. I swear. In the name of God, I plead with you, don't ravage—"

A soldier booted him and he fell. As he attempted to scramble to his feet, he was kicked again and again. His wife emitted a frantic shriek and sank to the ground; other women, wailing loudly, kneeled to revive her. The Thumbless and Heromavs, burning with impatience to fly at the tormentors, wondered at Shemon's perplexing demeanor. Ben-Habib's plight afforded the Romans an amusing spectacle. The legionaries nudged each other, slapped their thighs and screamed with laughter. What a sight that whining goatbeard made! How funny he was, writhing in pain, as time and again he rose and fell, staggered and crawled, trying to reach the garden. And his jabbering! By Juno!

"For the last time—" began the headman. He was interrupted by a soldier who leaned over to whisper, "I would say that the big lout looks like the horse thief. Look at his hulk and beard—exactly as described in the orders."

"You may be right," agreed the headman, "but let's say nothing about it until we have the girls. Then we'll have them, him and the reward too." The soldier nodded.

"For the last time," proclaimed the headman self-importantly, "I order you in the name of Commander Caunus to submit peacefully. The slightest sign of resistance and we cut you up like swine meat."

Elon translated sullenly. No one paid any attention to Abner, who was making stealthily for the Roman rear.

The headman, seeing no signs of surrender, grasped his sword hilt. "I will count ten," he said menacingly. "Unless you allow us to take the women, we will strike. One, two, three . . ."

To everybody's consternation, Shemon pushed Meredya away, advanced and, dropping his dagger, said with skillfully simulated impassivity, "Decurion, take the bride. I am her husband."

The Roman eyed him suspiciously. "Kick that dagger farther away from you," he ordered. Shemon obeyed. He turned to Elon. "And you, too, throw that knife down."

"Do it!" muttered Shemon in Hebrew, "and watch me."

Baffled, Elon threw his dagger down.

"Good!" the Roman unsheathed his sword. "Now all of you raise your hands and keep them up." The order was obeyed. He leered at Shemon. "I'll take your wife now."

Heading for Meredya, he came forward cautiously, his eyes on the crowd. Shemon stepped aside as if to allow the Roman to take his prize. Emboldened, the headman quickened his pace. Suddenly Shemon lunged and sent a stunning blow to the man's head. Without allowing him to crumple, Shemon seized him, lifted him high into the air and flung him at his charging comrades with terrific force. The body brought a number of them down; others tripped and fell over their sprawling comrades.

Elon shouted "Heromavs, upon them!" Knives flashed; young men surged forward, led by Shemon, Elon and Joel. On the other side, Abner charged with his axe. His eyes ablaze with insane fury, he looked the very incarnation of vengeance as he hacked and chopped and mowed down his mortal foes. "Here's one for my daughter! . . . Here's one for Ludd! . . . Here's one for defiling the Temple!" His pent-up hatred, once unleashed, was uncheckable. Fired by his fanatical fury and Shemon's cooler but even more devastating onslaught, the young men fought with frenzy. Sheer weight of numbers was now crushing the Romans. Even some of the women rushed in for the kill. They kicked and scratched and bit and pulled the hair of their would-be defilers. Before long the proud conquerors lay in a messy heap. The outside guards, as they ran to their comrades' aid, found a similar fate.

The battle was over; the dead were counted, the wounded tended and sentries posted. Shemon, blood-spattered, his tunic in shreds, sat down on the bloodstained rug where, but a few hours before, he had stood under the wedding canopy. Abner came and sat beside his son-in-law; so did Elon and Joel. Slowly the others congregated about them. Some momentous decisions had to be made. In the far part of the yard eight Israelite dead lay in a row, among them poor old Ahab and the deluded Yair ben-Habib, who had believed that evil would yield to pleas and persuasion. His heart had proved no match for the ordeal and he had been found dead in the garden.

The victims' nearest of kin sat or stood by their dead, lamenting and chanting psalms. Tamar and Meredya, who, with her sisters, was tending the injured who had been taken into the house, hurried to and from the well and outbuildings. Behind these the shepherd dog bayed and howled.

Abner removed his ripped mantle, examined what was left of it, smiled bitterly and, addressing no one in particular, said, "If it were the mantle only." He laid it aside and shook his head sadly. "Lo, the damage is done. There is no road back. We are in the fight before we are ready."

"God's will," said Joel.

Shemon, who was clasping his knees with his hands and staring abstractedly into space, said quietly, "Rabbi Akiba once said, 'The limit of endurance will be set by Heaven.' Now I know what he meant."

"There's little time to waste," said Elon. "Let us decide what to do. My thought is that we must leave without delay if Edomite vengeance is not to overtake us."

"Alas, alas!" moaned an elder.

"Perhaps," stuttered another elder, "if we tried influence, gold . . ."

"Ah!" snapped Abner impatiently. "Influence! Gold! You saw what happened to Yair tonight, may he intercede for us in Heaven."

"Uncle is right," muttered Joel.

Shemon looked up at the crowd. "It is clear we cannot stay. Does anyone disagree?"

A middle-aged, corpulent man coughed and said falteringly, "It is hard to disagree, but is it not cruel to leave the fruits of a lifetime of toil and one's forefathers' toil to plunder and destruction?"

"Would you rather that you and yours lose your lives into the bargain?" Elon asked caustically.

"God forbid!" protested the man.

"It is settled, then," said Shemon. "We are going. I will take you to the hills. Later each man can look out for himself if he so chooses."

"So be it," said Abner. No one objected.

"We must take along all we can carry," said Shemon. "How many beasts of burden are there in Zofith?"

The elders did some reckoning. "About four hundred, including fifteen camels."

"Besides our five horses," reminded Itamar.

Shemon reflected. "Not enough!" he said. "But we will do what we can." He turned to the elders. "You can't take with you all you possess, but you will take what is most important in the following order: the wounded, the children, the feeble, food supplies, weapons, our dead, clothing, tools and vessels. No cattle, of course, should be left."

"I think," interposed Abner, "that the caravan and the herds should take two different routes."

"Right," said Shemon. "My Thumbless will drive the cattle. How many men will you need, Itamar?"

"The three of us and two more."

"What will we do with these?" inquired an elder, pointing at the Roman corpses.

"We'll strip them," said Shemon without emotion, "and let them rot."

"They were men, even though they were pagans," the elder sighed.

Shemon shrugged. "There's no time for idle talk," he said. "The villagers are to be told, the cattle gotten out, the beasts of burden loaded." He enumerated the tasks and asked for volunteers.

Leadership was distributed among Abner, Elon and the elders, with Shemon in general command. It fell to Joel to return to Bnai Brak to notify Akiba. The rabbi, according to Hagarsi, was due back from Galilee that morning. Joel took hurried leave. Hagarsi mounted his donkey and followed. The villagers and their leaders hastened to their tasks. The mourners lingered on. Shemon went over to them and exhorted them to go and salvage what they could.

The mourners prostrated themselves and took leave of their dead. Bent with grief, they straggled out of the yard.

Shemon remained alone. With bowed head and heavy heart

he gazed at the corpses. It was easier to fight and inflict death upon enemies in a state of white heat than to contemplate the aftermath of battle. The tragedy of these first eight would be multiplied thousands of times before the rebellion was over. The realization of the magnitude of the impending struggle and the responsibility for it became more incisive than ever before; but just as incisive was the conviction that to retreat meant merely to augment and extend the tragedy, not to avert it.

The distant howling of jackals scenting carrion, and Raam's responsive yowl, woke him from his brooding. He walked over to the well and washed.

When he had shaken the water from his hair he looked up at the starlit sky. Its beauty was as refreshing as the water. It steered his reflections into serener channels. For the first time since the dance he thought of Meredya as his bride, and of his unconsummated love. He thought of her courage and fortitude and what a boon it would be to have such a wife in time of peace.

All the while Meredya watched him from the doorway of the house. Now that he stood gazing at the stars, his back toward her, she came stealing across the carpeted yard. His keen ears detected her footsteps but he pretended not to hear. She tiptoed close, flung her arms about him and rested her flaming cheek against his naked back. "So this is our wedding night!" she whispered.

He turned and pressed her close to his breast. She stayed there, quivering, her hot tears of release burning his skin.

The howling of the jackals came nearer. In the center of the village the blasts of rams' horns were summoning the people to congregate. From the house a shriek of pain pierced the stillness of the yard.

Chapter Seventeen

At daybreak trumpets sounded in the fort of Apollonia. The Roman eagle was hoisted high above the drum-shaped citadel, whose eastern side towered above the Plain of Sharon and whose rear bordered on the sea. Guards were shifted in the four lookout turrets that faced in as many directions, and at the eastern and western gates, one of which opened on a causeway linked with the coastal highway, and the other on a long jetty. North of the fort a clearing and citrus groves fringed the outskirts of the ancient Israelite city of Eintov, whose modest harbor accommodated the grain and fruit shippers of the region.

In the large court of the stronghold, heavy with stable odors and somber with the leaden early-morning light, armor clanged, commands were barked, feet shuffled and rows of men stood immobile. Once again a trumpet sounded, and the night watch was dismissed. The guards hurried into the barracks, where breakfast was being served. They stacked their spears, put aside their mantles and breastplates and lined up in the food queue. In their sleeveless tunics, kilts and strapped sandals they waited comfortably.

"Say, Gaius," said a dark, stocky legionary, apparently of Spanish origin, to a tall, flaxen-haired Nordic. "What do you think of headman Arminius? He never returned, the braggart. Promised us a good time and"—the sentry whistled meaningfully —"disappeared. No headman, no men, no girls."

"Probably drunk," said the flaxen-haired one indifferently.

"You don't think they sneaked in by the sea gate?" asked the stocky one.

"No. Why should they take the trouble?"

"Why?" The dark one laughed suggestively. "More privacy in the barracks above the second court."

"Nonsense," yawned the Nordic. "They would have had what they wanted before bringing the wenches here. Besides, I would have seen them from the turret. So many couldn't have sneaked in unnoticed."

"Maybe you're right. I wonder what's keeping them."

"They are drunk, that's all."

"I don't know. It isn't like Arminius. And the commander's temper has not been too good lately."

Centurion Catanus, second-in-command to Caunus, entered the mess hall. "Thirty-two men are missing," he announced. "Has any one seen them or Decurion Arminius?"

Most of those present mutely stared at the officer and at each other. A few ventured a hesitant "No." The centurion, a tall, bony, leather-skinned man with a shoe-shaped nose and chilling blue eyes, motioned to a big scar-faced soldier. "Decurion Treverius!"

The legionary wiped his lips with the back of his hand and hurriedly elbowed his way to Catanus.

"Finished with your breakfast?"

"Yes, sir."

"Take five good horsemen, fully equipped, and find out what happened to Arminius and his men."

"Yes, sir."

"Be off immediately."

"Yes, sir."

Some time later Treverius, flustered and perspiring profusely under his armor and helmet, stood before Caunus and Catanus in the center of the main court. The others watched from barrack windows, leaned against columns and stable entrances or loitered some distance away.

Caunus, short, corpulent, his bulldog face crimson and his small black eyes flashing with anger, plied the decurion with questions. "So not one of them was left alive?"

"Not one of them, Commander."

"Mutilated?"

"No signs of mutilation. Some of the corpses were gnawed by jackals."

Caunus cursed. "What an end for Roman legionaries! The circumcised swine!" Caunus resumed his inquisition. "And you, Treverius, what did *you* do?"

"Galloped with my men through the main street to see whether any of the townsmen were there and, seeing none, posted two sentries outside the town."

"Did you search any houses?"

"No, Commander. I did not risk it."

Caunus frowned and dismissed Treverius. For a few seconds he did not speak, manifestly overcome with rage. His thick lips were compressed, cruel lines drooping from their corners; the nostrils of his fleshy nose twitched and his goiterous second chin wobbled ever so slightly. At last he growled, "And this had to happen to me after the theft of the herds!" He stamped his foot. "I'll show them."

"Show them something they'll never forget," ventured the centurion frigidly.

"Forget? They won't be able to remember it!" He passed his hand over his cropped graying hair, now hot from the scorching sun. He had hurried out from his quarters bareheaded, anxious to hear Treverius' report. "I'll go up and get ready," he said to Catanus. "I'll take a century of cavalry; you take charge of the fort."

Catanus saluted. "You are taking Treverius with you?"

"Yes. Have the bugler sound general assembly."

Again the centurion saluted.

From the road at the foot of the hill where Caunus deployed his cavalry, Zofith seemed like a large sunlit garden set with drab stones—parapeted housetops. The lower, unparapeted dwellings, swallowed up by the heavy verdure, were not discernible from below. The fruit groves and vineyards, in various stages of bloom, climbed the slopes of the hill to its crest, throbbing with colorful life. Only the harvested barley fields to the south seemed to have succumbed to the withering sun, for they lay parched and cracking under a shriveling yellow stubble.

Caunus directed his horsemen to surround the little town. The sentries posted by Treverius reported that they had seen no sign of life in or outside of it. He ordered an advance, and encountering no resistance, instituted a house-to-house-search. Walls were smashed, articles of furniture broken and floors ripped open in the hope of discovering concealed treasures of coins and grain. But nothing of value was found.

Reviling the Israelites, Caunus accorded military honors to his dead, ordered the buildings and the surrounding groves to be put to the torch and, reassembling his men on a barren barley field, watched the leaping, sputtering flames blend into one gigantic pyre that consumed the rotting flesh of his warriors together with the dwellings and the living, growing, life-nurturing products of generations of toil and care.

Caunus turned his head to Treverius, waiting on his mount immediately in the rear. "Treverius," he said, "this is just the beginning. We must do something the country will remember for a long time. Any thoughts?"

"Shaarim lies a short distance south, in the plain," the decurion grinned suggestively.

"Is it not near Ekron?"

"The commander means Shaarayim. Shaarim is an old village, not far off. About one hundred families, and good prospects for fun."

"Yes, yes. I remember now." He mopped his face and winked at his subordinate. "Good prospects for fun, eh? Let's go."

Shaarim lay less than a parasang northeast of Antipras. Its inhabitants were peace-loving toilers who tended their fields, sheep, looms and a single tannery. Situated a little off the beaten track, Shaarim had survived the ravages of the countless foreign incursions and internal conflicts which had plagued the land. An old, low wall, with a high tower built before the Babylonian invasion, still enclosed the settlement. But the wall was crumbling and the tower tottering, and the two gates were battered, open and unguarded. The level of the main thoroughfare had risen in the course of centuries above the lower floors of the structures, which appeared to be half buried below the street. Only part of the stone ground floors and the upper stories, made of adobe brick, projected above the street level. Solid-stone stairways rose from small courts directly to the higher floors. Here and there vat-shaped rain-water cisterns stood in the courts.

As Caunus and his cavalry came within sight of Shaarim, children were playing in the streets, women were working at their spinning wheels or laundering, and the village elders were in session in the commodious tower court north of the west gate. Surrounding the village a full furlong before reaching it, and moving his force into a perfect circle so as to cut off escape, Caunus drove before him and through the wide eastern gate every tiller, shepherd and straggler and all the grazing herds. Panic-stricken, the cattle stampeded into the village, trampling children, stumbling and falling below the street level and causing pandemonium. Led by their commander, whooping, cursing, threatening and laughing, the Romans galloped behind the herds, two abreast, their gleaming spears ready to pierce.

In this fashion they reached the tower court, which only Caunus, Treverius and a few other headmen entered. So sudden was the intrusion that the elders in the court barely managed to escape into one of the rooms encircling it. Some of them halted in and about the doorway.

Caunus, perspiration dripping from his cheeks and chins, bellowed, "Who is the archon here?"

A gray-bearded, slightly stooping man in a black robe and skull cap stepped forward. "I am the archon," he said, bowing his head. Then, looking up apprehensively, he asked, "Why this unexpected honor? And the strange manner . . .?"

"Quiet!" Caunus checked him gruffly. "I will do the asking."

The graybeard bowed his head again and waited.

Caunus, mopping his forehead with tantalizing leisureliness, studied the men and the premises. "What is your name?" he said at last.

"Zerubavel."

"Have you any friends among the elders of Zofith?"

Zerubavel, unaware of the preceding night's events, appeared perplexed. "I know some of them. All Israelites are comrades."

"If so, you surely know where the Zofithians are now."

The archon's perplexity deepened. "Is it for me to know where they are?" he protested, his tone a blend of genuine innocence and perturbation. "Are they not where they belong?"

"They are not!" roared the Roman, clamping his helmet on his head. "Their place is on the gallows."

The old man and his fellow elders paled. "Whom have they wronged?" ventured the archon.

"They have murdered Roman soldiers."

Zerubavel gasped. "It cannot be. God help us!"

" 'It cannot be'?" Caunus repeated menacingly. "Do you doubt my word, you—?" He placed his hand on the hilt of his sword.

"God forbid!" stammered the archon. "What I mean to say is: I do not believe my ears."

"Show your ears more respect or I'll have them cut off." He enjoyed his quip, and looking back, was gratified to find his entourage appreciative.

"Well, Zerubavius," he bantered, "it will do you good to stop pretending and tell us the whereabouts of the Zofithians."

"If they are not in Zofith I know nothing about them."

Caunus, simulating anger, turned to his adjutants. "The man is as stubborn as the rest of his accursed race. He will have to be flogged. Strip him."

Treverius and another decurion dismounted.

"God is my witness," pleaded the archon. "I speak the truth. Flogging will disgrace me but it won't help the commander. If it is money that my lord desires, let him tell us how much."

Caunus eyed the old Israelite mockingly and chortled, "Money, you say? Ha, ha! Money. Not a bad idea. How much?"

"Perhaps we can scrape together five hundred silver shekels," Zerubavel said feebly.

The Roman guffawed. "Five hundred shekels!" he said contemptuously. "Do you think we don't know the value of coin? What do you think you are all guilty of? Trespassing? Nonpayment of taxes? You are accused of"—he raised his voice menacingly—"conspiracy against the Roman Empire! Five hundred shekels! Three talents of gold will perhaps be considered; and even so, the burden of proving your innocence will be upon you."

"Merciful God!" whispered Zerubavel. "The whole village is not worth that much."

"Merciful God!" echoed his associates. They approached to confer with him. Caunus watched them, a derisive smirk on his face.

Outside the gate, which was blocked from view by cavalrymen, the commotion was continuous. Men shouted, women wailed and shrieked, children cried and soldiers cursed. Suddenly a woman's scream, shrill and frantic, rose above the turmoil! "Murderers! What has my innocent baby done to you? Why did you crush him to death? Why? May God in Heaven smite you and your wicked rulers! May you and your Caesar burn in the Gehenna of Gehennas! Oh, my baby, my poor baby!"

The voice was smothered but sounds of a furious scuffle supplanted it.

"You see?" drawled Caunus sanctimoniously. "Insults, blasphemy, rebellion. How will you disprove that? This business will cost you another talent of gold."

Zerubavel threw up his hands in despair. "We are only men of the soil. We have no riches. If my lord will give me several days we will raise two thousand shekels. But if the money is wanted today we can collect perhaps one thousand shekels."

Caunus glanced at his headman insinuatingly. "Several days," he chuckled. "Ha! Several days." Abruptly he changed his manner and bellowed, "I want the money now! Immediately!"

"At this moment we have only five hundred. If the commander will give me an hour and let me out of here, I'll raise five hundred more."

Caunus turned to his headman and muttered, "I'll get what I can. Their wealth may be hidden and we may not be able to find it." Treverius grinned his approval.

"I agree," Caunus announced to the archon. "Treverius will accompany you. Meanwhile we are hungry and thirsty. Will the other elders see that we get food and drinks? And I don't mean only water. If you, too," he said, addressing himself to the other elders, "must go outside the court, my men will go along to help."

Disconsolately the elders bowed their heads. Caunus dismounted, and followed by his retinue, went into one of the rooms.

When Zerubavel returned with the money, he was shaking like a man in a violent distemper from the effect of the sights he had witnessed. The mangled bodies of children had lain in the streets; mothers had been assaulted in the presence of their families; screaming young girls had run in a frenzy, hounded by raving, guffawing soldiers; men resisting with their bare hands had been felled like trees. Seeing his people thus afflicted despite the promised ransom, he had refused to proceed, but, threatened by Treverius with the complete destruction of the village, Zerubavel had had no alternative but to yield. Some of the families he had approached for contributions had already sustained casualties, and only God knew how he had felt as he had waited for the head of such a family to produce his dole of silver to mollify the murderers of his dear ones.

But the utter futility of his tragic efforts did not dawn upon Zerubavel until his return to the tower court.

Caunus, his headmen and a befuddled, boisterous mob of legionaries clustered about firepots, over which meat sizzled on spits. The carpet was bespattered with blood and spilt wine. Bones, broken bread loaves, empty wineskins and jars were scattered about the men, together with untouched cruses of ritual wine plundered from the synagogue. Horses, standing in their droppings, were tethered to monoliths in a corner of the court, while in another corner entrails of animals and sheepskins lay in messy heaps. In a large room opposite the court entrance the archon's colleagues, trussed, were propped up against a wall. In another, girls were herded together under guard.

Zerubavel's return evoked an outburst of hilarity. "Welcome, welcome, Zerubavius," shouted Caunus drunkenly. "Come here. Make way for the first citizen of Shaarim. By Venus! he is a man of his word."

The old man came closer and laid the little bags before the Roman. "Nine hundred and forty," he whispered, purple-lipped. His eyes were dull, his face yellow and shrunken, his feet unsteady. His mental agony seemed to sap his physical strength, but an impalpable moral force sustained him. His sense of communal responsibility, his instinctive urge to perform his duty to the last, and his faith gave him courage to plead, "Will not my lord now stop the horrible game?"

The Roman blinked. For an instant he was disconcerted by the impertinence of this doddering old Israelite. Then he said sardonically, "Not if you are short sixty shekels, Zerubavius,"

The archon shook a trembling finger at Caunus. "God in Heaven sees thy misdeeds, Edomite. A day of reckoning will surely come."

"Well, well. So you are insolent enough to threaten me. Quite courageous for your age. I must somehow reward you for it." He turned to his men. "Mustn't I?"

They greeted the suggestion with a boisterous whoop.

"I'm sure you've never been to the arena, Zerubavius, so you don't know what a good spectacle means. To atone for my wickedness I'll let you see one before you die. That will also give your God an opportunity to show what *He* can do."

The old man bowed his head and whispered unintelligibly.

Caunus commanded, "Take the old blackguards out of that room, stand them up against each other as they are and tie them up like a sheaf of straw."

Several soldiers rushed to obey the order. Knotted together like faggots, the elders were placed between the horses and the refuse. They uttered no sound; only their lips moved in prayer. Zerubavel turned away.

"Now, that will not do, Zerubavius. If you do not watch them, you will join them and watch something else."

The remark produced a hilarious howl. Then Caunus commanded, "Fasten him with the others. In front of them—that will give him a good view of everything."

This order, too, was promptly obeyed. The archon shut his eyes.

"And now the girls."

The men on the ground leaped to their feet and all surged for the coveted prize.

"No haste, no haste!" their commander restrained them. "Be patient and don't spoil the spectacle. Treverius, take five men and bring the girls."

The decurion grinned broadly and saluted. His task proved an easy one. The girls showed no resistance. Resignedly they followed their captors and were lined up in a row opposite their elders. There were ten of them, the proudest belles of the village. Some of them were daughters of the doomed men, and one, Bathsheba, was Zerubavel's granddaughter. They stood there, eyelids down, their dresses ripped in an earlier struggle, their long hair falling to their waists.

Caunus, a sensual smirk on his face, inspected them as one would horses, and suddenly roared, "Strip them!"

The command swept the girls out of their lethargy. The moody apathy bordering on stupefaction which their faces had seemed to reflect at once gave way to that type of insane fury which comes of utter despair. As the men approached, the girls all but leaped at them. They hit and kicked and clawed and spat and cursed. The hands and faces of their tormentors were bruised and torn, but in the end the girls were subdued and their tattered clothing lay trampled in heaps at their feet. Covering their breasts and faces with their disordered tresses, they wept, their bodies pale and helpless in the afternoon sunlight. As the men in the rear pushed closer and closer, they swallowed their saliva, laughed short, snorty laughs and huskily grunted lusty obscenities.

The old archon opened his eyes for a moment and absorbed the scene. Then he shut them again. "Poor little Bathsheba!" he murmured, hot tears streaming down his cheeks. "Poor beautiful daughters of Israel. Father in Heaven," he pleaded, "for the sake of our mothers, Sarah, Rebecca, Rachel and Leah, save these virgins from defilement and take me from this wicked earth!"

The second part of his prayer was soon to be fulfilled, for even as he was uttering his last words, Treverius was setting fire to the elders' beards. Now the torch was set to his. The odor of singed hair hit his nostrils before the rapidly rising fire touched his skin.

"Hear, O Israel!" he chanted, "The Lord is our God, the Lord is One." From the other elders came the same immortal chant, the words of Israel's everlasting faith, Israel's challenge to a godless world. As the flames enveloped the elders' faces, the Romans emitted a roar of jubilation. The girls looked up, shuddered and shrieked. That was the signal for the final orgy.

Part Two

A Star Rises

Chapter Eighteen

When the dead had been buried and the fugitives sheltered in the caverns and the gorge, Shemon gathered the people of Zofith and spoke to them: "You are safe here in the Cave of Vengeance. The enemy will not easily find us, and if he does, he will not easily overcome us. But life will be hard; food may be scarce. Young and old will have to help, each according to his strength and skill. We have not yet decided whether our safety will permit us to allow anyone to leave. But if there be among you such as would wish to go, speak up now."

Young men and women looked at each other, and their glances carried their silent resolve; the older ones whispered to one another or gazed confidently at the powerful man before them. Only one, an elder, spoke up, and he seemed to voice the sentiments of the assembly: "The Almighty has thrown in our lot with yours, Shemon. We have lost our vineyards but not our faith. Freedom and happiness may yet be ours. Lead us, and may the Holy One, blessed be He, guide you."

When they were dispersed and only those closest to Shemon remained, he conferred briefly with them and assigned the most urgent tasks. Abner was given the responsibility for supplies; Elon, for the guard; Itamar, for the housing and comfort of the people; Meredya and Tamar, for the injured; and Issachar, for the herds and beasts of burden. Nadav was sent to Caesarea for news. The tasks distributed, Shemon moved from point to point to supervise, encourage and give a helping hand.

The morning was well advanced before Shemon was able to think of Meredya as his bride, and of himself. When he had secured Meredya's belongings from his father-in-law, Shemon loaded a donkey with bulging sacks and bundles and led it into an olive grove on the hillcrest opposite the Bowl. Here, on a plateau sheltered by the grove, Shemon pitched a tent, made it comfortable with rugs and cushions, and decorated it with shields, swords, a spear, a quiver of javelins and Roman uniforms, all trophies of his encounters with the enemy. At the entrance he put the package of his bride's belongings. A few yards away he built a shed, in which he placed a large vat, water jars, an assortment of pots and other kitchen utensils, as well as a modest supply of food.

On the opposite summit, at a dangerously narrow and easily removable wooden span built by Asher of Kfar Haroob for emergency crossings, a passing sentry had paused to watch.

"Where is your post?" Shemon called out to him.

"Further on," the man responded, and pointed at a clump of bushes quite some distance away.

"Who put you there?"

"Elon of Zofith."

"Go there, then, and keep out of sight," Shemon directed. "The best watchman is he who is not seen."

Shemon found Meredya in a booth beside the tent of the wounded. Still in her bridal gown, now soiled and ripped, she sat drowsing, her hands clasped about her knees. From the tent of the wounded Tamar could be heard speaking softly to another woman. As Shemon entered, Meredya started, opened her eyes, and with a gasp of joy, ran into his arms.

He held her close, fondled her and asked solicitously, "Are you well, my love?"

She looked up at him with the heart-warming smile he loved and whispered, "I've been waiting for you years and years."

"We are going up the hill now," he said huskily.

When they reached the crest, he pointed to the nearest and lowest of the undulating hills. "Down there," he said, "Leveah, my pet lioness, lived. Here is our olive grove; I'll show you its secret—a hidden well. Come."

He brought her to a clearing in the grove where old ivy-covered boards and sharp stones were heaped in several places. The crumbling foundation of a building gaped in the center. From one of the heaps he removed the top two planks and some small stones. A square brown board came into view. This he lifted. In the murky depths water glistened. Close to the top an iron ring was hooked into a heavy beam above the mouth of the pit. A stout rope, fastened to the ring, descended into the depths of the well.

"A real deep-water well!" she exclaimed. "There is water here for many people for a long time." She looked up at him, flushed with excitement and admiration.

"This is your well," he said. "Others don't need it now but we cannot foretell the future. Since you let Zarooba return to her village, I'll fill your vat for you every morning. When I'm away you will draw the water yourself; but you must keep the well covered, just as we found it. Let the well stay open now for a few minutes. I will fill the vat for you."

"But where is my vat?"

"Come."

He put his arm about her shoulders and led her to the plateau. She stared at the breath-taking panorama; at the strange, seemingly rickety span uncannily thrust across the abyss; at the large tent that was to be her honeymoon home; at the makeshift kitchen; at the huge domes, undulating in the sun's glare; and at the eagles soaring in the dazzling blue, their shadows trembling on the mountainsides. There was mystery and grandeur in the vistas. The giant beside her belonged here; she knew it with a sudden awareness. He and she and the vistas and the light were strength and love and faith and freedom under God.

Leaning against him, she stood as in a trance. A premonition of disaster was taking hold of her. Those kingbirds above and the abyss below—were they not omens of things to come? Would not Shemon's and her destiny hover between the heights and the abyss? Which would it finally be?

She was about to speak her thought when she became aware of a faint din, rising, it seemed, from the depth of the opposite hill. She pointed toward it. "What is it?"

"Our men are building fortifications in the Bowl."

"May I see it?"

"You may, if you wish to cross this board."

She caught the glint in his eyes and knew that he was jesting. She wondered whether anyone at all would risk crossing the dizzying span. The board was about forty feet long, two or perhaps three feet wide. It was completely flat, without the slightest protection against a fall. Was there no other way of reaching the opposite side? Could not a safer bridge be built?

Without speaking her mind she held tight to Shemon, peered into the abyss and shuddered. Instantly, however, she berated herself for her momentary cowardice. How could she, who had thrown in her lot with such a man, shrink from crossing a small bridge even if it looked a little narrow and shaky! "I will do it," she said, but not as resolutely as she would have liked, "but not today. If you let me hold on to you I'll cross it tomorrow."

He took her in his arms and kissed her. "You are a brave girl, my lovely one. I was testing you. You need not ever cross this board if you don't want to. It is a makeshift bridge for me and a few others. Let us forget it now. We must eat. I'll bring the water. Your clothes are at the tent door."

She cried out in delight and ran to her bundle while he picked up the vat and a water jar and strode off. Then she started a fire. After he had brought the water she went to the rear of the tent, washed, and put on a light gown.

When they rose from their meal, he took her hands and murmured a verse from *The Song of Songs*. She shut her eyes. The silence about them had deepened; the faint din from the Bowl had come to a lull. She slipped into his arms. They stood still, galvanized by the contact of their bodies.

Suddenly an eagle's cry ripped the stillness and countless similar cries reverberated far and wide. Startled, she shrank from him and looked up. There were no eagles in sight, but on some of the hill crests armed men appeared and a shaggy head bobbed up above a boulder on the opposite peak.

He took her hands again. "Be not frightened, my love," he said. "It is only a signal. Our sentries are being tested."

"Oh!" she smiled feebly. "I thought the Edomites were coming."

The cry was repeated twice and the guards vanished. She waited, and when the stillness was complete she again glided into his arms. He lifted her and carried her into the tent.

Chapter Nineteen

The Shaarim massacre deepened the despair of the meek, shook the placidity of the wary, ignited the wrath of the courageous and whetted the determination of the rebellious. Young men began to seek out the Thumbless and the Heromavs of their own accord. The secret smithies worked feverishly, preparing arms. At the Cave of Vengeance and Bnai Brak men were taught warfare day and night, and Zevulun had begun deliveries of food and war supplies. Nevertheless, the community as a whole, though seething within, had not been stirred enough to rise in force.

It was early in the month of Ab. Shemon, in linen breeches, a kerchief protecting his head from the scorching sun, galloped on horseback hither and yon, putting a company of his riders through wild paces. His commands echoed through the mountains and perspiration glistened on his face and mighty torso. The men, dressed like Shemon, were divided into several opposing groups. Shouting ferociously, they charged at each other with long rods, wielding them like spears. Now and then a rider dislodged his opponent from the saddle, but the loser would promptly remount his horse—to roars of approval or reproof, depending upon his agility.

The riders were tiring. Shemon looked up at the sun. The afternoon was well advanced. He raised his hand; the day's training was over. Shemon handed over his mare to an attendant, exchanged a few words of banter with the men and bade them *Shalom*.

The sun was low when Shemon, his head on Meredya's lap, lay on the dry, yellowish grass in front of their tent. Some distance away another tent had been pitched by Elon, but he and Tamar were now in the gorge. Meredya, playing with her husband's coppery curls, was singing his favorite song, about a shepherd who left his flocks and his beloved, exchanged his *halil* (fife) for a dagger and joined a rebel band.

It was good to relax, to feel the warm softness of her legs, to hear her soothing voice, to forget the burden of responsibility for a great and perilous undertaking. But his tense nature and restless mind made complete abandon difficult to achieve. His thoughts were drifting to flaws in the training of his men, to the continuing lack of horses (Zevulun had encountered obstacles in securing them), to a thousand eventualities which he could not cope with if they arose now, to disturbing rumors about a serious clash with the Romans in the region of Kfar Haroob.

Discovering his absent gaze, Meredya stopped singing and called softly, "Shemon."

"Yes, pleasure of my heart," he responded without looking up, his voice still distant and blank.

She leaned forward, took his face and turned it toward her. "Your thoughts are not of me, my dear."

He smiled at her guiltily. "In a manner of speaking they are, even if they are not," he said apologetically, "for I divide my thoughts between you and Israel, and whichever I think of, you, my love, are in them."

She kissed him on the lips. He sat up and took her in his arms. But his love-making was interrupted by a signal from a sentry outside the grove; someone was coming. In a matter of seconds Nadav, in a beggar's disguise, appeared in the clearing. He was barefoot, his black hair was matted and his face was soiled and dripping with perspiration.

Shemon greeted him and invited him to sit beside them.

Nadav cast off his ragged sackcloth. His ritual vest and linen breeches seemed to cling to his body. "I bring you word from Judith the seamstress."

Meredya hastened into the kitchen shed and brought water for him to wash. While he was washing, she came with a trayful of food. Refreshed, he sat down, whispered a prayer and gulped down the milk. Meredya resumed her seat beside her husband.

Nadav wiped his mouth with the back of his hand. "Eat," urged Shemon. But Nadav spoke: "Jerusalem is being plowed under."

His words fell like a thunderclap. Meredya opened her eyes wide in unbelief. Shemon stiffened. "What, now, do you mean by 'ploughed under'?" he demanded.

"The Temple site on Mount Moriah and the holy ground rising up to the Mount of Olives are being cleared of ruins and ploughed under. This the Edomites always do before building." Nadav spoke gloomily, haltingly, as if feeling personally guilty for the acts of the Romans.

"What will they build?"

"Houses of idolatry, Judith says. A building wizard—a Greek, Achillas by name—is already in the Holy City, and images of naked men and women have been brought from across the Jordan."

Shemon's face darkened. He rose, paced up and down ferociously, and, upon halting, demanded of Nadav: "Proof! Has Judith given you proof?"

From a pocket in the back of his ritual vest Nadav produced a parchment and handed it to Shemon. "Ruffina wrote this," he said.

Shemon snatched the scroll out of Nadav's hand, swiftly absorbed its contents and stamped his foot. "May they burn!" he swore. "The, the . . . !" He was choking with rage.

"Sit down, my love," Meredya said anxiously. Shemon stormed up and down the clearing for a while, and regaining his equilibrium, sat beside his wife. "What does Ruffina say, my dear?" she inquired gently.

"Little more than what we already know." He paused, reread the parchment and continued, "The architect's name is Achillas of Synopai in Pontus. A great planner and builder, he. Erected palaces in Rome and Athens, designed the stadium in Caesarea. Now he is to build a new city on the holy site. Two temples— one to Jupiter and one to Venus. Two bathhouses, a theater and seven new districts—"

"For the heathen to live in," Nadav interjected, his mouth full (he had finally begun to eat), "and for the glorification of the emperor-god!"

"Aelia Capitolina," Shemon uttered scornfully. His bitterness mounted as he continued, "Hadrian has truly come to believe himself a god, the great benefactor of humankind. The Athenians completely turned his head when he last visited them. Their servile cajolery went beyond all bounds."

"Can you not set his head right, my dear?" Meredya said. He shot a quick glance at his wife. She meant what she had said. The smoldering hate he had perceived in her voice was mirrored in her eyes.

"His head is far, pleasure of my heart, but the heads of his servants are near," he said ominously. "We will strike at his vaingloriousness through them." A long silence fell. Then he asked, "Have you more to tell, Nadav?"

Nadav swallowed his last mouthful, wiped his lips, thanked the hostess and replied, "At the seashore in Caesarea they say cedarwood and marble and all manner of dyes and ornaments are being brought to the Holy City and stored on the site. It is also said that Galileans came to grips with Edomites near Soosita."

"Soosita is on the eastern side of Lake Kinnereth, near Kfar Haroob," corrected Shemon. "You are the second man who brings me these rumors. There must be some truth in them. If so, we will soon hear from Asher."

Shemon paused, clasped his knees and sank into thought. Above the darkened hills a baby crescent rose and countless unexplored worlds began to flash their golden signals.

At last he stirred. "My love," he said softly, "make a fire. I will confer with my men." Meredya rose and went for fagots. "And you, Nadav, get some sleep. You will go to Caesarea at midnight and see Judith early in the morning. Through Ruffina or some other friend we must obtain a blank parchment bearing Rufus' hand and seal. If necessary, Judith can use the gold we have given her. But you must get that parchment tomorrow." Nadav made no remark and Shemon continued, "You will dress in Edomite garb, take a fast horse and ride to Bnai Brak. Give the tidings to Joel and tell him we will, with God's help, destroy the enemy's designs. We may not need Joel's men, but let them be ready." He reflected for a while. "Today is the first day of the week and the fifth day of Ab. See me the afternoon of the fourth day of the week under the Five Palms, south of Kiryat Yaarim, above Jerusalem."

"In what garb?"

"Edomite."

"Is Joel to tell Rabbi Akiba?"

"Let him use his judgment."

The leaders huddled about the fire for hours. At first Shemon's plan appeared to them recklessly daring and fantastic. They argued that no band of plotters could enter Jerusalem without risking an encounter with the Tenth Roman Legion, Fretensis, which, in full strength, garrisoned the Holy City. But Shemon convinced them. They gave painstaking thought to every detail.

It was midnight when they rose, fatigued, content with their decision but still a little apprehensive. The air was sharp despite the season; the fire had long since died and only solitary embers still glowed in the ash heap.

"This will be our first real blow against them," Elon observed. "We must give them no cause to laugh at us."

"Laugh at us?" Itamar snapped. "We will laugh at them!"

Shemon smiled tolerantly, looked at the stars and yawned. "I will set out an hour before dawn. Every man knows his duties. Under you, Elon, the camp will be in good hands." He turned to Abner. "And my father-in-law will speak to the elders of Kiryat Yaarim the day after tomorrow."

Abner embraced his son-in-law and they all bade each other a restful night.

When Shemon entered his tent, he found Meredya waiting for him. He undressed and lay beside her. "You should have slept," he chided her gently.

"I wanted to be loved," she whispered. "Are you leaving at dawn?"

"A little earlier."

"Take me with you," she said abruptly.

He was astounded. "You cannot mean it, my love."

"Why not?"

"Whoever heard of women going to war?"

"Judith of Bethulia went. She slew Holofernes."

"In his sleep, pleasure of my heart," he murmured with gentle mockery, "in his sleep. The men we will encounter will, to our sorrow, be awake. Besides," he continued more earnestly, "we need no womanly wiles and we will slay only if we must. There will be only a few of us, hard and tested men. You, my love, would hamper us and perhaps bring disaster to all of us."

She swallowed a lump but did not cry. "I thought I would put on a boy's clothing and be your armor-bearer. I want to share your dangers with you, not only your food and bed."

He took her in his arms and she clung to him ardently. "Lovely of lovelies," he whispered. "Are you not sharing enough dangers with me by being my wife?"

She kissed him stormily.

Chapter Twenty

At Kiryat Yaarim, a mountain village off the highway west of Jerusalem, Abner visited the elders. They had already heard of the ground-breaking on the Temple site and listened to him receptively. He spoke in hints and parables and revealed no secrets. But they understood and assured him that the villagers would be deaf and dumb about anything unusual that might arouse their curiosity.

Abner then went to see the local blacksmith, Elhanan, a big, swarthy, taciturn young man with a leonine head and small, tense eyes. At the mention of Shemon's name, Elhanan became eager and attentive. Upon hearing what was expected of him he laid his apron aside and said briefly, "I will tell my men."

"And will they do what is asked of them?"

The blacksmith glanced at the older man with mild reproof, as if to say, "Unnecessary talk," but he only muttered, "Sure."

Abner, reassured, bade him *shalom* and rode up to the Five Palms. There he left a message under a designated boulder and returned to the caves.

The next day no one asked questions in Kiryat Yaarim when a number of choice young men were seen leaving the village in beggar's disguise, one by one, at given intervals. Some of them, including the blacksmith, went down the coiling highway; others disappeared over goat trails in the back of the vineyards. Nor were comments made when, toward evening, a solitary rider, by his attire an Edomite, appeared under the Five Palms and was soon joined by other horsemen, headed by a huge Roman. They tarried for a while and then cantered off toward Jerusalem.

It was dark when the riders who had been observed at Kiryat Yaarim reached a crumbled building northwest of the Mount of Olives and dismounted. Without relinquishing the reins they sat amid the ruins. No one spoke. From there, it was said, Titus had directed his long siege against the tenacious defenders of their holy capital. Did Shemon deliberately choose this spot for his first direct challenge to Hadrian? Did he believe that fate demanded that on this spot, where the beginning of his people's downfall had been engineered, the beginning of its rise, too, should be engineered?

Shemon tethered Ayalah to a battered monolith, hung up his shield and lifted himself onto the top of a still-firm wall. The scent of cinnamon was in the air and it was very still. In the amber light of the young moon the contours of the new Roman Jerusalem, and about it, the endless mounds of devastation, lay pallid, mysterious and forbidding. From the vast frozen sea of desolation which rolled from Mount Zion through the Valley of the Cheesemongers; through the Lower City; up Mount Moriah, where the ploughed ground could not now be discerned; and high up north, where once the proud Tower of Antonia had stood, voices seemed to reach Shemon. Perhaps they were the voices of prophets or crucified martyrs, of warriors who had fought to the last or of babes smothered by their anguished mothers; or perhaps the broken marble of the Temple courts, the buried sacred vessels or the torn priestly vestments had been given voices. Or perhaps they were the wails of remorse of the self-seeking leaders whose folly and sins had brought on the destruction; or perchance they were faint echoes of the last unfinished prayer of the Levites who had died on their feet, proclaiming the Oneness of His Name, and playing to their last breath the *magrepha* (a wind organ), the oboes, the lutes and shofars to magnify and sanctify His glory even at the hour of blasphemy and destruction.

It could have been any one of those voices, or all of them together, striving to be heard from the depth of the crushing ruins and succeeding in bringing forth to the surface no more than a faint whisper, audible only to such as Shemon. Deep was the effect of these indiscernible voices upon him, but he shook it off and called to Itamar and Nadav to join him on the wall.

"Has the blacksmith signaled?" asked Itamar.

"Not yet," replied Shemon, "but we should see his signal soon if all has gone well. Meanwhile look down there." He pointed at the dim outlines of Roman Jerusalem. "Do you recognize the three long shadows rising above the dark line in the north?"

"Yes," they replied simultaneously. And Nadav added, "They are the towers of Hippicus, Phasaleus and Mariamne."

"They are the northeastern bounds of the Roman quarters. Herod built the towers and Titus preserved them for posterity. Well, now"—Shemon smiled—"they are a good landmark for us even in the dark. There is a secret gate in the wall between the towers of Phasaleus and Mariamne, but we will not attempt to use it unless we fail in our stratagem." He paused briefly, and then continued, "If we are allowed to enter without suspicion, all we need remember is this: Via Praetoria runs from east to west, and its exit in the east is on a line with the Golden Gate. The Praetorium is in the northwestern end of the street; the prefect's house and the dwellings of other ruling Edomites are nearby, and Achillas of Synopai, too, is surely there. The main thoroughfare is Via Principalis, which runs from north to south and has a southern gate that leads into the Lower Market. This is the gate we will enter, and we will ride along Via Principalis until it meets Via Praetoria. At the intersection are a small stadium and the baths. There we will turn west, unless otherwise instructed by the Edomite guard. We must keep away from the eastern wall, where the barracks are located."

"But," Itamar wondered, "the holy site is in the east, and the broken ground is in its northern part. So are the images. Will we not go there?"

"Not if all goes well. That is where the 'beggars' will be," Shemon explained. "They will enter through Bar-Goria's tunnel."

"They are in already," Nadav interrupted. "Look."

Upon the upper reaches of Mount Moriah two lights, which from that distance seemed no larger than small apples, were blinking.

"The signal," Shemon said with subdued elation. He watched the lights for a while before he repeated, "Yes, the signal. The lights are slowly moving up and down. Let's go."

As the small cavalcade approached the southern gate, Shemon, who, to avoid detection, had dyed his hair, turned to Nadav. "Is my beard still black?" he asked.

"As black as the night," Nadav replied.

"Who goes there?" a challenge came.

"Friends," Shemon responded in Latin, and the horsemen rode up to the gate.

One of the two sentries called the decurion of the watch. "Who are you?" demanded the decurion.

"We are members of the procurator's guard and bear word from His Excellency the Procurator of Judea to His Nobility the architect Achillas of Synopai," said Shemon.

"What would the procurator want of the architect at this hour of the night?"

"When we set out the sun was bright, and it will be bright again when we return."

The Roman raised his lantern to scan the speaker. "Cunning talker, you," he said. "Show me your authority."

Shemon produced two parchments—one, unsealed, identifying him as Decurion Valerius Zarus of the procurator's guard; the other, sealed, addressed to Achillas of Synopai.

The Roman scratched the back of his head with one finger and muttered, "Seems in order." Then he came out of the gate to have a better look at the horseman. "By Juno! A whole legion —twelve of you! Why so many to carry a parchment?"

"I obey orders," Shemon replied, feigning slight annoyance at the inquisition. "The roads are not too safe of late. And I was given to understand that the architect may be coming with us to Caesarea."

"You'll make too much noise in the streets. It is past the ninth hour," the decurion procrastinated.

"I will leave half my men at the gate if you wish," Shemon offered to allay the Roman's suspicion.

The decurion returned the parchments to Shemon. "Be it as you say." He ordered the gates opened. "You will go up Via Principalis and turn west on Via Praetoria at the baths," the Roman directed. "You will find the architect in a villa one half-stadium before the prefect's."

"Thank you, Decurion."

While the Roman was showing half the horsemen where to wait, Shemon whispered to Itamar, whom he was leaving in command, to strike the watch down and hold the gate if he, Shemon, did not return in an hour.

The market place was deserted. The stalls were closed. A solitary tatterdemalion, apparently asleep, was leaning against a wooden stand. He was muttering in his slumber, and as Shemon came trotting by, the derelict stirred and mumbled, "The images are already broken, and so is the watchman's head."

Shemon kept going, his men behind him. There was little life and light in the streets. Porticoed dwellings, fenced off by jagged stones, sprawled far apart on each side of the street. Some were surrounded by young gardens; most stood bare and lonely amid lawns of yellow stubble and graveled walks.

At the intersection of the principal *via*s there were four smoking oil lights at the corners and a marble sundial in the center. A solitary guard was pacing up and down. He halted to eye the riders. Shemon greeted him, told him whom he sought and received final directions.

Where the villa placed at the architect's disposal stood, Via Praetoria was wide and rich with verdure. Old cinnamon trees which had escaped the Roman axe exhaled their pungent scent. Only the white columns of the structure, hidden in a luxuriant garden, could be glimpsed through the foliage. Shemon alighted, handed the reins to one of his men and knocked at the iron gate.

A heavy, bulldog-faced domestic responded. "Your wish?" he asked curtly.

"I carry an epistle from the Procurator of Judea to Achillas of Synopai."

"Let me have it."

"I am instructed to deliver it to your master in person."

The man growled something unintelligible and went away. He soon returned and opened the gate. "Follow me."

Shemon was led to the magnificent portico of an elaborate dwelling. His quarry, attired in a loose, gold-embroidered tunic and sandals, was reclining on cushions under a bronze seven-wicked lamp, studying a tablet. A patina of grapes and fresh figs stood within reach, and a censer containing burning incense stood behind his cushions.

Achillas acknowledged Shemon's greeting with a casual nod and, continuing to examine the tablet leisurely, extended a plump hand for the parchment. Shemon handed it to the Greek and waited.

Popping grapes into his mouth, Achillas broke the seal and, with an expression of boredom, began to read. Suddenly he sat up, and then came to his feet. "By Zeus!" he exclaimed. "What is the meaning of this incredible thing? The Syrian legate is in Caesarea and desires to discuss the modification of my plans? Why? The plans have been approved by the Caesar himself! And why can't my going wait until tomorrow?" He realized full well that no answer could be expected from a mere courier, but stared at him as if the matter were a grievous error which the man somehow could correct.

Shemon coughed modestly and said nothing.

"Thundering Neptune!" cried the architect. "Have no instructions been given to you by word of mouth? Do you know nothing further concerning this matter?"

Shemon cleared his throat. "A man of my rank," he said with a barely perceptible touch of mockery, "is not favored with the legate's confidences. But," he added with feigned hesitancy, "if I may venture . . . Is it not possible that the legate has had word from His Divine Majesty the emperor himself?"

"Of course it is possible. Of course. But nothing so strange has ever befallen me before." He paused to reflect. "Ought I not to consult the prefect before going?"

Again Shemon coughed deferentially. "The prefect is not at home," he lied. "He has unexpectedly been called to the barracks."

"To the barracks? At this hour? Did anything untoward happen? And how do *you* know?" he demanded.

"I was told by a guard," Shemon replied without blinking.

Achillas scanned the soldier dubiously, but providentially help came from an unexpected source. The bulldog face of the attendant appeared inside the radius of light and a husky voice said, "A little while ago I saw the prefect ride off east."

What a miracle! thought Shemon.

Achillas swore mildly, reread the parchment and began pacing up and down the portico. He was a man in his early forties, middle-statured, flaccid, bald-pated, round-faced and clean-shaven. He also had distinctive features: a high forehead, astute eyes and a full, generous mouth. "By the Fates! It seems that I will have to go," he said cheerlessly, and added, hoping against hope, "Could you not wait until morning?"

Shemon shook his head. "No, my lord. It is cooler and better to ride at night. No prying eyes, too, in an unfriendly land."

Achillas sighed resignedly. "Have you enough men for my protection?"

"More than enough, Your Nobility."

"Bring me my clothes, Nicholas, and have my horse saddled," Achillas ordered the invisible attendant, and briskly went inside.

When Achillas, riding with Shemon at the head of his horsemen, reached the Lower Market, the tatterdemalion, who was still sitting on the ground dozing, his head propped against the empty wooden stand, suddenly jumped to his feet and, running alongside the horses, wailed, "Mercy, good Romans, mercy on a poor wretch! Here," he gasped, beating his chest, "it burns! It burns, but no one can see it. It burns! And the flames will soon reach the sky."

"Begone, you creature! Begone!" Shemon cried contemptuously. "This is no time for begging."

"Pitiful," muttered Achillas, and tossed the beggar a coin.

"Thank you, kind lord, thank you," the derelict chanted queerly as he caught the alms. Then, falling back, he resumed his wailing: "It burns! And the flames will soon reach the sky!"

"What an odd creature," observed the Greek.

"Demented," muttered Shemon.

As they reached the southern gate and the other half of their men rejoined them, Shemon looked up. Only myriads of gems set in black velvet hung over Mount Moriah. But later, when the riders were high in the mountains and Shemon looked back, a red glow tinged the sky over the Temple site.

"Faster!" he commanded. "Faster, horsemen!"

It was still pitch dark and the cavalcade was galloping briskly downhill toward the Judean plain. Suddenly Shemon, who was at the head of the column, swung sharply into a wide curving bypath.

Achillas, rather surprised, followed, and close by him rode Itamar and Nadav. "Where are we going?" he asked. But no one appeared to hear him. "Listen, you, Decurion!" he shouted. "Caesarea is north of here and we have turned south."

There was no reply. The Greek spoke to the men beside him, behind him, but they were strangely unresponsive.

They reached a clearing. A wagon, to which a mule was harnessed, was waiting. Two men were leaning against the wagon. Achillas sensed a trap, and fear crept through his flesh. "What is the meaning of this?" he murmured.

Shemon swung his horse around and rode up. "Achillas of Synopai," he said, and there was a new, imperious ring in his voice, "we are Israelites. We have taken you captive to thwart Hadrian's wicked scheme. We mean to do you no harm unless you resist. You are a great artisan and builder, but Hadrian has brought you here to use your skills for evil, to desecrate God's chosen site. It will not be. The graven images have tonight been broken, the marble statues smashed, the timber and ornaments burned."

Achillas regained his bearings. To him there was nothing as disturbing as peril combined with mystery. Here the mystery was clearing. "Your cunning is great," he said. "But is not Hadrian's power greater? Are there no other statues and gold and ornaments in his domain?"

"Hadrian's power and riches are no more than specks of dust before the Lord," Shemon was quick to retort. "We serve Him and He will be our mainstay."

"Without wishing to offend," the Greek said slowly, and a note of disparagement crept into his voice, "I doubt it. For if it were true, why did your God permit His shrine—?"

Shemon cut him short. "We haven't brought you here to convert you to our faith. Where we mean to take you, men of learning will answer your questions when you ask them. What we wish to know is: Will you do as you are directed without resisting?"

"What will you have me do?"

"Where you are going, you are neither to see nor to be seen until you are in your room. Will you, therefore, climb into the coffin which is on the wagon?"

Achillas shrank back in horror. "A coffin? Gruesome!"

"There are openings in it for air," said Shemon as convincingly as the subject permitted, "and no bodily harm will come to you."

There was a long silence; then the innate philosopher in Achillas asserted himself, and he laughed. "After all, it is better to play the corpse for a little while than to be dead forever."

"Sound reasoning," Shemon smiled.

"How long will you keep me?"

"In the box or in captivity?"

"In either."

"Hardly an hour in the box. The length of your captivity has not yet been decided."

Achillas contemplated the coffin, sighed and then laughed again. "My litter does not look too comfortable. It would be best to take some of my clothes off." He spread his toga on the bottom of the coffin and began pulling off his tunic. There was an outburst of laughter.

Day was breaking when Achillas found himself in a spacious room, comfortable with rugs and cushions. It faced a garden, but tall cypresses blocked the view. Guards were heard below and at the door, and from a distance behind his room came the sounds of men and beasts of burden, mingled in a mild hubbub. His clothes were neatly spread out on a bench, and in a corner there were towels and water for washing.

Soon the door opened and a tall, bearded man brought in a patina containing fresh fruit. He bowed and his eyes twinkled mirthfully as he said, "I was told that my lord had been enjoying grapes and figs when he was taken from his house. The interruption is regretted. He may continue without interruption."

With this, the man turned to go. For a fleeting moment the architect stood speechless with amazement; then he burst into uproarious laughter, in which the bearded attendant joined as he closed the door.

Chapter Twenty-one

Shemon returned to the caves at night and went straight up the hill. In an olive grove he came upon Elon, who had just completed his nightly round of inspection. They embraced.

"Well done," Elon said warmly. "Spirits are high here and the men are eager to do more."

"They will. Let us first see what Tyrannus will do."

The friends walked slowly toward the clearing.

"Why did you not do away with Achillas?" Elon asked after a brief pause. "Rufus will turn heaven and earth to find him. Why should Nitsa and the whole of Ludd be endangered? Dead and buried, the Greek would never be found and could never talk."

Shemon knitted his brows and said with conviction, "There

is good in the man, Elon. He is not an Edomite and he has done us no wrong. Above all, Rabbi Akiba was against harming him."

"What will you do with him, then? How long can you keep him at Nitsa's?"

"As long as necessary. He may yet prove useful to us."

"I hope you are right," Elon said darkly.

"I am." Shemon laughed and put his hands on his friend's shoulders. "And do not be gloomy. There will, before joy comes, be more important reasons for gloom."

They bade each other *shalom*.

Meredya, in a white gown, bathed and scented, had been waiting for Shemon. Upon seeing him emerge from the grove with Elon, she held her breath until the other man had gone into his tent. Then, with a palpitating heart, she ran to meet her husband.

"My lovely one, my lovely one!" he murmured, holding her close. "How did you know I would come tonight?"

"I did not. I was hoping you would. I was waiting for you last night, too."

"All night?"

"Until after the change of the midnight watch." He kissed her ardently. "Come," she said, freeing herself, "you must eat. There is a meal spread out for you."

He washed himself hurriedly and sat down with her. They could not keep their eyes off each other.

"I did not come yesterday, as the others did, because I had to go to Bnai Brak."

She was glad he had explained of his own accord.

"Father thought so, too. Last night and tonight he spent a long while with me." She paused and added very softly, "You are all I had hoped you would be, my beloved. Everybody is proud of you. You've saved us from infamy, humiliated the enemy. And all that without losing a man! How did you do it?"

"With forethought, pleasure of my heart," he replied, and swallowed his mouthful. "With a little forethought, inspired by the Almighty, we captured Achillas." He observed her eagerness to know more and continued, "As for the destruction of the idols, I would say that in the sorrows of the past were planted the seeds of a little joy for us. About two years ago, when, one night, my men and I were probing deep into the ruins of Jerusalem outside the present Edomite walls, we came upon a forgotten underground hide-out, one of those which Bar-Goria had dug during Titus' siege. Hundreds of men had died in it; it was cluttered with human bones. Then we stole in night after night, buried the bones and cleared the tunnel. It was a long tunnel with tricky twists, one of which led to the northeastern corner of the present Edomite fortress. Right into it, Meredya. 'God-sent!' we said. 'Someday we will use it.' And we did. So you see, beloved, it was all providential."

She gave him an impulsive kiss. "And what will you do now, my dear? Free Jerusalem?"

"Not yet, pleasure of my heart. We are not strong enough to free Jerusalem; and if we took it by stratagem, we would be besieged and could not hold it. We must keep gathering strength."

He was through with his meal now and she nestled up to him. A great wave of love rolled through him and he gathered her up in his arms.

That morning Shemon had spent much time in the gorge and on the training field, and now was resting on the grass, his head buried in his arms. Meredya was preparing the noonday meal in the kitchen shed and Tamar was singing in the grove.

Suddenly, a huge, burly man, naked save for a loincloth and a bandage on his right knee, appeared on the span between the two hills and, paying no heed to the violently shaking board, proceeded at a dangerous pace toward the plateau where Shemon lay. His chestnut hair, except for the earlocks, was cropped; his thick, sharp-edged beard sprawled in every direction; his full lips were parted in a smile, revealing large, strong teeth, and his brown eyes shone with the excitement of anticipation. When he was a few feet away from the plateau, he could contain himself no longer and roared, "Shemon, my friend! Shemon!"

Shemon looked up, jumped to his feet and ran to meet the newcomer. "Asher! I have been waiting for you."

They hugged each other wildly, shook and lifted each other and emitted loud whoops dating back to their adolescent years. The commotion brought Meredya and Tamar to the scene.

"Women!" exclaimed Asher without excessive enthusiasm. "Women! What are they doing here?" Then he remembered. "Your wives!"

"One of them is," Shemon smiled.

"One of them? I'll tell you which." Asher paused, glanced swiftly at each woman and announced, "The taller one."

Shemon slapped him on the back. "Right," he said. "Meredya, this is Asher of Kfar Haroob."

Asher studied her for a moment, and then rendered his unsolicited verdict: "Worthy of you, Shemon. Fine woman."

Meredya flushed, smiled at Asher and rushed back into the kitchen shed. Tamar, fascinated, kept staring at him.

"And who is this petal of a woman?"

"Elon's wife, Tamar."

"Elon of Zofith?"

"Yes."

"Fine woman, too," he laughed, "but a storm will surely blow her away."

She stamped her little foot. "It will not," she shouted. "I will stand against any storm like any one of you." With this, she ran into her tent.

"Asher will break bread with us," Shemon called out to his wife, and the two friends retired to a distant corner of the plateau, where they sat on the parched grass.

"What are the tidings, Asher?"

"Bad, Shemon. We killed some Edomites. Then hosts of them came and besieged us. We blundered—we came out and fought them. Time and again. We fought well. We took a heavy toll, but we lost in the end and Kfar Haroob was lost. Not many of us escaped."

"Where is Noah?"

Asher's head drooped and a solitary tear rolled down his hairy cheek. "We were both on the ground for a while," he groaned. "I had received a heavy blow on my knee. It was then that the men of Haroob cried, 'The brothers are dead,' and gave up. But I rose; Noah did not."

"May the righteous Judge be blessed," whispered Shemon.

There was a long silence. Then Asher spoke: "My guilt I confess to you, Shemon. I did not listen to your counsel. My hatred for them blinded me. Know you that even before Zofith and Shaarim they came to towns and hamlets on both sides of Lake Kinnereth and hunted out Nazarenes for the slave marts. Now, we have our differences with the Nazarenes, but they are human beings. And peaceful. But the accursed Edomites showed them less pity than I would a wild beast. Then Shaarim came. My mind went loose." Moaning, he beat his fists against his temples. "My brother's blood cried out to me from the soil. I could not rest and went out to many towns and villages in Galilee. Now I can say this to you: I will deliver three thousand men in a week if you give the word." He paused, waited for Shemon to say something, and finding him silent, pleaded, "Give the word, Shemon, my friend. Give the word. Let's swoop down on Jerusalem and take it."

Shemon shook his head gravely. "No. The time is not yet, Asher. Would you see me err with Jerusalem as you have with Kfar Haroob? Would you pit our full strength against Jerusalem, where the enemy holds almost a full legion, and leave all the fortresses in Judea and Samaria unmolested and sending men to strike us in the back? Or to besiege us? Are we ready for a siege? Are we strong enough to overcome three legions?"

"What will we do, then?"

"Prepare more, Asher. Prepare more, and hit them wherever we can, as often as we can. Make them afraid, confuse them and then take their coastal fortresses."

"What will I do?"

"You will not be idle, Asher. You will be given men to lead, but you are also a wizard in carpentry and ironwork. Build us battering-rams, the kind the Edomite uses. We will need them soon."

Asher brightened up. "That I will do, Shemon. But I will need a sample to follow."

"We will provide it, Asher. Zevulun—I will tell you about him later—will deliver some from Alexandria."

"Soon?"

"Very soon."

At this point Elon came out of the grove and ran toward them. "Ovadya has just arrived from Caesarea. Rufus has decreed the proscriptions and has raised the price on your head fourfold."

"So he has done it, the swine!" Shemon exclaimed. "Call a war council for the fourth hour this afternoon."

Chapter Twenty-two

To Tinneus Rufus, Achillas' unsolved abduction was the deepest humiliation of his career. The issuance of the decree did not heal the smarting wound. Among his counselors and officers, except for those connected with the unceasing search, no one spoke about the matter, but it preyed on his mind nonetheless.

Where there was no solution, there was the eternal solace—wine. And there was a pretext for celebrating—the decree. And so Rufus gave a lavish banquet at which he promised his debauching friends more gold, women and slaves than ever, and an era in which no obdurate Jews would live and the living Jews would be Romans.

At the same time the rebels emerged from their war council with the slogan: *The Edomites do not let us live as Jews; we will not let the Edomites live.*

Even as Rufus began to enforce his proscriptions, Shemon began his raids upon patrols, foreign caravans, small garrisons. The procurator's calculations went awry. The troops intended for policing and foraging had to be shifted to scout and escort duties and the strengthening of garrisons. Tax collections were dropping with alarming rapidity, for sworn tax collectors were in fear of their lives. Fines levied on villages for their proximity to the localities of raids could be secured only by punitive expeditions. Even these gradually became ineffective as the inhabitants, rather than be subjected to their oppressors' cruelties, deserted with their movable possessions. Some found refuge in the larger towns, others fled to mountain hide-outs; many made their way to Shemon.

Rabbi Akiba, defying the proscriptions, continued to instruct, but few disciples sat at his feet. The mature, able-bodied ones had gone to their homes, to secret training centers throughout the land or to other points designated by Shemon. Among the latter was Masada, an immense rock amid the chloric and sulphurous wastes of the Dead Sea, on the rim of Southern Judea.

To the freedom-hungry this forbidding cliff, rising above dizzying chasms to a height of sixteen hundred feet and unscalable on its eastern side, was an undying symbol of defiance and invincibility. On the fertile plains of Masada, within walls and turrets erected by Jonathan the Hasmonean, a band of nine hundred and sixty valorous men and women had held out for three years, after the fall of Jerusalem, against the might of Rome. All the ingenuity and fury of Flavius Silva had failed to subdue them. When the last wall had become untenable they had died by their own hands—still free.

Hither Shemon had dispatched Amitai with a small unit to prepare and wait for a propitious moment to seize the stronghold. It had long ceased to be an object of interest to the Romans. The poisonous exhalations of Sodom's sepulcher and the sword of Rome had driven the inhabitants west, inland or east into Moab, across the lifeless lake. There were no prospects for revenue and no danger of invasion. A small Roman post, commanded by a decurion, was still maintained on the rock as a mere precaution. The ten soldiers devoted most of their time to dice, rough sport, petty quarrels and impatient waiting for their relief shift, which came once a month. But the strategic value of Masada, in the rear of all the important centers of Southern and Central Judea was clear to Shemon. The rock was to be captured by surprise.

Amitai and his men, well supplied with food and arms, took cover in a Mount Targum cavern in the same region. There they waited for the signal to strike, which was to come from nearby Ein-Gedi, the town of terraced vineyards high above the Dead Sea, and the home of Abner's kin.

Shemon's fortifications and preparations for attack progressed rapidly. Several thousand men were made ready for action, the secret training centers teemed with volunteers and the underground smithies worked day and night. But he was still short of horses and food reserves.

Then, after the Feast of Tabernacles, Zevulun delivered a

shipment of grain and arms. There were still no horses but the cargo was a valuable one. One night, when everything had been securely stored away, Shemon and Zevulun wrapped themselves in robes of camel's hair—the nocturnal air in the hills was already sharp—and settled themselves on the grass to discuss further plans. Serious action could not be delayed much longer, assuredly not long beyond the early winter rains. Life in the caves would soon become hard, the eagerness of the rebels to fight would grow and the depredations of the Edomites would rise in proportion to the rebels' failure to act. And how much longer could they watch the torment of their people without striking?

Zevulun proceeded to tell Shemon what he had accomplished with the aid of Pappus and his friends. They had acquired four strong triremes that would be in fighting trim in a matter of weeks. On their biremes they had erected innocent-looking poop decks, from the shelter of which the exposed decks of the enemy's galleys would be easy targets. Even for their smaller craft they had contrived arched shelters with holes for darts. These would be carried in sections and put up when the craft were out on the open sea. The sons of Pappus and Andreas, Shemon's kinsmen, on hearing of Leveah, had banded themselves with their friends into a Brotherhood of Lions to support the rebels with men and arms. Some of them were learning seafaring. Despite its secrecy, the Brotherhood had branched out to Memphis and Sais, and as far south as Thebes.

Zevulun left at daybreak. Shemon was elated. The glow of the early sun on the verdant mountainsides seemed to reflect the glow of his own spirit. The world about him looked beautiful and cheerful. Autumn is the second spring in the Land of Israel. The first drizzle of the season had fallen and the grateful earth had brought forth its riches. The grass was high and alive again; the barley and wheat sprouted from the soil; fig trees, scattered on the slopes, abounded with fruit; the olives were green; here and there a date palm added its touch of grace to the exhilarating scene. He now was confident in the success of the revolt.

Chapter Twenty-three

Shemon was on the training field when Nadav, dusty and perspiring, rode in to report: "Israelites and Nazarenes from Galilee and Transjordan are on their way to the Gaza slave mart. They are shackled and moving slowly. By nightfall they are likely to reach Eintov or maybe Apollonia."

"How many?"

"One hundred and twenty-six."

"How many guards?"

"Ten, not counting the headman; horsemen all."

Shemon reflected. "Is someone following the captives?"

"Yes, Shemon. Yair of Zofith, the nephew of Ben-Habib, the parnas who was killed at your wedding."

"I remember him," said Shemon, "a short, sturdy lad with a strong likeness to Joshua Hagarsi."

"It is he."

"Let him see me in the hills below the Fox's Ears before sundown."

Nadav touched his forehead and was off.

Shemon called to Asher and Issachar, "There will be work tonight. More than a hundred slaves are on the way to the mart. They must be freed."

Issachar smiled and wiped the perspiration from his flat nose. Asher rubbed his hands, shook Issachar with a slap on the back and laughed, "Ho, ho! A lively evening."

"We may do more than free the captives," Shemon, infected by the exuberance of his friend, said with a twinkle in his eyes. "The evening may stretch into the night. Come up to the olive grove after the noonday meal and we will lay the plans."

It was evening and Shemon and his Thumbless, divided into two companies of horsemen and infantry under Asher and Issachar, waited in the hills overlooking the Plain of Sharon. Yair had just left and had been told to be on the lookout near the slaughterhouse in the northern suburb of Eintov. The slave convoy had been delayed by some accident and was now moving at a snail's pace, still furlongs away from Eintov. An ambush inside the town's suburb would have been more advantageous, but because of the delay Shemon decided to attack on the road and at once. "Issachar," he said, "we will wait no longer. Take ten men and cut the guards off from the rear. You, Asher, take ten men and cut off the road in front. I, with some of my men, will do the rest. Let all the others wait here."

With thirty chosen stalwarts Shemon swiftly moved through the hills until he caught sight of blinking lantern lights on the road below. He brought his men down to the foot of the hill. "Their lanterns," he said quietly, "make the guards easy targets. Move forward and aim at their unprotected stomachs and faces. We outnumber them three to one. If three javelins are aimed at each man, all of them cannot miss. I will aim at the headman." He paused and commanded, "Prepare," and then, "Quietly forward!"

The soft sand did not reveal their approach until they were thirty paces away from the road.

"Who goes there?" challenged a Roman. A volley of deadly javelins was the response. There were agonized cries and gasps of pain. Horses snorted, neighed and reared; one fell, burying his rider beneath him. A solitary survivor, apparently unhurt, raced madly toward Apollonia, only to fall victim, farther up the road, to Asher's double-edged sword.

The prisoners were stupefied. In horror they watched the sudden death of their tormentors and the onrush of the wild-eyed horsemen. They might be liberators but they might just as easily be slave traders of a fierce Arabian tribe. The slaves went down on their knees or prostrated themselves. Some, in fear, called out, "Hear, O Israel!" Others ecstatically invoked the name of Jesus Christ.

Keys to their shackles were found on the dead Roman head-man. Shemon ordered the chains unlocked. Weeping tears of gratitude, many of those freed fell to the feet of their deliverers and kissed their hands.

Asher and Issachar, with their men, rode up. Shemon directed that the bodies be taken to the hills to be stripped and buried, and that the liberated captives be led to an unfrequented part of the caves. Then Shemon and his rebels rejoined their waiting comrades.

"Not enough revenge," grumbled Asher.

"The night is only beginning," muttered Shemon.

He was considering his next move when Yair came panting up the hill. "The Eintovites have ushered in the New Moon," Yair reported excitedly. "The first half of the congregation is gone and soon the second half will come. Avishai, the head parnas, who had been there with the earlier worshipers, will be there again. I overheard him say, 'I love all my townspeople equally well. And if I stood in peril of my life with some of them, I must do so with the others.' "

"Avishai is a brave man," Shemon observed, and turned to Asher and Issachar, who had been listening. "Here is more work for tonight. Caunus' men will surely bear down upon the worshipers."

"What would you have us do?" Asher asked.

Shemon paused to think. Ayalah shifted restlessly and he patted her. Then he bent forward, visibly animated. "Asher," he said, "if all goes as I think it will, Shaarim and your brother will truly be avenged tonight."

"May your words go straight up to the throne of His glory," Asher responded piously.

"Listen carefully," said Shemon. "You and your men, Issachar, go to the groves south of Apollonia, and wait noiselessly until you hear our cry. You, Asher, lie in wait in the dark carob woods. If Edomites come out of the citadel and go through the carob alley toward Eintov, let them go unmolested. On their way back, undo them silently, strip them, put on their garb. Should they discover you first, fight hard. Yair will go with me. Give him a horse. And remember this: Have at least a dozen of your men cut their beards to the skin to look shaved like the Edomite. Understand?"

"Need we really do this? There are bearded Edomites."

"There are, but most of them are shaved. *You* need not do it."

"Will you do it?"

"It is necessary for the success of my plan. The beard will grow back soon enough."

The town of Eintov extended from the Plain of Sharon to an escarpment, high above the sea, which from days immemorial had been one of the ideal spots in the country for greeting the new moon. The ceremony was a mystic rite, enveloped in legend. Some linked the ritual with the moon-worshipping cult; others, with colorful conspiracies against foreign oppressors, when plotters, masquerading as worshipers, had spun their schemes in the moonlight. It was said that underground temples with openings for lunar shafts were still to be found in various parts of the country.

From the Apollonia fort the Eintov escarpment, about six furlongs away, was visible in the daytime. But at night, in the luminescence of the young moon, light objects were not easily detectable against the tan background of the dunes. Shemon and Yair passed the walls surrounding the slaughterhouse yard and quietly moved into the shadows of the nearby storage sheds. From there the flat top of the mound was plainly visible as men in white robes and skull caps stole toward it from the center of the town. A number of them, headed by Avishai, were wrapped in fringed white-blue prayer shawls as they paced, grim-faced, after their leader. Though the moon service required no ritual attire, they wore their shawls in token of the solemnity of the occasion, the defiance of the proscriptions. Violation of the decree anywhere in the land was perilous; in proximity to the turrets of the ill-famed Caunus, it was an act of fanatical courage.

Avishai said something and the worshipers separated into groups of ten and, gazing at the young crescent, began to sway. Avishai stepped close to the brink of the escarpment, raised his hands heavenward and began, "Hallelujah! Praise God in Heaven; praise Him in the lofty spheres!"

Yair became restless and whispered apprehensively, "If the Edomites come, will we stand alone against them?"

"We will do what I think right, Yair," Shemon replied coldly.

"And a good warrior asks no questions." He turned to watch the worshipers.

"Blessed be thy Creator! Blessed be thy Molder! Blessed be thy Conceiver! Blessed be thy Redeemer!"

Swaying, clapping their hands ecstatically, lifting themselves on their toes as if springing, they chanted, "As I dance before Thee and cannot touch Thee, so may my enemies fail to touch me with evil intent."

This they repeated three times; then they turned north toward Caesarea and shook their fists. "May fear and terror descend upon them, and may Thy mighty arm silence them into the silence of stones."

They paused, huddled close to each other and muttered conspiratorially, "David, King of Israel, lives and endures!"

Now they turned to Avishai, their leader, as if seeking confirmation. He declared solemnly, "David, King of Israel, lives and endures!"

As if deriving joy and comfort from the declaration, each man bowed to his neighbor, saying, "Peace be upon thee! Upon thee peace!"

The enchantment of the young moon; the mystery of the dark sea beneath the luminous firmament; the spell of the ritual; the release, however inadequate, of their bitterness; the comfort that came from sharing and facing danger together in the name of the all-embracing ideal, God—all these buoyed them up and fortified their spirits. Now, once again raising their eyes moonward, they intoned, "A good omen and good fortune will come to us and to all Israel. Amen!"

This was the end of the ceremony; now a psalm was to be chanted. In a body the worshipers faced eastward toward Jerusalem. *"Shir lamaälot—A* song to the heights: I will lift up mine eyes to the hills, whence cometh my help. . . ."

Shemon, certain that the Romans could not help but discover this defiant performance, began to wonder whether he had not erred in his judgment and whether the men of Eintov would not go home in peace after all. His daring intentions might for the present go to naught.

Even as he wondered, still tensely alert, he became aware of a faint rumble. Jumping off his horse, he laid his ear to the ground, and, remounting, exclaimed, "Hoofs! Edomites!"

Motioning to Yair to stay where he was, he bolted into the open, stunning the gathering by the suddenness of his intrusion and by his huge frame and voice. "Save yourselves! To your homes! Edomites are coming!"

Petrified, the worshipers stood gazing at him.

"In the name of God!" he cried in desperation. "Why do you tarry? Run! The enemy is upon you and you are unarmed. Run for your lives."

At last the portent of his words took effect and some of them ran toward the town. The rest, hesitating, stared at him in fascination and at one another in indecision. The rapid approach of the Roman horses was now audible. There was some uneasy shifting but no further attempts at flight.

Avishai, a middle-aged man of imposing stature and deportment, raised his hands. "What is it that we have done that we should run as thieves? We have prayed. That is our duty and right, and no mortal shall deny it to us."

"Israel needs men like you, but first learn how to uphold your faith with swords. Until then, save yourselves," Shemon pleaded.

But his plea was futile. Already the shadows of the oncoming cavalry, as it climbed the eminence, were distinguishable.

His plan demanded avoidance of a premature clash with the Romans. With sorrow in his heart he dashed back into the shadow of the buildings. "I will stay here for a while," he said to Yair, "and you go through the groves to Issachar and tell him, Thus said Shemon: Whatever you see, and however hard it may be to contain yourself, do nothing until you hear the cry. But be ready."

Avishai, erect and fearless, his hands uplifted, his silver-threaded black beard swaying, his eyes all but shut as if in exaltation, went forward, followed by the others, drawing fortitude from their inner fountain of faith and chanting ecstatically, "As I dance before Thee, and cannot touch Thee, so may my enemies fail to touch me with evil intent."

The Romans, under Treverius, were now mounting the escarpment, yelling and cursing. They had been instructed to terrorize, punish and arrest, but to avoid promiscuous murder. Expecting no opposition, they had no shields and spears with them, only swords and whips.

The decurion flushed with rage on discovering a defiant mob where he had anticipated cowering suppliants. Ordering his cavalrymen to surround the Israelites, and spurring his horse, he bore down upon Avishai and lashed him across the face with a lead-tipped cowhide whip. Avishai staggered but did not fall. A frightful welt marred his face and blood trickled onto his beard.

The decurion plunged into the advance rows of the crowd and lashed out ruthlessly. His blood lust sated, he returned to Avishai and shouted, "Are you the head of these men?"

Avishai nodded.

"What were you doing here?"

"Praying."

"Praying to whom?"

"To the God of Israel, to the Almighty God of the universe."

"You stinking barbarian!" exploded the Roman. "I'll beat the insolence out of you." Releasing his foot from the stirrup, he kicked ferociously at Avishai's head. Avishai toppled to the ground, unconscious. As the Israelites bent to help their leader, Treverius motioned to his men, who charged at the crowd with sadistic fury.

Shemon could no longer watch the gruesome spectacle without losing his self-control. He had seen all he wanted. Silently he rode his mare into the groves, patted her mane and said gently, "Now go, Ayalah. Go fast!"

When all signs of protest had been smothered, Treverius halted his men and ordered that Avishai be raised to his feet. He had regained consciousness but was unable to stand unsupported. Two of the younger and stronger members of the community, tears trickling down their bloodstained faces, helped him.

"This will teach you a lesson, you circumcised dogs," Treverius taunted, glaring menacingly at the crowd. "You should be grateful that you are alive. I am taking you to the citadel, where you will explain your insolence to the commander. Come on, move!"

The prisoners, limping, groaning and supporting the badly injured, were prodded by whips and obscenities toward Apollonia.

As Treverius entered the carob alley he placed his horsemen on each side of the prisoners. It was difficult to ride under the low, intertwining branches of the carobs and the Romans took to their feet, leading their horses by the bridles. The alley, beneath its umbrella of boughs, was very dark and, save for the fall of feet and hoofs, still.

Suddenly a jackal wailed and another responded. All at once shadows stirred on each side of the alley. Figures leaped from behind trees, from above, from below. Before the Romans had time to realize what was happening, their throats were clutched by powerful fingers that would not relax or relent. One by one, with hardly more than a gasp or death rattle, the legionaries slumped to the ground and lay limp. Treverius alone, who marched in the center of the alley, managed to draw his sword. But before he could smite, a javelin-thrust from behind paralyzed his arm and a fierce, shaggy, bare-armed man in sackcloth flung him down and shut his breath off.

Before the prisoners were able to collect their wits the attack was over. Asher, rising from the decurion's body, uttered tersely, "Silence and attention!"

The Eintovites, paralyzed with surprise and fear, were scarcely able to do anything but follow the order. To them these terrible shadows which had destroyed the enemy with such speed and precision, and which were now stripping the corpses, were apparitions, angels of retribution, a miracle.

"We are the Thumbless," declared Asher. "We are not finished. To succeed we must fool the watchmen at Apollonia. Therefore be silent and obedient."

The Eintovites no more than stirred. Avishai alone whispered his gratitude to Heaven, and opened his eyes with an effort.

The Thumbless donned the Romans' uniforms and hid their own clothes in the woods. Asher, assisted by another man, tied the fully clothed decurion to his horse and led it to the ingress of the alley, where the cover of branches was higher. Here they raised the corpse to an erect position, roped it to the mount's neck and hind parts to prevent it from falling and tied the reins to the dead man's hands. Its face swollen and its eyes bulging beneath its helmet, that which a few minutes before had been Treverius looked grotesque. But the grotesqueness would escape the turret guards in the dark.

Meanwhile the men of Eintov, flanked by the masquerading Thumbless and the captured horses, moved up. Now Shemon, with Ayalah trailing behind him, stepped into the alley and mounted her directly behind the dead decurion. Asher mounted his charger. A rider came forward and the two men flanked Shemon. Then the Heromavs with the shorn beards lined up behind and Shemon spoke. His voice was restrained but loud enough to be heard only in the alley. "We will take you into the fort, as was ordered by Caunus. Our plans are well laid. What we ask of you, men of Eintov, is not to betray us by a false sound, word or gesture. Act as though you were still in the hands of our enemies. As soon as we have completed our task, you will be free to do as you choose."

"We will do as you say," declared Avishai.

The vanguard moved forward to enable the others to mount.

"In the name of Almighty God and of Israel's freedom," commanded Shemon in the same measured accents, "forward!"

Cautiously the procession moved through the dark and lifeless village of Apollonia and out into the open area about the fort. The moon was no longer visible and in the starlight identification from the turrets was impossible.

"Is it you, Treverius?" called a sentry from above.

"Yes," responded Shemon in the Roman vernacular. "I'm bringing a rich haul with me."

"Any women?"

"No, not this time."

An obscene interjection expressed the sentry's disappointment.

They arrived at the road linked with the causeway, which ran for about one hundred feet above an inconsequential moat and rolling dunes. In the groves close by the highway Issachar and the bulk of the Thumbless lay stretched, swords in hand, darts on their backs. Their tethered horses were engrossed in munching the grass.

The procession stepped onto the causeway. The decisive moment was at hand. Avishai prayed with quivering lips. Two sentries stood directly in front of the gate. Shemon thought: *Good! Where they stand, the turret guards cannot see them and will no longer see me.*

"Salutations, Decurion," called one of the sentries. "Good work, by Jupiter!"

"A good haul," drawled Shemon. "Is everybody in the yard?"

"No. It is past the night bugle. Only two decurions are waiting."

"Your voice sounds strange, Treverius," observed the second sentry.

Shemon coughed. "A little hoarse from excitement." He covered up his mouth, pretending to choke and chuckle simultaneously.

The sentries, amused, turned to unlock the gate. Shemon and Asher, now barely fifteen feet from the entrance, dug into the sides of their horses, which leaped forward. Before the sentries could turn, their heads rolled on the causeway. Asher dismounted, flung open the gates and stepped aside. Shemon, driving Treverius' horse before him, rode into the court, which, enclosed by the high fort walls, was completely dark. The two waiting decurions called out a greeting. Their voices betrayed their location. That was their undoing.

Matters now progressed swiftly. Shemon admitted the Eintovites into the court, herded them into a corner, sent four Thumbless up to each of the turrets to eliminate the watch and posted reliable men at the stables and himself at the gate. Never did time pass so painfully slowly. It seemed to have frozen. Actually the sixteen Thumbless returned sooner than Shemon had expected. The bloody swords in their hands told the story.

From an upper window Catanus called out somewhat impatiently, "Are you coming up to report, Treverius? The commander is waiting."

"At once, Centurion," replied Shemon, and turned to Asher and his men. "Now, quietly into the barracks and avenge Shaarim and Kfar Haroob!"

They needed no further urging. It was then that Shemon stepped onto the causeway, and in a voice that rang out clear as a clarion call in the stillness of the night, cried out, "Issachar! *Heruth o mavet!*"

The carnage did not last long. Darkness and panic were the allies of the Thumbless. Only a handful of soldiers, barricading themselves in their officers' quarters, attempted to resist. Lacking effective arms, which had been stacked away in their barracks for the night, they and their second-grade centurion, Catanus, surrendered.

In the next room their commander was crouching in a corner, sword in hand. A short dagger lay beside him on a bench. His eyes glowed with the fierceness of a wildcat as he watched Shemon standing in the doorway, huge and grim, with bloody sword ready, Nemesis incarnate. The Roman had one slight advantage; he was in a dark corner, hard to see, while the Israelite, in the dim light falling upon him from the adjacent room, was a good target.

"This is your *Jus Primae Noctis,* Caunus," said Shemon, his restrained passion smoldering in his voice. "Come out where I can see you, and fight."

"Die, first!" snarled the Roman, and sent his short dagger flying at Shemon's face. But it came high and only knocked his helmet off.

"You foul coward!"

Shemon had seen him now, and lunged at him. The duel was brief. The Roman was corpulent and clumsy and his reach was short. All he could do was to ward off his foe's relentless blows. Their swords crossed only three times. The fourth thrust cut off Caunus' right hand at the wrist. The fifth severed his head from his body.

The victors assembled in the courtyard. Their elation was high. Their losses were light; their booty exceeded all their expectations: horses, cattle, food supplies, clothing, arms and a battering-ram.

Shemon was happy but sober. There was no time to waste. The wounds of the injured had been washed and bandaged and those who needed it had been given a little wine. "Men of Eintov," said Shemon, "we shall leave this fort before dawn. We cannot hold it. If we did, our forces would be split and defeated separately. Now, what will you do? If you go back to Eintov, you and your families will be in mortal peril. If you come with us to the hills, you will be outlawed but safe. Make your choice now."

There was a long silence. They all waited for Avishai to speak. He hesitated, burdened by the weight of the decision he was called upon to make. "It is as bitter as death," he groaned at last, "to decide. If we stay, an end to our suffering may come swiftly and the gates of Heaven may be opened to us. If we go to the hills, who knows how long our suffering will last and what the end will be? Were we possessed of the spirit of warriors, we would take up arms with you. But we are merchants and tradesmen and growers and students of the Torah; we are men of peace. Is it not best for us to stay and leave our fate in His hands?"

There were protests and grumbling; not all were of one mind with their leader.

"Was not Mattathias of Modin a man of peace and a dignitary in Israel?" Shemon parried. "And did not he and his sons fly to the Judean Hills from the wrath of the Syrians and Greeks, only to return and defeat them? No man is born for war, but few men are born so weak as to be unable to strike a blow against the beasts of prey which would devour them. God is merciful, but is it not said that He is also a Man of War?"

"To face death by staying where one lives," retorted Avishai, "amid the fruits of one's lifelong labors, asserting thereby one's right to be there whatever the peril, is also war; but it is war of the spirit. That is my choice. Let those who decide otherwise follow you."

About one fourth of Avishai's party, preponderantly middle-aged and older men, decided to return to Eintov. The others were willing to cast their lot with Shemon.

It was still necessary to establish what the other Eintovites wished to do. Shemon took all the men, horses and beasts of burden he could spare and went to Eintov. There numerous families had already packed their belongings, waiting for him to take them to the hills. The livestock and booty he sent, under Issachar, to the caves. Asher and a small number of Thumbless remained behind to dispose of unfinished matters.

When a courier arrived with routine orders the next day, he found that Caunus' head, with glazed eyes gaping, had been substituted for the head of the Roman eagle suspended high above the turret facing the highway. And on the open gate of the fort there was a papyrus reading:

> You will find Catanus and some of your brave
> soldiers trussed up in the centurions' quarters. Catanus
> is entitled to the proclaimed awards, for he knows my
> name and description. I warn all Romans: Refrain from
> savagery and pillage if you would avoid Caunus' fate.
>
> Shemon.

Chapter Twenty-four

Rufus summoned a war council. It included the Military Prefect of Jerusalem and Southern Judea, the tribune of legionaries and the Acting Prefect of Tiberias and Upper Galilee, as well as all the cohort commanders and first-class centurions. The procurator demanded to know what had become of their military skill and cunning. How long would they suffer a lowbred Hebrew to degrade the glory of Rome? The Roman eagle had been humiliated, a fortress taken. The roads were not safe; the law was defied! And where was Achillas of Synopai? Was their martial tradition and pride gone? Had not the standards of their legions penetrated the forests and marshy fastnesses of the wildest and fiercest Germanic tribes; the Treveri, Suabi, Marsi and Chatti? Had they not subjugated the Britons, crushed the savage Danubian hordes? And here in Judea the hideout of a small band of cutthroats could not be found! What did they think the imperial legate at Antioch would say? And would they be happy if the news, as it stood today, reached Rome? Drastic action had to be taken. What were they proposing to do?

The Tribune of Tiberias observed that it was easier to fight a strong enemy in open battle than a handful of elusive bandits. He promised to search every Galilean hill, but there was no telling, he reminded, what might be going on in skillfully concealed caves. Canopus promised to do likewise in his own territory. So did the Centurion of Emmaus. Valentinus recommended that he and Canopus join forces to converge on a given point in the hills. One of the centurions remarked that the action would take the Roman forces across Samaria, and the Samaritans, who thus far had stayed out of the rebellion, would object. The Prefect of Jerusalem thought that locating Shemon might not stop the revolt and that it would be best to suspend an unworkable decree; but if that was undesirable, he continued, prominent hostages, under threat of death, should be taken throughout the country and the remaining leaders told to deliver Shemon and his band within a specified time. The policy of intimidation hitherto pursued had failed, he argued, because it had been directed against suspected or guilty settlements rather than the whole community.

The prefect's idea found favor with the procurator. One hundred prominent figures were singled out for arrest. The name of Rabbi Akiba headed the list.

Dedius, as he listened to the discussion, was torn inwardly by two conflicting loyalties: to his conscience and to his government. His reason, accustomed to evaluating the relationship of man to man and people to people on the basis of the patrician tradition, dictated unswerving loyalty to Rome. He and a few thousand others like him *were,* in fact, Rome. If they ceased to uphold each other, Rome, as a concept and as a personal convenience, and most certainly as an empire, would cease to exist.

On the other hand, a voice stronger than his cold logic, rising from inexplicable sources deep within him, spoke boldly against the monstrous crimes Rome had to commit to maintain her power. True, according to her ethical standards, no act aiming at sustaining her power was a crime. But Dedius had too long been in contact with people and ideas adverse to those standards to accept such crimes without challenge.

And so, during the proceedings, he either stared at the floor or permitted his large blue eyes to travel sadly from one speaker to another. When, early in the discussion, the procurator had asked Dedius for his views, he had muttered, "There are wiser and more experienced men here."

When the officers were dismissed, Dedius, his conflict still unresolved, sought out Ruffina and shared his doubts with her. She upbraided him for his weakness, and as soon as he left she sent for Judith.

Achillas was reading. On a patina before him was citrus fruit. A gentle breeze rustled the leaves in the garden and carried the early autumn scents into the room.

During the first weeks of his captivity Achillas' loss of freedom and of commanding position had depressed him and kept him tense with thoughts of escape and hopes of sudden liberation. But as time had rolled on and the vigilance of his captors had not slackened, while the search for him had ostensibly failed, Achillas had decided to accept his position philosophically and be content.

Being a bachelor, far from his native land, he had no memories of a family to disturb his peace of mind, and no thoughts of anyone who would, as a friend, be unduly concerned about his absence.

Before long, Achillas had come to like certain aspects of the situation—above all, the nightly strolls in the dark garden and the discourse with the slight, animated man, with the silver-streaked beard, who had asked to be called Noon. There also was the other one, Alef, the long-legged, black-bearded one with the huge nose, who had brought the grapes and figs the morning of Achillas' arrival and attended him ever since. This Alef, too, was a pleasant companion for the walks, but vastly inferior to Noon in the discourses.

The place of man in the scheme of things, the nether world, the seven heavenly spheres, the Supreme Being versus graven images, slavery, war, love and astrology were among the topics of their discourses. The most frequent subject was God. As a follower of Plato, Achillas listened with mounting sympathy to the tenets of faith expounded by Noon, who was none other than Nitsa. They commanded Achillas' ever growing interest, as he found them, with rare exceptions, to blend harmoniously the rational with the spiritual. When Nitsa once asked jocularly whether Achillas was ready to enter into a covenant with the Lord, Achillas replied earnestly, "Perhaps. But may I not first speak to your great man, Rabbi Akiba?"

That was a delicate request, and Nitsa laid it before the sage. To see the architect meant not only to violate the decree, but also to become an accomplice in the most rankling act of the rebellion. Akiba, however, decided to visit the Greek.

To avoid prying eyes Akiba, accompanied by Hagarsi and Joel, arrived at Nitsa's long after sundown. Before being taken to the isolated room on the upper story of the hostelry Akiba and his escort were entertained at their host's house. Elon, who had meanwhile arrived at Bnai Brak to forewarn the rabbi about the impending arrests, was unable to deliver the message, as Akiba had left in strict secrecy.

At about the same time orders reached Marcus Saturnius, the centurion in charge of Ludd and its environs, to arrest the rabbi and send him to Caesarea. Nitsa, for the present, was to be kept under surveillance.

The order put Saturnius in a predicament. Over the years he had become genuinely fond of Nitsa and a respectful admirer of Akiba. He understood the significance of the procurator's order and could not cold-bloodedly execute it.

He was a big, scar-faced, easy-going plebeian who had risen from the ranks in twenty years of campaigning. His method of dealing with the natives was simple: friendliness and persuasion. He did not relish the prospect of having his old wounds cut open. He neither loved nor hated the people and their God.

He avoided questioning orders; they had to be obeyed. But if an order was glaringly unreasonable, he displayed no zeal in ferreting out disobedience. In connection with the proscriptions, he reported no case of circumcision. "I am a soldier," he had said upon hearing of them, "not a midwife."

Gloomy as a thundercloud, he stamped up and down his quarters in the citadel, snapping at his children and ignoring his wife's solicitous inquiries. After a long time he snatched his helmet, lighted his lantern and went to Nitsa.

Akiba was already closeted with Achillas when the Roman came. Joel and Joshua had posted themselves at the door, and Ben-Dov, the Heromav who, with Amitai, had won the sapling-pulling contest, guarded the entrance to the hostelry. Abiezer, upon seeing the centurion, ran to apprise his master. Nitsa, alarmed but outwardly unperturbed, invited Saturnius into a secluded room in his house.

When they were seated, the Roman announced bluntly, "I have an order to arrest your friend, the sage of Bnai Brak, and to watch you."

"Why?" asked Nitsa, maintaining his outward calm.

"I don't know."

"What do you intend to do?"

"I do not want to find the rabbi home when I come there very early tomorrow morning."

"You will not find him there," Nitsa smiled gratefully.

The centurion grunted. "I am betraying my governor," he said, "but I expect nothing from you. Why am I doing it? I don't know. I have taken many gifts from you in the past but never felt I was doing wrong. Now, perhaps, I am doing wrong, but I want no gift."

"Maybe you have come to believe in our—" ventured Nitsa, but was interrupted.

"No, Nitsa. When it comes to gods, I find it hard to believe in them when I see them, and as hard or harder when I do not. I am a soldier, not a philosopher. But I am tired of killing. I never had special qualms about it—that was how I made a living. But it never made me happy. When you began offering me gifts seven or eight years ago, I said to myself, 'I'm as tired of making others miserable as I am tired of fighting. Nitsa does not mean to harm us. Why not take what he offers? It will keep him and his people satisfied and my government will lose nothing.' I was right. Now, when one grows tired of killing and raises a family, as I have, one sometimes thinks of the value of men. They are like vases. Some are made of clay, others of crystal; and of the crystal ones, some are inlaid with gold. I wouldn't think much of breaking a clay vase, but a crystal one inlaid with gold . . . "

Nitsa reached out across the table and pressed the Roman's rough, hairy hand. "One like you," he said, "will some day see the true light."

The centurion shrugged and lifted his big, sprawling hulk. "I do not mean to harm myself, either," he said brusquely. "From now on, I'm going to keep my eyes open. You will receive no further reports from me."

"You have already done more than I can thank you for and I will hold nothing against you," said Nitsa.

While Nitsa was closeted with the Roman, Abiezer alarmed the guards. They wondered whether the centurion's untimely visit was a coincidence or the result of treachery. Whatever the answer, the danger was great. It was thought best to whisk the rabbi away at once. Joel went down to join Ben-Dov at the entrance, and Joshua Hagarsi, with many apologies, entered the room and whispered into his master's ear.

The rabbi shook his head. "No," he muttered. Joshua, persistent, whispered into the rabbi's ear again. Akiba looked up coldly and said with finality, "No. I will stay here until the purpose of my coming is accomplished. Leave me here and go, if you fear."

Hurt and depressed, Hagarsi left the room. Achillas, sensing peril, and realizing that the old sage chose to face it rather than run, gave him a broad, encouraging smile.

When Saturnius, accompanied by Nitsa, came outside, he recalled that upon his arrival he had caught sight of a tall man, wearing a *palnis* (a blanket-like robe), standing at the entrance to the hostelry. He glanced in that direction, and to his surprise, there were two of them and their demeanor was suspicious. Without saying anything to Nitsa, the Roman went toward them. Nitsa hurried along anxiously.

"Who are you and what are you doing here?" demanded the centurion of Joel and Ben-Dov.

"They are friends and staying here overnight," Nitsa hastened to reply.

But Joel also spoke: "We are enjoying the fresh air. The night is beautiful and cool."

"Why not be in the garden, then? Wherefore stand here like guards? May you not perchance be guards?"

Without waiting for anyone to reply he pushed the two aside and stepped into the hostelry. Joel and Ben-Dov looked at each other and then at Nitsa in angry bewilderment, and Ben-Dov was about to draw his dagger.

"No," whispered Nitsa. "No! Let us wait and see. He is not a bad man."

The three followed the Roman into the house. He kicked several doors open and, holding his lantern high, looked into the rooms. "Nothing to show people are staying here," he charged. Nitsa attempted to reply but Saturnius, not heeding his friend, went to the upper floor, Nitsa and the others close at his heels. Catastrophe seemed inevitable.

"I will strike the Edomite down," muttered Hagarsi through his teeth.

"If you do, it will be the end of Ludd," admonished Abiezer.

"To me, Rabbi Akiba excels. . . . "

Joshua did not complete his sentence, as the Roman had reached the landing and was now glowering at the two men by the door. The even rumble of voices could be heard from within. Saturnius moved forward. Nitsa, Joel and Ben-Dov came up close behind. The Roman pretended to ignore them. "Abiezer," he demanded sternly, "I want to see who is in that room and what they are doing."

Abiezer gathered up his courage. "I do not think the centurion need see them," he said sternly, trying to avoid undue provocation. "The centurion may be assured that the men inside are highly esteemed, peace-loving personages."

"Wherefore, then, all these guards and mystery?"

"Do you not know, Saturnius, that we always guard our esteemed personages? Do you not guard things precious to you?" Nitsa interposed.

"I do. But I would not tremble over them as though I had stolen them."

"After our conversation a while ago I am grieved to hear you say that, Saturnius."

"I warned you, Nitsa, that I would henceforth do my duty. Please open the door."

"No!" Hagarsi snapped, and planted himself against the door. "No! We will not open it."

Saturnius laughed and looked about him. "By Jupiter!" he exclaimed with feigned nonchalance, "I'm surrounded. Surely no harm will befall a Roman in Nitsa's house?" When the reply was grim silence he said earnestly, "I am outnumbered. But do you forget the consequences?" He looked straight at Nitsa. "I have always admired your sagacity, my friend. Surely you will not lose your mind now?"

Before Nitsa could retort, the door was opened from within and the venerable figure of Rabbi Akiba appeared in the doorway. "I've heard the voice of Rome," he said simply, and his gaze fell upon Saturnius. "Will the centurion come in?"

In the general consternation the most flabbergasted person there was the Roman.

"Please come in," repeated the rabbi. "There will be no battle here. There is no cause for battle."

For a while Saturnius stared at the rabbi as though he were seeing an apparition. It was cruel that of all men Akiba, whom he had come to forewarn, should have been found in that room. As the immensity of his dilemma dawned upon Saturnius, cold perspiration covered him, and tilting his helmet slightly, he brushed the dripping sweat from his brow. "I beg the rabbi's pardon. I am a servant of the law. I will, with the rabbi's indulgence, take one look into the room."

Akiba stepped aside. The Roman came forward and paused in the doorway. What he beheld was a corpulent, black-bearded, bald-pated, middle-aged man with a smiling, benevolent countenance. Reclining on cushions amid tablets and parchments and two platters of fresh fruit, apparently in great comfort, he gazed at the centurion with amused indifference. He wore a Roman tunic, sandals and a small black skull cap which, on his large cranium, looked like an isle in a lake. The silken, gold-embroidered tunic was distinctive and clearly patrician; the skull cap, plebeian, native.

The incongruity struck the Roman. "And who may my lord be?"

"A seeker after truth, sitting at his rabbi's feet," replied Achillas cheerfully.

"Instruction by rabbis is prohibited."

"No one is instructing me, Centurion." The Greek kept smiling imperturbably. "I have merely been seeking information from an older and wiser friend."

"But who are you and what are you doing here?"

"My name is Mehilla," replied the Greek, and glanced at Nitsa as if seeking his approval, "and I come from foreign parts. I am a merchant and brought a shipment of timber and dyes with me. It was I who asked for the privilege of talking to the great rabbi, and it was to save me from embarrassment that our meeting was kept secret. I trust that I have set the centurion's mind at rest."

The centurion grunted. He did not appear to be convinced. "I trust that my lord," he said quietly, "will save himself and us from further embarrassment by returning to his foreign parts as soon as possible."

With that, he swung on his hobnailed heel and left.

Nitsa rushed forward to thank Achillas. Akiba closed the door and said solemnly, "Tonight, Achillas, you have bought yourself a place in the world to come. *Mehilla* means "forgiveness," a high estate. It was in your hands to give us away. You have chosen to forgive. We, too, have forgiven. Whether you enter into the covenant of Abraham or not, you are a good man."

Achillas, breathing heavily, lifted himself to his feet. "I am too lazy," he said, chuckling deprecatingly. "I am too lazy to be wicked. What I've heard from you, Rabbi, and from you, too, Nitsa—I know your real name at last—evokes a response in me.

In your faith, Rabbi, the rational blends beautifully with the divine. That is how your tenets become livable." He reflected for a few beats and then continued, "Yes, livable, but not always enjoyable. I am a great admirer of Plato, but also an Epicurean. I am attracted to you not by your abstinence, but by your steadfast courage. You have discovered what you regard as a great truth, and you defy kings to uphold it. Plato, too, defied a king at the peril of his life. You are defying the most powerful Caesar at the peril of your lives. I would be a knave to betray you. As for entering into your covenant, let me think about it." He smiled warmly, looking from one to the other. "And now, I suppose, we must think how best to heed the centurion's advice."

"We will heed it," Nitsa assured him eagerly. "We expect a fleet of boats very soon. You will be taken to Athens or any other place you choose."

"Thank you, Nitsa."

"Meanwhile we will have to give you more comfortable quarters."

Achillas laughed. "I understand, my friend."

Nitsa turned to Akiba. "And it is too late to go back to Bnai Brak tonight. A fine, comfortable house is at the rabbi's disposal in Ludd."

Akiba fixed a long, searching stare at Nitsa, concluded that there was a good reason for what his friend had said, and sighed resignedly.

Chapter Twenty-five

Elon returned from Bnai Brak with news. The important seat of instruction was now a dead town. The rabbi had been prevailed upon to stay in Ludd until the storm abated, and the members of his household and his remaining disciples had gone to join him there. The rabbi had been reluctant to abandon his home and the fig trees under which he had dispensed the Word for so many years. Nitsa, however, had insisted that when the very life of a man like Akiba, the proud possession of Israel, was at stake, Israel, and not Akiba, knew best what was good for Israel. "Your arrest," Nitsa had told the rabbi, "would cast the House of Israel into despair and weaken the hands of the fighters for freedom. Your voice will be heard from a house in Ludd no less than from your seat in Bnai Brak. In Caesarea your voice will be silenced, perhaps forever."

Concerning the rumors that Canopus and Valentinus, with strong forces, would soon comb the Hills of Ephraim to find and destroy Shemon, the old sage had said, "I do not think they will. Their war machines, and even their foot soldiers in their heavy armor, would bog down in the mire. The rains are already here."

Elon considered it remarkable that Achillas had not betrayed his captors. He was still convinced that in wartime neither the enemy nor his servants, however highly placed, should be given quarter. But Achillas' case seemed exceptional. For Akiba's sake some divine power must have guided the Greek. He was still under that influence, Elon surmised, for in Joppa, where he was waiting for the boat which was to take him to Greece, he had said, "I may return to this land, and if I do, it will be to become one of you and to help you build it for your welfare."

In conclusion Elon informed Shemon that old Johai had returned from Alexandria without having achieved much. His son, Simeon, was still there and met frequently with Shemon's kinsmen, old Pappus and Andreas; his, Elon's, brother-in-law Shilo, and other eminent Alexandrians. It was not quite certain whether a delegation would go to Rome; but it was certain that ever increasing help in ships, treasure, supplies and even men would come from their Egyptian brothers.

When Elon left Shemon, it was time for the evening meal. He sat down at the table, deeply absorbed in his thoughts, and began to eat. Akiba's opinion notwithstanding, the possibility of a powerful attack by the Romans was still there, as the strong rains had not yet come; and the arrests of the hostages had robbed Shemon of his peace of mind.

Despite his abstraction he became aware of quivering lips

across the table. Meredya was on the verge of tears. In the dim light of the flickering, sputtering oil wick her beautiful eyes glistened strangely and her cheeks seemed bloodless.

He took her hand. "Are you not feeling well?"

She shook her head and looked away.

He came over to her side, took her face and turned it gently toward him. A solitary tear was rolling down her cheek. "What is the matter, my love?"

There was a long pause. "You no longer have an eye for me."

Woman's nature was foreign to him and her reply was puzzling. "How can you say that, Meredya? I have an eye for no one else."

She slipped her fingers into his hair. It was thick, tangled and rough. "You hardly seem to notice me. Lately your thoughts are far away."

He laughed and took her in his arms. "There's a hard war to fight, my dear. It takes much thinking if we are to win it. When the Edomites are driven out, I'll devote all my thoughts to you."

She knew that he was right. The war assuredly took precedence over everything. The future of a people depended upon its success; her very existence depended upon it. Yet she was jealous and hurt; hurt at her passive role, at being in the background, at not being loved enough. It was easier, she thought, to die once fighting than to wait in anguish when he was away and again feel uncertainty upon his return.

But these thoughts she kept to herself. It was too good to be near him to risk spoiling the pleasure with unnecessary words. She pressed closer to him. Her warm, vibrant softness stirred him. Suddenly he became aware of hill crests weird with pallid gold and of a large orange moon trailed by a brilliant star. Meredya, too, was looking up. "That bright star is yours," she said.

"No," he objected. "I will have it fashioned into a jewel for you when Edom is driven out."

She pulled his head toward her. Their lips met, and as on the first day of their marriage, he carried her into the tent.

Later, when the cry of the watch woke her, she lay thinking

for a long time. Her love for the man beside her was as immense as the hills, as the endless sky. She loved him not only for what he was, but also for what he strove to accomplish. Somehow she had hoped to be beside him always. But she found herself alone most of the time. And together with her disappointment she was torn by longing and dread. Dread. Powerful as was his body, it was but of flesh; and to poisoned arrows and wall-splitting stones all flesh was alike. Why could not the Almighty, since Israel's cause was just, destroy the oppressors with one of His invisible weapons—a flood, a plague, an earthquake? "Spare the man for me and my people," she whispered prayerfully. "What a powerful builder he would make! With the gifts Thou hast bestowed on him he constructs fortresses against the enemy. What gardens and orchards he would plant, what towns he would build, what ships he would send to foreign parts, if Thou wouldst allow him to use his brain and strength in peace."

"What are you whispering?" he muttered drowsily.

She did not reply, pretending to sleep. But after an interval she turned and nestled up to him. "I have something to tell you, Shemon." He waited. "I'm with child."

He held her close, without speaking, for a long time. Then he said tenderly, "May God protect you for your sake and his. Guard him well, for he is a descendant of the House of David."

She lay breathless. What a surprise! Her husband was of royal descent! He wanted a son—a prince. What if a girl came?

In the morning they brought the good tidings to Abner. Moist-eyed, he embraced his daughter, but his happiness, he said, was marred by the arrest of the hostages. More than eighty of them were already in jail, among them Rabbi Uziel of Caesarea and Avishai of Eintov. And in Eintov, in addition to the slayings, they had flogged every fifth man. Deliverance and retribution, he knew, would come, but it was hard to wait.

There was a long, gloomy silence; then Shemon said, "I seek your judgment, Father. I do not wish to wait until I can see Rabbi Akiba."

"What is your question, Shemon?"

"Among the freed slaves there is one named Nicholas

Malanos, thirty-three years old, an imposing man, good to look at. He is a Cilician Christian, wears his hair and beard like a Nazarite. Looks one straight in the face; has a gentle smile, but there is strength behind it. He found favor with me. His companions in misfortune spoke well of him. He hates Edom as much as we do. He says one of his ancestors was torn by beasts in Rome. He wants to join us. But that is not all. He wants to go to Galilee and across the Jordan to secure the help of other Christians for our cause, which, he says, is also their cause."

Abner bristled. "How is it their cause? They do not circumcise, do not eat clean food; and they switched our Sabbath to the first day of the week."

"What is most important, Father," persisted Shemon, "is that they believe in the same God and are persecuted for it. Did we not save this Malanos from slavery? Had he been born in our fold and turned Christian, he would have been a renegade. But he is a foreigner, born of Christians. What can we have against him? Are we not trying to secure aid from the Parthians, who are heathens?"

"True. But can we be hasty in a matter so grave? Since the days of Saul of Tarsus many harmful falsehoods have been spread about us in Cyprus, Lycaonia, Cilicia, Antioch and Alexandria. In Antioch and Alexandria, to say nothing of Rome, the falsehoods caused bloodshed. Should we admit the Christians into our ranks, how can we be sure that the thoughtless and ill-willed among them—or among us—will not stir up old hatreds and new dissensions? And will they agree to deny themselves unclean food and abide by other rigors of our Law as long as they camp with us?"

Abner's observations seemed potent to Shemon. He was also mindful of the fact that his father-in-law might have been an ordained rabbi, had it not been for the part he had taken in the uprising against Trajan's regime. His judgment in such matters could not be taken lightly.

"My dear father," he said, "I agree that in a matter so grave we should not be hasty, nor should we dismiss it lightly. This young Nicholas seems a man of knowledge and character and would not himself have spoken lightly. Please go down to see him. If he satisfies you, do what is right. You have a free hand."

Abner agreed. The following morning he and Malanos were seen on camels, heading north.

Chapter Twenty-six

It was early in the month of Heshvan. In the evening, rain fell for a while. Toward midnight the wind developed into a storm of great ferocity. The clouds burst and streams came down like waterfalls. Thunder crashed continually, and its peals, breaking against the mountainsides, echoed and re-echoed as countless explosions. Shemon rose promptly, wrapped Meredya in his camel's-hair cloak, threw over his shoulders a square blanket and, against her protests, carried her down into the caverns. Up he went again, packed their belongings and brought them down. The tent, he told Meredya, had been ripped by lightning.

In the general cave excitement was high. Women shrieked as thunder crashed; children yammered; defenders, frowning, strode up and down; old men in corners chanted psalms, and in an adjacent cave cattle lowed.

Shemon took his wife into a section of the cavern where there were a few young women, among them Tamar, who had left the plateau earlier. She was happy to have Meredya with her again and they began to plan how to cheer up the weak and frightened among their people.

At the height of the storm Nadav came and brought word from Judith and Ezra Harrar that in the first week of Kislev, about one month hence, the hostages would be cast to the beasts unless Shemon surrendered or was delivered to Rufus. It became necessary to confer with Rabbi Akiba.

Abner had not yet returned from his journey with Malanos, and Shemon, anxious about his wife in his absence, sought out her nearest of kin, Joel, who had joined them in the caves after Akiba had taken refuge in Ludd.

Shemon found his friend in the animal cave. The brook in the gorge had turned into a seething river, pounding stubbornly against the unyielding rock. The inside channel had overflowed and under Joel's direction it was being embanked. Unlikely as an attack was from that direction on such a night, armed men were guarding the iron door.

Shemon smiled his approval, took his cousin aside and told him about the hostages. "I will set out for Ludd before the night is over," he concluded.

"Alone, Shemon?"

"Why not, Joel? I'll dress as a peasant and ride a donkey, and my beard is not yet its former self since that night in Apollonia. No one will know me. Besides, there will be few people on the road."

"You've always had good luck. May the Lord keep favoring you." He turned abruptly to one of the workers. "More sand on the left side. There. Right."

"Tell the others and see Meredya whenever you can. Peace, Joel."

"Peace."

Shemon selected a donkey, some sackcloth and a bag of dates, and went to take leave of his wife. He found her with Tamar in the general cavern.

Her eyes were brilliant with emotion. She was reciting Isaiah's Chapter of Consolation while Tamar was strumming a lute, the gentle strains harmoniously blending with the cadences of Meredya's voice.

> O thou that tellest good tidings to Zion,
> Get thee up into the high mountain;
> O thou that tellest good tidings to Jerusalem,
> Lift up thy voice with strength;
> Lift it up, be not afraid;
> Say unto the cities of Judah:
> Behold your God!

The people were listening raptly and Shemon decided that it was best not to interrupt.

He snatched his camel's-hair cloak and slipped past them. At the exit, where he had left his donkey, he covered the beast with sackcloth, wrapped himself in his cloak and, taking the beast by its halter, began to climb the mountain.

The wind was slackening but the rain continued steadily. The hills had turned into quagmires. Pools had formed in cavities, and muddy rivulets leaped over rocky projections. It was impossible to proceed and Shemon descended to the plain. The slush, the darkness and the donkey's mood made progress slow and thinking unavoidable.

Now that the heavy rains had come, an attack upon his mountain fastnesses would fail, however strong the force. The old sage had been right, as usual. But why did not the Edomites act before the arrival of inclement weather? Shemon was not aware of the two reasons for their holding back: a confidential pledge given to Rufus, and signs of collapsing faith among some Israelites.

After the arrest of the hostages and the procurator's stern warning, a small group of wealthy growers, shippers and bankers visited him secretly. They belonged to the class that stood to lose most from disturbed conditions and Rome's displeasure. These men gave him their solemn assurance to use their wealth and influence to deliver Shemon into Rufus' hands or to force his surrender. Their power to corrupt was great and the ruler took their pledge seriously. Neither he nor they understood the sentiments of the people.

But a very small minority, living in close proximity to more privileged neighbors, had weakened under the relentless Roman lash. This minority was located in Ephraim, where mixed populations of Samaritans and Israelites were common. In this zone, lying between Lower Galilee and Northern Judea as these regions had been redistricted by the Romans, several Israelite communities, the first of which was Dennushahan, had renounced their creed to adopt that of the Samaritans. Though the original Samaritans had sprung from the tribes of Benjamin and Ephraim, they had long since diluted their tribal purity through intermarriage with pagan peoples, largely Assyrians and Babylonians. Conspicuous among these had been the Cutheans, whom the Assyrian king Shalmaneser had transplanted from Cuthath in Parthia to Samaria after carrying off a large number of the original Samaritans into captivity. In the Holy Land, "Cuthean" had become interchangeable with "Samaritan."

Professing, as they did, their faith in God, the Samaritans were guided exclusively by the Pentateuch; they rejected the Prophets, the Sages and the Writings accepted by the House of Israel. The rejection meant, in effect, lax observance or non-observance of many of the injunctions of the Pentateuch, which, taken literally, were often ambiguous or unworkable. These had been elucidated, codified and made usable by the Israelites under two broad categories: the relationships between God and man, and between man and man. The failure of the Samaritans to adopt the Israelite code had resulted in a way of life closer to paganism than to Judaism. Foreign wives were allowed to bring idols and heathen customs into their homes, and images symbolizing God had been placed in some of their temples.

In the absence of an acute religious division the attitude of the Romans toward the Samaritans was tolerant. Rufus regarded the interlopers as the harbingers of an early general collapse among the Israelites. With the bulk of them contrite, the handful of intransigents could be disposed of in short order.

Shemon reached the populous mart center of Shukpatris. Linked by a good arterial road with the coastal highway to the west, and located almost midway between two ports, Joppa and Eintov, it served as a caravan junction and produce and business exchange. Here was the meeting place of fruit cultivators from all over the country; of cattle breeders and woolgrowers from the south; of wine producers from Judea; of potters from Sichin and Kfar-Hanania, high up in Galilee; of iron and copper miners from Transjordan; and of importers of fine silks and precious rugs from Antioch and Parthia, marble from Egypt and high-grade timber from the Lebanon. There were few articles that could not be obtained in the stalls of Shukpatris.

The arcades, except for the vendors, were almost empty, and the dazzling finery displayed beneath smoking oil lamps was tempting. Shemon had passed the point of greatest danger and permitted himself a few moments of indulgence. The attraction of the colorful silks, trinkets, scent in quaint phials and other oddities, never of interest to him before, was now strong.

"Come here, come here, King of Bashan," a huckster, dangling a string of beads, urged with good-natured mockery. "What will you have for the light of your heart? A lace kerchief? A wrist bracelet? Or perhaps a silver hair clasp? No? Look at these ankle bracelets with tiny bells to announce the coming of your love. Made in Damascus. Nothing finer."

Shemon fingered articles of wear and finally chose a silk robe and a pair of gaudy slippers. *These will surely please Meredya,* he thought, *but when will she wear them?* Nevertheless, he paid for them and stuffed the package into his date bag.

Satisfied, he clucked to his donkey and headed for the highway. The rain was subsiding. The clouds were still thick and low and it was very dark. The densely populated villages off the road were awakening and indicated their presence by odors and sounds. Soon there appeared north- and southbound caravans, led by bell-dangling camels; loaded donkeys, with their barefoot masters plodding beside them; occasionally a drove of donkeys, urged on by a solitary driver; ox-drawn carts, and pedestrians in blankets, burnooses and sackcloth.

The morning was gray but the rain had subsided when Shemon reached Nitsa's yard. Abiezer, who was already up and about, took Shemon to the hostelry.

Later he had a hurried breakfast with Nitsa, who had to go to the town council, of which he was the president. Abiezer was told to escort Shemon to Akiba.

Shemon had not seen Ludd for years and strange emotions stirred in him as he strode beside Abiezer through the ancient town. Some of the streets, which had survived the ravages of time and man, were so narrow that Shemon could cross them in one stride. Structures, as a rule, had crumbled and their architecture was no longer distinguishable. Large plots between them were covered with rubble. Workshops, smithies, carpentries and wool-carding and weaving shops in half-sunken old buildings could be found on such streets. A considerable distance away square, flat-roofed structures of more recent architecture could be observed. Within enclosures, cattle were kept. Next to the older streets came a labyrinth of wider lanes, with narrow walks above gutters that were paved with square stone blocks. There a bakery or a cobbler's or butcher's stall could be seen now and then. Pedestrians and beasts of burden mingled in the gutter, while the walks were blocked by sacks, baskets, boxes and wooden forms employed as benches by barbers and hairdressers. Once in a while one encountered a larger and more imposing structure, with a row of side steps leading to an ornate entrance. This was a house of worship and instruction. Here, during hours of worship, beggars loitered and a scribe served the illiterate. Before one of the synagogues Shemon paused to listen and smile, for a faint chant of young voices came from within. Abiezer, as if divining Shemon's thoughts, remarked: "Children studying the Torah. They are warned when an Edomite is near."

Later they reached the center of the town, where the arcaded mart, the inns and, farther on, the better dwellings were located. In the Ludd stalls one could buy as many articles as in Shukpatris. Here the raucous voices of criers mingled with the pleas and castigations of half-crazed tatterdemalions, would-be prophets, and with the plaints of blind lute-strumming bards.

An area of gutted ruins marred the otherwise pleasant neighborhood. Here Shemon tarried, contemplating with dimming eyes the cracked walls, the smashed doors and charred articles scattered amid stones and bricks, the tree stumps, the twisted helmets and a large, weather-worn signboard: THESE RUINS MAY NOT BE REBUILT. LUCIUS QUIETUS, PROCURATOR, PROVINCE OF JUDEA. This was where his family had perished. Abiezer, his bronzed face taut, watched Shemon from the corner of his eye.

"The sign," muttered Shemon, "the sign!"

"Yes?" said the overseer respectfully.

But Shemon walked on without replying. Abiezer knew the answer. He turned his eyes west, to where the battlements of the Roman fort dominated the town. "That must go first," he said in his heart.

The house occupied by Akiba was at hand. The three-story building stood in a walled-in garden and was spacious enough to accommodate the rabbi, his staff and his remaining disciples. In good weather he was able to lecture in the garden, as he was also wont to do at Bnai Brak. Occasionally local students waiting for the call to arms would slip in to hear God's Word.

On its ground floor the structure had a colonnaded passage opening onto service rooms and the living quarters of the household staff. The first story consisted of an anteroom and a large, high-ceilinged hall, from which doors led to a portico with a stairway to the garden. This was the hall of instruction and prayer. The remaining two stories consisted of libraries and sleeping rooms.

The gatekeeper who admitted Shemon showed him into the hall, where the rabbi had just ended his discourse and was dismissing his disciples. Akiba took his visitor aside and Shemon came to the point. "I have come to ask the rabbi: Is it not time to strike? Might we not begin by freeing the hostages?"

"Are we strong enough for open warfare?"

"We may not be ready for a long war yet, but war itself will help us gain the means for it."

The sage brought his long, bony fingers to his temples and seemed to stare into space. "My son," he replied slowly, "if your faith in your power to free the hostages is as great as our faith in the Lord, then strike."

Shemon's eyes flashed with happiness at the word "strike" and he grasped Akiba's hand.

"Come up with me," said the rabbi, "and let us talk."

Chapter Twenty-seven

When Nitsa reached the council house an unusually large and restless throng was waiting in the court. Most of the people were as strange to him as he was to them, judging by the indifference or impatience with which they regarded him as he elbowed his way to the councilors' room. There, to his surprise, he found a number of out-of-town dignitaries, among them Rabbi Johanan ben-Torta, famed for his acrid disagreements with Akiba; Ezra Harrar of Caesarea; Eusabbatis of Sepphoris, who was a banker, reputed to be one of the three wealthiest in the country; a dye manufacturer from Hebron, and several other men of substance from Jerusalem, Joppa, Shukpatris, Ein Gedi and Tiberias. They rose to greet him cordially enough, but there was an air of belligerence about them. The room was crowded with scribes and people who had come to register births and weddings, to draw up contracts of betrothal and to file complaints about trespassing, short weight and the like.

"My lords," said Nitsa, "I suppose a serious matter brings you here. Let us go up to the tower room, where there is more comfort and privacy."

He motioned to the chief scribe of the council, who picked up some papyri and followed Nitsa with the others. They climbed a winding stone stairway to the first floor, where an attendant admitted them into a large hall. At the far end of the hall, within an enclosure, there stood an oblong table for the archons and magistrates, small square tables for the scribes, comfortable settees for the officials and benches for complainants and witnesses. Several rows of rougher benches were outside the enclosure.

Nitsa seated himself with his visitors at the long table while the scribe assumed his usual place. Affable but guarded, Nitsa addressed his visitors. "The honor is great, my lords and teachers. What can I do to deserve it?"

"Where is Rabbi Akiba?" asked Rabbi Ben-Torta curtly. He was a tall, gaunt man with a pointed beard of fading yellow. His eyes squinted and seemed to stare coldly at Nitsa and the others simultaneously.

Nitsa sensed little friendliness in him, but retained his affability. "I might say: Am I the guardian of the old master? But what I will say is: Wherefore this sudden interest?"

"Have you heard that one hundred of our best men have been jailed by Rufus?" said Eusabbatis. He was a stocky, paunchy man with a puffy face and scented round beard, and had the self-important air of a man spoiled by cajolery.

"Alas, I have," replied Nitsa with unfeigned sadness.

"Do you not think the venerable rabbi should take an interest in them?" exclaimed Ezra Harrar, his pink face reddening. "The distressed wives and kinsfolk of the hostages are waiting in the court to ask this question."

Nitsa was annoyed. "Do you not know," he parried icily, "that the venerable rabbi was first on the procurator's list of hostages and could be of no help in this matter?"

"Yes he could!" exploded Ben-Torta. "Let him denounce that enemy of Israel, that murderer, Shemon bar-Koziba."

"Is it for me, a mere layman," said Nitsa sadly, "to remind the worthy rabbi of the adage of our sages: 'The words of the wise are spoken in moderation and heard in calmness'?"

Ben-Torta brought his fist down on the table. "This is impertinence!"

"Now, now," interposed Eusabbatis appeasingly. "Will anger free the prisoners? Nitsa, my friend"—he suddenly grew mellow—"the misfortune is great and no one can save us but the Lord and Rabbi Akiba."

"You've heard this man—" began Ben-Torta, but Eusabbatis laid a restraining hand on his arm. "Nitsa," he said, "if Rabbi Akiba would publicly denounce Shemon and appeal to his misguided followers and fugitives, Shemon would remain alone and surrender or be caught."

Nitsa looked down so as not to betray his agitation. "And what will stop Rufus from murdering them wholesale on their return? Are *their* lives worthless?"

The banker looked meaningfully at his colleagues and replied, "We undertake to secure a promise of safety for them if Rabbi Akiba agrees to denounce Shemon."

Nitsa's ire was rising, but he was trying hard to hold it in check. "I cannot speak for the rabbi; nor will I broach your ideas to him; nor do I know whether or not he would see you."

"I will speak to the people!" exploded Ben-Torta, and rushed out.

"This will lead to nothing good," said Harrar ingratiatingly. "Please take us to Akiba. Perhaps he, in his great wisdom, will have a better thought. Can one like you, Nitsa, who have God in your heart, do nothing to help—?"

Nitsa cut in impatiently. "Since when, Ezra, has your heart become so soft? I beg your pardon," he hastened to apologize, "I did not mean to offend. I am bitter because our situation is bitter. Perhaps I ought to take you to Rabbi Akiba. But I fear that if his whereabouts becomes known to too many people . . ."

"I swear for all of us—" declared Eusabbatis pompously, "by our children I swear—that not one of us will breathe a word—"

A commotion on the stairway interrupted him. Nitsa rose angrily. "Rabbi Ben-Torta is stirring up trouble. That a rabbi should be so intemperate . . . !"

He called out to the attendant to shut and lock the door, but it was too late. Brushing the man aside, Ben-Torta led the excited crowd into the hall. Nitsa and the scribe hurried to the railing to block the onsurge. Immediately following Rabbi Ben-Torta were several bewigged matrons wrapped in *pellae;* their maidservants, adolescent sons and male attendants came behind. Hurrying close after them, but careful not to trip over their long, wide skirts, were young women in satin cloaks and kerchiefs, older ones in wigs and woolen robes and then kinsmen and servants. Flushed, sobbing and gesticulating, they shouted, lamented, pleaded.

"Speak up, Mara; speak up, Esther, and you, Annis," incited Ben-Torta. "Let the hardhearted hear."

Several women raised their voices simultaneously, some shrilly, others tearfully: "Take us to Akiba! . . . Allow not the destruction of the flower of Israel! . . . My husband, Zachariah, the parnas of Ramat Lechi, the breath of my life!—please save him! . . . Woe is me, woe is me! Will you let Pincas, the man of charity of Migdal, the pillar of his community, be devoured by beasts? . . . What will I do, what will I do? The love and apple of my eye! I cry to God and He hears me not! Oh, my husband, my husband! . . . Please save them! . . . Take us to Rabbi Akiba!"

Only by a supreme effort did Nitsa succeed in silencing them. "Was it Rabbi Akiba and I who cast your dear ones into dungeons, or a godless ruler? Is it in our power to set them free or is it in the hands of God? Were it a matter of gold, I would lay all my fortune at your feet here and now. But it is not gold—it is the lives of Israelites for other Israelites that is demanded. Who among us will be so arrogant as to decide who shall live and who shall die?"

"Shemon is an outlaw!" shouted Ben-Torta. "How dare you compare him with the best among us?"

"And will Rabbi Johanan tell us what house of judgment in Israel has ostracized Shemon?" countered Nitsa angrily.

"But, Nitsa," interjected Eusabbatis, "why can we not lay our case before our great sage? His wisdom has in the past saved us from troubles and disasters. Why should we be denied the opportunity?"

"Far be it from me," Nitsa said, regaining his composure, "to deny you the opportunity. But how can I imperil his security? It is not reasonable to ask me to take a mob to see him. Select a small delegation."

"Let us choose ten representatives," suggested a woman.

"At most, five," Nitsa declared firmly. "Even five are too many under the circumstances."

After some haggling Eusabbatis, Harrar, Ben-Torta, a merchant from Joppa and a dye manufacturer from Hebron were selected, and Nitsa took them to Rabbi Akiba's house.

When they arrived, Hagarsi, mindful of Rabbi Akiba's dislike for Harrar and Rabbi Ben-Torta, and disturbed by Shemon's presence, was reluctant to announce them. But Nitsa insisted and Joshua went up.

"Master," he said apologetically, "the fat of the land are here, Harrar, Rabbi Johanan and Eusabbatis among them. Nitsa brought them. The kin of the hostages besieged the council house."

Akiba frowned. "The men who, for the vineyards of this world, overlook the everlasting gardens of the other," he muttered as if speaking to himself. To Joshua he said, "So it is concern about the hostages that brings them here?"

"So it seems, Master."

"I am coming down."

Joshua bowed and left. Akiba rose and Shemon sprang to his feet. "May I come with the rabbi?"

"That would be very unwise, Shemon."

"I would like to hear what they say, dear rabbi; the future may bring them onto my path. I would like to know them. May I not listen from the portico?"

Akiba regarded him sternly, but almost at once relaxed. "You are my guest," he said, "and the whole house is yours."

The rabbi left. Shemon descended into the garden, tiptoed

up to the portico and halted at a curtained entrance to the hall. He knew Rabbi Ben-Torta's voice, for he had heard him preach. The banker's voice was also familiar to him, for he had heard Eusabbatis pronounce the benediction over the Holy Scrolls at the main Sepphoris synagogue. Counting Akiba and Nitsa, Shemon was able to recognize four if they spoke.

As he began to listen, Akiba was speaking. His tone was vigorous and determined. "That will never be, Johanan. I ask you not to repeat it, for it offends my ears. No Israelite, however humble, will ever be betrayed to save another, however consequential. We are all equal before the Holy One, blessed be He. We may die for each other in martyrdom or in battle, but not in ignominy. If that is all you have to propose, I am obliged to bid you—"

"That is not all, venerable Rabbi," Eusabbatis hastened to interject. "I agree that our worthy Rabbi Johanan is perhaps a little harsh. May I propose three things: Let us bring Rufus a peace offering in gold, so large that the temptation would be irresistible. Let the greatest rabbis in the country, headed by Rabbi Akiba, issue a call to the people to refrain from violence against Edom, and to all fugitives to return to their homes under a solemn pledge of pardon by the procurator. And let us send a delegation to Rome, headed by the venerable rabbi."

"Eusabbatis," responded the sage, "let me answer the first first and the last last. Not so long ago I gave Rufus more gold than you can imagine, and what followed you know. That man knows not the word 'honor.' The more you give him, the less he fears you, the more he demands, and the less he cares to keep his promise. Second, let those rabbis who wish sign such a call; I will not. Never again will I believe in Rufus' pledge, and I will not take the blood of the innocent upon my soul. Nor will I deprive those who believe in resistance of their hope, which is the last, next to their reliance on their Creator. Third, a delegation has gone to Rome from Alexandria. Simeon bar-Johai may soon bring us news. I expect nothing good, for I know Hadrian."

"But would not a delegation from here be more effective?" asked Harrar.

"No, Ezra. We have already shed Edomite blood. Our Alexandrian brethren have not; in any case, not during Hadrian's rule. Besides, it would take us longer to reach Rome than Rufus would allow the hostages to live."

"If so, what does the rabbi propose to do?" said Harrar with unconcealed impatience. "Shall we permit the hostages to die?"

"Their life and death is not in our hands, Ezra. Have faith."

"Faith, faith, faith!" exclaimed Harrar angrily, but Eusabbatis checked him.

"When the rabbi says 'faith'," asked Eusabbatis, "does he mean to give us hope that the expected reply from Rome may, with God's help, be favorable?"

"Anything may be favorable with His help, Eusabbatis, but the Almighty's ways are inscrutable, while the ways of Rome are clear. Hadrian will not relent. I spoke to him. I know. As pagans go, he is not a man of evil. But evil, to him, is not what it is to us. To him might is right. It is right that the strong should devour the weak, he maintains, for is it not so among the beasts? The most powerful of all beasts is man; what packs are to beasts, tribes and peoples are to men. The most powerful of all peoples is Rome; the most powerful Edomite is Hadrian. He rules the world; he is the highest god, and gods are fashioned after him. And to him goes everything that is enriching and pleasurable. This is his faith; this is paganism. Our faith—in the Almighty God of the spirit, of truth, of justice and love for man— is his deadly enemy. If Hadrian and his faith are to live, either we or our God—and may He forgive me, for I say it not in blasphemy—must die. That is why no delegation will succeed."

There was a long silence and Shemon thought that the conference was at an end. But, no; he heard Ben-Torta clear his throat.

"True as your words may be, Akiba, they will not save the hostages. I uphold Eusabbatis. Let us sign a call to the people and to those in hiding. They will return, and Shemon, abandoned, will surrender or be caught."

"Silence!"

That was Akiba's voice at its crescendo. His patience had come to an end. Only once, at the close of the rabbi's speech upon his return from Hadrian, had Shemon heard it rise to such power. His impulse to go in and upbraid the sanctimonious Ben-Torta vanished as the thunder of that solitary word fell.

The effect still lingered in the ensuing pause, when Harrar cried out, "The rabbi's shouts will not silence us; nor will they save the flower of our people, doomed to die a horrible death. The rabbi refuses to do anything to help. He is safe. He is in hiding, while the others will die. It is cowardly. . . ."

Several voices spoke up together. But that of Nitsa, quivering with passion, dominated them all: "How dare you, you sinner in Israel, cast aspersions upon our pride and glory; how dare you! Ask pardon; ask pardon immediately or I'll have you thrown out!"

Violence, it appeared, was near. He, Shemon, was the cause of it and the great man was suffering for him. Should he step in and take the burden off the old man's shoulders?

Akiba was speaking again. Now his voice was deep, old and spent. "If you think that my surrender will save the others, I shall be on my way to Caesarea before nightfall."

Shemon gasped. In the hall all seemed to burst into speech. Loud words mingled incoherently. Shemon no longer heard or cared. He had made up his mind that the shameful performance must end. He pulled the curtain aside and entered. With measured gait, in the silence of consternation, he went over to the cushioned seat upon which Akiba sat, his head drooping. "I am Shemon," he declared simply, and paused to stare at his vilifiers with annihilating contempt. "Your conduct is unworthy of men of distinction in Israel. I had and still have my own intentions about the hostages. If, however, you force the greatest man of our generation to incur martyrdom—which will not save the hostages— I will go with you to Rufus and perhaps save them. I warn you that my death will not halt the storm. It will break more fiercely. It will destroy you. A holy war like ours does not depend on one man. Here I am. Take me to the centurion."

The members of the delegation squirmed but dared not speak. Shemon towered above them as a colossus among pygmies. Then Harrar came slowly to where Akiba sat, bowed to him and murmured, "Forgive me, venerable Rabbi. I spoke in anger which came of pain for the others. Forgive me."

"I forgive," said Akiba.

"We shall have faith," declared Eusabbatis, but it did not sound convincing. The other members of the delegation also muttered something about faith. Rabbi Johanan alone was truculently silent.

"*Shalom,*" they said at last as they turned to go.

"*Shalom,*" replied Akiba, and went with them to the door, whence Hagarsi escorted them to the gate. Only Nitsa and Shemon remained in the hall. They stood there, watching the old master as, with head still drooping, he moved toward them. Suddenly something unusual occurred, something that stirred Shemon to the quick. The old rabbi, the glory of his generation, flung his arms about Shemon's neck and kissed him.

Chapter Twenty-eight

On his return to the caves Shemon dispatched messengers far and wide to Bnai Brak students, directed Amitai to take Masada and ordered the fortification of hills closer to the highway as well as the occupation of some strategic positions in the Samarian, Galilean and Judean hills.

In the evening he remained alone with Meredya—a rare treat, to her. Asher had walled off part of a cave for her and she had made it cozy with rugs and cushions and her husband's trophies. Now she sat on his lap, snuggling against him and listening raptly to the account of his journey, which he interspersed with words of endearment.

Suddenly he stopped. He had thought of the gifts he had bought for her and which, forgotten, still lay in the date sack. "What a fool I am!" he said guiltily and, lifting her gently, he seated her in his place and rushed out.

"What is it?" she called after him, but he kept her puzzling. He returned with the gifts and, grinning, handed them to her. "For you," he said.

She unfolded the robe, smoothed its silky texture, slipped into it and glanced at him for approval.

"No one like you," he exclaimed with genuine admiration. She smiled gratefully, then gloved her hands with the slippers and held them up to the lamplight. Her eyes sparkled with mirth. "The colors of the rainbow," she laughed.

"They'll bring fair weather, then."

She threw her arms about his neck. "Thank you, my dear."

Without warning, Joel burst in with the news that Zevulun had disembarked horses, supplies and men, and was waiting. Meredya dropped the slippers but picked them up again and, patting them mechanically, stood listening.

When Joel had received his instructions and departed, Shemon turned to her. She was pale and her large black eyes were moist, but she was trying to smile. He took her in his arms. "I must go, my love."

"I know," she said quietly. "Tonight waiting will be hard."

He pressed her closer and kissed her. "I will be back by sunrise."

Soon afterwards Shemon, with a company of cavalry, was speeding toward the seashore. Heading the same way, at a slower pace to protect the men and animals of the transport, were two hundred horsemen under Joel and Issachar. The night was cloudy and dark. There was no talk and only the fall of hoofs was heard. At given points on the road Joel and Issachar posted lookouts.

What Shemon saw upon reaching the shore exceeded his expectations. The beach, lighted by torches, was crowded and Zevulun, with some of his sailors, was in the center. Behind them was a jumble of bales, crates and packs, and behind these were horses surrounded by mounted armed men. In the crescent-shaped harbor numerous craft swayed between war vessels.

Shemon dismounted and the two commanders embraced. "God is with us, Zevulun. What I see is unbelievable. How did it happen?"

Zevulun grinned and slapped Shemon on the back. "Luck! Two Roman biremes pulled out of Alexandria with flat-bottomed boats. Some were in tow, some under their own oars. The boats were laden with supplies and hundreds of horses. The galleys moved slowly because of the weight of the boats in tow. Thank the Lord, we were ready and pulled out the same night. We had two triremes, two biremes and other vessels. Our crews were free men, not rowers chained to their seats, so we had every advantage. We were waiting for a favorable moment. Then a storm came. In the noise and excitement of the storm we cut the tow ropes. Before the Edomites knew what was happening, our biremes took the animal boats in tow and the triremes attacked the galleys. One we set on fire. She sank with all on board. The other was captured with no Edomites alive. We boarded her after the storm. The tribune and the hortator, as well as those members of the Edomite crew who had not been killed in battle, had been murdered by the slaves, who had broken loose. The small crews of the cargo vessels surrendered without struggle after throwing their supervisors overboard."

"And who are these horsemen?"

"Brothers of the Israelite Lions in Egypt. All fine riders. Some come of good families. Pappus' son's best friend, Isidoros, is their headman."

"And what happened to the slave rowers?"

"They are here behind the horses, waiting for your decision."

"Who are they? And how many?"

"Athenian Christians and Carthaginians, most of them Israelites. About four hundred in all."

"Will they fight with us."

"They say they will."

"And what are your further plans?"

"I will hide my fleet in a small harbor between Acca and Sidon and will attack galleys and shipping."

"Good! And where is this—what's his name?—Isidoros?"

Zevulun called out, and a graceful young rider advanced on a fine steed. "Isidoros, this is Shemon of Kozib."

The young man saluted. Shemon scrutinized him and was impressed by his steady, fearless eyes and perfect posture.

"How many men do you command, Isidoros?"

"Two hundred horsemen." His voice was unfaltering and resonant.

"You will do," said Shemon, "but not your Greek name. You come from the south; your name shall henceforth be the

Son of the South—Bar-Daroma." The young man smiled his assent. "I will talk to you a little later." Shemon turned to Zevulun and Bar-Daroma backed his horse.

The mariner motioned to a man waiting directly in front of the sailors. A stocky, round-bearded, begrimed man of Zevulun's stature approached. A tattered tunic protruded from beneath a hempen sack that served to protect him from the chilly air.

"This is Theodoros, Shemon. The slaves chose him as their spokesman."

Theodoros nodded.

"Now I must sail, Shemon," Zevulun continued, "if the Edomite fleet in Caesarea is not to catch me. I will see you soon." Once more they embraced.

"Theodoros," Shemon said, "there is work to do and I will ask you only one question. Life with us will be hard and dangerous. Are you ready to stand or fall with us?"

"I am ready, Shemon, and so are the others. We have seen slavery; nothing could be worse. We fear no one save the Lord."

"Good. You need clothing. I suppose the others do, too. You will receive whatever you need when we return to the caves. And now to work. I hear my men approaching with the beasts of burden."

Late that night the horses were placed in enclosures built by Asher, the booty was stored away in the caverns and the men were housed in tents.

Shemon was up at dawn, but Asher was already about. He had outdone himself. The Bowl and the plateau had been spanned by an adequate bridge, across which lumber and cut stone were being carried. Enclosures and sheds for animals and stores had been put up and tents pitched.

The forward mountain, named Tower Hill, was a beehive of activity. Hundreds of men and animals were working. Some of the men were digging, others were hewing or carrying stone and still others were helping the animals bring up lumber and stone.

It was still quite early when Meredya, wrapped in a warm

cloak, appeared at Shemon's side. She watched the scene with intense interest. Fascinating to her were the men who picked blocks of stone from crumbled fences and, securing them in loops of stout rope, placed them in pairs on the backs of asses or pack horses. "Shemon," she asked earnestly, "how long ago were those villages destroyed?"

"Those? Let me see, that was Vespasian's work. Sixty-three or sixty-four years ago."

"Before the destruction of the Second Temple."

"A year or two before."

After a silence she said, "I have been thinking, Shemon."

"Yes?"

"I have grasped the meaning of something. It is said, 'The stones cry out to Heaven.' I wondered what it meant. Now I know. For sixty-four years the stones of houses and fences broken by the enemy cried out to Heaven against the crimes. Now the stones have been heard. They are coming up to the hilltop to be a tower of strength. They are going to live again."

"Meredya!" Shemon exclaimed. "My darling Meredya!"

After breakfast he summoned Bar-Daroma. In broad daylight the Alexandrian looked handsomer than by torchlight. He was a well-proportioned youth with a straight, almost classical nose and a short black beard.

"Are all your men strong and well trained?" Shemon asked.

"They are athletes, Shemon. Some were prizewinners in Greek and Roman games. They can ride, run, swim and row. All have learned to throw the discus and the javelin; some are good swordsmen."

"And you?"

"I can hold my own in any of these things; and I can wrestle."

"Give me your hand," said Shemon.

Bar-Daroma did, and Shemon held it and pressed it. Bar-Daroma smiled. Tiny beads of perspiration appeared on his brow, but he kept smiling.

Shemon released the young man's hand. It was blue and numb. "Good," smiled Shemon. "If the others are like you we have two hundred new good warriors."

Chapter Twenty-nine

December came and Rufus announced elaborate spectacles and games at the stadium. The surprise of the festivities was to come on the last day, the Sabbath, when every fifth hostage was to be thrown to the beasts. Dedius, who was charged with the responsibility of maintaining law and order in and about the stadium during the week of the event, immediately informed Ruffina.

That night she, who had been grudging her wifely favors to Rufus, came into his bedroom seductively attired and scented with the perfume that stirred him most. But her wiles and pleas were to no avail. Rufus shouted that he would no longer let her befuddle his judgment and seduce him into acting against the interests of the empire. Israel's God did not frighten him. If Jehovah were all the accursed Israelites believed He was, why did He allow the Romans to destroy His Temple? The Judean vermin would be taught an unforgettable lesson. He, Rufus, would show them what their God was worth. Saturday, the day when the Israelite God and His people rested, would be the day when the most eminent and devout of the prisoners would be devoured by beasts. On that day God would assuredly have ample time to save His servants, and they to witness His omnipotence.

Shaken and humiliated, Ruffina left him. Not only had she failed in her mission, but she had been forced to submit to his lust.

When, in the morning, as was her wont, Judith called on her patroness, she was obliged to wait much longer than usual before being invited into the boudoir. She found Lady Ruffina in bed, her eyes red and puffed. The drawn curtains kept the daylight out of the huge room, illuminated by a triple-flamed oil lamp fed by bronze serpents. Ruffina motioned to Judith to throw back the silk mesh which, supported by four gilded rods, enshrouded her bed. She sat up, her shoulders white against the purple cushions and the gilded headboard on which the figures of Cupid and Psyche were carved. She gathered up her scattered hair into a knot, tucked the silk cover about her waist and asked Judith to hand her a phial standing on one of several marble-topped tables covered with scent phials, make-up palettes, trinkets and figurines. Judith did not mind those exquisitely carved statuettes that Ruffina regarded as amulets. They were too ridiculously small to be detested as deities. But she avoided gazing at the larger statues of Aphrodite and Minerva that gleamed white in the dimness of the far end of the room.

While her mistress was applying the perfume, Judith slipped out onto Ruffina's private terrace, with its double columns of black marble. The palace and the garden surrounding it were situated on a walled-in mound. To the west was the sea; to the east, the citadel. Judith looked down into the peristyle encircling the palace, scanned the paved walks and pergolas in the garden, and turned to an arch that indicated the invisible exit from the underground citadel corridor. *What a fine residence this would make for an Israelite prince,* Judith thought.

Ruffina called and invited Judith to sit beside her. Her freshened-up face had lost its puffiness and her eyes had brightened up. Now she was able to unburden the details of her misadventure. She told Judith everything, beginning with Dedius' visit. As her story unfolded, her cheeks colored and her eyes glowed with ferocity. What had happened the preceding night had by now become more than the denial of a plea for compassion, more than the rejection of an eccentric lady's whim. It had become the offended vanity of a beautiful woman and the loss of prestige of a wife accustomed to having her way. Henceforth the case of the hostages was to be fought out as a duel between her and her husband. Never before had Judith seen Ruffina so incensed against the procurator. "I loathe him!" Ruffina cried. "I loathe him!"

Clearly, Judith thought, the pagan woman, of whom she had become genuinely fond, was now ready to do anything to frustrate her husband's evil designs. The opportunity must not be neglected. Some plan of action must be devised.

Judith leaned forward. "I have a thought," she whispered conspiratorially. "Let the beasts be poisoned. It would take a long time to replace them." Her deep, dark eyes were fixed in keen suspense on Ruffina, who seemed frozen by the daring thought.

But in a moment she burst into laughter. "You little devil!" She pinched Judith's cheek. "You little devil!"

They discussed the scheme and decided that it was workable if Dedius agreed to relax the vigilance of his guard when the time came.

It was necessary to inform Shemon and to secure his help. As usual, Judith expected to transmit the message through Nadav, who called on her every day. But on that day he failed to appear, so she decided not to wait for him. To avoid suspicion she dressed as a peasant woman and went to Ovadya, who took her to Shemon.

He listened to her attentively and was grateful. But the answer was no for the present. He had some plan of his own, which would soon become known. If it should fail, there still would be time to accept hers.

All the way back her thoughts, against her will, drifted to Shemon. This had been her first personal contact with him and the impression he had made upon her was deep. She could not forgive herself for having let him see her in humble garb that did no justice to her beauty.

Later Nadav came to report. Disguised as a Greek freedman, he had been trailing the slave merchant Padulos. The latter had sustained a staggering loss on the liberated slaves. Padulos had castigated the government for its weakness in dealing with the accursed Israelites. Their insolence was growing, while the Roman authorities were becoming more timid. What was to happen to respectable, law-abiding citizens? he had asked. How were they going to earn their livelihood? Padulos had had the answer. He was gathering the dregs of Caesarea and, with the connivance of government officials, was preparing them to plunder and massacre the Caesarean Israelite community during the week of the festivities.

Shemon instructed Nadav to inform the community and to counsel temporary withdrawal from the Judean quarter. Nadav also received far-reaching instructions of a different nature.

"You remember," Shemon asked, "how Bar-Goria, the bitterest

enemy of Titus during the siege of Jerusalem, undermined the
Edomite breastworks after they had reached the height of the
outer wall?"

"Yes," said Nadav. "It was a remarkable feat. He dug beneath
the works, propped the thin layer of soil with beams and
crossbeams and, when the time was ripe, set fire to the beams.
The works toppled into the flames."

"Right," Shemon confirmed. "You are to do the same to
twenty-five feet of the Caesarean wall where it faces the plain.
Start digging from beneath a nearby building. You must be
ready not later than the night of the fifth day."

Nadav scratched the back of his head. "It will take many
men and much secrecy."

"The men you will have. The rest is in your hands."

"It will be done," said Nadav.

Chapter Thirty

As Shemon was making his final preparations for the attack,
news arrived that Amitai had seized Masada and Joel had
secured the crest of Har Hamelek, the highest mountain in
Samaria, to prevent the Romans from taking it. Spirits rose high.
The time for striking was ripe.

At last the command to advance was given.

Throughout the night Shemon's forces moved through the
hills where, nine months before, he had stood in the disguise
of a Roman legionary, facing Caesarea. Now he was there again,
in Judean attire, as the leader of the Judean host, as the
descendant of King David. Then he had aimed to retrieve
plundered cattle; now, to redeem human lives. Then the last
words of his uncle had been the mere injunction of a dying
revolutionary; now he, Shemon, young and strong, with a multitude of others to support him, was about to fulfill the injunction.

His forces—less than half of his total effectives, but including
the bulk of his cavalry—moved surreptitiously to striking positions. The remainder was left behind to defend his strongholds.

The night was cloudy and moonless, ideal for concealment. The horses' hoofs were muffled; talk was forbidden. Five hundred foot soldiers, under Issachar, had already descended from the hills and were quietly advancing across the plain toward the northern gate. A similar contingent, under Elon, was moving toward the southern gate. Two companies of cavalry on each side were coming up as reserves. A special task force of horsemen, under Bar-Daroma, was lying in wait off the highway to intercept all Caesarea-bound caravans and wayfarers. The center and the mound of the citadel were left for Shemon, at the head of five mounted companies. There was no gate in the center but Nadav had reported that the breach in the wall would be made. A few Greek-speaking Heromavs, impersonating local drunkards, had been assigned to appear near the jail at dawn. At the outbreak of the attack they were to stir up confusion and meet emergencies.

Shemon's prime purpose was to liberate the hostages. He had little hope of taking the citadel now. It was the strongest fortress in the country, and eight full cohorts of Romans were stationed in and around it. He aimed to crush any Roman forces outside the fort, to paralyze the bulk of the garrison within the citadel by besieging it and to fight a rear-guard action after the captives had been freed. The attack was to begin at dawn.

Thus far everything was going according to plan. All contingents had reached their positions. Nadav had signaled that he was ready. It was still very dark, a good thirty minutes before daybreak. Shemon, in his saddle, was in front of his force. Immediately behind him were twelve signalers with rams' horns, representing the twelve Israelite tribes. Each of them was a seasoned Thumbless who had shown his mettle in action. In their rear a unit of torch-bearers, trained to use torches as both signals and weapons, was waiting for the order to light. On their flanks were the commanders of the five cavalry companies and, behind them, their men.

"Unmuffle the horses," Shemon ordered.

It was still quite dark but in the east the blackness was thinning. He looked at the hill crests behind him, still no more than shapeless projections beneath a lightless firmament. The signalers and company commanders were watching him, and within several hundred feet of the city gates Elon and Issachar were waiting for a ram's-horn blast. At last, huge gray fingers rose above the hills; then a streak of purple broke through the clouds.

"Signalers, prepare!" Shemon commanded. He raised his hand, but suddenly shouted "Wait!" for he could hear something strange. From an indeterminate direction, or perhaps from all directions, there rolled a rumbling sound. It was nearing, growing in force, as though countless chariots were wheeling underground. Simultaneously the sky was graying and the sea and city emerging from the dark. Then, though there was no wind, the sea began to seethe. Mammoth geysers spouted high and whirled in the air. A mountainous swell heaved in the harbor, swallowing the anchored merchant craft and war galleys. All the time the underground rumbling grew in volume, until it burst into a terrific roar. The hill trembled, the horses neighed and reared in fear; but the ground beneath them held firm. Not so in the city. There the earth had been rent asunder. Dwellings, temples, theatres and baths were toppling and sinking; chasms had opened and the encircling wall had crumbled in a heap.

Then there was stillness. The earth had spent its fury. There was stillness in the hills. And in the stillness a confident, metallic voice, Shemon's voice: "Warriors of Israel! God is with us! Sound the horns! Charge!"

The survivors in Caesarea were in a state of such panic that the yelling, sword-brandishing riders galloping wildly through the streets failed to impress them except as part of the general pandemonium. Men and women, half-clad and unclad, ran about frantically, invoking the aid of their gods and calling the names of their dear ones. Small children, unheeded, toddled along or settled at the side of the road, crying. From the ruins of buildings voices of partly buried people came, pleading for aid. Here and there houses were burning. In some streets, crowded with surging throngs, frightened horses and cattle stampeded.

The Caesarean prison stood in a segregated spot southwest of the citadel and within its sight. It was a square, grim structure, built of large blocks of stone and enclosed within a wall. Beneath it were dungeons and above the surface were three stories of windowless cells with heavily grated iron doors. These opened onto rail-less balconies or landings that ran alongside the cells for the length and width of the building. A stone stairway on each side of the structure led to the lofty landings.

When Shemon and his horsemen reached the prison, Elon and his men had already overwhelmed the keepers and were swarming over the precarious terraces, unlocking doors with keys procured from the dead keepers, and smashing locks where keys would not readily fit. As the doors were opened and the prisoners emerged, there were scenes of unrestrained joy. The freed hostages blessed, embraced and kissed their liberators. Some wept; others demanded arms. Young Ovadya, who had joined Elon's men as they had swarmed into the city, was hurrying Rabbi Uziel toward a stairway. The portly rabbi, in his excitement, was tripping over his long black robe, to his own and the youngster's amusement.

All this was taking place under the hiss and whistle of arrows and javelins discharged from the ruins of the outer wall of the citadel. Here partly clad and insufficiently armed legionaries were hurriedly mustering for an attack.

Shemon, straight in his saddle, his kerchief aflutter, his black cloak falling in even folds to Ayalah's beautiful back, took in the situation at a glance and, raising his huge sword, charged, his men close behind. The zest and fury of the onslaught was such that the Romans wavered after the first shock and soon fled in disorder, pursued and mowed down by the rebels.

"God is with us!" yelled the Israelites in holy frenzy.

"The Copperhead!" shouted the demoralized legionaries as they ran for their main gate. But no safety lay behind it. The outer gate, like its wall, had collapsed. The moat, filled with heavy stones and debris, was passable. Shemon and his horsemen dashed after the enemy into the outer court of the citadel, slashing with their swords, piercing with their spears and trampling the enemy with their horses as the Romans scrambled for the entrance to the second court. Most of them succeeded in crowding inside and the heavy iron doors, operated from above, descended. Now an avalanche of stones and arrows came down upon the rebels. There was a fierce duel. The rebels threw burning torches through the grated windows. Here and there the woodwork caught fire. The rebels vented their fury on Jupiter and Juno, pelting the statues with stones and lumps of tar.

Rufus and Valentinus appeared at a window. At the sight of the mutilated statues the procurator shouted, "Beasts! Barbarians!"

An outburst of laughter greeted him. Stones crashed into the bars of the window at which he stood and Shemon galloped forward. Sharpshooters aimed their darts at him but he warded them off with his shield. "Here I am, Tyrannus," taunted Shemon. "You have set a high price on my head. Come down and take it. Come down and meet me in open combat. I will send all my men out and I alone will wait for you. No? You may take Valentinus with you—I will meet you both. No? You squirm? You rage? You pound with your fists? Cowardly thief! Assassin! Despoiler! The God of Israel has today shown His hand. Get out of this land or that hand will crush you and your wanton empire!"

The Israelite casualties were being picked up, and now Shemon ordered a slow retreat. "You will soon see me again, Rufus."

A Roman cavalry unit rushed out to pursue the Israelites, but it was caught between two forces as the contingent under Issachar suddenly appeared in the rear. Again there was pursuit, heavy casualties and a scramble for the inner court.

Sending the wounded forward, Shemon reorganized his columns and moved triumphantly through the streets. The first part of the dream he had dreamt for years had come true. The tyrant oppressing his people had been defeated and humiliated. The stadium had been reduced to a mound of broken stone and marble, with the beasts beneath; many temples of idolatry lay in ruins. The populace, by now recovered from its panic, lined the principal thoroughfare, watching sullenly. Mounted heralds, cantering some fifty feet in front of Shemon, announced at regular intervals: "There is no one like Thee among the gods,

O Lord, and there are no deeds like Thine! . . . Whoever is for God and against tyranny, join us!"

Now and then a bystander stepped forward and joined the rear of the column. The procession, singing, "This is the day in which we shall rejoice," reached the Judean quarter. There Shemon sent messengers to every house, advising the inhabitants to vacate with their portable possessions and to follow him, for with his departure their lives would be in peril. Many hastened to leave; others remained. Rabbi Uziel declared that as long as any of his flock stayed, he would stay. Shemon pleaded with him, but in vain.

The triumphant procession, augmented by the fugitives, left by the southern gate, which had remained intact, and lined up on the plain. Elon, radiating vigor and enthusiasm, came galloping up to Shemon. "A word before we set out," he cried.

"Yes, my friend."

"Would it not be wise to besiege them now, Shemon? Their losses are high, their courage is low, their fleet is on the bottom of the sea."

"No, Elon. We are not strong enough to starve them into surrender. They have other fleets. And almost all the fortresses in the land are still in their hands. If we stay, they will entrap us."

Elon smiled apologetically. "I spoke too soon."

It was early forenoon. The sun had broken through the clouds. Shemon looked back. Behind his columns, extending for more than a furlong, was the crumbled Caesarean wall; behind it, billows of smoke. Satisfaction and pride such as he had never known before possessed him. Now there was hope for his people. "Signalers," he commanded, "sound the horns."

Slowly the procession started toward the hills.

The same afternoon the Caesarean rabble descended upon the Judean quarter to loot, kill, rape and burn. Rabbi Uziel, with the holy scrolls in his arms, appeared on the steps of his synagogue. He was stoned to death, the scrolls defiled and the synagogue set on fire. Noah, Judith's old father, was strangled and his house pillaged. Judith had gone to Ruffina the preceding evening and had remained at the palace, intending to intercede on behalf of her benefactress in the event of an attack by the rebels. The palace had been spared. But nothing and no one would have been spared in the Judean quarter had it not been for Dedius, who marched in with a detachment of trustworthy soldiers and put the rioters to flight.

That was an indiscretion. It upset Padulos' calculations. The spoils were meagre. Dedius' behavior was reported to the procurator, who promptly called him to account. With patrician aloofness Dedius listened to a long, choleric tirade accusing him of conduct unworthy of a Roman officer and inimical to the empire. Dedius haughtily inquired whether the protection of peaceful, law-abiding citizens was a crime. Rufus, on the verge of an apoplectic fit, demanded to know whether rebels and murderers of Romans could be regarded as law-abiding citizens. The verbal duel ended in Dedius' arrest. He was ordered sent to Antioch to stand trial before the imperial legate.

On learning of Dedius' predicament Ruffina dispatched messages to powerful friends in Antioch, Alexandria and Rome, certain that they would come to his aid. Eventually she learned that he had been reduced in rank and sent back to Rome.

In the evening she again attempted to persuade her husband to suspend the decree and to make peace with the Israelites. Was it not clear from the events of that morning that the God of Israel was truly a fearsome Power? Could Rufus not see that the Israelites had a leader and were launching a new war against Rome? Whatever its outcome, she argued, the war, judging by its beginning, might not crown Rufus with glory. But he was adamant and abusive, and even threatened her with violence.

She decided to leave him and arranged through Judith and Nadav to see Rabbi Akiba. Attended by the seamstress, she came to Ludd, posing as a Tyrian lady of substance. Once in the old sage's presence, Ruffina discarded all pretence. She was extremely unhappy, she declared; dissatisfied with her husband, religion, environment. Now she was convinced that the Israelite God was the only one, that the Israelite creed was the only creed and that he, Akiba, was its unanointed high priest. Would he not allow her to stay with him? By serving him, by learning from him, by treading the holy ground which he trod, she should be serving God best and find a measure of peace for her tormented soul.

Akiba held her hand, stroked her hair and talked to her softly, as one would speak to a child. She did not understand, he said, how thorny and tortuous a path she was choosing. She must take time, study the philosophy and restrictions of the faith she desired to embrace. It meant self-abnegation. It entailed the acceptance of six hundred and thirteen do's and do-not's. The glamor there might be in the creed was not worldly glamor; it was a radiance derived from indefinable mystic sources. It shone from within, not to be observed by the naked eye.

If she desired to be helpful to the cause of Israel, let her go to Rome, he said. There she might appeal to Hadrian on behalf of Israel; she might enlist the influence of her powerful connections. Success was unlikely, but her sincerity, her beauty and her faith—if it was true faith—might achieve the unlikely.

Later, Ruffina announced to Judith that they were going to Rome.

Chapter Thirty-one

Shemon's great victory electrified the country. Messengers ran from place to place, heralding the tidings with ever growing exaggerations. Strangers greeted each other on the roads like old friends. Synagogues opened for worship and thanksgiving. Men and women who had gone about their tasks depressed and brooding now capered in the streets for joy. Roman soldiers kept out of sight. Shemon's slogan, *God is with us!* passed from mouth to mouth and was becoming the solace of the old and weary, the battle cry of the young.

Hanukkah, the Feast of Lights, came, and bonfires of revolt were lighted on the mountains throughout the land. From Dan to Beersheba volunteers responded. More strategic points were seized. Romans venturing to leave their camps and forts were attacked. A mocking message was sent to Rufus, inviting him to fight or get out of the country; copies of the message were distributed far and wide. Padulos was warned that he would die if a single person in the Judean quarter of Caesarea should thereafter be attacked. In his own domain Shemon urged those who bore no arms to return to their towns and villages. Treks of departing fugitives and arriving gift-bearers brought life to unfrequented hill paths.

Simeon bar-Johai returned from Alexandria and the leaders of the revolt met in a large tent on Mount Kharim, behind which rolled the hills surrounding the caves. Toasts were drunk. Akiba said a few words. Then Bar-Johai spoke.

The Alexandrian delegation to Rome, he reported, visited the leaders of eight congregations. It sought support for the liberation of the Holy Land and peace with Rome. To that end a council of eminent Hebrews and Romans was to be established to influence members of Hadrian's court, and eventually to get the emperor himself to rescind his anti-Judean decrees. Of the eight congregations, the three that responded wholeheartedly were the poorest. The Campesian and Suburesian congregations, located in the Campus Martius and Subura districts, contributed to a man; so did the Calcaresian congregation, composed chiefly of lime-burners and cobblers. They promised to continue their donations, but their political influence was nil. The members of the Augustinian, Agrippesian and Volumnius synagogues were divided on the issue. They gave treasure, but feared that the time for intercession was not ripe. Most of their leaders hesitated to identify themselves with the movement in the Holy Land, lest their status as Roman citizens be impaired. They were grateful, they said, that the decree had not been extended to include Hebrews in other parts of the empire. It would be unwise for them to make themselves unduly conspicuous. The Herodians were too wealthy and Romanized to be concerned. The Sekenians did not go beyond offering advice.

Simeon's manner was reserved and he tended toward understatement. But when a point was important, a gesture of his delicate hands, the glow of his deep, dark eyes in his pallid face, a nervous tug at his beard or a sign made up for the unspoken words. His reserve, it was felt, while partly due to good lineage, was mainly the result of control of a forceful, not yet completely developed personality. The more discerning among Akiba's disciples regarded Simeon bar-Johai, though at the time not yet ordained and barely thirty years old, as the rabbi's likeliest successor.

For a long while the sage pondered his disciple's report. At last he said, "If we cannot expect much from our kinsmen in Rome, let us look to our brethren in Parthia. They have already helped us considerably but they can do much more. They have nothing to fear. Parthia hates Rome. Hardly a generation goes by without an armed conflict between them. The Parthian government must be shown the advantage of striking at Antioch from the north while we are fighting the legions in the south. We may both win a lasting victory if we strike together." He was asked to choose a man for the mission.

That night far-reaching decisions were made: The leaders of the rebellion would proclaim themselves the Council of the People. Payment of taxes to Edom should be stopped. The taxes prescribed by the Law of Israel should continue. A special freedom tax should be levied on those who had not seriously suffered from the oppression. The main camp of the rebels would be shifted to the Valley of Rimmon, more accessible and more fitting for their rapidly growing forces. As for Rabbi Akiba, he would go back to Bnai Brak.

Shemon's personal influence and the ranks of the rebels were growing stronger, while the position of the Romans was weakening. Their numerical superiority was of little value because their forces, compelled to hold a considerable number of forts throughout the land, were scattered. They dared not leave their citadels to unite into a strong army, for they might be destroyed separately before achieving their purpose. The Roman forts were isles in a sea of hate where every man, woman and adolescent was an enemy and self-appointed spy.

Rufus realized, of course, that he could request reinforcements from the imperial legate at Antioch. But it would be humiliating to confess that within such a short time he had permitted the situation to deteriorate so badly. He also doubted the efficiency of the Syrian legions, which, stationed for many years in the large cities of that sunny and leisurely land, had grown soft and indolent, victims of the customs and vices of the natives.

On the other hand, he could not allow this state of affairs to continue. Stores were growing scant and signs of demoralization were appearing in the ranks. He decided to call by sea to Caesarea the bulk of the garrisons of the forts that lay directly on the Mediterranean. These were Gaza, Askalon and Apollonia, south of the capital, and Castra and Acca to the north. Thus, the Roman was able to muster for his attack twelve cohorts of infantry and ten centuries of cavalry—a total of seventy-two hundred men. He believed that this force would prove sufficient if he could surprise the rebels in their mountain fastness, for by now their forces, too, had been scattered and the superiority of organization and equipment was still on the Roman side.

Rufus waited for the peak of the winter to pass; and when his spies reported that Shemon was in the Valley of Rimmon, he ordered his forces to be ready.

On a night made bright by a glaring moon the procurator, dividing his army into two parts and keeping half of his cavalry in reserve, advanced at top speed into the hills. His battering rams and ballistae were drawn by powerful teams of mules so as not to impede the rapid advance of the infantry.

But Shemon's spies under Nadav were better. The procurator's plans had been known to Shemon almost from the outset.

The rebels were ready and waiting. As soon as Rufus' army had penetrated far enough into the hills, Shemon attacked from higher peaks and from the flanks. When the battle reached its height, a powerful detachment charged from the Cave of Vengeance and Rufus found himself surrounded. Fortunately for him, Valentinus, who led the second half of his army, heard the din of the battle and, shifting his course, advanced to relieve his chief. His maneuvre was only partly successful, for Shemon's forces also lay in wait for Valentinus. Rufus managed to save himself, but his losses were staggering. Most of his war machines and his best commanders, including Canopus, were lost. Valentinus was wounded by a poisoned arrow. To the Israelites, too, the engagement was costly. Among the fatal casualties was Itamar. But the spoils and the glory went to the Israelites.

It became imperative for Rufus to seek aid from Lolios Urbicius, the imperial legate at Antioch. Without losing time he dispatched three overland couriers to the Syrian capital. Before long their heads were found on the ruined city wall of Caesarea. Now Rufus was compelled to send others by the slower sea route. Weeks of troubled suspense followed.

Shemon had to go the Valley of Rimmon before returning to the environs of the Cave of Vengeance, but when he came, the young women, attired in white, went out to meet him with harps and cymbals. Led by Tamar and Meredya, who, although heavy with child, was still beautiful, they danced and chanted:

> Sing glory and praise to the Lord of Hosts,
> Who smileth again upon His people.
> From death and despair, from anguish and fear,
> He guideth us back to sunlit pastures.
> Sing glory and praise to Israel's sons,
> Who smote and humbled the iniquitous Edom,
> And praised be the Lord for the mighty arm,
> For the fearless heart, of Shemon, the man,
> The leader of men,
> The terror of foes.
> Shemon! Shemon! Hallelujah!

That night Shemon said to his wife, "Pleasure of my heart! You excel in singing and you excel in beauty even when your limbs are weighed down. But camp or cave is no longer the place for you. For his sake and yours, you must have rest and quiet. To which of your sisters will you go?"

Her eyes welled with tears. "I will not see you if I go from here," she whispered.

"You will see me later all the more."

She knew he was right and capitulated graciously. "Take me to Hemda, my dear."

He had a comfortable seat fixed for her on a donkey, and accompanied by an armed escort, he took her to Ein Gedi.

On his way back Shemon went to Ludd and asked Nitsa to see Saturnius.

"Centurion," said Nitsa, "I come as a friend. Shemon bade me tell you—and this because of my high regard for you and your many favors—that all the Roman garrisons in the country will soon perish. But you and your garrison can leave with honor.

You will be allowed to retain your swords and to march in a body, but without standards. Shemon's men will take you to Gaza."

The old veteran laughed bitterly. "Who would have thought a few months ago that we would come to this?" He paused to consider, staring at his rough, stubby fingers. "But my answer is no. You mean well, Nitsa. But I have been a Roman soldier in many a war. I do not run. Moreover, I will not be the first one to run."

"You will not be the first, Saturnius. Your procurator—"

"He still holds Caesarea," interrupted the centurion.

"He will not hold it long."

Saturnius remained adamant, but Nitsa pleaded for him and Shemon agreed not to molest the man for a while.

Upon returning to camp Shemon was greeted by his father-in-law, who brought good tidings from his journey with Malanos, whom he had come to hold in great esteem. They spent a long while together recounting their experiences and speaking of Meredya and the impending event.

Chapter Thirty-two

It was early spring when the bulk of the rebel forces, which by then numbered tens of thousands, concentrated in the new camp in the Valley of Rimmon. The stream of volunteers was incessant and their eagerness for action great. Zealous, well-equipped men were now also arriving from Numidia, a province of the former state of Carthage in North Africa, and from Cyrene, Darnis, Ptolomais, Tucheria and Berenica in Cyrenaica. Supplies, too, came in great quantities. A considerable portion of the grain and cotton which the Alexandrian Jews exported to Rome was diverted to the rebels; and Zevulun's fleet, which was becoming the terror of the Levantine coast, delivered much valuable booty.

Gratifying was the rapidly changing attitude of the Samaritans. Barely four months earlier they had been hostile and had regarded the acceptance into their fold of some of their weak and wavering Israelite neighbors as an act of grace. When Joel, in a surprise move, had occupied the Har Hamelek peak, the villagers of Kfar Hamelek, predominantly Samaritan, had warned him that they would not support him. Later, when Bar-Daroma had arrived with his Alexandrians to replace Joel, the villagers had still been unfriendly. But now a representative of these villagers was included in a Samaritan delegation which came to offer Shemon every possible aid. Their change of heart was important because of the geographical position of Samaria, midway between Judea and Galilee. Hostile, the Samaritans might have been a constant menace to the forces of liberation, which would have to cross and recross their territory and operate within its bounds. Now this source of possible vexation was about to be eliminated.

Pleased as he was, Shemon had little taste for these people. Like Rabbi Akiba, he regarded them as unprincipled, fawning before the strong. Whenever the fortunes of Judea ascended, they forgot their derelictions from Judaism and stressed their descent from the tribes of Benjamin and Ephraim. Whenever an invader scourged Judea with fire and sword, the Samaritans hastened to deny their Judaism.

Shemon therefore left the deliberations with the Samaritans to Abner, Joel and Simeon bar-Johai, and promised to join them after inspecting his camp.

Followed by a signaler and a runner on mounts, and leading Ayalah by the reins, he walked slowly along the main avenues of the encampment, permitting no detail to escape him. These daily inspections filled him with confidence. In his fondest dreams he had not visualized a camp more impressive than the one about him. It occupied a good half of the valley, which extended for three parasangs between the hamlet of Beth Rimmon, northwest of Shechem, and the stream Cyprus, skirting Mount Keyar and flowing southeast into the Jordan.

On each side of him there were perfect rows of tents, with water trenches around them and side lanes between them, a lane to every company. The trenches were interconnected and each row was joined to a canal that ran the length of the central avenue. Subsurface cisterns received the rainwater from the canal. Each company of one hundred men had a special tent housing the commander, and each unit of ten companies a booth accommodating the unit commander. Commanders' quarters were located in the center of their units, and the main head-quarters in the center of the camp. The latter consisted of a large number of huts for Shemon and his aides, guard and service tents and a platform with a high observation turret. They faced a large clearing. Adjoining the main camp was a special reservation for cavalry, transport services and supplies.

After the inspection Shemon joined the conferees and was handed a papyrus containing the proposed terms of the agreement. They were acceptable, but he was in no hurry to say so. The importance of an agreement, he thought, lay not in its wording, but rather in the good faith of the contracting parties. On this point he still had misgivings, but what was it one could do to assure good faith?

He raised his eyes from the papyrus and let his gaze wander over the faces of the seven delegates, as if trying to discover the answer in them. The appearance of the presidents of the Sebaste, Azkaroth, Ein-Kushim and Dennushahan communities aroused no apprehensions. Each of them looked neither better nor worse than the average archon of the average Israelite com-munity: middle-aged, portly, sober, with a touch of rectitude wrapped in self-importance. Even the head of the town of Baal, where, it was said, idolatry prevailed, was of the same familiar type. But Agrim of Shechem and Manashik of Kfar Hamelek were unmistakably different. Agrim, a man in his thirties, was somewhat undersized, with a sparse, blondish beard, a pointed nose and shifty brown eyes, too eager to respond and too quick to seek refuge from a fixed gaze. He wore a showy silk robe over a long, warm garment, though the season no longer demanded it, and a silk turban. Manashik, somewhat older than the other, was a tall, bony, yellow-bearded man with a long, fleshy nose, small black eyes beneath joined eyebrows, and a sepulchral voice. The color of his cloak and turban matched his beard.

At last Shemon spoke. "Is it your intention to join your first five thousand men?"

"Some of us are too old for war," replied the President of Sebaste hesitantly, "and some are undecided; but Agrim and Manashik will join."

Shemon paused to consider and again looked at the papyrus. "This agreement," he said gravely, "is based upon our victory. What will you do if we fail?"

The question startled them. Then Manashik's long face seemed to grow longer, the pupils of his eyes rolled upward and out of his thick-lipped mouth there came a chant such as seers intoned when inspired: "Adonai is a Man of War; God is His Name. From under the earth He sendeth His chariots to shatter the walls of our foe. With an invisible hand He smiteth the sea, and in rage it swalloweth the ships of Edom. Angels guard thy path, O Shemon, and ironclad warriors flee before thee. Mighty is thy arm and irresistible thy blows, for God is thy mainstay. Doubt not the will of the Lord, for He hath given the sign."

This sudden pseudoprophetic outpouring, coming from one whose very faith was in doubt, angered Shemon; it seemed to him to be a sanctimonious maneuvre to evade his question. "No one," he said coldly, "need reassure me of the Almighty's favor. I have asked a question and desire an answer. Will the Samaritans stand with us in adversity as in success?"

The delegates exchanged quick glances and Agrim, in a high-pitched voice, hastened to declare, "How can it be otherwise? We stand with you to the end."

His colleagues muttered, "To the end. To the end."

"There is another question, Shemon," said Bar-Johai in his subdued but firm manner. "Shall any of the Israelites who in the days of danger went over to the Samaritans be allowed to join our army?"

"No," replied Shemon.

"If you accept us," Agrim hastened to say, "why not them? Are we not now one—?"

"No," Shemon cut in. "There is a difference between you and them. You are Samaritans trying to come back to us; they are Israelites who have fled from us. We cannot trust them."

The agreement was signed and the delegation departed. That

very night the first two contingents of Samaritans arrived in camp from the neighboring Beth Rimmon and Azkaroth.

It was time for a decisive blow against Rufus. Before striking, Shemon took a flying trip to Har Hamelek and thence to Judea. He spent a night examining the environs of Jerusalem, a morning in Betar and a few hours with Amitai at Masada. From there he went to Ein Gedi to see Meredya. They enjoyed a few precious hours together in her sister's vineyard, dreaming aloud of the days when the oppressor would be driven from the land. In that daylight reverie she fixed their residence on the Mount of Olives in Jerusalem. There he would build a house of white marble, half of which would always be open to the needy and weary. PEACE. BLESSED BE THE COMERS would be inscribed on its portals. And over the portals of their actual residence large golden letters would read SHEMON THE LIBERATOR. From the windows of the residential half of the building their children must be able to see Mount Moriah, with the restored Temple upon it; the Tower of David on Mount Zion, looming over a new, impregnable wall; and, in the distance, the glimmer of the Jordan as it fell into the Dead Sea.

Chapter Thirty-three

In early spring Caesarea fell and Rufus fled to Antioch. The attack upon the Roman capital had been timed with simultaneous attacks upon the enemy strongholds in Galilee, so that Caesarea had been completely isolated from the north. All approaches to the city from the south had been previously severed. With no aid arriving from anywhere, his defences impaired by the earthquake, and his garrison depleted and demoralized, Rufus had been unable to hold out long against Shemon's fierce onslaughts. In the dead of night, in a lull between battles, he and the remnants of his cohorts were picked up by a fleet of small boats which had managed to slip into the private harbor of his palace grounds.

That week Tiberias fell to Joel; Cabul, to Elon; Acca, to Issachar, assisted by Theodoros; and Sepphoris, where Malanos had secured Christian aid from within, to Asher. To them Shemon sent letters of gratitude.

He remained in Caesarea for a week to establish a firm grip on the city. Then, alone, he rode to his uncle's grave to offer a thanksgiving prayer.

The morning of his return to the Valley of Rimmon he ordered the flower of his forces in Caesarea and the populace to assemble on the square before the damaged citadel. When they stood there, each unit with its banner, Shemon ordered his trumpets to signal and, in the stillness that followed, called out, "Nadav, the son of Hanan, will come forward."

Nadav, pale of countenance and wearing sackcloth, for he was mourning for his young brother Ovadya, who had fallen in battle, came forward slowly to the center of the square.

Then Shemon, attired in his best garments and holding a parchment, advanced toward Nadav and, in a voice which resounded far and wide, proclaimed: "Nadav, the son of Hanan! You were among the first to join me in an oath to resist the oppressor. Throughout the long struggle you served your people faithfully. You were the seeing, scouting eye of our forces. We won many a victory because of the timely information you gave us about the enemy. And you fought in every battle. You knew no rest and no fear, and I never heard you say, 'Impossible.' In the battle for Caesarea you were courageous and cunning and you smote the enemy where he did not expect you. Alas, you lost your brave brother, Ovadya, whom we all loved. Be consoled in our victory, which will lead to the early liberation of Jerusalem. In recognition of your services I, Shemon, designate you this day Commander of Caesarea, and I so proclaim it in the hearing of the army and the people."

He embraced Nadav, kissed him on his left cheek, where the old scar ran down to his neck, and handed him the parchment.

A great shout went up and Nadav, his brilliant eyes dim and his voice choking with tears, said, "Thank you, Shemon. This is a day of retribution, which the Lord above and you below made possible."

Passover was near and gift-bearers streamed to Rimmon. Flour, wine, eggs, fowl, lambs, ewes, nuts, fruits, a variety of delicacies suitable for the feast and many articles of clothing were brought by the affluent as well as by the poor, each according to his means.

The visitors pitched their tents or slept on the bare ground some distance away from the military camp. They set up field kitchens and marked off an area for slaughtering cattle. Their number was growing hourly, until on the eve of the holiday their encampment reached the banks of the streams, which skirted the southern and northeastern ends of the Valley.

Inside the military reservation special tents were pitched for distinguished visitors, among them men of wealth and learning who had previously been indifferent or opposed to the rebellion. Surprisingly enough, Rabbi Johanan ben-Torta also came, but Shemon received him with undisguised coldness. Still more surprising was the arrival of Eliezer, Shemon's uncle. He came riding a gaily decked pack horse, accompanied by his old house-keeper and a younger man, both on asses. The meeting of uncle and nephew was strained. Shemon dutifully invited the old man into his hut, to which several rooms had been added since Shemon's return. He offered one of these to Eliezer, observing that the adjoining room had been reserved for Rabbi Akiba.

Abruptly the old man came close to his nephew and said, "The Holy One, blessed be He, is the sole judge of men and their ways. Today I come to you as a friend. To show me His favor he sent a messenger into my path, one who bore good tidings so that I might bring them to you. Shemon, my son, *beseeman tov! Beshaäh mootzlahat!* Your wife has presented you—to give you joy for many years—with a son in Israel!"

Shemon stood speechless, color flushing his face, his eyes brilliant and moist. Suddenly he embraced the old man. "When did it happen?" he muttered huskily.

"Three days ago."

"Forgive me, Uncle. I must find her father." He rushed out.

A little later Akiba arrived. As erect in the saddle as a young horseman, he radiated joy and whispered benedictions as groups of enthusiasts, predominantly his former students, chanted,

"There is no one like God in Heaven, and no one like Akiba on earth! He fights the tyrants with divine fire and the faint-hearted with the lash of the word!" Abner, on his way to assure Eliezer that old differences had been forgotten, fell in with the cheering throng.

A scene of great joy was enacted in Shemon's hut when Akiba and his entourage learned that Shemon's wife had borne a son. "Great is our God!" exclaimed Akiba. "He perpetuates the House of David." Those who had not known of Shemon's descent were awed. Shemon invited all present to attend the rite of circumcision at Ein Gedi.

Late in the afternoon contingents of the victorious armies arrived from Galilee. Of the leading commanders, only Joel was able to leave his post for the holiday. The others sent their associates to represent them. Shemon was particularly sorry at the absence of Zevulun, for the mariner's share in the victory had been great.

Eliezer of Modin officiated at the services; Rabbi Akiba, at the Seder, the Passover night feast, the most memorable since the destruction of the Second Temple.

Although the main attraction was the Seder, the fighting forces and the more informed among their friends were looking forward most eagerly to the following afternoon when, it was said, something unusual would occur.

After the midday meal the soldiers and visitors assembled in the field to sing and dance. Inhabitants of the nearby towns of Azkaroth, Beth Rimmon and Sebaste also came, some to participate in the festivities, some to watch. The day was beautiful, the far-flung green fields were bathed in sunlight and the spirits of the people were high. Dances abandoned since the fall of Jerusalem were revived. Samaritans and Judeans, Israelites and Christians fraternized with one another.

The leaders and distinguished guests mingled with the festive crowds and, after a while, came to the spot where the revelers were exclusively soldiers, some veterans of many a fray, some recent recruits. Word went out that Rabbi Akiba would speak, and men began to gather from every part of the field and from camp. Upon an improvised platform were Abner, Eliezer, Akiba and other men of distinction. Immediately below were Shemon and his war leaders.

Abner welcomed the multitudes and Eliezer spoke first. He was distressed at the bloodshed, but since it had been pre-ordained he accepted it with humility. Soon, he hoped, even greater multitudes than those before him would flock to a redeemed Jerusalem. And now he invited all who wished to do so to come to the rite of circumcision at Ein Gedi, where wine would flow and meat abound for rich and poor alike. And all this would come from his, Eliezer's, own treasury in honor of his nephew Shemon, whom the Almighty had blessed with a first-born son.

A great cheer went up and shouts of *"Beseeman tov!"* passed from row to row and grew in fervor and volume. Abner reminded them that Rabbi Akiba was about to speak and the noise died down.

The old sage spoke of the need for setting the House of Israel in order. A small band of courageous men, headed by Shemon, had led the country to this happy Passover. Jerusalem and the whole of Judea would indeed soon be redeemed. But that would not be enough. They must strengthen the House from within, for peace as well as for war. The source of most of Israel's woes in the past had been dissension within. If but for one generation they could compose their differences and subordinate personal cravings to the interests of the common weal, Israel would grow strong and happy. Meanwhile the people, the humble as well as the rich, must uphold Shemon and give zeal and treasure for waging the war until their freedom was secure. They also needed a high priest. He, Akiba, and the distinguished persons about him believed that the man for that exalted office should be none other than Shemon's uncle, Eliezer of Modin, a kohen of great distinction, a man of learning and rectitude.

"And now," Akiba went on, "I come to Shemon himself. The Almighty has made him a Samson in strength and courage, a man of wisdom despite his youth, the son of one who died the death of a hero, a selfless man who loves his people above all and a descendant of the House of David."

A murmur of surprise passed through the crowd, and cries of delight were heard.

Akiba called for silence. "Need I tell you what Shemon has done for you and me, for Israel, for the Almighty?" he exclaimed, and the power of his voice was mounting. "If there were need to sing his praises, my tongue would be too feeble. To slaves he has given freedom; to the downtrodden, hope; to the wavering, faith. He is the Lord's choice. The Lord proclaimed it by rending the earth and shaking enemy strongholds into dust. We this day proclaim it in words. Shemon is our liberator. Shemon is our God-appointed leader."

The mounting suspense broke. The pent-up emotions of the crowd burst forth: "Shemon, our liberator! Long live Shemon, our liberator! Shemon, the son of David! Shemon, our king!"

"Yea," pressed on the old master when he had finally succeeded in stemming the crowd's fervor, "Shemon is our liberator. He will set the House of Israel in order. He will bring glory and redemption to our land. He is a star in the firmament of Jacob. He is a star in the constellation of David; hence, the scion of a star. And so his name shall henceforth be BAR-KOKBA, Prince in Israel!"

"Bar-Kokba! Bar-Kokba! Long live Bar-Kokba!" stormed the crowd lustily.

The rabbi gestured to Shemon. "Ascend, Bar-Kokba."

Slowly, reluctantly, Shemon came up. Through a haze, he heard Akiba's solemn voice continue: "On this first day of Passover in the year three thousand eight hundred and ninety-three we, the people of Israel, assembled in the Valley of Rimmon, have named thee Bar-Kokba, Son of a Star, Prince in Israel, by virtue of thy heroism and leadership and thy descent from the House of David. In the days of yore we anointed our princes with sacred oil, whence the name *Moshiah*—Messiah—is derived. Thy anointment will take place when the whole of our land has been redeemed and our Holy Temple rebuilt. Then thou wilt be our truly anointed prince and liberator, our Messianic king."

"Bar-Kokba!" roared the crowd. "Bar-Kokba! Our Messiah!"

This time protests came with the cheers. They came from some visitors, from soldiers and from the circle of notables about the platform. Of the protesting voices that of Rabbi Johanan ben-Torta was the loudest. "Sacrilege, sacrilege!" he shouted. "Thou takest too much upon thyself, Akiba ben-Joseph. Grass will sooner grow on thy chin, Akiba, than the Messiah make his appearance!"

Hagarsi hushed Ben-Torta, but in the crowd someone was yelling, "No Messiah can come before the Prophet Elijah descends from Heaven to herald him!"

"Every great Jewish king was a Messiah because of his anointment!" thundered Akiba in rebuttal.

But the noise was growing. Now Malanos and other members of his sect made themselves heard: "There is only one Messiah, and he has arisen from the dead. Jesus Christ is his name."

Shemon threw back his festive blue robe and gestured for silence with his long arms. "Our great master, Rabbi Akiba, spoke to you of unity. Is this how you strive for it? Will you fight each other rather than your mortal foe? And over what? A word? You have heard him say that there is our war to be won and our House of Israel to be set in order. Can this be accomplished without leadership? If you do not want me as a leader, I will fight with you and be as one of you and take commands from whomever you choose. Leaderless, you will perish. So name your choice now!"

"Bar-Kokba! Bar-Kokba! Lead us to victory! Long live Bar-Kokba, Prince in Israel!" The acclamation rolled on in stormy waves, unbroken by dissenting voices.

"Remember, I am one of you. I have no aim in life other than to give our land freedom. Let our great rabbis resolve, in calm deliberation at the proper time and place, their differences on the question of the Messiah. I do not lay claim to the title, and I respectfully ask that no one lay any such claim for me. You have honored me with authority enough to fulfill my duty. Let us, therefore, give thought to the task of driving the enemy from our land forever. And let the House of Israel be united and made ready for the true Messiah."

Again the Christians protested; this time it was not Malanos whose voice rose above the rest, but one of the newcomers, Khadi, a lean, swarthy, gaunt man of the fanatical-dervish type. His expostulations and threats to leave were repeated again and again until Bar-Kokba lost his patience. "Let those who wish to go—go! No one will molest them. But let them keep their tongues and hold their peace, for the fate of a nation is at stake. Woe unto those who are caught dealing with the enemy! Whoever wishes to go—go now."

Malanos rushed to Khadi to dissuade him from leaving, but in vain. He and a handful of his supporters elbowed their way through the jeering crowd and disappeared.

All eyes were again fixed on Bar-Kokba. And in the great silence his voice fell clear and sharp: "Now our thoughts must turn to Jerusalem."

"To Jerusalem! Onward to Jerusalem! Lead us, Bar-Kokba!" clamored the multitude, gesticulating, shaking fists, brandishing swords.

Rabbi Akiba and Eliezer of Modin raised their hands in benediction. Their pious words were drowned out in the frenzied roar of the crowd, which rushed onto the platform, lifted Shemon onto its shoulders and, singing and dancing, carried him to his hut.

Chapter Thirty-four

The circumcision festivities lasted until the end of Passover.

Meredya rejoiced that her son, named Elisha after Shemon's father, had come into the world "under a lucky star." "Is he not the son of the Son of a Star?" she remarked playfully. But there was pride in the words. She reminded her husband of the evening on the plateau opposite the Bowl, when she had predicted that the brilliant star trailing the orange moon was his star. "Does not the Almighty reveal things to people in His own grand way?" she asked. "If they believe in Him," Shemon agreed.

Bar-Kokba's nimble mind swarmed with schemes. They went beyond the liberation of Jerusalem, of which he was certain. He could not yet risk withdrawing sufficient forces from Galilee to lay siege to the city, but few of the supply-carrying caravans reached it. His detachments were everywhere and struck mercilessly at everything foreign that dared take to the road north of Gaza. This warfare of attrition would eventually force the garrison to surrender or to venture out into the open and accept battle on terms favorable to the Israelites. It would never be too late, though it would undoubtedly prove costlier, to take Roman Jerusalem by storm. The underground passage which had helped to defeat Hadrian's construction plans would also be of incalculable value in seizing the fort.

Bar-Kokba's thoughts traveled beyond the immediate future. What if somehow fortune should turn against him? Or if, in the course of time, another nation should attack Jerusalem? It would take many years and staggering amounts of gold to make the capital impregnable. More walls—and more powerful ones than before—would have to be erected over a miles-long perimeter, for had not those which had been deemed invulnerable fallen? If a height more favorable than Jerusalem for fortification, and central enough to protect the capital as well as the most valuable region of Judea, could be found, that height should be fortified without delay.

During Bar-Kokba's recent inspection of Judea, Betar had impressed him as answering these requirements. The town was perched on a mountain three thousand feet high. Situated only seven miles southwest of Jerusalem, the mountain commanded all roads north and south and was a more formidable protection for Southern Judea than was the Holy City. Parts of a wall erected many years before by Herod were still intact, testifying to the fact that the ground was suitable and that a king who had a flare for building had also chosen the site as a fortress. To make doubly sure, and to establish what it would cost and how long it would take to erect the type of citadel he visualized, Bar-Kokba requested Nitsa to send him a trustworthy and able architect. Bar-Kokba also asked for Asaph, the Betarian, who might act as their guide.

And so, shortly after Passover, the architect, Bar-Kokba and young Asaph roamed the environs of Betar. The town, in addition to gardening and sheep breeding, was known for the manufacture of the inexpensive blanket-like upper garment known as a *palnis*, the prototype of the Roman *paenula* commonly worn by the poorer classes. There were as many as eighty workshops for this manufacture in Betar. The Betarians, too, could be fully relied upon not to betray any building operations that might be initiated while the Romans were still in Jerusalem. They would be loyal not only for patriotic reasons, but also because of the glory a fortress would bring to their obscure town.

All conditions but one favored Betar as the site for the stronghold. The drawback was an inadequate supply of water. There was only one well with an abundant water supply, and it lay in the lower reaches of the hill. A fresh-water spring, high on the steep side of the mountain, was neither adequate nor readily accessible. The bulk of the townspeople saved up rain-water in cisterns; in the arid weeks they were compelled to go down to the well below and, if that dried up, to even more distant streams, of which there were three in the surrounding dales. After careful examination of the soil the architect under-took to dig a tunnel to the spring. A tunnel to the well below was not feasible. Although the water problem had not been settled to Shemon's complete satisfaction, the construction of the fortress was decided upon. Asaph, familiar with every nook and cranny in the surrounding country, was directed to remain in Betar.

In the months that followed, the People's Council prepared the country for self-government while Shemon destroyed or forced the capitulation of Roman strongholds. Jotapata, in the north; Apollonia, in the Plain of Sharon; Emmaus, in the Judean Hills—these fell one after another. Shemon's fame and prestige rose to great heights and aid came from near and distant lands. Ever growing support in gold and products arrived from Alexandria, and among the donors were Israelites hitherto cold or hostile to the rebels. It was said that these Alexandrians had also sent a delegation to Rome to offer a compromise, although no one in Israel had authorized them to do so and the nature of the compromise was unknown.

After the fall of Emmaus, Nitsa went to see Saturnius.

"Shemon will wait no longer," he said. "You must decide within twenty-four hours or be destroyed with your men. Sorry as I am, there is nothing I can do. . . . "

Aged and miserable, the centurion stared at the floor. "I have never surrendered in my life," he said hollowly.

"Your death and the death of your men will not help your empire. If you live, you can still serve your country, and that, you must understand, is against Bar-Kokba's interests. The fewer the men serving Rome, the more secure are those who fight her."

"Will he allow us to take our standards with us?"

"No. The display of images is objectionable to us. All you will be allowed to take are your short swords and a supply of food. What is your decision?"

"We will go to Gaza," groaned Saturnius, "and will be ready at sundown."

Chapter Thirty-five

The fields had been harvested, more men were ready to serve than Shemon could train and equip, and the cry "Onward to Jerusalem!" echoed and re-echoed throughout the land.

Shemon was about to yield to the popular demand, when six cohorts of the Jerusalem garrison, undernourished, irked by inactivity and despairing of being relieved, mutinied against their prefect and struck out south of the ancient city. Over bad but unguarded roads, pillaging and murdering as they went, they crossed the Jordan below Jericho and marched through the desert toward Egypt, reversing the route of the early Israelites. Bar-Kokba was elated. His judgment had been correct. Time had proven an ally. Now he would dispose of the remnant of the Jerusalem garrison with few losses to his army.

Just then word reached him that preparations for an invasion had been completed at Antioch and that an army of four legions and their auxiliaries would strike from two directions. Marching in a body to the confluence of four other streams with the Jordan, the invading forces would separate into two armies. One, under

Lolios Urbicius, the Imperial Legate of Syria, would attack through Transjordan, while Rufus would cross the Jordan high in the north and invade Galilee.

Acting swiftly, Bar-Kokba gathered his best-trained and best-equipped units in the vicinity of Gamala in Transjordan, sent his less-experienced units to man the seaports and requested Zevulun to be ready to meet a possible invasion from the sea. Having secured his western flank, Bar-Kokba, despite the midsummer heat, marched at high speed to Caesarea Philippi and occupied advantageous positions in the Mount Hermon range, where the hills rose from three to eight thousand feet in height. Below, passes led through narrow ravines and gullies, perilous to invaders.

Here, on the summit of a mountain overlooking the city, Bar-Kokba made his headquarters. For miles in every direction he could see the far-flung, tortuous highways and byways and the treacherous passes through which the enemy was to come, and the terrain on which the early history of his people had been inscribed.

To the south lay his own glorious land; to the north, the country from which the patriarch Abraham had come. This very mountain Moses had conquered. Yet the western side of its summit was marred by a challenge to Moses. There a huge statue of a rooster, a war deity, arrogantly cocking its head, stood above a palace of white marble, a gift from Herod to Caesar, a symbol of subservience. But no compromising hand could alter the mountainside below the idol. Grim and steep, it fell precipitously into a deep chasm where a dark pool of water lay silent and mysterious. From its unfathomable depths the water flowed through subterranean arteries which, finally bursting to the surface, became the fountainhead of the Jordan. From there the river headed south into Lake Kinnereth. On its banks, as on the shores of the lake, towns and hamlets, walled and unwalled, nestled amid fruit trees and flowers. In those habitations, as in the hills in the background, lawgivers and seers had lived and died, and prophets of peace had trudged their dreary, often martyred way. They had preached and presaged, but had brought no peace. Would it be given to him, Bar-Kokba, to bring that precious gift?

Before the first day of their encampment was gone, some of his officers and men approached him with the request to be allowed to destroy the abominable rooster.

Bar-Kokba laughed. "Would you undo that which will help you win?" he chuckled. "Whatever may have been the reason for the presence of this rooster here," Bar-Kokba continued, "it will now be an instrument for victory in our great God's hands."

The men were puzzled.

"This image," Bar-Kokba explained, "is the god and guide of our enemies. To destroy it means to forewarn them of our presence and to keep them out of the snare we have laid for them. You will do with the idol what you please after the battle."

Providentially, the battle came on a moonless night. So sudden, swift and devastating was the attack that the enemy, crowded into narrow passages between towering mountain walls, had no opportunity of organizing resistance. Immense boulders crashed down upon them from invisible heights, and burning lumps of tar added to the havoc. Exits and entrances seemed blocked by mad devils on horseback. Where stones were not falling, men possessed by implacable hate, shouting war cries and names of kin and places destroyed by the enemy, charged from the mountainsides. Nor was that all. Bar-Kokba had taught the Roman signals to his buglers and now they were confusing the Romans into slaughtering one another. Thousands of dead were left in the passes as Rufus and Urbicius fled with their battered forces; and a huge amount of booty, including horses, fell into the hands of the Israelites.

Jubilantly they turned and swept through the country to Judea, and thence on to Jerusalem. In three days the demoralized and starved remnant of the Roman garrison was destroyed and Bar-Kokba, now the unchallenged Prince in Israel, entered the ancient capital of Israel in triumph.

With Meredya, moist-eyed with emotion, riding proudly beside him on a captured horse, he responded warmly to the cheering throngs. To honor those who had aided him in abducting Achillas and destroying the statues, he took the route he had followed that night, lining up his vanguard on the highway at Kiryat Yaarim. There Levites in white—trumpeters, drummers, lutists and singers—rendered praise to the Lord and to the brave and faithful sons of Israel. Sons of Kiryat Yaarim had distinguished themselves, and foremost among them was Elhanan the blacksmith, now commander of one hundred men. The elders and the inhabitants of the village, in their Sabbath finery, listened gratefully and proudly.

Coming from the west, the procession went downhill to the southern gate of the now-broken Roman wall and through the Lower Market, and then headed north, going up and up on Via Principalis until it reached Via Praetoria, where it turned east and went on and on to the ruins of the Golden Gate. There the priests, led by Eliezer of Modin, blessed the multitudes, the Levites chanted a hymn, and only the commanders and men of consequence accompanied Shemon and Meredya to the Mount of Olives, where they were to reside.

Many men and women from the surrounding villages had come to the Holy City to see their liberator, and now, upon beholding him, shouted with the Jerusalemites: "Long live Bar-Kokba! Long live our prince!" and also the most popular slogan of the revolt: "David, King of Israel, lives and endures!"

For a week the country was mad with joy. Huge bonfires were kindled on the hill crests of Jerusalem and on hundreds of summits throughout the land. Elements of Zevulun's fleet lay decorated in the main ports and were illuminated at night. Mass ceremonies of thanksgiving and processions carrying the holy scrolls were visible everywhere. In the capital a provisional altar of unhewn stone blocks was erected on Mount Zion and old Eliezer, in the sacerdotal robes of a high priest, in the presence of the army and a mass of pilgrims, offered an oblation of gratitude. At last the people were free to worship God as they saw fit and to mold and remold their lives.

Bar-Kokba found few Israelites living in Jerusalem, for more than one reason: They had been banned from the city some time before; later, when the ban had been lifted, they had been frowned upon by the other inhabitants. Most of their dwellings had been sacked by Titus and the government had not encouraged reconstruction. Foreigners and heathens—predominantly Roman reservists and adventurous Greeks from Egypt,

Syria, Cyprus and elsewhere in the Near East—had attempted to colonize the city and its surroundings and to lay their hands on whatever easy spoils or crumbs of spoils filtered through the fingers of the Roman officials. The colonists had been hostile and overbearing, and their arrogance had found expression not merely in offensive acts and language, but also in crimes, for which, as a rule, there had been scant redress. The sight of the glory that had been Jerusalem lying in ruins, its holy places repeatedly defiled, had been unendurable to most of the Israelites. While they had come periodically to mourn and lament, they had not been able to bear to live there. And so, few had remained in their own capital, and these few were divided by wide social gaps. They lived either on the upper or on the lower rungs of the ladder—there were no intervening rungs. Those in the lower strata were in the meaner trades and occupations— they were barbers, cuppers, shopkeepers, bathkeepers, ass and camel drivers, peddlers. Beggars, though alms were scant, were still in evidence; so were dream interpreters. The few in the upper strata belonged to ancient families whose possessions had shrunk but not entirely disappeared. Their wealth, part of which had been passed on periodically in bribes to Roman officials, had made their lives in Jerusalem bearable.

Of these, a descendant of the House of Abtinas, dealers in incense, turned over to Bar-Kokba his palatial mansion on the Mount of Olives. The mansion became the seat of the government, and here, too, Meredya and their infant son, Elisha, were installed. Part of Meredya's daydream had come true. From her lofty windows she could see in the bright sunlight the incomparable scenic design of hills, valleys, fields, streams and deserts extending to the banks of the Jordan and the Dead Sea; this colorful panorama made the desolation and the sight of vestiges of vanished glory more endurable.

Before long, suitable quarters on the slope of the Mount of Olives were found for Rabbi Akiba, Eliezer, Abner, Elon and other members of the government. At the recommendation of Akiba, who divided his time between Jerusalem and Bnai Brak, a government mint was established and new coins were struck. On the obverse side the first coin bore a palm tree with the words

SHEMON, PRINCE IN ISRAEL, and on the reverse, a vine and the date FIRST YEAR OF LIBERATION.

Shemon and Meredya were playing with little Elisha when Eliezer of Modin was announced.

The prince hastened out of the bedroom and into the huge, luxurious reception room. "What brings my venerable uncle to me this warm afternoon?" he asked amiably. "Will my uncle take a refreshing drink?"

The priest rose from a sumptuous couch, and with quick, short steps, too quick for a man of his age and temperament, approached his nephew and thrust a parchment into his hand.

"What is it?" demanded Shemon, sensing agitation in Eliezer's unusual conduct.

The old man's eyes were aglow with anger and his hands shook. "Read it," he said brusquely. "Read it and see for yourself."

Bar-Kokba unfolded the parchment. "An epistle to Hadrian!" he exclaimed, and read on rapidly. The old man sat.

"The snakes!" Shemon cried out bitterly, and went stamping up and down. "The snakes in our bosoms! Ha!" The "Ha!" was a bark rather than a laugh. "Ha, ha! They no longer have anything to do with us or with our faith. They seek the protection of just and man-loving Edom, whose legions, as is well known, are ever ready to help the downtrodden peoples. Fools! Sons of Belial!" He paused in front of Eliezer. "And what would my uncle call these serpents in our midst?"

"Traitors, Shemon, traitors."

Bar-Kokba reread the parchment. "It was written before we took Jerusalem," he said more calmly, "and it is marked *Copy*. Is it known with certainty that Hadrian received the epistle?"

"It is," Eliezer declared emphatically.

"The cowards! The cowards!" Shemon flung the parchment on a low olivewood table. "Who are they, this Quadratus and this Aristides? Are they foreigners or Israelites with foreign names?"

"They are foreigners, Shemon. Nazarenes of Greco-Syrian descent. Uncircumcised. Swine-eaters. They never were true believers. Neither they nor their forbears."

"If so, what are they doing in the Holy City?"

"It is the city where the one they believe to be their Messiah found his death. They thought Jerusalem would never again be in Israelite hands. They have been against you, Shemon, since Akiba proclaimed you the Messianic king. And now that you have proven them wrong, they hate you all the more."

For a time Bar-Kokba paced the room in silence. Then, facing Eliezer, he asked, "How did the parchment come into my uncle's possession?"

"One of my men came upon Khadi—do you remember him, the one who would not stay with us in the Valley of Rimmon? The man followed Khadi to Quadratus' dwelling place and watched the house. When no one was in it he searched it." Eliezer glanced at his nephew and said firmly, "There can be no doubt about this writing. It was sent and delivered to the emperor. I have inquired into the matter."

"If so, would my uncle tell me whether the whole Nazarene congregation is of one mind with Quadratus and Aristides?"

"As far as I know, Shemon, it is so."

"Since the punishment must be severe, I think it would be best to inquire further into the matter."

The next day Shemon sent for Malanos and commanded him to investigate and to deliver the leading offenders for interrogation. When the Christian confirmed Eliezer's findings and reported that the main offenders had fled, Bar-Kokba posed a straightforward question: "Did you, Malanos, know of this epistle before I sent for you?"

"Only vague rumors reached me in Galilee. I was too far away to know." Malanos paused, and then added with deep sincerity, "That protection of Nazarenes could be sought from crucifiers was unbelievable."

Bar-Kokba was satisfied and posed another question: "What, Malanos, would you do if you were in my place?"

Malanos' honest countenance grew tense. His predicament was great. It was hard to speak against men of his own faith and it was impossible for him to speak falsely. He wavered for a long time, and in the end his integrity won. "They did not believe in you and in your people," he said with deliberation, "and sought the rule of the heathen. Now, then, let them go to the heathen."

"So be it," decided Bar-Kokba. And thus it came to pass that the Nazarenes of Jerusalem were banished to Transjordan.

Demands to commence the reconstruction of the Holy City and the restoration of the Temple became more persistent from day to day. They came from Eliezer of Modin, rabbis, members of priestly and Levite families and men interested in reviving trade and production, and from pilgrims. Among the most fervent pleaders for reconstruction was Simeon bar-Johai. To him, Bar-Kokba's victories, though he did not underestimate their importance, were no more than a narrow and bloody preface to the restoration of the glory and holiness of the Temple. To all these pleas Shemon had one reply: "Not yet. But with God's help, in His own good time."

Bar-Kokba did not treat the matter lightly. It was constantly on his mind. Early in the morning and, at times, after sunset he wandered through the ruins of the city and over the grounds of the desolated shrine. He pondered, planned, calculated. Often he would be carried away by emotion and conjure up visions of the splendor and magnificence that were no more: The domes covered with solid gold. The white marble, a mirage of snow-capped mountain peaks bathed in sunlight. The silver doors and marble courts. The beautiful cloisters. The mighty turrets and the walls that encompassed the city for eight miles. All that had been the handiwork of generations of faith, love and genius. How could such an edifice and such fortifications be restored in haste? The removal of the ruins should perhaps be attempted . . . but even that was a stupendous task.

Amid the piled-up blocks of stone he found a chunk of solid gold one day, and brought it to Meredya. "This is from a Temple dome," he told her. She held it with trembling hands, then pressed it to her bosom. "Keep it," he said. "Some day you may donate it for the rebuilding of the Temple."

"When will that be?"

"I know not. If God wills it, we may start four years from the day we entered Jerusalem?"

"Why so long?"

"We must be sure, pleasure of my heart. Our peace is but a

lull in the war. The enemy gathers his forces; he leaves and comes; he is driven out and returns. It took Vespasian and Titus four years to reconquer the land. If that does not happen within the next four years, we may take it as a sign that we are really free, that the Almighty has relented and that He will again reside in our Holy of Holies."

"But can you not clear the stones in the meantime? When I look at them and see above them Herod's three towers that Titus the Wicked deliberately left standing to torment us, I mourn. The ruins give me no peace."

Shemon took her in his arms. "We will begin tomorrow. I remember what you once said about the stones crying out for salvation. With God's help we will give them life. They will live in the walls of our new fortress, Betar."

She kissed him.

That week a thousand men began the arduous task. With infinite patience they dislodged the undamaged blocks and carried them on their shoulders or in their arms for seven miles to Betar. These stones were too sacred to be placed on the backs of animals. Their way led them past Rachel's tomb. There they would halt to chant, "Mother Rachel, Mother Rachel, pray for us; bless these stones! May no enemy overcome them."

Chapter Thirty-six

The disastrous rout of Urbicius and Rufus shocked Rome and aroused the senate and the emperor. Demands that the pernicious Judeans be taught a memorable lesson became loud and persistent. Old slanders were unearthed and magnified. The bitterness was directed against the God and customs of the Israelites rather than against their stinging rebellion. Rebellions of conquered peoples were nothing new to the Roman senate, but the spread of a theistic philosophy that was beginning to take root in Rome itself and threatened her civilization was something else, and had to be suppressed with determination. Vilifications successfully inveighed against the Hebrews in the past by authorities already defunct, such as Senator Lucius Annaeus Seneca and the historian Tacitus, were revived and widely quoted.

"They refuse to worship the emperor. They mutilate their bodies. They let their fields lie fallow every seven years. They even deny to parents the right to dispose of their own flesh and blood as they please," raged Senator Alfenius. "To quote Tacitus:" he cried, " 'It is a crime among them to kill any newborn infants.' Unheard of! We must put an end to the peril that this barbarous, narrow-minded people presents to our established customs. They are bad to the core, but their badness attracts the lowly. I again quote from Tacitus: 'All the Judean customs that are at once perverse and disgusting owe their strength to their very badness. The most degraded out of other races, scorning their own national beliefs, brought to the Judeans their contributions and gifts.' "

Alfenius expressed the sentiments of the senate. That revenue should be contributed by foreigners voluntarily and not exacted by force was an intolerable thought and a danger to the empire. The principle of enforced rest from work, particularly one whole day's rest every week, was even more disturbing. Rest might corrupt the toilers and make inroads into the profits of the greedy. "The Sabbath is responsible for the waste of one-seventh of the working life of man." These words had been spoken by Seneca some decades before, and now they were brought to life again. "The customs of this criminal nation," he had asserted, "are gaining ground so rapidly that they already have adherents in every country; thus the conquered force their laws upon the conqueror."

Fear of the moral force of the conquered was the real cause of the clamor. Hence nothing but the complete extermination of the bearers of this moral force would satisfy the senate. That august body was all the more vociferous because Hadrian shared its views. The course to be pursued was clear. All that had to be determined was whether the punitive expedition should be entrusted to a general or led by His Divine Majesty himself. The emperor chose Caius Publius Marcellus, a loyal veteran of many wars. But when all preparations had been completed, Hadrian, beset by misgivings as to the state of affairs in Antioch itself, decided to join the expedition.

Ruffina reached Rome at the height of the anti-Judean storm. Undaunted, she broached the subject of her mission to influential friends. They discouraged her; nevertheless, she approached the emperor. When he heard the purpose of her visit, he forbade her to mention the matter again. Through Judith she made contact with some local Israelites. They appeared to be dismayed rather than gratified by her interest. In view of the rage against their coreligionists in the Holy Land, they deemed it hazardous to project themselves into the situation. Reticence, they felt, was the more judicious course. She could not understand this attitude.

Later the Alexandrian delegation sought her out. Having come all the way from Egypt, they could not be content merely to wait. But they had been unable to make headway; even their friends among the senators had refused to see them. Ruffina was their last resort. She listened to them and promised to lay the matter before the emperor at the first opportunity. With that, they returned to Alexandria. In the course of the succeeding months she, at the risk of arousing the emperor's displeasure, again and again sought to see him, but to no avail. Finally, at a reception given in his honor shortly before his departure for Syria, she managed to speak to him, but she did not go beyond requesting permission to be included in his entourage. Since her husband was still in Antioch, her request was granted.

It took many months to bring the preparations for reinvading the Holy Land to their last stages. Two crack legions were brought from Italy and one from Cyprus; and out of the forces in Cilicia and Antioch, at least two more legions were being brushed up for the drive. The armada which escorted the emperor to Seleucia, the port of Antioch, twenty-one miles west of the Syrian capital, was also scheduled to participate. The campaign was being planned carefully.

The day of retaliation was at hand—so thought Hadrian as

he stood atop his palace in the heart of Antioch. The large roof was sheltered by latticework that was supported by carved wooden columns inlaid with gold. Vines creeping over the shelter, palms in huge gilded vases, a fountain of black marble, flower beds, graveled walks and soft couches, gave the roof the appearance, shade and scents of a garden and the restfulness of a bower.

The emperor had just dismissed Marcellus and was waiting for Ruffina. He was well disposed. The general had pleased him. He had appeared to have good sense. He would not repeat the errors of Rufus and Urbicius. He would surely clean up the mess. Hadrian came close to the parapet. The afternoon sun was mild and soothing; the crowds below, colorful and gay. The interview with Marcellus had taken less time than he had expected and there were a few minutes to while away.

He looked down. Four members of his Praetorian Guard, erect and good to behold, their helmets and unsheathed swords glistening in the sun, stood on each side of an ompholos on which Apollo, lyre in hand, was seated. The statue dominated the marble-paved square, from which far-flung colonnaded avenues ran in several directions. Its back was turned to the senate house and the museum, which faced the forum across the street. The basilicae on the fourth corner housed the hall of justice and chambers for public assembly. The avenues were lined with two- and three-story buildings and shops, intermingled with temples, baths and sport palaces. Pedestrians in costumes from many lands, gaily decked litters, military and civilian horsemen and chariots moved in an unceasing stream. At this hour traffic was densest at the south end of the avenue, where crowds filing out of the theater and the amphitheater on the slopes of the Silpian Hill were heading north. Moving down the avenue, they turned into numerous intersections running east and west toward the outer walls of the city. These turreted walls, with hundreds of towers, climbed up and down the hills of the Casian range. They looked down upon a rich alluvial plain washed by the magnificent Orontes and its torrential tributaries, Parmenius and Phryminus.

Hadrian was fascinated by the frothing Parmenius as it crashed down from the steep eastern hill slopes and across the

Iron Gate viaduct to the south and spilled its waters into the city to join its mother stream. Sated, the emperor glanced north, past the elaborate Bridge Gate, and marveled at the beauty of the White Lake, which, like a huge pearl set in silver bars, hung above the isle of the extinct Seleucian dynasty. If there were no Rome, Antioch would be the ideal seat for an emperor.

But now boredom was creeping up. Hadrian's large, bold eyes narrowed, his perfectly arched eyebrows contracted and he yawned. He was about to move away when his glance caught a rich litter adorned with a patrician emblem. The litter, carried by four black slaves, was approaching the ompholos. As it came close to the palace he recognized the symbols of Ruffina's house.

Presently an officer of the guard announced the lady. The emperor received her cordially, even jovially; he complimented her on her charm and attire and offered her a cooling drink. For a while the conversation centered on pleasant trifles. Then cautiously he mentioned her husband. Had she seen him lately? Did she intend to see him? Her blunt "No," though tempered by a ravishing smile, indicated her sentiments. He had not yet decided what to do with Rufus, so he did not press the point. It was now up to her to state the object of her visit. He waited.

Ruffina understood, smiled bewitchingly and said, "Will Your Majesty allow a lady who adores her emperor and who is deeply concerned about the welfare of his empire to transgress just once?"

"Transgress?" The wide nostrils of his strong, straight nose distended, his sensuous mouth opened and he laughed. "Transgress?" he repeated, and took her hands. "What do you mean?"

"Transgress your orders for Your Majesty's sake," she replied, and gently withdrew her hands.

"You are quite mysterious, my dear. Be more explicit."

"Thank you, Your Majesty," she said, and paused to formulate her thoughts. "Your Majesty, before more Roman soldiers are killed and—how shall I put it?—more misery inflicted on a small but extremely stubborn nation, I would like to tell you of a visit of a group of people to me before our departure from Rome."

He frowned. "Confounded Judeans, I suppose. Now I recall.

I forbade you to mention their obnoxious name, did I not?"

"But Your Majesty has given me permission now. Just this once."

"I have not," he said uncertainly. She pouted while her eyes pleaded. He softened. "You are a sorceress," he said. "Speak."

Now she was on surer ground and spoke unhestitatingly. "The delegation came from Alexandria. No one in Rome would see them. They are loyal to Your Majesty, would not like to see your empire lose any of her benefits and certainly not her dignity. Naturally, they would like, if possible, to prevent the complete destruction of a land holy to them."

Hadrian rubbed his cropped blond beard impatiently and frowned again. "Holy! A good word for scoundrels to lean on. I do not trust any of them."

"Divine Caesars," she cajoled, "need neither trust nor mistrust people. They are sagacious enough to know, powerful enough to be just."

He liked the flattery. "I suppose I must listen to the end," he sighed with simulated resignation, "if for no other reason than to be gracious to you."

She rewarded him with a grateful smile and resumed: "The trouble in Judea, the delegation asserted, always comes from hasty decisions by procurators and the presence of too many troops. The army is sent to assure a certain amount of revenue and certain products for the empire. Recently, they said, Your Majesty was interested in the bitumen of the Dead Sea. The Alexandrians said they would undertake to induce their people in Judea to pay the revenue as heretofore and send the necessary products on condition that our army is kept out of Judea and that only a procurator with a small police guard resides in the country. Rome would have what is due her and the Judeans their freedom."

"No," snapped Hadrian.

"But is not such an arrangement preferable to a new and costly war?"

"No," he repeated, a glint of cold hatred in his eyes. "The Judean revenue is now of little moment. They have killed Romans and have defied me and our gods. They stubbornly insist that their ways and their God are best. This cannot be tolerated. We have punished them many times, but they do not change. If we are lenient with them, the whole empire will soon be torn by revolts. We must wipe them out."

"But what if their God should interfere with Your Majesty's plans?"

He flushed. "Do you realize, Ruffina, what you are saying?"

"I mean no offense, Your Majesty. I am distressed. Their God has shown His anger. He has shaken the earth and destroyed our fortresses. We have lost many men. I am in mortal fear. How can we tell what this invulnerable God may do to us?"

"Stop," he interrupted angrily. "Enough. You are a superstitious woman. Earthquakes occur everywhere." He rose, and added a little less harshly, "You are also a charming woman. If you wish to enjoy the influence which is rightfully yours, do not meddle in matters which do not concern women. I may wish to see you again after I have settled my most important affairs here." He nodded.

Her eyes welled. She whispered, "Thank you," gathered up her palla and hurried out.

She had failed, but her failure had taught her something. She had discovered *the irreconcilability of Rome and Jerusalem.* She had heard that very expression from Akiba. But merely hearing it had not been enough. She herself had had to become part of the struggle in order to grasp its full significance. Now she understood. Now she realized that here was more than a clash of physical forces. Here was a clash of two ideas so incompatible that one of them was bound to perish. The people upholding the idea of God was physically the weaker; it would be the one to perish. That was an unbearable thought. In her heart she had accepted God. How could she calmly stand by and allow those who supported the God-idea to perish? She did not feel strong enough to align herself openly with them. If she had a man like Akiba to lean on, it would be easier; but he was unattainable. How could she possibly remain passive? But what effective help could she render?

She discussed her dilemma with Judith, sought the advice of a local synagogue president and finally decided that she could not go beyond keeping the Israelites informed as to what was transpiring at Antioch. To put this plan into effect she dispatched Judith to Rabbi Akiba.

Chapter Thirty-seven

While Hadrian was preparing for assault, Bar-Kokba was preparing for defense. In the course of the year that had elapsed since the Roman rout, he had fortified several hundred towns and villages in Galilee and Samaria. Their defenses could impede an enemy's progress but were not strong enough for serious resistance. Nevertheless, in the event of a sudden break-through these towns could be relied upon to hold out long enough to complete the fortification of a few real strongholds. Of the major strongholds, the Har Hamalek citadel was one.

While progress in fortifying the country had been made, the numerical strength of the defenders had temporarily diminished. Fallow fields, neglected vineyards, destroyed villages and seasonal crops had demanded hands; so tens of thousands of workers had gone back to their peacetime pursuits. The backbone of the army, however, remained sound. The veterans of the early battles had practically all stayed and the Heromavs continued to draw volunteers from Rabbi Akiba's disciples.

Upon reaching the Holy Land and observing the surprising changes that had taken place, Judith decided that it was preferable to see Shemon. She was told to proceed to Har Hamelek. There the dedication of a new wall and towers, named "Tur Shemon" in Bar-Kokba's honor, had just taken place, and he was most likely to be found there.

At the village she learned that none but the military and bearers of special passes were admitted. Even the villagers were not allowed inside the fort. Judith was in a dilemma. She might seek aid from Nadav at Caesarea or go to Bnai Brak after all, but either course would entail a loss of time. She decided to try her luck with the guard. Bringing her donkey close to a gate of the citadel, she called out, "Watchman, if you have God in your heart, you will see that Bar-Kokba is told that Judith of Caesarea prays to see him."

"Many wenches crave to see the prince; he sees no one."

She was hurt. "I am no wench, watchman. I have come all the way from Antioch with an important message. I must see Bar-Kokba."

"Fair to look at and fairy tales, eh?" joshed the sentry.

"You annoy me, man. See you not by my dusty clothes and donkey that I come from afar? Please tell Bar-Kokba or a headman. Tell him that Judith of Caesarea, who once saw him with Ovadya, wishes to speak with him."

"Ovadya of Caesarea? Never heard of him." He temporized, scratching his head, but finally descended into the tower. Reappearing in a little while, he said, "Wait."

Presently two armed men admitted her into a large, high-ceilinged chamber, from which steps hewn in the outer wall led into the tower. There they questioned her at some length, asked her to sit, secured the donkey to an iron hook in the wall and departed.

After a considerable wait a tall, handsome young man in a flowing black robe appeared. He glanced at her dusty dark-blue linen cloak and sandals, then at the long silk kerchief that failed to hide her curls, greeted her cordially and introduced himself. "I am Bar-Daroma, the commander of the citadel. What brings you here?"

"Bar-Daroma?" she asked in surprise, and stared at him incredulously.

"What is it, Judith? Have I frightened you?"

"No . . . yes," she stammered. "Bar-Daroma has been dead for sixteen or seventeen years. I was told he died defending this very mountain."

He smiled sadly. "It is so. Bar-Kokba told me about it. He named me after Bar-Daroma so that his name might live. I came from Alexandria bearing a Greek name."

"Oh," Judith sighed in relief. "It was strange to hear the name. I hope you will be luckier than the other Bar-Daroma."

"Thank you. To come back to—"

"Forgive me," she said uncertainly, still wavering. "Forgive

me if I still prefer—without meaning to offend—to see Shemon—
I mean Bar-Kokba. I bring him a grave message."

"You will not be able to see him unless I decide that the
message is important enough."

She saw the futility of further insistence. "I was sent by
Ruffina, Tyrannus' wife. It concerns another attack by the
Edomites."

"Oh. And how did you come to Ruffina?"

"She took me to Rome as her personal attendant."

"And Bar-Kokba knows you?"

"I spoke to him once, before the fall of Caesarea."

"Come with me." He took her through a narrow circular
alley into another chamber, similar to the one she had left, and
asked her to wait. She had just managed to shake the dust out
of her dress and to adjust her kerchief when Bar-Daroma returned
with Shemon. Her heart seemed to stand still when she saw him.
Well-groomed and confident, he was a picture of commanding
power.

"I remember you," he said, and seated himself on a stone
bench beside her. "You are a brave woman to travel all the way
from Antioch alone."

She caught her breath. "I traveled with a caravan. I was
dressed as a man and changed at Gamala. There I bought an
ass to bring me here."

"You are brave," he repeated, "and comely, too. Now speak.
Bar-Daroma may stay. If we can trust him with a fortress, we
can trust him with a secret."

She told Bar-Kokba briefly what had transpired in Rome,
how large an armada had escorted Hadrian to Antioch and what
other legions had come subsequently, and gave him the details
of Ruffina's visit to the emperor. "Ruffina's direct message is:
'Expect attack in two or three weeks. It will come by land and
sea. Land route still uncertain. Ports of landing probably Acca
and Caesarea.' "

"Judith," said Shemon, "you have rendered a service to
Israel. For this you deserve thanks. But we seldom thank each
other; the satisfaction that comes from doing one's duty is the
greatest reward. Would you serve us further?"

Her heart was aflutter with excitement. *Would* she! Aloud she said, "I have always tried to serve Israel. I will do as Bar-Kokba commands."

"Good. Rest you, then, in the village and tomorrow morning I will send two men with you to Cabul. There you will see Theodoros, a Christian, who will have received word about your coming. Tell him how to see Ruffina; what to say to her he will already know. You will then go to Gamala and wait for his messages, which you will send to me. My horsemen will come to see you daily. Confide in no one who gives you no watchword. I will give you the first watchword in the morning; new watchwords will be brought to you from time to time by the Thumbless. Is it all clear?"

"Yes, Bar-Kokba."

He rose. "Bar-Daroma, see that Judith is taken to Bathsheba's house in the village and given all she needs." He turned to her. "No woman ever stays in this fort. Until the morning, Judith."

"Until the morning, Bar-Kokba." And in her mind she added, ". . . Prince in Israel."

When she had gone, Bar-Kokba went into action at once. He had Ayalah saddled and raced at top speed for Cabul, arriving there before sundown. Theodoros was now sharing the command of the town with Ben-Dov, the Heromav, who had taken over from Elon, who had been called to Jerusalem.

Bar-Kokba found Theodoros inspecting the fort stables. He turned his mare over to a stableboy, freshened himself up at the well and called Theodoros out. "Let us go up to your room," he said. "I have something important to discuss."

"Theodoros, the pagans are about to strike again. We must defeat them as we did before. To know the enemy's plans and to attempt to foil them is half the battle won. We already know that the attack will come in a matter of weeks. We must know the exact time and place. Antioch is where we can find out. You told me you had friends there."

Theodoros nodded.

"I take it that they will be of help if necessary?"

Theodoros nodded again.

"Good. Will you go, then?"

Theodoros replied simply, "I will."

While they supped, Shemon gave Theodoros instructions. He then hurried on to Acca to see Zevulun. There the two friends strolled for hours along the craggy seashore, trying, as was their wont, to foresee all eventualities and to evolve counteractive schemes. At midnight Shemon was on his way to Bnai Brak. The following day a confidential call to arms was issued to the men who had gone back to their peaceful pursuits.

Chapter Thirty-eight

When he reached Antioch, Theodoros, supplied with ample funds, made his quarters in a fashionable guesthouse close to Ruffina's mansion and within easy distance of Daphne. The first two days he devoted to establishing contacts with Christians and Israelites in the upper sections of the Heracles and Iopolis quarters, where a few important congregations were located. Here he found old, reliable friends and secured a number of volunteers to carry his messages to the Holy Land, to watch military barracks and encampments and to be helpful in emergencies.

Then he visited Ruffina. He told her that Judith had delivered her message, and that she had not returned because she could be of greater service to her people by staying in her own country. The purpose of his visit to Antioch, he went on, was to obtain and transmit accurate information on military and political developments in Syria.

Despite the confidence his reserve and honest face inspired, Ruffina was wary. Hadrian might have become suspicious of her and was perhaps testing her; or Rufus, whom she persistently declined to see, might be plotting to destroy her. Knowing nothing of this Theodoros, she must be careful. Surmising her hesitancy, he submitted his credentials. They were in Hebrew and he offered to leave them with her for verification. That was agreeable. The next day she showed the credentials to the president of the Hebrew congregation to whom Judith had introduced her, and when Theodoros came again, she was communicative and candid.

After weeks of repression she again was able to discuss freely the problems that troubled her most. She no longer doubted the omnipotence and omniscience of God. What she could not understand was why He tolerated the evil and wantonness of the strong and the misery of the weak and the faithful. Salvation in the hereafter was, of course, a great comfort, but why should the wicked be allowed to reign even temporarily? Theodoros was neither a missionary nor a preacher. He could merely quote some of Christ's parables and Paul's and Peter's teachings. The story of their martyrdom only accentuated the disquietude behind Ruffina's query. She had known of their martyrdom; she knew of countless other, more recent martyrdoms. She dreaded the thought of what was to come if Hadrian prevailed. Was there not someone who might foretell the future? Were all the prophets dead?

Theorodos suggested that they go to Daphne and consult the Sibylline oracle. Ruffina declined. She knew those oracles too well. Then would she try the one *he* knew of? There were no temples or statues or dancing priestesses about this oracle. Jews and Christians congregated nightly underground to hear the "Voice of God" speak through a mortal. Ruffina agreed and they went.

From a simple, arched, unguarded entrance, steps led into a subterranean vestibule opening onto a large chamber. An eerie bluish light fell upon a multitude of men and women sitting on a carpeted floor. Upon entering, visitors deposited coins in containers on tripods, removed their sandals and rinsed their hands in basins of water provided by attendants in long white robes. Against the eastern wall there stood a closed arklike platform with an opening in the center. A silver plate, fashioned after the biblical Urim and Thummim except for its twelve slits and a loophole in the middle, had been inserted in the window. Above and below it were mystical symbols composed of ancient Hebrew characters. From the ceiling a glass eye stared down upon the ark. Two votaries, in gold-trimmed blue-silk robes and miters, stood on each side of the ark.

When the chamber was full and the door had been bolted, the votaries called upon the audience to ask their questions. The women were to address one votary; the men, the other. Some questions were about marriage, divorce, death and revenge; others, about dear ones lost in wars and travels. Most were concerned with the outcome of the war with Judea and the fate of Babylon.

"Why are they interested in Babylon?" whispered Ruffina.

"Because here 'Babylon' means 'Rome,'" replied Theodoros.

"Why?"

"Because there are pagans in the audience and one must be careful."

When all the questions had been asked, inscribed on papyrus and inserted into the slits, the eye in the ceiling flooded the ark with light. An invisible choir began to intone a weird tune and a woman's voice in a monotone gave the personal answers:

"He is dead. . . . He hath betrayed his God for the body of a heathen woman. . . . He went down with his ship. . . . Widow, wait not for thy husband's brother to marry thee, for he hath taken unto himself another woman. . . . Keep thy peace. The Almighty will revenge thee. . . . Thy dream means: Thou wilt bear a son and he will bring thee fame and fortune."

Upon the conclusion of the personal replies a shofar sounded, the blue light was extinguished and against the chanting of the unseen choir rose a dramatic voice. It grew in force or dropped to a near-whisper, it waxed passionate or quavered with sorrow, in keeping with the successive moods of the speech:

"Hear, ye men and women of the great faith, and ye who move in the paths of idolatry and sin. Ye ask what the fate of Judea and Babylon will be? A fire from Heaven will deluge many lands, lay waste the fields, destroy the habitations. Men, like beasts, will flee from place to place and live in swamps and jungles. Then a comet will strike at Babylon, Babylon the sinful and the wicked, where many faithful saints of the people of truth have perished; where palaces are full of matricides; where men sin with their mothers and daughters, and in their utter wantonness, lie with beasts. No more will these men, clad in armor, march out of their city of stone and corruption to murder the innocent and pollute the chaste. Babylon will be laid utterly desolate, even, alas! as Jerusalem was for the deeds of those who turned from the path of God. But Jerusalem will once more be restored and sanctified. The Almighty will set her up again upon her beautiful hills, and in her center He will build a mighty tower of righteousness guarded by pillars of flame. Then the peoples of the earth will know that the Holy One, blessed be He, hath returned to His chosen seat."

The eye in the ceiling closed, the dazzling light vanished, the blue dimness reappeared and men and women sat motionless and speechless under the lingering spell of the oracle's words. Then the door was unbolted and the crowd began filing out.

Ruffina whispered, "The oracle did not say *when* all this would happen."

Chapter Thirty-nine

After Ruffina's visit Hadrian had a bad dream. In a raging storm invisible hands carried him into his throne room, which was dark. As flashes of lightning fell upon the walls, he saw countless ghastly eyes oozing blood. The storm grew in fury and thunderclaps rocked the walls. Slowly they swayed backward and forward, and as lightning flashed, the solid mass of blood-oozing eyes advanced and receded. In terror he rang for his guard, but no one came. He called out to Jupiter, but no one responded. Suddenly a fiery comet broke through the clouds and lashed against the walls. They collapsed. Out of the storm a bull came charging. Hadrian drew his sword, but it broke against the beast's horns. He raised his shield, but the bull gored his legs, shook his throne.

Hadrian awoke drenched in perspiration. Deep in his heart he was as superstitious and disturbed by the baffling and mysterious as was his lowliest subject. The inexplicable and uncontrollable belonged to the sphere of the gods; they could not be ignored. While some gods were part of the imperial political scheme—and of these, Hadrian, as a deified Caesar, was the most potent—there were others that represented the mysterious forces of nature not as rationalized symbols, but as embodiments of the truly divine and incomprehensible. Through these gods came the auguries; from them favors were sought and to them sacrifices were brought. Had this dream not come on the heels of his conversation with Ruffina and before his impending campaign, Hadrian would probably have dismissed it, but under the circumstances it gave him no rest.

Seeking relief in wine and amusements, he ordered a banquet in his palace. He found himself bored. He thought of summoning dream-interpreters but decided to try the shrine of Apollo first. In disguise he went to Daphne, whose nature was in harmony with what its principal shrine, a temple of Apollo, stood for in relation to its name. While the suburb Daphne was the paradise of the amorous and the hunting ground of the debauched, the name Daphne was that of a chaste nymph, the daughter of the river-god, who, rather than submit to Apollo's amorous advances, had called upon her father to transform her into a laurel tree.

Daphne was the magnet of Antioch, which was itself the magnet of the Middle East. If one found no satisfaction at the shrine of Apollo, there was the temple of Bacchus, the wine god, with his revels; of the Syrian Astarte, with innumerable forms of sensuality; of the Python, with her serpentine maidens; of the Furies, for seekers of terror and hair-raising mystery; of the seductive water nymphs; of an assortment of Egyptian divinities, of which Isis, represented as a woman with the horns of a cow, was the most important. Everywhere sex played a leading part in the rites and was the principal attraction for all visitors.

As Hadrian strolled through the lanes and groves of Daphne, he was appalled by the large number of debauching soldiers. Drunk and boisterous, they were on the porticoes of roadhouses, staggering and raucous in the alleys, rolling in the bushes in various stages of undress—and not alone. With civilians they crowded the temple of Apollo, cursing, guffawing, shouting bawdy remarks. In disgust the emperor hurried back.

The following morning he summoned Marcellus and upbraided him for permitting legionaries under his command to indulge in such conduct a fortnight before their campaign. "Their legs," Hadrian stormed, "shaven or plucked, were either too fat or too thin, and their arms, by Juno! were as flabby as the arms of middle-aged women."

Marcellus protested that those were soldiers corrupted by local customs during their long stay at Antioch; the recently arrived troops, he said, were strong and tough. But Hadrian, unsatisfied, demanded that Daphne be forbidden to the army until its return from the campaign, that the training be intensified and that a review be held the following week on Campus Martius, across the Orontes.

After dismissing his general Hadrian summoned the presidents of the eighteen districts into which Antioch was divided. He informed them that he required the interpretation of a strange dream and desired to see the best priests or soothsayers of their parishes.

On the appointed day the high priests in their regalia appeared before Hadrian in the presence of senators, district presidents and high officials. Hadrian, tall and stately, his middle-age abdominal bulge concealed under the splendor of purple and gold, greeted every one separately before ascending his throne. When he sat down, conversation ceased.

One of the two archons who shared the responsibility for the civil administration of Antioch, to whom the eighteen district chiefs were subordinate, stepped forward, bowed halfway to the ground and announced, "If it please Your Divine Majesty, the district presidents have chosen four priests and one priestess worthy of the privilege of standing before Your Divine Majesty and interpreting a dream."

"Let them come forward," muttered the emperor.

The archon nodded and five impressive figures in flowing silk and miters advanced, the woman in the center. Behind them trailed priestesses carrying ritual vessels.

"Speak," said Hadrian, "so that I may know who you are and what you are."

The priest on the woman's right, a big, heavy man in a black robe on which the image of Zeus appeared in white, stepped forward. "I am the high priest of the temple of Zeus-Jupiter, the mightiest of gods, ruler of the world, keeper of the bolts of lightning."

The emperor nodded, the priest stepped back and the one on the woman's left came forward. He was a colossus in a carmine robe upon which a chariot hitched to winged horses had been embroidered in light green. "I am the high priest of the temple of Ares-Mars, the god of war, the patron of thy great empire, O divine Caesar."

Again the emperor nodded. The priest retired and a third advanced. He was a paunchy, middle-statured man in a yellow robe on which the profiles of Hermes and Aphrodite, each facing outward, appeared in deep green.

"I am the high priest of Hermes, the patron of Antioch; god of roads, commerce, inventions, cunning and theft. Likewise, I am the priest of Hermes Trismegistus, god of Thoth, known for his mystical wonders."

"I am the high priest of Apollo," said the fourth, a tall, slender man, "the god of music, poetry and love, and, jointly with Aesculapius, the god of medicine. I am authorized to speak and perform in the name of Isis, goddess of fertility, wife and sister of the great Egyptian god Osiris." His robe was pink; it bore the image of Apollo in front in gold, and that of Isis in light blue on the back.

The woman was last. Her gold-fringed green robe was decorated with variegated serpents coiling up and down. She wore a gold-green turban fringed with tiny bells. "I am the pythoness, priestess of the serpent Python, the soothsaying spirit. Apollo slew the Python's body, but her great spirit, which knows the frailties of man and the mysteries of nature, is immortal."

"Each of you," said Hadrian sedately, "is a person of power in his domain and draws his wisdom and strength from the gods. Tell me, then, the portent of this dream: The walls of a kingly palace are made of blood-dripping eyes. A storm rages, and a planet breaks down the walls to give a red bull freedom to attack the king as he sits on his throne."

There was a long pause. The priest of Zeus took an incense burner from his attending priestess, murmured an incantation and declared, "Your Divine Majesty, the blood-dripping eyes are the widows of the Roman soldiers who fell in battle. The storm is Jupiter's anger at Rome's foes. And the bull is the god of the rebellious province."

The emperor looked indifferent. "Thank you," he said.

The giant priest of Mars stepped forward without ceremony and announced, "Mars is angry at our enemies, Your Divine Majesty, and storms and weeps at the inaction of our army. The bull is his messenger."

Hadrian covered up a yawn and murmured an impassive "Thank you."

The priest of Hermes took from his priestess a glass and a bowl into which she had poured some water from a silver ewer. While he waved his hands over the bowl and chanted an incantation, the attending priestess, with the aid of another, tied to a tripod a yellow globe held up by golden chains. The priest touched the water with his wand and it turned red. He then placed the bowl beneath the suspended globes and intoned again. While some of the onlookers appeared to have been impressed with the transformation of the color of the water, Hadrian fidgeted, his boredom manifestly mounting. Finally the priest spoke: "Your Divine Majesty, I see great armies clashing on the frontiers of our country and thence veering into the heart of Judea. I see many men dying, cities desolated and commerce at a standstill. I see widows weeping—"

Hadrian interrupted him impatiently. "But what is the bull, the bull?"

"The bull, Your Divine Majesty, is your anger, which charges against the throne of an imposter king."

The emperor laughed. "Not bad," he chuckled, "not bad," and abruptly turned to the pythoness. "And what," he said with a faint touch of mockery, "would you say, O priestess of the serpent?"

She bowed gracefully, took a large basket from her attendants and removed its cover, and a python lifted its head and stared in surprise. The onlookers recoiled. An attending priestess whipped out a flute and began to play. The pythoness, dropping her robe and baring the upper part of her body, began to dance round the serpent, invoking its spirit to reveal the mystery of the dream. Suddenly she halted close to the basket, extended her arms over the python toward Hadrian, closed her eyes and spoke as one in a trance:

"The dripping eyes, O great and divine Caesar, are your vengeance-seeking enemies. The storm is the uprising of Judea. The bull is its red-haired leader. The planet is the divine Titus, warning Your Divine Majesty no longer to neglect our gods. A bull must be sacrificed to destroy the Judean bull. In the temple over the bridge where the rivers Parmenius and Phryminus join the Orontes stand the sacred bulls made of the bronze brought by the divine Titus from the Jerusalem Temple. There our gods must be appeased and the oblation offered."

Impressed, Hadrian rose. "Prepare the oblation for the morning," he ordered. "I shall be there."

After the sacrifice of a choice bull with gilded horns, the distribution of wine to the populace and the review of his troops, whose appearance had allayed his fears, Hadrian was able to banish the memory of his nightmare. In fine spirits, he saw his army off, himself riding behind Marcellus to the end of the marble road in the south that Herod had built for Caesar. When, in parting, the emperor asked waggishly, "When will I see you in Jerusalem, Marcellus?" the old general replied earnestly, "Before the beginning of the rains, Your Divine Majesty."

But he had reckoned without Bar-Kokba, for even as the ruler and his faithful old soldier were parting, a courier bearing vital information from Theodoros was riding posthaste toward Galilee. The messenger reached Judith before the Romans covered the first lap of their march. Encumbered by the heavy equipment of its foot soldiers and war machines, the Roman army was obliged to move slowly and to rest frequently. Bar-Kokba, on the other hand, had moved his main forces to Emek Zevulun, the plain of dunes between Mount Carmel and Acca, so that he was within a few hours' march from his principal Galilean forts and close to the three ports from which invasion might be attempted.

Judith promptly delivered the message to Bar-Kokba, who

at once informed Zevulun. Zevulun realized that the Romans were ignorant of the strength of his fleet, for the escort for the troops assigned to invade by sea was barely half the strength that Zevulun had at his command. Without waiting for the Romans to reach Palestinian waters and enjoy the benefit of being ready for the battle, Zevulun decided to sail at once and take advantage of the element of surprise.

Bar-Kokba, in adopting the same tactics on land, was pursuing a well tested course. With his customary speed and precision he proceeded to carry out his plan. This time the Roman route lay along the course of the Orontes, whose fountainhead was in the Lebanon. Marcellus intended to continue south through the Abilene district in Syria in order to cross the River Karmyon, also known as the Litani, where it swung toward the sea, thus reaching the northernmost point on the Galilean frontier. To march against Jotapata from there would be a simple matter. A second column was to land at Tyre, where the Karmyon fell into the Mediterranean and, proceeding along the seashore, to take Acca. Nor was this all. A third column was to disembark at Caesarea, where a good artificial breakwater favored such action, and to strike at Bar-Kokba from the rear.

But these excellent intentions proved futile. Bar-Kokba, at a forced march, took his cavalry and crack troops across the Karmyon at Hatzor, one of the towns conquered by Joshua ben-Nun. Thence he took part of his forces to a valley between Zuban and Baal Bekhi. While his foot soldiers encamped in the north of the valley, he placed his cavalry in the surrounding hills. The Cabul, Sepphoris, Jotapata and Tiberias garrisons took up positions between Jotapata and the Karmyon, while the Acca garrison was reinforced.

When the battle was joined in the plain above Hatzor, Bar-Kokba, feigning retreat, drew about half of Marcellus' army across the river. While the Romans were crossing, Bar-Kokba's cavalry charged at their flanks from the hills and his retreating foot soldiers suddenly turned and delivered a frontal attack. For twenty-four hours the battle raged, the Romans endeavoring to hold both banks of the river, and the Israelites pushing them into it from the north and south. The next day the Galilean garrisons arrived and the outcome was decided. Though the battle continued for two days, it was, on the part of the Romans, no more than a rear-guard action, aimed desperately at staving off a rout. They were pursued deep into the mountains of Lebanon, sustaining heavy losses in men, food and equipment. Marcellus himself, in a vain attempt to encourage his soft Antiochene legions, was wounded.

The outcome of the sea battle was crushing. Zevulun attacked the Roman armada at night, after it had anchored off Tyre. The Romans put up a gallant and stubborn fight, considering the inferiority of their numbers and the position in which they had been caught. But it was a losing fight from the outset, though it proved costly to Zevulun. Few of the Roman vessels escaped.

After this victory even Bar-Kokba's rabid opponents among the affluent and the rabbis with Sadducean propensities came to think of him as an invincible warrior, one who, like the early kings in Israel, might yet bring to his people lasting deliverance from the foreign yoke. Seeing that he was unbeatable, Rome might yet come to some understanding with him, and trading with the empire might become even more profitable than before.

Since the liberation of the hostages the opposition of the upper circles of society to Bar-Kokba had been largely passive. A good deal of this passive opposition stemmed from Sepphoris, a Galilean center of rich landowners, descendants of priests and wealthy families who had escaped from Jerusalem before its destruction by Titus. While the city boasted eighteen synagogues, the Roman influence had been strong there; it had been exerted through the Romans' patronage and the sports house and theater that had been built under government pressure. However, under untutored Asher's military rule all decisions of the People's Council had been obeyed, though grumblingly. Now this group was ready to carry its burdens with better grace.

And so, upon Bar-Kokba's return from the field, all joined in acclaiming him, and the welcome was such as befitted royalty. Valuable gifts were tendered to him personally and to the state. An impressive delegation, followed by a choir of garlanded maidens in white, met him outside the city gates. Flower arches were erected along his route, and flowers were strewn in his path. From windows and parapeted roofs men shouted, "Here comes our liberator! Here comes Bar-Kokba, our prince!" And from doorways mothers with male babies in their arms rushed toward him, each beseeching him to bestow his benediction so that the infant might grow up "to be a hero in Israel." In the evening there was a great banquet in honor of the conquerors and wine was distributed to the army and to the populace.

With varying degrees of pomp and clamor, these ceremonies and festivities were repeated wherever Bar-Kokba passed. In Acca, at Shemon's insistence, Zevulun rode beside him to receive acclaim as the hero of the fleet.

A council of war took place. Spirits were high. Elon expressed regret that Marcellus had not been pursued "even, if need be, to the walls of Antioch, and annihilated." Joel, enthusiastic, declared himself ready to besiege Antioch if necessary. He believed that in the present condition of the Roman army it was possible to march against Antioch and take it. "Let us," he exclaimed, "once and for all destroy this unending menace. For centuries this wicked city, even as Rome herself, has given us no peace. Now we can destroy the evil at its root."

Zevulun was not carried away. "Fighting here, we are as a sea that floods an island," he said. "Fighting there, we will be the island and our enemies the sea. Here, if we lack supplies, our people share their last measure of grain with us; there, what is clean will be hidden and what's unclean we cannot eat. The walls of Antioch, too, must be reckoned with; it may take us years to break them down. And will Edom be idle in the meantime?"

Bar-Kokba's words ended the discussion. "Before we carry God to the heathen, let us re-establish Him firmly in our midst. Let us make our still bleeding land strong within its borders; then we will think of what to do beyond them. We have torn men away from homes and work. Their dearest wish is to go back and build. Let them. The better their homes and their vineyards, the better they will fight to hold them."

Part Three

A Star Falls

Chapter Forty

At Caesarea, Shemon encamped on the plain. Again he went up to his uncle's resting place to offer a prayer, and from there to Tower Hill and the Bowl to greet old friends.

Toward evening Shemon returned to Caesarea and found Nadav at the head of a delegation waiting for him. The two old friends greeted each other with the exuberance of youngsters. Shemon was glad to hear that most of those who had been evacuated from the Judean quarter had returned to their homes and were prospering. To the delegates, there was no greater man on earth than Bar-Kokba, and to stand within four feet of him was a privilege. But Bar-Kokba was happy to sit with them as the Shemon of yore and to drink to their prosperity.

Delegations from nearby towns and villages arrived incessantly, and he celebrated with them all. He was stirred to see the representatives of Eintov, headed by Avishai. The community president had aged; a scar marred his face and one of his eyes was closed. Bar-Kokba received him with singular honor. He embraced him, and said in response to his words of salutation, "It is *I* who am privileged to greet you, Avishai. You fight with the spirit as I do with the sword, and such as you were the first to fight."

Late in the evening a huge bonfire was made and soldiers and visitors regaled themselves throughout the night.

After midnight Bar-Kokba, heavy with wine, retired to his tent. When he had removed his cloak and sword, washed his feet and thrown himself on his bed, he heard a woman pleading with the sentry to admit her or at least to announce her, for she had something important to confide to the prince. Bar-Kokba, recognizing Judith's voice, sat up and called out, "Let her come."

She slipped in and paused at the tent flap, which had closed. Shemon had never seen her look so feminine before. Her kerchief had slipped from her curly hair, clasped in a glittering headband that added luster to her glowing eyes. Her bosom, accentuated by the tight bodice of her dress, rose and fell in agitation which she vainly tried to conceal. Her face was flushed and dimpling in a smile, expressing a mingling of hesitancy and greeting.

"Come forward, Judith," he said, somewhat huskily. "What brings you here?"

"I . . . I came . . . I came to talk to Shemon about my house, my father's house," she stammered.

"What about your father's house?"

"It is ruined. . . . It burned down the day of the earthquake." She caught her breath and advanced a little. "And . . . now I have no home."

She had scented herself with a stirring perfume, which, as she came closer, roused his blood.

"No home," he repeated mechanically, unable to think of anything appropriate to say. His thoughts were like mired wheels, sinking deeper with every effort to extricate them. He could see only her glowing eyes and the rise and fall of her bosom. "No home," he said again. "Gamala was no home. . . . I sent you to Gamala, did I not?"

"You did," she said, growing bolder and coming still closer. "But now I have nothing to do there, so I came back to Caesarea."

"Yes, you have nothing to do there, and no home. Alone. A young woman alone . . ." He spoke heavily, grappling with the befogging wine vapors, her perfume and his tingling blood. She was too close, and he had been away from Meredya too long to win the struggle.

Slowly he rose and stepped toward her. "I will build you a home," he muttered. "You are beautiful and brave. . . . You are beautiful, Judith." He took her into his powerful arms and she clung to him.

In the morning he called in witnesses and, without rites or ceremonies, legalized their union.

The news of their marriage, which quickly spread through the camp and beyond it, brought Joel to Shemon. "Is one good woman not enough for you?" Meredya's cousin recriminated. "You know that our sages do not favor many wives."

"Don't exaggerate, Joel, my friend," Shemon laughed. "Not many—only two, and both good ones."

Joel eyed him sullenly. "How can you jest about it?" he grumbled. "Meredya is the mother of your son. She is young. She has stood with you in adversity. Now, when she is waiting for you, you take another woman."

Shemon knitted his brows. "Don't preach to me, Joel," he said. "Meredya stays first in my heart. Judith is comely and I was a little drunk, so it happened. I am only a man."

"Why did you have to marry her? You know that nothing good ever comes from indulging with women."

"I lay with her, Joel, and she is no harlot. I would not expose her to obloquy and shame."

"Why not send her away now?"

"There is no hurry," Shemon snapped, and the friends parted coolly. But on the morrow, when Joel was leaving for Tiberias, Shemon came to see him off and they embraced each other.

Accompanied by Judith and Nadav, Shemon went to the Judean quarter in Caesarea to examine the buildings destroyed or damaged in the riots. A number of people were living in palm-branch-covered booths or in tents put up beside the ruins of their former dwellings. Shemon discussed with the occupants their problems, offered immediate assistance and ordered the construction of a better-planned Judean quarter. Meanwhile he took Judith back to camp.

Shemon had a snug little hut built for Judith and, in the absence of pressing problems, spent a good deal of his time in it. She had a beautiful body and knew how to arouse his passion, but away from her charms, he would all but dismiss her from his mind. He transacted his business from his own tent, and in moments of leisure his thoughts drifted with tenderness to his wife and son in Jerusalem.

A few weeks went by. One morning, as Shemon was issuing routine orders to some of his headmen, he heard a commotion. He came out. Some distance away men were gathering about a small caravan, and Abner was helping Meredya alight from a camel. Shemon stood flabbergasted. His headman, who had emerged from the tent with him, promptly retired. Then his father-in-law and Meredya saw him. Motionless and pale, Meredya gazed at him with beautiful, wide-open eyes. Abner, slightly stooping, came forward slowly, staring at his son-in-law reproachfully. At the same time Meredya made one hesitant step and Shemon saw a flicker of a smile on her face. Her wrap slipped from her shoulders and she stood, tall and graceful, in an exact replica of her wedding dress. He recalled how the original had been torn; the scene in which that had happened rose before him in a flash. There was a powerful tug at his heart, and oblivious of Abner and the strangers about the caravan, he ran with outstretched arms toward Meredya. With a little cry, she flew to meet him. Judith, who had been watching from the doorway of her hut, slammed the door shut and threw herself onto her bed in a paroxysm of rage and tears.

Later, when Meredya sat close to Shemon in his tent, she avoided all reference to Judith. She spoke of the long months of fear and longing, of the thrills and elation that his triumphs had brought her, of the handsomeness and brightness of their growing son. When, in reply to his question, she informed him that Elisha had been left in her sister Hemda's care, he said abruptly, "Time to return. You and I, pleasure of my heart, will again enter the capital together. A second triumphal entry." She flung her arms about his neck.

Early the next morning Shemon came to take leave of Judith. She had lain all night without undressing, and as she sat up, her hair was tangled, her face haggard and waxen, and her eyes blurred. Somewhere in a distant nook of her mind a hope had been ticking faintly that he might perhaps not abandon her. But when she looked up at him, the ticking stopped. She saw only cool commiseration in his gaze.

He spoke gently. "You will be amply provided for, Judith. Your house, too, will be ready soon. Sorry that it went this way."

There was a long silence. Then she stammered brokenly, "Can't I come too? Only to be your handmaiden . . . only to see you." She attempted to embrace his legs, but he stepped back, shaking his head. She summoned all her power to keep from breaking down. "Then why do I need the house?" she gulped. "I'll go back to Ruffina."

Without replying he raised her, kissed her and went out.

Chapter Forty-one

The second defeat of the Roman army came as a great shock to the emperor. The speed of the blow, the heavy loss of life and the sinking of his Levantine fleet were incredible. To watch old, much-decorated Marcellus carried on a stretcher through the South Gate, followed by bedraggled and decimated legions, and to hear the jeers of the mob was a bitter experience. The whole business was all the more humiliating since he, Hadrian himself, had the misfortune of finding himself at Antioch, so close to the scene of the battle. Though he had not actually commanded the army, and so was not directly responsible for the defeat, public opinion at home would find it difficult to dissociate him from it. His enemies in the senate would gloat over the debacle and lay it directly at his door. Clearly, he could not return to Rome without rehabilitating himself and the army. But equally clear was the fact that the rehabilitation could not come easily, that it must be planned and executed painstakingly and that the best military forces and generalship would have to be mobilized to assure success.

After discussing the problem with his closest local advisers Hadrian dispatched special orders summoning Caius Julius Severus to Antioch. Caius Julius was his most brilliant general and commanded the famous Fourteenth Legion, styled "Conquerors of Britain." Hadrian also ordered M. Statius Priscus, rating next to Severus in ability, to equip with the finest weapons and bring to Syria as soon as possible at least six of the toughest and most experienced legions. Moreover, the emperor directed the Roman fleet, with the exception only of such craft as were required for the protection of the home waters, to escort the legions under the command of Admiral-Prefect Sextus Cornelius

Dexter himself and to be provided with sufficient supplies and slaves for a lengthy campaign.

The dispatch of these grave instructions did not dispel Hadrian's fears. What if this incredible Bar-Kokba chose to follow up his victory by attacking Antioch? Would the demoralized Antioch garrison be able to hold out until relief arrived? While Hadrian sought to attribute the debacle of his Syrian army, first, to its inefficiency and mental slothfulness and, secondly, to the cleverness and intrepidity of the young Judean leader, there lingered in the recesses of his mind the memory of his nightmare. What, he asked himself, if he were really contending with a supernatural force? How could even his hardiest legions and ablest generals overcome something which spears could not pierce or war machines shatter? As weeks rolled into months and the emperor's spies brought reports of the reconstruction and reclamation activities in Judea, of the new fortifications, of the mounting happiness of the people and of the rising popularity of Bar-Kokba, who might yet be anointed king, Hadrian felt that the success of the forthcoming struggle required that the gods be placated. If divinity was to strive with the Judean God, a worthy opponent must be selected. And which one would that be? Assuredly not one of those who had recently failed him. It would be, rather, the sun-and-weather Baal, and Hadrian would bring a human sacrifice to him, a perfect male less than thirteen years of age. The emperor made known his decision to the Antiochene archons and immediately a search for a suitable victim was instituted.

Once the native Syrian had considered signally honored those families whose sons were chosen for sacrifice to Baal. Mothers, whatever their innermost feelings, would themselves adorn their sons and bring them to the ritual. But now, under the influence of Jews and Christians, the practice was waning and victims had to be kidnapped, purchased from needy prolific parents or taken from slaves. A slave child, naturally, was not as welcome to the sun-god as one born free. For a ceremony ordered by the emperor himself it was imperative to obtain an unblemished offspring of free parents.

And so the *bloodhounds of the lictors,* or the *bloodhounds of the priests,* as the procurers of the victim were nicknamed by the natives, drove a bargain with a Syrian in the slums of the Heracles quarter. He was one of those typical moneyless Antiochenes who rested most of their lives so that they might give their wives no rest. Their calling was indolence; their labor camps, the banks of the Orontes; and their shrines, taverns. They subsisted on the intake of their slaving, childbearing wives and on occasional windfalls from tourists and drunken revelers. To bolster their income they, under the protection of Hermes, at times reverted to thievery if it entailed no effort or danger. Such was the type of man with whom the bargain was driven. The boy, one of a brood of nine, was snatched away despite the hysterical pleas of his mother, who was soon silenced by a blow from her husband.

Only a select group of notables and high officials participated in the ceremony. Escorted by a detachment of his Praetorian Guard, the emperor and his party rode in the dead of night through the East Gate and the Vicus Agrippae district to the foot of Mount Casius. There they dismounted, leaving their horses in charge of a few guards. Slowly they climbed to the open-air shrine on the summit.

They were requested to assume seats in a small amphitheater facing the shrine. The temple, a roofless tetrastyle with a solid marble wall at its western end, faced east. In a large circular opening paved with polished snow-white stone and adorned with red and purple mosaics, the Baal was mounted on a high base. Legless, with a horned sun disk for a head, it towered, immense and ugly, above a spacious platform and altar of Parian marble. Huge arms extended eastward toward the sun from the torso, and wings spread westward toward the sea and wind. The stomach, ordinarily shut by a circular door, was now open, belching fire directly above the altar and sending sparks into the starless night. South of the shrine a palatial dwelling was provided for orgies and escape from inclement weather.

As Hadrian and his party took their places, priestesses, in

blood-red veils and with small golden sun disks on their heads, lined up on the right and left sides of the altar. In the glow of the fire their young bodies, nude under the transparent veils, could be seen shivering in the brisk, misty atmosphere.

Daybreak was near; the damp air was penetrating. Hadrian and his entourage, wrapping themselves in their togas, yawned and whispered. The imperial guards, standing at a respectful distance, nudged each other, avidly eyeing the alluring priestesses.

After a wait a deep voice was heard. It was that of the high priest, chanting as he emerged with the victim from the adjoining building. He was robed in scarlet and wore a raylike gilded crown on his head. Directly behind him two votaries, similarly robed but crownless, carried lamps and long knives. The boy in the high priest's arms was wrapped in a scarlet coverlet. His hair had been shaved to the skin, his eyes were shut, his mouth was open but gagged, and his bare shoulders protruded from the coverlet. As the priests began to mount the carpeted platform steps, the priestesses, waving incense burners over the altar and swaying rhythmically, joined in the high priest's chant:

O Baal, O Baal, O great Baal-Sun,
Dispenser of sunshine and bounty and life!
We bring thee a sacrifice, guiltless and pure,
A mother's fondling, a perfect youngling boy.

When the high priest reached the top of the steps, the nearest priestesses removed the coverlet and the glow of the belching flame fell upon the nude body of the trussed boy. The priest glanced at the sky. The darkness was thinning, revealing heavy clouds. The child was placed on the altar. The touch of the cold marble, together with the heat of the furnace, shocked him. He opened his eyes, stared in horror, and straining impotently at his bonds, wriggled and tossed his little body. One could almost hear his stifled cries of horror. But those about him were unmoved. The old priest calmly held the boy fast and the priestesses anointed him with an oily unguent.

The darkness was dissolving and low clouds were emerging. They hung in heavy masses, hopelessly concealing the rising sun.

That was a bad omen. The Baal apparently was displeased, but the cause of his displeasure no one knew. The ritual, however, had to be completed, in the hope that the god might be mollified.

The high priest took one of the knives and began to mutter while the girls danced, chanting:

> For thee, for thee, O Baal,
> We knife this life,
> We cut this sapling tree,
> This fount of mother's joy.
> For thee and the glory of thy name
> We consign him to the flame,
> For thee. . . .

Suddenly a light flashed through the clouds, thunder pealed and rain began to fall. The priests paused to stare at each other in dismay.

The emperor, chafing at the bitter disappointment, was now incensed. "Finish it!" he cried.

The high priest promptly raised his knife. But as he was bringing it down to the child's throat, a blinding flash of lightning, seeming to strike at the shrine, glanced between the victim and the priest, tearing away part of the altar and flooring the man. The priestesses shrieked in horror and ran. Hadrian and his entourage stood up in consternation. The votaries were raising their stunned chief from the ground. The rain now was falling in heavy streams, lashing at the nude, helpless child and smothering the Baal's fire.

The emperor, his lips livid, turned to his guards and commanded shakily, "Save the boy!"

Chapter Forty-two

Shortly after the incident on Mount Casius, Caius Julius Severus, after successfully dodging Zevulun's fleet, reached Antioch with his celebrated Fourteenth Legion. He had taken the northern route, through the Aegean Sea, instead of the customary southern course, through Alexandria, that Zevulun had expected him to use.

It did not take Severus long to realize that two evils had to be corrected before the actual campaign against the Holy Land could be launched: the laxity of the local legions and the attitude of the natives. To wage serious warfare with an unpredictable population in the rear was as dangerous as fighting with an army that ran faster *from* the enemy than *at* him. Severus had been told that the fickle Greco-Syrians had lately added insolence to their indolence. High Roman officials, the army and even the emperor himself had become the butt of widely-circulated quips. Roman dignitaries were treated with disrespect in public places, the collection of taxes was falling off and reverence for the priesthood was declining.

Severus was a cool-headed, cold-blooded man, devoid of sentiment. He disdained all gods, regarding their priests as grotesque comedians; he derided all premonitions, dreams and auguries and believed only in reason and will. A great tactician and strict disciplinarian, he handled men and problems with directness, speed and ruthlessness.

One of his first acts was to take over the policing of Antioch. That done, he bore down on persons guilty of lese majesty. There were no arrests or trials, but every day hundreds of would-be wits careless enough to vent their satire in public found themselves nursing broken heads or ribs. To further impress the natives he paraded his "Conquerors of Britain" through the length and breadth of the city. Grim, aloof and powerful, holding their spears in perfectly even lines, they looked like armored walls in motion as they marched in the bright sunlight.

Even as he restored Roman prestige among civilians, he reintroduced Roman discipline among the lax local troops. Placing them under officers and drillmasters from his own legion, he imposed severe penalties for personal slovenliness and neglect of animals. Two legionaries twice apprehended at Daphne without passes were beheaded. Under these measures the army rapidly regained its discipline and zest, and the populace its respect for the rulers.

January was in its last lap when the Roman fleet and the cream of the imperial army arrived. Hadrian instantly chided himself for having succumbed to superstitions. How could one possibly disagree with Severus' cold logic? "Your Majesty," he had said, "had you had no misgivings, you would have had no dreams; had you stayed in your palace, you would have seen no miracles. There is but one god—the superior man. And who is superior to a Roman?"

Bar-Kokba was at Caesarea, watching the refortification of the city, when the powerful Roman fleet, bound for Seleucia, passed in full view of the shore. Unlike Severus, Dexter had deliberately chosen the southern course to draw out the Israelite fleet. But Zevulun could not accept the challenge. Outnumbered overwhelmingly, he preferred to delay a seemingly foredoomed action. Given time, he might perhaps be able, as in the past, to fritter away part of the Roman strength by sudden raids, or something providential might occur.

The size of the enemy's armada indicated to Bar-Kokba the gravity of the impending events and he promptly issued a call for total mobilization. By March two hundred thousand men stood under his banner. He placed half of this force on the northern frontier and the other half along the coast and at danger points in the south. This was an army of fervent, eager, Rome-hating citizens, but, with the exception of some fifty thousand veterans, it was untrained in the art of warfare. It consisted largely of foot soldiers and was therefore slow-moving. Its equipment, too, despite Elon's efforts, was far from satisfactory. This army was to be pitted against ten Roman legions, of which seven were the choicest in the empire. With their auxiliaries the Romans could bring against it a force of about one hundred thousand men, not counting the naval crews.

Theodoros, who had been in continuous contact with Bar-Kokba, was unable to furnish specific information. Try as he might, he could learn nothing definite concerning Severus' or Dexter's plans. Ruffina was equally unsuccessful. Either the general's tight discipline had sealed the mouths of his officers or the secrets were confined to a small inner circle.

To keep his large army patient, Bar-Kokba was obliged to spend most of his time on horseback, riding from fort to fort and from camp to camp. The easily inflammable Judeans were chafing under the boredom of inactivity. A war of waiting, with no enemy in sight, was hard to understand. They had left their fields, groves, vineyards, workshops and schools. What was the use of wasting their winter when they might not be needed till spring or summer? Why could they not be called a few days before the actual attack, rout the enemy and go home? To keep this element under control was a trying task, and the uncertainty aggravated the difficulties. It robbed Bar-Kokba of that calm and confidence which had meant so much in his previous victories.

Hoping that someone else might do better than Theodoros, Bar-Kokba requested his father-in-law to go down to Antioch, but Abner had scarcely crossed the frontier when things began to happen and he was obliged to return. Israelite caravans began to disappear; reconnoitering patrols failed to come back. There were even cases of arson in the border zone, and their perpetrators could not be determined.

Suddenly the Roman fleet appeared in full force above Tyre, holding course on Acca. Further dodging was impossible and Zevulun made ready for battle. Bar-Kokba rushed reinforcements from Cabul, thinning his lines there. But the Romans, keeping within sight but not coming close enough for action, sailed leisurely on. Zevulun had no alternative but to follow. Clinging close to the shore for whatever advantage it might offer, he watched the enemy. The Romans pretended to sail out into the open sea, but suddenly they returned and lined up in battle order off Caesarea. Zevulun prepared to meet them. Bar-Kokba was in a dilemma. Was he to shift the bulk of his forces to the coast and expose the frontier, or should he stay as he was? He decided to stay.

Nadav, who had been on the alert, brought his garrison to the harbor and beach, placed his war machines on elevations and sent a courier to Bar-Kokba.

The Romans launched their attack in semicircular formation, aiming to hem the Israelites in. Their heaviest galleys, going at high speed, bore down on Zevulun from the center. Maneuvering cleverly, Zevulun left only small stone- and fire-throwing boats in the path of the big ships and thrust the full weight of his largest vessels against the weaker Roman flank. The first two ships to go up in flames were Roman. In a rage, the Roman center and unopposed flank went for the small Israelite craft, trying to sink them by ramming them and pouring missiles into them. But the small boats, darting like fish, dodged the prows of the galleys and, from the cover of their poops and arches, inflicted heavy punishment on their foes. Zevulun, with a number of triremes, had crashed through the Roman flank and now attacked the dangerous center from the rear. The Romans reversed part of their force to meet the attack, and the conflict veered away from the harbor. Before long the battle zone extended for several miles, in which countless craft of varying sizes ran, circled, rammed, burst into flames, split up, sank or swerved to fight on amid the clatter of falling stones and darting arrows, the sounds of gongs and trumpets, and the cries of cursing, groaning, jumping, swimming and drowning men.

Commencing in the afternoon, the battle was still raging at midnight. By then it had shifted close to the harbor, now clogged with the protruding masts and bows of sunken boats. From time to time the desperate voices from the stubbornly fighting Israelite galleys that had survived could be heard exhorting the enemy's rowers in Aramaic, Hebrew and Greek: "Slaves, stop rowing! Mutiny! We are fighting for God and freedom! Your freedom, too! Slaves, mutiny, mutiny!"

What the response was no one could tell. Toward morning all was still; only the crackling flames of drifting or sinking boats and the swishing of the heavily depleted Roman fleet, reforming on the graying horizon, was audible. In the long, ominous silence a few score survivors, swimming wearily, reached shallow water and were helped to the shore. Zevulun was not among them. Nadav dispatched small rowboats in search of the gallant skipper, but they found no trace of him. The camp was plunged into deep sorrow, but there was no time for lamentation.

Later in the morning the invasion of the beaches began, the harbor itself having become impassable. Nadav fought gallantly and determined hand-to-hand combat forced the enemy back into the sea for a time. But eventually Nadav's resistance became hopeless. While he dealt with the frontal attacks the enemy landed north and south of the city, out of range of Nadav's machines. Without letup, wave after wave of Romans came wading through the shallow water. They formed in columns on the sunny beach and soon they would close in from both sides. To retire into the citadel would be suicidal, Nadav realized, for its fortifications had not been completed and no siege supplies had been stored. Caesarea had to be abandoned. Nadav sent word to the inhabitants of the Judean quarter to flee while he slowly retreated to the hills.

Bar-Kokba had not responded to Nadav's call. He had not been able to, for even as the fleets had joined in battle, strong Roman forces had attacked Jotapata and Cabul. There, too, the battle had raged through the night, but the result had been different; Bar-Kokba had thrown the enemy back.

When Prefect Dexter and General Priscus reported the results of their synchronized attack to Hadrian and Severus, they were grim.

"We have lost one third of our fleet," grunted the prefect.

"They are fiends," grumbled the general. "That man Bar-Kokba must have been born a Judean by mistake. We have brought back in fighting condition only half of the two participating legions."

"If it please His Majesty, we will change our tactics," declared Severus. "What we have learned from the experience is that it is dangerous to pit our massed forces against the Israelite massed forces. We will wear them out by tricks if the fleet will blockade the coast from Seleucia to Alexandria."

"Blockade the coast, Dexter," directed the emperor, and the war of attrition and stratagems began.

Severus decided to achieve three results, which, if successful, would inevitably lead to Bar-Kokba's defeat: to terrorize the noncombatants, to undermine the morale of the combatants and to starve both groups by destroying everything that grew. With outside supplies cut off by the blockade, famine would eventually set in.

Severus proceeded to put this plan into effect. After the first few open villages in Galilee had been sacked and the surrounding groves and meadows scorched, Bar-Kokba understood his opponent's intentions. To frustrate them he strung out his forces into a line thinner and longer but still solid enough to deal with raiding parties. He laid traps for them, and many a grove became their grave.

Modifying his tactics, Severus began sending out strong contingents for simultaneous attacks on the thin line at widely separated points. One of them was wiped out by the Sepphoris garrison and another was badly punished by the defenders of Tiberias, but the others devastated sixty villages and the surrounding areas. The perpetrators, fast-riding cavalry units, were able to escape with few losses because the Israelite cavalry was inferior in numbers and of necessity distributed to protect too many points.

When Bar-Kokba arrived on the scene and saw the charred hovels, the black pastures, the mutilated, unidentified corpses, and the whining dogs roaming in quest of their masters, he cried out, "God Almighty, what have we done that Thou turnest Thy favor from us? Do not let Thy people be destroyed! If Thou wilt not help us, I pray, do not help our enemies. If they, too, are unaided by Thee, we still can defeat them."

In retaliation, he swooped down on Caesarea and destroyed every Roman in sight. The bulk of the invaders, however, managed to escape into the inner citadel, which by then had been repaired. He ordered the fort besieged and returned to the Galilean frontier.

A new seaborne invasion, launched against Apollonia, Castra and Caesarea simultaneously, lifted the siege. Within weeks the Jotapata garrison was evacuated for lack of supplies. When, by the middle of the month, one hundred more villages had been devastated, and Bar-Kokba, while protecting the more fertile frontier lands and beating off assaults on strongholds, had allowed the Romans to consolidate their forces in the seaports, Severus gleefully announced to Hadrian, "Your Majesty, the tide has turned. We will win the war. I am moving my command to Geresh in Transjordan. It is safe again to send a procurator to Caesarea."

Hadrian preferred not to hurry. While the Romans were able

to hold the seaports, where the long-range ballistae of the fleet provided effective support, they were unable to move any appreciable distance inland.

With the reverses, those who had been the last to recognize Bar-Kokba were first to urge a negotiated peace. "If now, when we still have strong fighting forces," they argued, "we should offer to recognize Edom's sovereignty and right to revenues on condition that the edict be abrogated and the procurator's powers restricted, Rome would probably consent. Is it not worth trying for the sake of stopping the bloodshed?"

Foremost among the advocates of this view were the men who had sought Shemon's surrender to Rufus and some of the leading Samaritans. Reb Eliezer, too, indicated his sympathy for this standpoint, but did not press it. Agrim and Manashik, though covertly in favor of it, refrained from supporting it openly because of their written agreement.

Bar-Kokba lost his patience. "Just like the false mother who appeared before King Solomon, you are willing to cut in half the child you neither bore nor reared. How come you to think that Edom will give us concessions? Know you not that even when our victories were at their peak, Hadrian refused to consider concessions? He is determined to destroy us—not for what we now do, but for what we are. Since we will remain what we are when we stop fighting, Rome must still seek our extermination, for she, too, will remain what she is. I advise you not to try my patience with these offers again. I will fight to the last."

But the defeatists did not desist. Unable to sway Bar-Kokba, they influenced others. Gradually their propaganda bore fruit. It spread to the army and caused defections. The impending Passover and the harvest coming in its wake also drew men away. The Samaritans, with many excuses, left in large numbers. Peasants who had been glad to share their grain with the army now kept it back, frightened by the specter of famine.

In this situation Severus continued his hit-and-run tactics, murdering, plundering and burning everything inflammable above ground. Bar-Kokba struck back hard whenever he caught the enemy, but the punishment he took was greater than the damage he inflicted. Large areas in Galilee lay desolate; supplies in forts were dwindling; thousands of refugees, flocking to Samaria and Judea, interfered with the movements of troops, and general demoralization was setting in.

The time was now ripe for Severus to bring his main forces into play. Reinforcing the recaptured citadel ports, he launched synchronized land and sea attacks against Acca, Cabul and Sepphoris. While Bar-Kokba fought back desperately, Severus moved inland from Caesarea and, breaking through, left part of his forces behind for rear-guard actions and advanced northward to threaten Bar-Kokba's rear. To avoid encirclement and a hopeless siege, Bar-Kokba ordered the evacuation of the Galilean fortresses and moved the bulk of his army to Tur Shemon, the strongest position in Samaria. In Galilee, Tiberias alone, well fortified on its surrounding hills and stocked with ample provisions that could be replenished with fish from Lake Kinnereth, was able to hold out.

To gain time for reorganizing his main forces, Shemon left along the route of his retreat detachments of Heromav and Thumbless riders to delay the enemy's advance. They accomplished the mission valiantly but at high cost. In these conflicts Nadav and numerous disciples of Rabbi Akiba, including Ben-Dov, laid down their lives.

At Tur Shemon the People's Council met in an atmosphere of gloom. Rabbi Akiba could not attend because of illness. Joel and Simeon bar-Johai were in besieged Tiberias. Agrim failed to appear, for reasons unknown. Abner looked haggard and aged. Religious duties kept old Eliezer away; through Abner, however, he sent word to his nephew to sue for peace on condition that worship, study and circumcision not be interfered with. Bar-Kokba received the message with a bitter smile.

The session was brief. Elon reported that the fortification of Betar had been completed and abundant supplies stored away. Contact with Alexandria had been re-established and provisions in small quantities were arriving through the desert. Shemon announced that he had decided not to fight in Lower Judea, should further retreat become necessary. This might save the region from destruction and provide places of refuge for the homeless. Was there not another Zevulun in Alexandria who might at least establish a pirate fleet? Nitsa could not answer the question satisfactorily. His contact with Egypt at present was kept up only through the desert. As far as he knew, old Pappus had few ships left. Besides, it was impossible to obtain a written word from him. Zevulun's fate had shattered the old man's spirit and thrown him into despondency. To determine the possibilities of receiving any effective aid from there, it would be necessary for someone to go down to Alexandria by way of the Sinai Desert. He, Nitsa, would make the arrangements. Elon volunteered.

Bar-Kokba suggested that another attempt to approach the Parthian government be made. That, of course, would entail sending a second emissary, since communications with Meir had been severed. Abner, smiling somewhat wearily, said, "If you have no objection, I will go. The trip is hazardous, but is life here safe? Besides, I am the oldest among you and my life is worth less." There were, of course, objections. But in the end he was empowered to go.

After the meeting, Abner took his son-in-law aside. "If you should find time to see Meredya," he said, "do not tell her about my journey. She worries enough about *you*."

"What of my son?" Shemon asked quietly. "I have not seen him for a long time."

"He is quite big, runs about like a little colt and pulls my beard," reported the proud grandfather.

Bar-Kokba was pleased. "A rebel!" he laughed heartily. "And does Meredya see much of Tamar?"

"Yes, she sees her every day. Her music cheers Meredya. Now that Elon is going to Alexandria, Tamar, poor girl, will also be lonely."

For a fleeting moment Shemon's heart grew heavy with longing for his wife and child. But duty's call lay elsewhere. It was imperative to see Rabbi Akiba. He ordered his mare saddled, and after cantering down the Har Hamelek slope, sped on to Bnai Brak.

Despite his indisposition and the lateness of the hour, the old master got out of bed when Hagarsi announced Bar-Kokba. By way of greeting he laid his trembling hands on Shemon's head. "Things no longer go as they should," he said wearily as they sat down.

"That is why I am here." Briefly Shemon acquainted the rabbi with the latest developments and the decisions of the council.

"How are my disciples?" Akiba asked quietly.

"We have recited the mourning prayer for many of them," Bar-Kokba responded gloomily, "and but yesterday Ben-Dov fell."

The old man bent his head. "May God bless his memory," he whispered. "I am told that in the three weeks after the beginning of Passover not a day went by without some of my students dying. Is it true?"

"Alas, it is."

Akiba closed his eyes. Slowly a tear rolled down his cheek and disappeared in the silver of his beard. "This is the period of counting the sheaves," he said after a long and oppressive pause. "I will see to it that this period is decreed one of mourning in Israel." Bar-Kokba bowed his head. "And now proceed, Bar-Kokba."

"My dear Rabbi, some of the faint hearts have begun to waver. I wish to say that my eyes will never again look upon a subjugated Judea. As long as I breathe, it will be a fighting Judea."

"That is how it should be," murmured Akiba.

"If so, why has the Almighty turned away from us? What sins have we committed since the earthquake at Caesarea, where He gave us His sign to throw off the yoke of our oppressors?"

"To ask this question, my son, is a sin. Time and again I have said that the ways of the Holy One, blessed be He, are inscrutable. He does not hurry to mete out punishment or grant rewards for deeds evil or good. We may misunderstand His signs; we may not be aware of what He, the Omniscient One, knows; again, we may suffer for long-forgotten misdeeds. A mortal's scheme of things is reckoned by scores of years; but *His* scheme of things, by thousands of years. For it is said: 'A thousand years are as one day in Thine eyes.' The Lord's acts, as we see them, are but fragments of scenes enacted over the span of ages. It may well be that generations in the far-distant future will receive the answer to your query."

"Your answer, Rabbi, may explain our troubles but does

not alter them," muttered Shemon. "And," he added, "trouble comes to us not only from our enemies."

"You allude to the peace-seekers?" muttered Akiba.

"Yes, and my uncle among them."

Akiba sighed. "Judge them not too harshly, Bar-Kokba, for peace is God's creation—war, man's. Peace, too, is a purpose, and war but an instrument."

"But we are wielding this instrument now," Bar-Kokba said vehemently, "and to abandon it—"

"No, no, no," interposed the old sage, "we are not to abandon it. Peace now would mean nothing but ignoble slavery. We must carry our burden to the end. God will live through those who die for Him, just as He will eventually be with those who live for Him."

They parted, neither realizing that this was to be their last meeting.

At about the same time a week of victory festivities was decreed by Hadrian, to be wound up by a farewell banquet on the eve of his return to Rome.

During that week he summoned Rufus. "I have decided to return into your keeping the province which you lost and which we are retrieving at high cost," he announced. "As an administrator, you do not deserve it, but I never forget old, loyal servants. Rule with an iron hand; enforce my edict. If the obnoxious race will not accept us, let them accept death. Stamp them out. We will colonize others in their stead. Plow Jerusalem under as soon as our troops reach there. Erect a temple to Jupiter, as I have planned, and let the city forever be known as Aelia Capitolina. Severus reports that many young Israelites have been captured. Let them die in the arena. Since it will take time to rebuild the Caesarean stadium, stage your spectacles at Gaza."

"If it please Your Divine Majesty, I will call those spectacles the 'Hadrian Games.' "

"Agreed; and I will set up a special fund for them."

Rufus bowed as deeply as his paunch permitted. "No words are equal to the gratitude I feel, Your Majesty. Your Majesty's kindness is as great and your greatness is as unlimited as those of Jupiter himself."

"That was quite a speech, Rufus," the emperor laughed. "It must have taken you some time to memorize it. My rascally secretary must have apprized you of my intentions. But I am not finished."

Rufus glanced at Hadrian apprehensively.

"You managed to lose not only a province, but also a beautiful wife. She has some strange notions in her sentimental head, but you can get them out if you treat her as her loveliness deserves. I have ordered her to return to you. I promised her that you would apologize." He pulled the gong cord.

"Your Divine Majesty, I do not know how to thank you. . . ." began Rufus with mixed feelings.

An attendant appeared.

"Call in Lady Ruffina from the adjoining chamber," the emperor ordered. And to Rufus he said, "Come down on your knees when she approaches you."

The emperor's eyes twinkled. The scene should be amusing. Not much of a punishment for the fool.

Chapter Forty-three

Upon returning to Caesarea, Rufus confirmed the proscriptions, ordered the reconstruction of his palace and all other important buildings and went down by sea to Gaza to discuss the Hadrian Games. Though a good many captives were available, the time was not yet propitious for the spectacles. Savage fighting was taking place in the Hills of Ephraim and Benjamin. The siege of Tur Shemon was proving a costly affair, Judea was still inaccessible to the Romans, roads were insecure and the actual rule of the reoccupied part of the country was still in Severus' hands. Under the circumstances, no turnout commensurate with the degree of Rufus' personal vengefulness could be anticipated. Certain, however, that by autumn the rebellion would be completely crushed, Rufus made tentative arrangements for a sport meet and spectacle in November and returned to Caesarea. Free from excessive administrative duties, he concentrated on developing an effective spy organization and unleashing it on the surviving Galilean communities.

While a small number of Samaritans still remained with Bar-Kokba, their towns and villages, first singly, then in groups, declared their fealty to Rufus and Rome. In thirteen of these the Israelite communities joined the Samaritan defection. Denounced by Akiba, the leaders of the apostates insisted that their act was merely a subterfuge for the preservation of Judaism. Clandestinely they would continue to observe the Law until open profession of God would again become possible. On hearing this, Akiba rent his garments and cried out that their subterfuge was not against the enemy but against the Lord; that they were lickspittles and renegades and would, even as the Samaritans, become a mere shadowy memory, while those who fought to the last would perpetuate Israel and his God.

Stubbornly Bar-Kokba fought on. Though he had been seen with Bar-Daroma on the walls of besieged Tur Shemon, to the astonishment of the populace and the dismay of his enemies, he would appear in the most unexpected sections of the Hills of Ephraim and Benjamin to waylay, to seize food and weapons and to determine the outcome of local skirmishes. From Har Hamelek to the Valley of Rimmon, from Mount Gerizim to the Jordan, he harassed the legions. To put an end to these costly encounters Severus ringed with powerful forces the two main centers of resistance in those mountains, as well as Tur Shemon and Tower Hill, and began a stadium-to-stadium search for rebel lairs. To his chagrin, whole maniples of soldiers tracelessly vanished in the dark labyrinths of the Cave of Vengeance system. Severus gnashed his teeth but persisted. He placed groups of sentries at all suspicious openings in the hills, and kept these sentries linked and supported by cavalry patrols.

His main forces had in the meantime battered down the outer wall of Tur Shemon and discovered the underground passage through which communications with Bar-Kokba had been maintained. The discovery made the early fall of the fort imminent. To save its garrison Bar-Kokba decided on a simultaneous two-way attack upon the besieging Romans. To synchronize his own operation with that of the defenders of Tur Shemon, he sent instructions by a carrier pigeon. But the Romans intercepted the bird and foiled his plans. The battle between the two main armies materialized nevertheless; it proved too costly to Bar-Kokba and compelled him to retire to the Judean Hills. The Romans then overwhelmed the fortress.

Bar-Kokba took his army to Betar. There he found Elon, who had returned from Alexandria. The results of his trip were not comforting. There would be no new fleet, not even pirate raiders. No second Zevulun could be found and few boats were available. Some food supplies might reach them if they could maintain contact between Southern Judea and some predominently Philistine point on the coast between Askalon and Gaza. In that case the Alexandrian Brotherhood of Lions would, once a week, risk sending a small boat to that point.

Bar-Kokba said that they could maintain such contact, and summoning Amitai from Masada, put the problem before him. "There are two fortified points in Southern Judea," he said, "from which you can operate—Goren and Ziklag. Ziklag is close to the coast. Would you undertake the task?"

"I would," answered the big, dusky Amitai.

"We do not need the food now. We have stocks for two years. But it is good to have more. Fugitives are coming."

Leaving Elon in charge, Bar-Kokba now went down to Jerusalem to see Meredya and his son and to transfer to Betar what was left of his government. His heart was heavy, as unheralded, he entered the borrowed mansion that would soon revert to its owner. From an upper floor came the carefree voice of his son. Bar-Kokba had not seen the boy for many months and wondered whether he would know his father. Slowly he mounted the steps. From an inner room Meredya came running to meet him. Seeing him unkempt and worn, she halted for an instant, her eyes moistening.

"I am still here," he said.

She rushed forward and flung her arms about him. "My prince!" she cried, choking with emotion, "my prince!"

302

The little tot came over timidly and stared. His father took him in his arms.

Elisha gazed at his father for a while and touched his rough beard. *"Abba,"* he said. "You're my *abba,* Bar-Kokba. I wanted you. Where were you?"

"Away fighting the enemy, my son."

"Who is the enemy, *Abba?*"

"Edom, the accursed."

"What is 'the accursed,' *Abba?*"

"When you grow up, you will know," Shemon said, and pressed the little one to his heart.

"I know from Tamar that Father went to Parthia," said Meredya. "Have you heard from him?"

"No." Bar-Kokba, holding his son close, began moving toward an inner chamber.

"Yair was here this morning," Meredya continued. "He brought news from Issachar."

Bar-Kokba turned sharply. "Bad news?"

"He would not tell me. He went to Betar, hoping to find you there. He will probably be here again later."

In the afternoon, while the child rested, Shemon took his wife's hands and hesitantly began to speak to her. "Pleasure of my heart," he said sorrowfully, "we have not seen much of each other since our marriage."

"I knew that would be so when I married you," she said bravely, "but you were my choice, and I have not erred."

He patted her. "We are sending everything to Betar," he muttered haltingly. "Even Uncle Eliezer is going."

"I know." She moved up close to him. "Now we may be together for a long time."

The talk was becoming more difficult for Shemon. "That is what I wanted to speak to you about; we may not be.' '

"Why not?" she demanded.

"Because, for our son's sake and yours, I would like you to be in a safer place."

"Safety without you, when you are making your last stand, would be unbearable."

"It should not be. You will bring up a son who may finish what his father began, if . . ."

"No!" Meredya cried out. "No!" Her eyes dimmed and her lips trembled with emotion. She looked away and said more calmly, "His father himself will finish what he began."

"He may," he said moodily, "if Parthia comes to our aid, if other peoples in the East rebel, or if the Almighty turns His face to us again." He was silent. Then he reverted to his subject. "Elon will ask Tamar to do the same," he said gently. "You may both go to Ludd. Nitsa and his wife will look after you."

"No," she repeated firmly. He looked at her reprovingly and she turned to pleading. "You are my master and my prince, Shemon, and Prince in Israel, and your will is law. If it is the law that I am to obey, I must go; but if it is my heart, then" she was choking—"wherever thou goest I will go. . . ."

She broke into sobs. Bar-Kokba took her in his arms and said no more.

Yair made his appearance the following morning. He was haggard, emaciated and ragged and his eyes glowed unhealthily. "I bring you greetings from the dead," he said blankly.

Bar-Kokba stared at him. "Issachar? Everybody? The Cave of Vengeance, too?"

"Everybody, everything!"

Shemon offered him food and wine. Yair ate but pushed the wine away, murmuring, "Are we not in mourning?"

"We are," Bar-Kokba answered. "But we are at war, too. And preserving our strength for war comes first. Drink the wine."

Yair obeyed. After a while he spoke more freely: "They stormed Tower Hill first. Then they bridged the precipice to the Bowl. We opened the trap doors and hundreds of them rolled in. But they built a mountain of earth in the gorge, a mountain higher than the Bowl. Then, to bury us, they showered earth and stones into the Bowl. So we had to flee through the caves. But the exits had become blocked. So most of us were caught and killed. Some were taken prisoner. Me, too, they took, but I escaped. They were sending us to the Valley of Rimmon. Prisoners were coming there from everywhere. Maybe the Edomites chose Rimmon for revenge. They can laugh at us better on the site of our camp. I'd like to cut their throats and bellies. One after another, without pity, as they do to us. As they do to us!"

The last words Yair shrieked hysterically. Bar-Kokba squeezed his hand, and the pain brought Yair to his senses. "The prisoners are coming from everywhere," he whispered, spent. "From everywhere. I know not what they'll do with them."

In the Valley of Rimmon the early July heat hung in the air, fiery and oppressive. Starved, verminous, tattered and almost black from the merciless sun, the prisoners lay or sat on the withered grass. Guarded by bulky, scowling sentries, they were waiting for their doom. But it was slow in coming. Every day new prisoners arrived, some from nearby points, others from small forts on Lake Kinnereth.

"Is Joel still holding out in Tiberias?"

"Yes."

"Is Bar-Kokba still fighting in Judea?"

"Yes."

Weary, sunken eyes would light up. "Blessed be the Lord; not all is lost yet."

The number of prisoners mounted. Five thousand, six thousand, ten thousand. Then some of those taken earliest succumbed. Perhaps a deep sigh or a slight convulsion indicated their passing. Their comrades, submerged in their own misery, would rarely know about it until the stench of the decomposing bodies became pronounced. Under Roman orders, the corpse would stay where it was, putrifying the air and hastening the end of the others. Now and then moans would be heard: "Lord of the universe! What are they waiting for? . . . Why don't they kill us? . . . Great God, be merciful! Send us death, send us death!"

But the Angel of Death was overtaxed with work. More war prisoners came, and then women and children, refugees or captives. They were taken from highways and byways, from hideouts, from homes—thousands and thousands of them. They did not weep; they did not lament. They stared with blank eyes at the men who had fought for them and lost. If they recognized husbands or brothers, a stray tear or a gulp was the only sign. There was no outcry, no recrimination. What was the use? And why amuse the scowling sentries? Children alone expressed their feelings without restraint, and heightened the torment of their parents.

One morning a large body of soldiers surrounded them all and the women were ordered to strip. When they refused, the soldiers began to strip them by force. But the worn, starving, unkempt men threw themselves upon their tormentors. They hastened their own ends.

The carnage lasted for hours, and the blood of the slaughtered streamed in innumerable torrents from the sloping valley into the Cyprus River and thence into the Jordan. Crazed women leaped into the dark-red waters to be carried with their men's blood to their deaths.

In the afternoon, after the soldiers had rested from the butchery, they herded the children together to be sent to slave marts. Then they lined up the women on the river bank to await the arrival of the commander. He came in a matter of minutes. His punctuality was rivaled by the impeccability of his dress and the irreproachableness of his bearing and conduct. By his smile, which did not quite smile, and by his eyes, which were not quite cold, culture and good breeding could easily be divined. He did not touch a single woman, but scrutinized them all before speaking.

"Your men are dead," he said finally, "and most of you are young and comely. My soldiers want you. They will stay here, and they need wives. You can be their wives and live in peace. Your children are no longer yours." Some women wrung their hands and wailed. Disdainfully he waited for the noise to subside. "They are no longer yours," he repeated, "but you can have other children, begotten by strong, healthy Romans. And your new children will never be slaves. The unwilling will die. Let the ones who agree step forward."

There was a long silence. No one stirred. A solitary vulture soared above and the bloody waters lapped the bank.

Then one woman came forward. "Edomite," she cried out, "your words are as sweet as your heart. Wild beasts have more compassion than you. They do not devour their own kind. You do. We spit on you and your blackhearted race! Be accursed!"

An arrow struck her in the heart and she fell. The commander shrugged and walked away. The last act of the slaughter began. The blood of the women mingled with that of their men. Some bodies rolled into the river and were swept into the Jordan. For days the Jordan ran red, carrying its toll of bodies into the Dead Sea, which held them on its surface in the glare of the sun.

Chapter Forty-four

The Roman blows were as hard and unceasing as the heat was unbearable. Askalon surrendered and Ludd was reoccupied by Saturnius. Then a confidential message from Theodoros was brought by one of his men, masquerading as a Roman: Abner had been caught near Antioch and hanged. That was the hardest blow of all, for with Abner's death the hope of Parthia's assistance vanished. But Bar-Kokba shook it off and took care to conceal the news from Meredya. Finally scouts reported that a large Roman army, under Severus himself, was slowly marching on Judea.

It was time to abandon Jerusalem. Shemon told Meredya that they were leaving the next day. All essential business had already been disposed of. The records and the mint had been transferred, and the scribes and attendants had gone to Betar with old Eliezer. Tamar, too, was gone. Like her friend Meredya, she had refused to seek safety in Ludd.

Toward evening Bar-Kokba, as had been his habit in better days, roamed through the ruins of Jerusalem. The City of Peace— that was what his people had named it. Of all the nations on earth, his alone had named their capital not for a hero or ruler or god, but for peace. That was what they had wanted the city to be. Not so others. Others had made it a peaceless, woe-stricken city. He had hoped one day to do justice to its name and to the will of his people. Now that hope was slipping, fading. This, perhaps, was the last time he would be treading the holy ground. From there the Temple stones had been taken for the walls of Betar. He had been right in his precautions. If only he had been wrong!

The evening was far advanced when he found himself near Rachel's tomb. Lonely it stood, beneath a few palms, amid the sweeps of rising and falling hillslopes and curving roads again and again tramped by foreign hosts. The tomb was like his country; his country was like his people. He clenched his fists. The struggle was not over. God might yet relent. Here, at this tomb, the stone-carriers had halted and pleaded for intercession. Perhaps Mother Rachel would yet intercede. Surely she could not abandon her children forever.

Dim-eyed, he turned to go back. The road was sandy and led uphill. In the moonlight its color was ghastly, like that of the skin of an embalmed corpse.

When he awoke the next morning, Meredya was pale and her eyelids were red.

"What is wrong?" Shemon inquired solicitously.

"I had a terrible dream," she answered. "It is all a jumble now. I remember one thing: I heard voices from the Dead Sea and moans from the Jordan. The river moaned and moaned and filled me with terror."

Shemon muttered unconvincingly, "It is because you worry."

Later, as they waited for the animals to be loaded and saddled, they went to a window. The hills and dales lay bright in the sunshine. The three streams running from Jerusalem to the Dead Sea were dry. Vultures were circling over Mount Scopus; their shadows trembled on its slopes. One by one they paused in the air, turned southward and winged away.

"Vultures!" exclaimed Bar-Kokba. "Vultures over Jerusalem. A . . . a . . . an omen." He had been about to say, "A bad omen," but had checked himself in time.

Suddenly Meredya seized his arm and cried, "Look!"

"What is it, my love?"

"The Jordan is red! And where it falls into the sea, the Dead Sea is, too."

Bar-Kokba looked, saw, understood. A chill ran through him.

"Maybe the moans were real, too," she whispered. "Maybe our kin and friends were calling."

"They were all our kin and friends," he said with a sudden gruffness that was intended to conceal his emotions. She understood, and looked at him sorrowfully. He turned away, muttered something about speeding up their departure and left hurriedly.

The approaches to Betar teemed with men, women and children, beasts of burden and herds of cattle fleeing from the advancing enemy. Inside the fortress the streets were packed with people, most of whom carried their belongings, and beasts of burden that could move no farther. The heat of the day was augmented by the heat of steaming bodies and irritable tempers, and men and women fought for elbow room with abusive words and even with blows. With great difficulty Bar-Kokba and his little family made their way to the upper citadel, closed to all but the fighting forces. Placing Meredya and Elisha in prepared quarters, Bar-Kokba returned to the lower fort. As matters stood, the refugees would bring disaster to themselves and the defenders.

Bar-Kokba mingled with the crowds and exhorted them to assemble outside the gates. But it soon became apparent that, barring some drastic action, the people would not budge. They simply could not move even if they wanted to, for everyone was in everyone else's way. He ordered the town cleared by force.

When none but the local residents remained, he addressed the crowds from the wall. He reminded them that he had refrained from fighting in the Judean plain and in the northern half of the hills so that they might stay where they were. By coming here, far from helping themselves, they only imperiled the defenders, who were here making their last stand. The enemy was still quite a distance away, and some of them still had time to return. That they should do at once. Those who could not do so should move on to Hebron, Eglon and Ein Gedi and across the Jordan. For their own sake and for that of the outcome of the war, let them stay away from fortified towns. Should the fortunes of war go against the Israelites, whoever was found in such towns would be slaughtered regardless of his guilt or innocence. And while the fate of the inhabitants of unfortified towns might not be too enviable, the majority of them would at least be left alive.

As he concluded, women wailed and lamented. Men, beating their chests, shouted that they would rather die with Bar-Kokba than live under the accursed Edomites. Others proclaimed vehemently that they wanted to fight. The crowds began to move, and by nightfall only about a thousand irreconcilables remained; they insisted that they wanted to fight, and were therefore admitted.

Later strong patrols were placed on the roads to divert other refugees from Betar. Exceptions were made for those who insisted that they had come to fight.

After midnight Bar-Kokba summoned his leading commanders and the remaining members of the People's Council. He was pleased to see Malanos among them, but the presence of Agrim and Manashik aroused his ire. He desired to know what had brought those two there when most of the Samaritans had so ignobly surrendered to the enemy. Agrim replied that his and Manashik's part in the war was known to Rufus, that their heads were wanted and that for them there was no alternative but to fight to the end.

Bar-Kokba described the weak and the strong points of the three walls of the fortress. He told them that their food supplies, barring the unforeseen, would last for two years; that their water supply was satisfactory if the enemy did not discover the location of the spring; that further food supplies were expected to arrive through a secret subterranean channel. No one should take his unwillingness to be more explicit about this channel as indicating a lack of confidence in his lieutenants. Men often revealed information unwittingly, and in a stage of siege even walls had ears.

"Let us not think that we have gathered here to die," he concluded. "We have gathered here to fight our most stubborn battles while Heaven decides our fate. Let us pray that the decision be in our favor. Almighty God is our greatest ally and commands the most effective weapons. He has in the past wiped out besieging armies by plagues and earthquakes, and has buried them under the molten metal of fire-belching mountains. As for us, we will not wait for the enemy to storm us. We will give him no rest. We will fight outside the walls as often as it will be to our advantage. To fight well, we must be of one mind and of good cheer in all circumstances."

When the meeting was breaking up, Bar-Kokba asked Elon, Asher and Malanos to remain. "Friends," he said, "our scouts report that the enemy was in the hills late this afternoon, about thirty furlongs from Kiryat Yaarim. He will probably encamp for the night and reach here tomorrow night. I mean to give him the first blow before he encamps—a telling blow. How many first-class horsemen and horses can we rely on?"

"Fifteen hundred," Elon responded.

"The Edomites have six thousand. Here is what we will do. You, Asher, with five hundred men, will wait in the grove behind the bend of the hill below. Take Yair to assist you. I and one thousand men will be in the woods across the valley. I'll have Malanos with me. Even if the enemy arrives before nightfall, he won't be able to see you. You, Elon, will man the walls with thousands of men, as if expecting an immediate attack. You know how the Edomites march: First come the foreign auxiliaries, never anxious to fight; next, the engineers and masons; third, the commanders' baggage; fourth, the commanders, with a guard; fifth, the pikemen; sixth, the horsemen. The main body of the army, preceded by their tribunes, cohort commanders and eagles, follows the horsemen. Our purpose is to destroy their engineers. They are the ones who will set up the camp and build the fortifications to counter ours. You, Asher, charge straight into them and cut without mercy. I will have the auxiliaries confused by false signals. The road will be blocked by their own forces and it will take some time for the horsemen to come up. When they do, run for the fort. They will pursue, and I'll come up from behind to repay them part of the debt for the Valley of Rimmon."

The following evening the attack was carried out. Half of the Roman engineer corps was annihilated and serious losses were inflicted on the auxiliaries and cavalry. Among those who distinguished themselves was Elhanan the blacksmith, who tricked his enemies and smote them with his hammer with deadlier effect than many a sword. The Judeans fought with the zest and fury which they had exhibited in the battles early in the year. The results were heartening to them, for Severus' plans were disrupted and the siege retarded. But their success was marred by their losses, the foremost of which was that of Asher, captured by the enemy.

Chapter Forty-five

With Betar besieged, the ports regained, the coast blockaded and Amitai's raids confined to Southern Judea, for which Severus was responsible, Rufus was now free to enforce the proscriptions with the utmost ruthlessness. He enlarged and perfected his spy system, announced attractive rewards for the denunciation of transgressors and rebels, and treated archons failing to report violations in their communities as cruelly as the violators themselves. Fanatical mothers who went into hiding with their circumcised infants drew death upon themselves and their offspring when caught. The bodies of executed transgressors, like the bodies of rebels killed in action, were not allowed to be buried and became carrion for ravenous beasts and birds. Numerous groves and forests were destroyed to provide lumber for Severus—and to reduce the number of hide-outs. Men nailed to crosses marred the appearance of roads and mountainsides and drove tradesmen from market places. The teaching of the Law was all but stifled, and the instruction of small children, when it was dared, took place underground.

Only Rabbi Akiba persisted in his defiance of Rufus. He rejected all pleas to leave Bnai Brak. Though but a select group of disciples listened to his discourses, he was content. Every day brought them closer to ordainment; men who defied death for the privilege of being ordained would be worthy carriers of his tradition. When Nitsa warned the old master of the imminence of his arrest, Rabbi Akiba said, "Bar-Kokba holds his fort at Betar. I will hold mine at Bnai Brak."

At the end of the summer, shortly after the Day of Atonement, he was seized and lodged in a special jail in Caesarea. The night over the people of Israel had thickened.

One day a palace attendant whispered to Judith, who had returned with Ruffina, that an Israelite was asking for her at the gate. She wondered who it might be. Few of her compatriots remained in Caesarea, and those who were there knew how to reach her in a different way. She ran through the garden. As she approached the iron gate, she saw a middle-statured man in sackcloth contemplating moodily the marble blocks of the entrance walks. Upon hearing the patter of her feet he looked up. She recognized Joshua Hagarsi. He was unkempt and his eyes were bloodshot.

"Joshua, peace be with you. What brings you here?"

"Our master is in jail," he replied.

She put her hands to her heart. "Where?"

"Here, near the ruins of the stadium, in a secluded house where the keepers of the beasts used to live."

Her eyes filled with tears and for a while she could not speak. Then she told him to wait and ran to find her mistress. Ruffina was shocked at the news. Her first impulse was to see Hagarsi and hear the story from him. But then she thought better of it. Who knew what her husband might do under the present circumstances? He had been courteous enough since their return from Antioch, and more avid than ever for her. But beneath his passion and honeyed words she could sense that memories of injured pride and unforgiven jealousies were rankling; at the first opportunity they might break out and incite vengeful acts. So she decided to proceed cautiously and merely asked Judith to ascertain where Hagarsi lodged.

After dinner that night she gathered up courage to broach the subject gently to the procurator.

He bristled at the very mention of Akiba's name. "I warn you not to interfere in matters of state. This old rattlesnake is the most dangerous seditionist in the country. I was lenient with him once, and paid a heavy price for it. No more. He will be taught a lesson as an example to others."

"What will you do to him? He is a very old man."

"You will see."

"Tell me," she implored. "Surely you don't mean to kill such an old and venerable man."

"Venerable?" he snarled. "Poisonous!"

"I know that you hate him. But he can no longer do you any injury. If you think that his presence in the country is undesirable, send him away. But please don't kill him."

Rufus stared down like a bull before charging. She realized that her case was hopeless, but tried once more. "He cannot harm the empire any more. If you kill him, he will haunt you to the end of your days; if you spare him, it will add to your glory."

Still he was stubbornly silent. She began to hope that he might be wavering, and laid her hand on his. "Please tell me what you will do."

He leered at her. "I see that you are extremely interested in the old swine's fate. I promise that you will see it." He rose. His eyes were bloodshot, his cheeks were crimson and his jowls shook. "You will see it!" he repeated, almost choking, and stamped out of the room.

Autumn passed and winter approached but the Romans made no appreciable progress against Betar. They inflicted serious losses on the defenders but suffered no less themselves. Bar-Kokba's losses would have been much lighter had it not been for his frequent sallies. Though men lost were irreplaceable, the high morale of those living more than offset the loss. And that high morale was creditable largely to the sallies that Bar-Kokba personally led to foil any signs of Roman progress. If the Romans began to build iron-cased wooden towers from which to menace the defenders on and inside the walls, Bar-Kokba would charge and destroy the bases. If the Romans attempted to bring their big battering-rams close to the wall, under cover of testudines or massed archers, Bar-Kokba would cry, "At the Nicos!" (a name for the battering-rams since the days of Titus) and the defenders would rush out to smash the engines. Small detachments, at times disguised as Romans, would creep out of the subterranean passage in the rear of the Roman camp at night, slash the throats of sentries, steal or burn supplies, maim horses and vanish. Amitai, too, engaged in acts of sabotage, but more frequently he attacked Roman patrols and kept Bar-Kokba in contact with the rest of the country.

Akiba's arrest plunged the defenders into grief. Elon volunteered to make a desperate attempt at rescuing the rabbi by taking a party of disguised Heromavs to Caesarea in small rowboats. Bar-Kokba discouraged the plan, not so much on the ground of its unworkability as because of its ultimate futility. It might be possible to reach Caesarea and set Akiba free, but to bring him safely to Betar was another matter. And even if that should succeed, why expose him to the jeopardies of the siege?

Chapter Forty-six

The weeks went by. One night, as Agrim wandered through the lower fort, he observed Amitai emerging from a house in a lane adjoining the wall. He waited, and presently a party of men carrying baskets and bundles came out of the same doorway. He followed them and took note of the building where they stored their supplies. Assuming that the house near the wall was in some manner connected with the underground passage used by Amitai and his men, he was curious to see its layout. He retraced his steps, but found that people were talking in the house. Apparently they were waiting for Amitai, who undoubtedly had gone to the upper fort to see Bar-Kokba. Agrim decided to satisfy his curiosity the following night.

In the upper fort Bar-Kokba listened glumly to Amitai's recital of the latest events. It was tormenting to hear such news without being able to do anything more effective about it than to hold Betar and occasionally to destroy some Romans.

Amitai told Shemon that the second spectacle of the Hadrian Games had taken place at Gaza. After the sports meet, in which legionaries as well as athletes from Antioch and Alexandria had participated, the spectators and the contestants were treated to a show which in its wantonness and cruelty exceeded the one staged the month before. Mad dogs, wolves, fire and mass combats, in which the fighters were prodded with glowing iron prongs, were used as means of destroying men; and between the acts naked Adonises declaimed odes in honor of Hadrian. Asher's end was terrible. He wrestled with a well-known wrestler of the Antiochene Plethrium, who had been condemned for some ugly crime. It had been expected that the Antiochene would break Asher's neck and limbs, thereby evoking Rufus' gracious pardon. But Asher upset the plans by breaking the man's head. Rufus, who presided, ordered Asher thrown to the tigers.

Amitai followed his harrowing account with a recital of the daily misdeeds of Rufus' regime. These had made life so intolerable that the whole community had begun to think of self-destruction. To find some way out of the catastrophic situation a secret conclave of leading rabbis was held in Nitsa's attic at Ludd. There, after a discussion which lasted from noon till the following morning prayer, it was unanimously decreed to absolve the people, when death was the alternative, from the guilt of transgressing all rites and all laws except those covering adultery, incest and murder. An attempt was made to obtain Rabbi Akiba's vote from jail. Hagarsi, who was allowed to bring food to his master, was entrusted with the task.

"Are they weakening?" Akiba asked unhappily. And he then declared, "I will not vote, nor will I question the decision of the conclave. The wisdom of the majority rules."

Bar-Kokba communicated Amitai's story to his colleagues and commanders.

Reb Eliezer rose to comment. "It is not my intention to recriminate, but rather to save the little that is left," he said somewhat shakily. "I warned Shemon, when he was merely my nephew and not yet Bar-Kokba, that rebellion would lead to disaster. Now we have it. Already we have lost that which we strove to uphold. But things can still be worse. We cannot foresee what the wickedness of Sodom may invent. Let us save our people from the abyss. The month of Tebet is here. In five or six weeks the strong rains will have ceased and Severus will again begin to build his fortifications to bridge our walls. He may fail once, twice, three times, but he will succeed in the end. What then? If we sue for peace now, we may not be allowed for some time to live according to the Law, but we will be allowed to live. If we cause no trouble, the oppressing hand will gradually relax, and eventually the proscriptions will be withdrawn. If we bear our lot with fortitude, we may expect a change for the better. They will not do unto a submissive people as they do unto a rebellious one. . . ."

Bar-Kokba, his patience gone, brought his fist down on the table. "Enough, enough! Sit down, Uncle. We all know exactly what life will be like if we surrender. Death is sweeter to me, and to the death I will fight! Let us vote. You, Elon?"

"I fight to the death."

"You, Malanos?"

"With you to the end."

All the others except Agrim, who was noncommittal, voted to fight. Old Eliezer seemed to shrink and grow older with every vote. When the last man had spoken, he rose, trembling, and, leaning heavily on his cane, turned to go. With his first steps he almost lost his balance, but Agrim hastened to his support and helped him out. The old breach between uncle and nephew, between two attitudes, had reopened and deepened and became an unbridgeable gap.

A week passed and Amitai came and departed. The following day Agrim confided a grave secret to his friend Manashik. "Bar-Kokba," he said, "did not consider us worthy of knowing the secret of the underground corridors and the water. The secret of the passage Amitai uses I already know."

"How did you come to find out?"

"By accident. Last week I happened to see him bring supplies out of a house. I was able to learn nothing till last night, after they had gone off with their bundles. Then I slipped in and found an open trap door. It looked like one solid block of stone, two cubits long and as wide and thick. I examined it, and found that it was fastened to strong iron hinges. I tried to budge it, but I could not. I still don't know how they work it. But I went down into the passage. By the lights they had left I saw that it was very long. I was curious to know more about it, but could not risk going far. I went back. What I had really wanted to know was where the passage led to. That I found out because I heard the men speak. It leads into a grove behind the Edomite camp. One of the men said that the Edomites had chopped down some trees in the grove, and that he hoped they wouldn't chop down any more. 'They may discover the exit,' he said, 'if they do.'"

"What do you mean to do?" inquired Manashik cautiously.

"Nothing," said Agrim, equally cautious.

"Why are you telling me, then?"

"I thought you might like to know."

"In case things should grow worse?"

"Yes." Agrim paused, and then added as an afterthought, "They *will* grow worse."

"Why?"

"There will be dissension inside. Reb Eliezer told me that some time soon he would preach peace."

"Which may arouse brother against brother."

"That is what I was saying. And the Edomites will soon again be attacking hard."

"Yes. Are you longing for Samaria?" asked Manashik.

"Are you?"

"I am."

"So am I."

They paused and eyed each other meaningfully.

"I suppose," Agrim said, "we will work together if I think of some good plan?"

"Most assuredly."

They shook hands.

Chapter Forty-seven

Pressure was brought to bear on Rufus to release Rabbi Akiba. Delegations arrived from Alexandria, Antioch, Cilicia and even Cyprus. Of the members of the local moneyed class, Eusabbatis, Harrar and Nitsa came. Huge sums were offered for the old sage's redemption. But the procurator remained adamant. Here was one man whom he had to destroy. With the other Judeans, as long as they behaved, he would eventually have to arrive at some understanding. The country must again bring revenue to Rome. With such men as Eusabbatis, Nitsa, Harrar, he would deal. Their foremost interest was business. But rabbis he would not tolerate; they were the root of all trouble—especially this old seditionist. This persistent intercession on his behalf merely proved the extent of his influence, and therefore indicated the danger of keeping him alive.

Suddenly it occurred to Rufus that it might prove even more advantageous to break the old man's spirit than to crush his bones. What a triumph to hear the great rabbi say, "I am sorry." And how humiliated Ruffina would be! Thus inspired, Rufus went to see Akiba.

He found the old rabbi standing at his heavily barred cell window, which, partly below the street, abutted directly on the walk. Save for a solitary stone bench, the room was devoid of furniture; the bench to which Akiba was shackled by a long iron chain was his bed, chair, table.

As the guard opened the door for Rufus, Akiba, without acknowledging the procurator's mocking greeting, plodded over to his bench and sat down.

"A poor beginning, Akiba," muttered Rufus. "You are as arrogant and intractable as ever."

Akiba made no reply.

Rufus' eyes fell on an earthen water jar and some dry bread on the bench. He recalled that, except on the Sabbath, when Akiba was permitted to have a broiled egg and barley soup, bread and water was his daily diet. Rufus nodded at the dry bread. "Are you not tired of it?"

Again Akiba ignored him.

Rufus tried to keep his temper under control. "You behave," he said, "as though I were the prisoner, and not you."

Akiba retorted quietly, "You are."

The procurator laughed uproariously. "I? Am I confined to this hole, or are you? Am I shackled to that stone bench, or are you?"

"You are shackled to a heart of stone, and your chain is a chain of wickedness."

The blood rushed into Rufus' head, but he laughed off the offense. Then he said gruffly, "Listen, Akiba, you and your God have lost. You have stung us but you have definitely lost. Only a fool won't admit that, and you are no fool. I have come to make you an offer. If you accept it, I will not only pardon you but elevate you. You may choose whatever title and position among your people you desire. All I ask is that you publicly renounce your God. He is of no use to you. He exists only in your imagination. He does not answer when you pray; He does not help you when you fight or suffer. He does not exist. If you agree to say that publicly, your people—most of them, I am sure—will follow you. Life will then become more bearable to them; in time they will become prosperous Roman citizens. You have it in your hands to put an end to their suffering and yours."

But even as Rufus was speaking, Akiba had begun to whisper in Hebrew.

"What are you whispering?" demanded the procurator.

"I have been praying," responded the sage calmly, "that the God you blaspheme should forgive you so that you may live to see His glory."

Rufus shrugged. "You are not susceptible to reason, Akiba. I warn you—and this is my final warning—that unless you recant, you will die a horrible death."

"There can be nothing more horrible than to live under your rule," said Akiba without emotion.

"You will soon find out that there can be," Rufus snapped. To the head keeper he said, "Henceforth this man's attendant is to be barred. No one is to see him except those bearing permits under my seal. The prisoner may still have his bread and water, but only through you. And double the guard."

The date of Akiba's execution was set for the end of the month of Shebat, when the rainy season waned and intervals of sunshine grew longer. Rufus took care to publicize the event throughout the land, so that friends of Rome might jubilate and foes be stricken with fear.

A temporary wooden amphitheater, with a special loge for the procurator, was erected in the stadium square, in sight of Akiba's cell. In the center a high platform was built, flanked by huts for guards and executioners, and upon it a revolving crosslike wooden contraption was constructed.

When building operations had been completed, a strong guard was thrown about the structures. The street of Akiba's cell was closed to traffic, but pedestrians were allowed to use the walk across the street from the jail.

With the visitors who came to enjoy the spectacle, a number of Akiba's disciples arrived. Disguised as hucksters, now one and now another went tramping by. Pretending to shout their wares, they posed debatable questions which Akiba alone could resolve. Standing at the bars, he would, as if asking for the prices, give them his decisions. On the eve of the execution, together with their last questions they sent him their farewell.

The last to pass was Joshua Hagarsi. "Needles for sale!" he cried. "Needles—oh, master, my master!"

Sobs stifled his last words and he shook with emotion. Across the street the guards eyed him suspiciously, and he hurried off.

That day Ruffina arranged with Judith to see Akiba after sunset. She meant to tell him that she had not forgotten him, that she had tried hard to save him, that she was brokenhearted at her failure. But when evening came, they found that the palace guard had been instructed not to permit anyone, even Lady Ruffina, to leave the palace grounds without the procurator's written orders.

Raging with anger, Ruffina ran to her husband's chambers. Not finding him there, she ran to the baths, the stables, the guest house. But he was nowhere to be found. Spent, she retired to her boudoir, flung herself on her bed and wept.

In the morning, when Rufus came to invite her to the execution, he expected to find her rebellious. To his surprise, though pale and a little puffy under the eyes, she was dressed and ready. He told her how gratified he was, but she said nothing. In her heart she had decided to attend in the hope of being able somehow to convey to Akiba what she had been prevented from telling him the preceding evening.

She followed her ermine-robed husband into their sumptuous loge, ornamented with the imperial eagle. In boxes immediately behind were high military and government officials and local Greek and Roman notables. The loge was scarcely more than twenty feet away from the platform. The instruments of torture, thumbscrews and long, sharp iron combs, as well as the executioners, two huge, dull-faced Teutons, were already there. A band of trumpeters and drummers stood between the platform and the loge.

As Rufus and Ruffina entered, the dense crowd in the amphitheater rose and cheered. The procurator bowed to the large assembly and sat down. After a brief interval a detachment of lictors appeared from the northeastern corner of the square, where the ruins of the stadium lay. Here, some three years before, Bar-Kokba had humiliated the Roman army. Now, in the same place, a proud Israelite would be made to pay.

The drums began to rumble. The lictors advanced into the square. A few paces away, flanked by two powerful soldiers, Akiba, barefooted, bareheaded and dressed in a single linen robe, trudged slowly, dragging his shackles. A second detachment of lictors closed the procession.

The amphitheater mob began to jeer and the drummers increased their tempo, but the old rabbi betrayed no emotion. He held his head high, his gaze directed at the backs of the lictors. Only the beads of perspiration glistening on his bald skull betrayed his effort.

As the lictors reached the platform, they lined up on each side of the steps. Then Akiba mounted the steps slowly. The executioners unshackled him. The drumbeats stopped. The jeering, in which the throngs in the surrounding streets joined, increased in volume. Akiba lifted his head higher and fixed his eyes on the boisterous mob. Once again beneath his tablet-like forehead shone the pools of light which Shemon had seen at his first meeting with the master. Now only Judith and a few of his disciples, disguised and mingling with the mob, saw that light.

The executioners removed Akiba's linen garment, and save for his loincloth, he stood nude. His body was thin and bony from undernourishment and age. His long arms, once powerful, hung loosely at his sides—but not for long, for the executioners roped them behind him and seated him on a bench.

The trumpeters sounded a signal. An official mounted the platform, unrolled a parchment scroll and read the charges. When he was done, he called out in a loud voice, "For the last time, will the prisoner, Akiba ben-Joseph, renounce his Judean God and abandon his criminal ways?"

The sage glanced at the official with disdain and said nothing. The official then nodded to the executioners.

All this time Ruffina had been vainly trying to catch the rabbi's eye. Since she could not speak to him, she wished at least to smile a greeting or to send a look of encouragement, one solitary message of sympathy from the vast amphitheater of hate and derision. But he did not rest his eyes on her or on any other individual; he seemed to gaze through and beyond the assemblage into space.

The executioners brought the thumbscrew and placed it at Akiba's feet. One Teuton inserted the rabbi's toes into the machine and held his calves while the other slowly turned the screw. As the pressure increased, Akiba paled and his face and head moistened with perspiration, but he uttered no sound. When his joints began to crack, he sank his teeth into his lower lip, still uttering no sound. From a distance the torture looked like an innocent pastime, but from near by its horror was unmistakable. Ruffina felt a rising nausea. The procurator thought, *The old devil is brave.*

Since no sound had escaped Akiba and the executioner apparently could turn the screw no further, the official ordered Akiba's toes released. His feet were limp and livid and his toes, oozing blood, seemed to hang in their skin.

The official glanced at the procurator, and the latter nodded. "The combs," ordered the Roman.

The executioners seized Akiba and all but carried him to the crosslike contraption, to which they secured him with thongs. They ripped off his loincloth, and his body, now completely nude, became exposed to view. Slowly the contraption, operated from below the platform, began to revolve so that all the spectators in the square might see. When the Teutons grasped the iron combs, Judith, who could endure the sight no longer, slipped away. Hagarsi and other disciples shut their eyes but stayed.

The executioners began to comb Akiba's flesh. Blood spurted from his back; strips of skin dangled amid the bloody trails. That was what the crowd had been waiting for, and it howled with delight. The procurator, too, was visibly gratified. Only Ruffina presented a discordant note; as white as the face of the tortured man, she slumped to the side of the loge in a swoon.

Akiba's flesh had been shredded from neck to heels before he lost consciousness, and all the while his lips had moved in inaudible prayer. Covered with his white robe, he was taken back to his cell.

Toward evening Rufus came to taunt the dying man for the last time. He was unaccompanied. Through the bars the glow of the setting sun fell on the blood-soaked robe. Akiba's face was whitish-yellow, but his eyes still flickered with life. His lips were moving; he was whispering his evening prayer.

"I warned you it could be worse," said Rufus, as if continuing their recent conversation. "Now you have tasted it."

Akiba smiled wanly. "It is not worse; it is better," he whispered. "The Holy One, blessed be He, has tested me. I am happy." He gathered his waning strength and added, "I have been granted the privilege of loving God with all my heart, all my soul, all my might." His breath failed him and he stopped. He struggled to say something, but his last strength was gone. He closed his eyes and sighed. It was the end.

Rufus stood in the vanishing daylight, contemplating Akiba's lifeless face. Despite his hatred for the man, he had to acknowledge that there was something uncanny in his fortitude. "I killed him," Rufus reflected, "but I did not conquer him."

Outside, he found ten men in black waiting for him across the street. Hagarsi stepped forward. "Rabbi Akiba was our master, Your Excellency. We want his body for burial."

The procurator wavered. Bodies of rebels were supposed to go uninterred. But this man had not fought with the sword. What he had fought for had not been killed, and what *had* been killed might be more harmful unburied.

He turned to his head keeper and ordered him to release the body.

Chapter Forty-eight

When Bar-Kokba informed his men of the manner of Akiba's death, the hate in their eyes and their cries of "Revenge!" expressed his own feelings. Whatever the outcome, they could not let the wanton act pass without a bloodletting, and so Bar-Kokba ordered a daring sally.

Its ambitious objective was to capture Severus. To gain the objective it was intended to set the large Roman camp on fire from four sides, and feigning as many attacks, to throw the weight of the charge into the center of the camp, where Severus' hut was located. Night, the suddenness of the assault and the ensuing confusion were to be Bar-Kokba's allies. With a little luck, such an attack might even turn the tide of the war.

But that little luck was missing.

The sally indeed disorganized the Romans' camp and caused them great losses in men, horses and stores. Bar-Kokba even succeeded in bursting into Severus' hut, ready to kill. But the general was elsewhere and the sally failed of its objective—and cost Bar-Kokba two thousand men. Of these, almost half were native Betarians. So telling a loss plunged the town into deep mourning and gave rise to bitter complaints at the useless sacrifice of life. Nor did the Romans rejoice. Severus was so deeply stung as to lose his customary equanimity. He was hurt not merely by his losses, but also by the fresh evidence of the unbroken spirit of the besieged. Hence, he resolved to speed the downfall of Betar by more vigorous tactics and an attempt to demoralize the defenders.

Not long afterwards, as Bar-Kokba, from one of the twelve towers of his upper fort, watched the far-flung Roman camp three thousand feet below, he observed unusual activity. Earthworks, designed to encompass the scalable sides of the Betar eminence, were being constructed. Large quantities of lumber were being brought up. Infantry was being drilled, and contingents of cavalry, with large catapults behind them, were heading for the outer rim of the camp.

These were signs of preparations to storm the fortress, but there was little by which to judge how long these preparations might take. Bar-Kokba gazed down the steep western incline of the mountain which faced the camp, and thought that he would welcome such an attempt if it were to come now.

From the valley the mountain rose steeply for about five hundred feet to a wooded plateau, thence in a difficult slope for fifteen hundred feet, and from there, in varying degrees of steepness, to the wall of the fort. The height of the wall was sixty feet, and above it rose four towers, each thirty feet high. One aspect of the mountain was advantageous to attackers: sec-

tions of the hill were covered by underbrush, which might provide cover. Bar-Kokba would long since have done away with
these shrubs and wild plants, had not some of them concealed
the vital spring. It would not have done to leave only one
section covered, moreover, for the Romans would at once have
surmised its importance. The slopes on the other sides of the hill,
except on the north side, were more favorable to attackers; but
this was not true of the ground below, full of pits and depressions.

Suddenly the Roman cavalrymen went into action. Shunning
the steep western side of the hill, they dashed to its flanks. The
charge was puzzling. Even if it were successful, the cavalry could
not be expected to mount the walls; nor was the number of the
attackers sufficient; nor was there evidence of adequate support
by machines and other essential branches of the army.

Bar-Kokba ordered the walls manned and waited. The purpose of the attackers became apparent as they reached points
high on the slopes. They were shooting arrows bearing messages.
To each missile a small parchment roll was attached. Enough
of them landed on the walls and inside the forts to bring them
to the notice of the defenders. Each read: *I will pay one hundred
thousand denarii for Bar-Kokba's head or for information about
your underground passage. Severus.*

One of the rolls of parchment came into Agrim's hands.
That evening the Samaritan dropped in to see his compatriot.
He showed him the message. "Have you seen this, Manashik?"

"No." He glanced through the parchment and opened his eyes
wide. "How did it come to you?"

Agrim told him.

"You can buy much for one half of one hundred thousand
denarii," ventured Manashik.

"And get your freedom for nothing, into the bargain," added
Agrim, his shifty eye pupils dancing.

"Yes," Manashik agreed, squinting at his friend. "And I
suppose you already know all you need to know about the
passage?"

"No. But I think I know enough. I know, for instance, that
it is necessary to solve four or five riddles before one can cross
that corridor."

"What do you mean—four or five riddles?"

"That many walls across the passage block it. Amitai's men talked about it. I could not get past the first one."

"So you do *not* know the secret?"

"I know enough for the Romans. I know where the corridor leads to. Once they know where the door is, they can stop others from coming in, even though they may not be able to enter themselves."

"And how can you let them know?"

"The way they reached us—by arrow."

"And what if they do not find it, or if Bar-Kokba's men find it?"

"You are right, Manashik; it is dangerous. Whichever way we do it, it is dangerous. But if we wait till the fortress falls, we will surely die."

"It is so, Agrim. What do you propose to do?"

"I told you, Manashik. An arrow will tell them to tie their answer to a rope that will hang from the lower wall at a fixed hour. I will tell them that the rope will hold nothing heavy, so that no one will attempt to climb up. Then you and I will take turns in putting out the rope and watching it."

"Good. Let us try."

A fortnight later the news spread throughout Betar that two of Amitai's men had been caught by the Romans and that communications through the subterranean passage had been cut off. The lower well had been cut off, too. This was a serious blow. Some believed that the discovery had been accidental. Others, Bar-Kokba among them, suspected treachery. But there were no clues. It became necessary to maintain a strong, frequently shifting guard inside the corridor and to devise other means of keeping in touch with the rest of the country.

Bar-Kokba summoned Asaph. "Only you and I know that there is another passage leading to the southern side of the fort. That side, which would take anyone using it southeast, onto the Bethlehem road, and up back to occupied Northern Judea, should be used only in an extreme emergency. The passage will do no good to many; it can save a few." Bar-Kokba paused, and then said quietly, "We are all mortal. If anything should happen to me, tell Elon about this exit."

A blow far worse than the blocking of the passage was destined to follow soon. A week before Passover the lower fort stores, containing three quarters of the reserve foodstuffs, went up in flames. More than half of the cistern water was used up to prevent the fire from spreading. The charred remains of the sentry, who had apparently fallen asleep, were found inside one of the buildings. What had prompted him to go in was as deep a mystery as the identity of the perpetrator of the arson. That it was arson, and that a traitor was therefore at work, no one doubted by this time.

Dire peril threatened the fortress from inside. It was imperative to discover and punish the betrayer. This was not a simple matter. With the refugees, close to one hundred thousand people crowded the town in addition to the twenty thousand veterans of Bar-Kokba's army. There were still some Samaritans, Christians and recent proselytes among Bar-Kokba's forces, and the refugees were even more heterogeneous. By a process of elimination Bar-Kokba came to the conclusion that Samaritans were the likeliest suspects. Again he summoned Asaph. "See that Agrim, Manashik and their closest friends are watched."

Meanwhile the great loss of irreplaceable food reserves demanded a drastic curtailment of daily rations. But even these semistarvation doles could not last for more than three months. The strength of the defenders would be sapped at a time when the Romans were intensifying their activities and the warm weather was fast approaching.

On the first day of Passover, when the main synagogue was jammed with worshipers, Eliezer preached a sermon of surrender. His arguments did not essentially differ from those he had advanced a few months before. But then he had had a small and unsympathetic audience; now it was a large and receptive one.

"The war against Edom," he said, "was begun so that we might be free to live according to the Law of God. That war, alas, we have already lost. Of the six hundred and thirteen laws which it is incumbent upon us to observe, our great rabbis were forced to absolve us from observing six hundred and ten. It is true that here in Betar, thank God, we can still observe them all. But how long will that last? If we persist in fighting an unconquerable foe, we will surely die. If we sue for peace now, we will live. Our lives will be unhappy for two, three, five years. But then we shall regain our rights. The Almighty in Heaven, He and He alone, knows why we suffer, when the expiation of our sins will be complete and when we shall again be privileged to enjoy our share of earthly happiness. Let us therefore demand that Bar-Kokba sue for a reasonable peace now."

After the services the congregants came to petition Bar-Kokba, but his reply was brief: "We have fought too long and too hard to be given quarter by Severus. Suing for peace now means death to most, slavery to the rest of us. To us, who have fought for Israel without asking for your approval, and who will die for Israel without asking for your approval, slavery is worse than death. Those who would rather live like worms than die like men will be free to leave this fort after the holiday. Whoever leaves it will not be allowed to re-enter. And now, go in peace."

Some upheld Bar-Kokba, but others cried out in anger, "Not Bar-Kokba, Son of a Star, art thou, but *Bar-Koziba—Son of a Lie!*"

For days stormy meetings were held. On the last day of the holiday Bar-Kokba was informed that six hundred dissenters, including a handful of Samaritans and Christians, were ready to leave Betar in the morning.

"Is Eliezer with them?" he asked.

"No," was the rejoinder. "He disagreed but would not secede."

"Let them go," ordered Bar-Kokba, and his heart was heavy and bitter.

In the morning he watched them go. Elon, Malanos and Yair stood beside him in gloomy silence. The peace-seekers, their women and children in the center, were leaving by the south gate, whence the mountain sloped toward Atzmon and the Valley of Tears. At the foot of the hill, north of the stream Akor, which sliced the valley, earthworks had already been built; and as the procession started down the slope, Romans came out from behind the slope and trained their arrows on the moving crowd. The men raised their hands and shouted, "Peace! We want peace! We renounce circumcision! We want peace!" They repeated these cries incessantly, loudly and in unison so that the Romans should not mistake their intentions. Hate contorted Elon's face and he shot an arrow at them. But Bar-Kokba pushed his arm and the arrow went wide. Down went the dissenters, shouting their renunciation until they reached the enemy lines. The Romans met them with jeers and buffets and kept them outside the earthworks for hours. When they had their fill of fun, they took the peace-seekers to the nearest tribune.

Chapter Forty-nine

Hard days came; days of privation, irritations, defeats and ever growing losses of men and animals from warfare and disease. The heat increased and took its toll of the undernourished defenders and populace. Horses died from lack of fodder. No news arrived from outside. The world as a functioning, striving, event-producing reality ceased to exist; it existed only in retrospect. It had dwindled to the limited space and functions of the stronghold, and the space and acts of the hostile camp. Even Jerusalem, to the northeast, and the Dead Sea, to the south, clearly visible from this height, had become to the defenders mere dreampoints in the unattainable outer world.

The most terrible reality was the Roman camp. Like an immense rattlesnake, it rolled upward from the south, southwest and southeast. Tightening its death coils as it climbed, it sounded its approach with hammer and axe, trumpet and catapult. New engineers arrived and filled up the depressions and pits. They laid iron roofs on stout poles, under whose cover the attackers built their trenches and ramparts. As the rings of earthworks increased in number and filled up with soldiers, Bar-Kokba's assaults against the builders became more risky and less effective. And so it was from day to day, from week to week and from month to month—until the ruthless midsummer heat came to add to the defenders' woes.

Old Eliezer, who had reconciled himself to his fate, spent his mornings and late afternoons studying the Torah in the shade of old sycamores belonging to his hired dwelling. Over the low shrubs fencing his little garden he could be seen poring over his parchments and chanting in a deep, cracked voice. To many of the inhabitants he had become a holy man. In their eyes his studies and prayers played a vital part in the defense of the fortress. Were a miracle to turn the tide of the war, they would ascribe it as much to Reb Eliezer's influence in the Heavenly Spheres as to the defenders' valor.

Agrim, whom Bar-Kokba continued to suspect, came to visit the old priest from time to time. Again and again the Samaritan urged the old man to renew his advocacy of surrender. He even intimated that the Romans would certainly arrange terms with Reb Eliezer, for was he not the high priest? And was not a high priest in Israel imbued with at least as much authority as a commander? But Eliezer's answer was a steadfast "No!"

Asaph, without knowing their content, reported these conversations to Bar-Kokba. His uncle's previous conduct, Bar-Kokba felt, lent a peculiar color to his association with the suspected Samaritan. The matter was grave.

Despite Bar-Kokba's reluctance to have any dealings with his uncle, he went to see him to clear up the matter. But Reb Eliezer refused to explain. No one had the right, he insisted, to meddle in his private talks with people or in the choice of his friends.

Thus the matter stood when the Romans, under cover of night, launched a fierce three-pronged assault on the fortress. Hitherto they had been unable to attack from the steeper western side. But since, south and west of the fort, they had reached points less than half a stadium from its lower wall, they were able, with the aid of engineers and their impregnable iron-roofed shelters, to strike at some western points. The attack was repulsed with heavy losses to the assailants, but early in the morning Bar-Kokba was horrified to discover that the Romans had dug in and built ramparts around the spring. He rushed into the narrow tunnel connected with the spring. The tunnel had not been discovered but its mouth was blocked.

"Soldiers," he shouted, "our water is cut off!"

The defenders, weary and weakened from almost incessant action and guard duty, were exhausted after the night's conflict.

"Men," Bark-Kokba shouted again, "our fortress is lost if we do not regain the spring! In the name of God, who goes with me?"

Two thousand followed him. But the Romans were ready with fresh and overwhelming forces. The battle veered back and forth for six hours. At midday Bar-Kokba was compelled to return with only seven hundred battered and weary men. The spring was lost.

Inside the upper fort Bar-Kokba slipped into a secluded tower chamber, and beat his head with his fists in despair. Then, in utter exhaustion, he dropped to the floor and slept.

It was dark when someone aroused him from his sleep. "It is I," he heard Asaph's familiar voice say. "Will the prince come with me."

Bar-Kokba sat up, shook off his drowsiness and hurried down to the lower fort. The narrow streets, with their squat, flat-roofed dwellings, were silent and few lights were on. In the fort tower sentries talked across space to keep each other awake, and from neighboring avenues the stamping of patrols was heard now and then. Bar-Kokba and Asaph ran past several houses whence weeping and lamentations issued. These mourners bewailed their yet-unburied dead.

They reached a point in a lane parallel to the southern wall where two men were holding a third. When Bar-Kokba came close he recognized Manashik. "Why is he being held?" he asked.

The two men pointed to a stone to which a rope, flung over the wall, was attached. Bar-Kokba looked down. As far as he could see in the dark, the rope reached to the ground. He pulled it up. A small papyrus was looped to the end.

He called for a light. Asaph ran to the nearest tower and returned with a burning taper. Shemon unrolled the papyrus and read: *Our work is done. We will steal out of the citadel in the tenth hour tomorrow night. We will wear black robes and no headgear. See that there is no mistake.* The note was unsigned.

"What has Manashik to do with this?" inquired Bar-Kokba with ominous calm.

"We saw him tie the rope to the stone and throw it over the wall."

"Did you see it too, Asaph?"

"Yes, Bar-Kokba."

"Lower the taper so that I may see his face," ordered Bar-Kokba. Manashik's eyes were bulging with fear and his lips were trembling.

"Who wrote this note," demanded Bar-Kokba, "and who is 'we'?"

Manashik attempted to say something, but only a gurgling sound escaped him. Bar-Kokba pushed the two men aside and struck the Samaritan across the face. Blood began to trickle from his nose and mouth as he staggered against the wall.

"I don't know," he gasped.

"Tell me who your accomplices are."

"I don't know."

Bar-Kokba seized him by the throat. "Tell me, tell me. Do this one good deed before you go to perdition. Tell me!"

No answer came, and Bar-Kokba's fingers tightened on Manashik's throat. "Tell me, tell me, tell me!"

Manashik, writhing and choking under the relentless pressure, suddenly hung limp. Bar-Kokba relaxed his grip and shook him, but Manashik was dead. Bar-Kokba tossed him to the ground and wiped his moist forehead. "Throw the reptile overboard," he said. "Let the Edomites see that he arrived with his message in person."

He turned to Asaph. "Find Agrim, bring him to my tower and wait for me if I am delayed."

"Where will I find you in an emergency?"

"At my uncle's."

Reb Eliezer was frightened by the pounding on his door and opened it with trembling hands. It took him a long time to light a lamp, and when the yellow flame began to flicker, Eliezer's fear deepened; he had never before seen his nephew so frightening in appearance. His tunic was soiled and torn, his hands were bloody and his pupils glowed like fireflies.

"What is the matter, Shemon?"

He stared at his uncle piercingly. "I have just killed Mana-shik."

The effect was not what Bar-Kokba had expected. Eliezer merely recoiled a little and whispered, "Blessed be the just Judge."

"You do not ask me why. You do not happen to *know* why?"

"I have no right to ask and certainly do *not* know why."

Bar-Kokba came close to the old man. "Listen, Uncle," he said harshly, "I have condoned many evils, but I will not tolerate vile treachery. Unless a miracle happens, the fortress is lost. The secret of our water has been betrayed, and in the cisterns there is hardly more than two days' supply left. Tens of thousands of people are doomed to death, infants among them. That was Manashik's work. But he had accomplices. At least one. I know who he is, but I must be sure. I must have a witness. I can no longer let this wolf stay in our midst. You must tell me what Agrim was talking to you about."

"Agrim?" The old man was clearly taken aback. "Agrim?" he repeated, and there was fear in his eyes. He had suddenly realized that what Agrim had been suggesting to him had led to treachery. If he were to reveal that to Bar-Kokba, Agrim would surely lose his life. And what if the Samaritan had merely spoken, and had *done* nothing wrong? Then he, Eliezer, would be the source of an innocent man's death. No, he could not disclose that information.

His uncle's hesitation deepened Bar-Kokba's suspicion. "Uncle, I ask you not to try my patience any longer. Tell me."

"I cannot tell you, Shemon; and I cannot tell you why not."

Shemon's eyes flamed. "You are protecting a traitor. Suspicion falls heavily upon you. . . ."

"Upon me? Great God! Shemon, you are mad. . . ."

"Reb Eliezer, in the name of God, I ask you for the last time: What did Agrim talk to you about?"

"I will not answer."

Bar-Kokba's head spun with fury. Hardly realizing what he was doing, he brought his fist down on Eliezer's head and the old man crumpled to the floor. Instantly Bar-Kokba was overwhelmed with remorse. He lifted Eliezer, placed him on his bed and forced a few drops of water into his mouth. Eliezer opened his eyes, looked at his nephew, whispered, "I forgive thee," and closed them again.

During the night he died. Thousands of men and women escorted their high priest to his last resting place. Their sorrow was deep and unrestrained. They could not believe in the high priest's guilt. They were certain that whatever he might have done he had done for their welfare, as the intermediary between them and Providence. Now their holy emissary was gone and calamity became inevitable. As they trudged after his simple wooden casket, as they lamented and chanted psalms, it seemed that it was themselves and their freedom that they were escorting to the crowded graveyard.

The only emotion which Bar-Kokba felt was stern determination. The old man had been responsible for his own fate. This the people must understand. He must have Agrim's confession. But Agrim had vanished.

After Eliezer's funeral Bar-Kokba placed a strong guard about the city wall, confiscated all the water left in private cisterns and concentrated it in a reservoir in the upper fort. Out of this a quarter of a cup a day was allowed for the healthy and half a cup for the ailing and infirm. For these pitiful rations the populace stood in long lines in the merciless sun and, as they waited, cursed the day of their birth. The defenders on active duty were given the same rations as the infirm, but those off duty got no preferential treatment. Meredya insisted on standing in line with the others and receiving an equal dole. At times, when the plaints grew loud, she would, despite her own suffering, endeavor to soothe the people with words of faith. She was a source of strength even to Bar-Kokba. Whenever, in the rare moments which he managed to spare for her and their son, she read dreariness and despair in his eyes, she would whisper love and encouragement to him. Caressing him and pressing his heavy head to her breast, she would say, "He who saved Jonah from the whale will save you and Israel."

But there were no signs from the Savior of Jonah. Misery was growing and spirits were rapidly sinking. Few believed that the fort could hold out much longer. Every night famished men and women gathered in their synagogues and, with lips parched with thirst, prayed for a miracle. Every night men and women collapsed at the services, and if they died, there were those who envied them.

Animals, given no water at all, died faster than men. To harass the Romans, dead horses and donkeys were thrown over the walls. The Romans would move up to bury the carcasses so as to avoid disease—and Israelite sharpshooters had their targets. This, however, gave them little comfort, for the enemy was closing in. He was now scarcely more than fifty feet from the southern wall and was bringing up his heavy battering-rams.

One day a *hamseen*, the like of which even the ancients could not recall, blew in from the desert. Before nightfall it had scorched all vegetation a lifeless brown. In the morning the streams Akor and Sair, in the valley, and Nahal Kidron, below Jerusalem—all flowing into the Dead Sea—stood still. At sunset they were dry.

Bar-Kokba took Elon aside. "Elon," he said, "we have been in this from the start. Outside of Meredya, there is no one dearer to me than you." Elon, sensing what was coming, looked away. "I would not ask you to do this, Elon, if it were a mere matter of friendship. It is more than that. It is something that will perhaps save what we have done from being completely fruitless." It was not easy to say what he wanted and for a while Bar-Kokba stared at the floor. But it had to be done. "This is my request: Save Meredya, Elisha and your wife and her unborn child, from our fate."

"How can I? And is it right?"

"You can, and it is right. I will tell you how and why. There is an underground exit, leading to the Bethlehem road, about which only Asaph and I know. Through that exit you and Asaph can take the women and Elisha out. Once you are out, you should have no trouble. The exit is a good distance past the Roman camp, and except for occasional patrols, the road to Bethlehem should be clear. What I ask you to do is right, for if it is not done, all our sacrifices will have been in vain. Who knows but that Israel's fighting spirit may go down with us? Elon, my friend, I want that spirit to live through our children;

that is why I want our children to live. I wish I could do as much for every family in Betar. But I cannot. If many go out, they will be caught. If few go out, they may escape."

Elon put his hand on his friend's shoulder. His eyes were sorrowful and pleading. "Let me stand with you to the end, Shemon."

"It is painful to say no. You have done your duty until now; what I ask you to do is part of your duty. I ask you to sacrifice the privilege of dying for Israel, so that our spirit may live on in Israel."

"I will go."

There was a long silence. Then Bar-Kokba said, "Here is the plan. Meredya will not go of her own free will. We will give her a sleeping potion in her water. You and Asaph will carry her out. Once out of the tunnel, she will wake and be able to walk. You will find yourself behind the Roman camp and close to Bethlehem. Nitsa has stores and a relay station there, and Asaph, who worked for Nitsa, is well known. You will get food and donkeys and proceed to Ludd as peasants."

"I will try to come back, Shemon."

"No. I order you not to. Stay with your wife and try to help my . . ." The words stuck in his throat. "Let us not fail at least in this," he concluded abruptly, and walked away.

Elon caught up with him and they embraced.

Chapter Fifty

Tamar slipped past the clump of shrubs concealing the mouth of the underground passage and looked about. There was no one in sight. A short distance away the dusty road could be seen in the moonlight. She pushed aside a dry shrub and called into the opening, "There is no one about. Give me Elisha."

She placed him a few paces away and went back to part the shrubs while Elon and Asaph brought Meredya up. The little boy looked about in bewilderment at his mother, still sleeping, strangely; at the large, reddish moon; at the high mountain in the background, and at the road descending mysteriously into the eerie distance. "When will *Imma* wake?" he whispered. "I am afraid."

Tamar cuddled him. "Soon, Elisha, darling, soon. Be a good boy and do not cry." She spread her mantle on the ground and the men placed Meredya on it. They rested a little and Asaph went over to the road.

"Not a soul in sight," he said as he returned.

"Let us not waste time, Asaph," decided Elon. "The farther we are from here, the better. We'll take turns in carrying her. I'll take her now. And remember, in case anyone asks us: 'She has fainted from the heat.'"

They went some distance down the road and Meredya began to stir. Elon carried her a little farther, until she opened her eyes and asked drowsily, "Where am I?"

He sat her down by the road and they waited. Tamar released Elisha's hand and he ran to his mother and hugged her stormily. "*Imma!* You slept so long. I was afraid."

She caressed him, rubbed her eyes and looked about her, still half-dazed. Tamar came over. Meredya yawned. She looked up at her friend, patted Elisha's hands which were still clinging to her neck, and said, "I am thirsty. It is so quiet here. Where are we?"

No one replied. She was almost awake by now but still incapable of coherent thinking. She gently moved Elisha's hands and stood up. The Betar mountain loomed large behind her, and southeast, barely a mile down the road, she discerned the contours of a village which might be Giloh. Then came the impact of the realization that she was out of the fortress. "Surrendered?" she whispered.

"No, no. They are still fighting," Tamar hastened to assure her.

"They? So why are we here? Has something happened to Shemon?"

"No, Meredya," Elon interposed. "Shemon is well and will stay to the end, but we are here by his orders. We are going to Ludd. And," he added, "there is no time to waste."

She stood still, trying to grasp the full significance of what she had heard. "I do not wish to be saved," she said at last. "Life without Shemon means nothing." She took Elisha by the hand. "Take me back, Elon. It is not far." Suddenly she broke down and wept. "I did not even say *shalom* to him." Elisha withdrew his hand and gazed at his mother without understanding, ready to cry out of sympathy.

Tamar took Meredya into her arms. "It is for Elisha's sake that he sent us out," she said quietly, struggling to keep her own tears back. "He wants to live through his son."

Again Meredya wept.

"You have always been a brave woman," said Elon. "You are Bar-Kokba's wife. I know that you have been and will be worthy of him to the end."

Her sobbing stopped abruptly. Yes, Elon was right. She had to live up to the proud name of a prince in Israel, her prince, the Son of a Star. Now there was the little prince to take care of. She dried her eyes, gathered Elisha up in her arms and covered him with kisses.

"Do not cry, *Imma*." He brushed a tear off her cheek with his little fist.

At Giloh they were given drink and food and they rested briefly. They reached Bethlehem without mishap and found the expected accommodations there, as well as animals for the onward journey.

The *hamseen* lasted for seventeen days. In the daytime, purgatory itself seemed to have moved up from the nethermost regions; at night stifling vapors arose from the earth. Dead birds dropped from the fiery air; scorpions and snakes became unusually bold and vicious. The water in the upper-fort reservoir evaporated and even the ailing went without drink. Men and women crept into their cellars to die, walked about muttering insanely or lay in the streets groaning, biting into their veins to suck their own blood.

Bar-Kokba was everywhere at once, sleeping little and encouraging his men with words and deeds. He took the place of many a collapsing guard, operated stone-throwers, visited the ailing, and fortified the spirit of the depressed. Fortunately, there was no serious fighting, for the heat was heavy upon the

Romans, too. Nevertheless, they pushed on with their building operations, most of the work being done under cover of night.

Early in the month of Ab the height of their ironclad towers reached that of the lower walls of Betar. The Roman battering-rams, whose effective operation had hitherto been frustrated by the defenders, could now do their work with little interference. The Romans might now also attempt to bridge the wall.

Most of Bar-Kokba's men were incapable of resistance. Gasping for air, they lay or leaned against the walls in the tower chambers or closed courts. Their spirit was unbroken, but their bodies, after months of incessant duty, undernourishment and, finally, waterless days in desert heat, refused to obey. However, from the ranks of the veteran Thumbless and Heromavs Bar-Kokba mustered a few hundred men to meet any eventuality in the lower fort. As night came, he went from tower to tower to see that the sentinels were awake, while Yair, Malanos and Elhanan looked after the guards at the gates.

Toward midnight a breeze began to blow from the sea, driving the furnace air back into the desert. The breeze grew in velocity— and then something extraordinary occurred. Clouds gathered and soon the stars disappeared from view. From where they had lain, resigned to their fate, people got up to pray. "Almighty God, Thou art omnipotent!" they cried, their faces turned toward the sky. "Take pity, take pity; give us rain! Let the miracle come!"

As if in answer, thunder rolled, the clouds opened and the rain began to fall. Men and women held out their cupped palms to it and sipped, or threw themselves down on the ground to let it pour into their open mouths. Pans, bowls, pails and vats were rushed outside to collect the precious water. Some of it accumulated in the cistern. In a few minutes Bar-Kokba's dying army became virile again.

Providence had at last relented. A greater miracle might yet come! And even while the frantic hope stirred within them, rain turned into hail. Huge hailstones came down with ever gathering speed. The vessels bearing the precious rainwater which, with strict economy, might last for two or three days, were hurried indoors.

The *hamseen* did not return. But the heat, with only carefully measured drops of water being dispensed each day, was like salt in an open wound. Frenzied men and women again ran through the streets of Betar demanding water, cursing their fate and reviling Bar-Kokba. There was a rumor that Agrim, in disguise, had been seen among the crowds, had been heard instigating them against their leader. "First he sent his wife away," the Samaritan was said to have declared, "and now he himself will flee and leave you to the mercies of the enemy."

Knots of wild-eyed townsmen stood below the upper fort shouting, "Thou betrayest us, Shemon! Thou wilt flee as thy wife hath fled! Not the Son of a Star art thou, but the Son of a Lie! The Son of a Lie!"

Suddenly the heavy pounding of the Roman battering-rams could be heard. The defamers, terror-stricken, subsided. The more circumspect citizens filed out into the streets and proceeded to Bar-Kokba for guidance.

He came out to them. "Brethren," he said, "the last battle is beginning. You can help us by bearing your suffering with fortitude. Those who are still strong enough can help man the second and upper-fort walls if the first is breached. We will give up nothing easily. Nothing is ever lost if it is not lost in one's mind. So your minds must be set for victory, only victory. If your fate is to die, with that thought you cannot lose. You will lose only if the enemy takes you alive. Torture or slavery will then be your lot.

"This, too, I must say. And not to dishearten you. Ab is a fatal month in our history. Both our Temples were destroyed on the ninth of Ab. Masada fell on the ninth of Ab. Let us resolve to fight on past that fatal date, however tormented we may be with thirst and hunger. Perhaps the evil spell will be broken. Go now and prepare. Bring anything that will hurt the enemy. God help us all!"

Solemnly they murmured, "Amen," and hurried off to do their duty.

The battering-rams smashed at the outer wall until nightfall without causing any visible damage. An exchange of stones and arrows went on all day, and vain attempts to bridge the wall were made by the Romans until they called a halt at sunset.

During the night everything that was portable but heavy enough to hurt the enemy was brought to the second wall: stone benches, wooden chests, small stone tables, copper pots, millstones, hammers, axes. Tar was distributed in small vessels to be handy for action. All this was stored on a ten-foot projection, five feet below the top of the wall.

With daybreak the battering of the outer wall was resumed, and in response the Betar ballistae began to rattle. Shemon, assisted by Elhanan the blacksmith, was in charge of the forward wall; Yair, of the second; and Malanos, of the third, in the upper fort. Bar-Kokba, dashing from point to point, co-ordinated action and inspired the men by his presence. He seemed to have a charmed life. As he ran along the wall, missiles whizzed and fell about him without touching him. He hurled back some of the stones that crashed at his feet.

As the morning wore on, the wall began to crack. Bar-Kokba ordered Elhanan to abandon the towers and to line up his men between the first and second walls. At the same time he directed Yair to be ready to meet a full-scale attack. Even sooner than expected, a section in the forward wall, near the southern gate, collapsed. The Romans rushed for the breach, but the blacksmith and his men were in it first.

As other parts of the wall crumbled, retreat became inevitable. Under the shelter of testudines, the Romans began to move the battering-rams against the second wall. Several cohorts of foot soldiers followed the machines. When the Romans got into position, Bar-Kokba's men and the Betarians came to the rim of the wall and, with a fury incredible in men so worn, let loose an avalanche of the articles brought up during the night. Immediately the Roman stone-throwers opened up from their improvised towers.

The battle lasted throughout the day. Mounds of corpses formed on both sides of the wall. Several battering-rams were smashed. Before sunset the Romans withdrew to their original positions and, when it was dark, returned to remove their dead. The Israelites had already begun to count their own.

Tiny portions of water—the last—were distributed before dawn, and the battle was renewed at sunrise. Almost at once the Romans attempted to storm the wall, but they failed. The fight developed on the lines of the preceding day, except that the Romans continually threw in fresh reserves, while the ranks of the defenders dwindled. Bar-Kokba, in the forefront of the combat, exhorted his followers to hold out until after the fatal ninth day of the month, but their strength was flagging. By afternoon the wall was littered with headless and disemboweled corpses. On the projection, five feet below the top of the wall, exhausted men lay asleep or gasping for breath. An obdurate handful fought on. Amid the piles of their own dead the Romans began to pound the second wall. When nightfall came, Yair's body was found among the corpses.

After a few hours' sleep Bar-Kokba met with Elhanan the blacksmith, Malanos and the other surviving commanders. "I do not know," he said gloomily, "how many will be able to rise to the defense at dawn. I will ask you to count them soon. But whatever the number, we shall not have enough men to keep the enemy out of the lower town if the wall is breached. Let us, therefore, conserve whatever strength is left for the defense of the upper fort. Only a few will hold back the battering-rams so that the enemy may not know what condition we are in."

"What about the people?" asked Malanos.

"Those who want to go into the upper fort may do so. But they must stay in the covered courts without moving about."

"And if all of them want to come in?"

"We will have to let them. It is for them that we are fighting."

"It will help neither them nor us," said Elhanan.

"There is no other way. We must share one fate."

There was a long silence. Then Bar-Kokba said huskily, "In an hour like this it is our custom to forgive and ask for forgiveness. Do forgive me, brave and loyal comrades, for any harsh word uttered, for any hurt unwittingly caused you."

As one, these tough men saluted and their response, though unspoken, glistened in their welling eyes. He embraced each one of them. To Malanos he said, "To you I am doubly grateful. You are a Christian, and not one of our race. You stood with us to the last. Not until such loyalty is understood by all will there be happiness for all."

To which Malanos responded: "As well as to the Lord God,

I owe my life to you. Can I do less than lay it down with you for the same God?"

The following night, the eve of the ninth of Ab, the battering-rams hammered against the last Betar wall. The Romans gave the exhausted defenders no respite. They moved their machines and reserves over their own dead.

Inside the fort all men still able to resist stood in rows behind the wall or lay flat on top of it, their weapons ready. The best sharpshooters were in the towers, waiting for daylight.

In the courts and in the narrow streets of the citadel men and women huddled in groups, leaned against walls murmuring psalms or lay half-conscious on the ground. Here and there families of mourners squatted, swaying and intoning unintelligible prayers.

From his tower, above which his flag still fluttered, Bar-Kokba could see in the dark the gilded Roman eagles where the first Betar wall had stood. Down below in the valley, burning torches and faint sounds of marching indicated the arrival of new Roman reserves. Far to the south, flames leaped into the darkness— undoubtedly they marked the end of the forts that Amitai had been defending.

Bar-Kokba watched the picture spelling the end of his struggle. He no longer felt the dull despair of the last few days. His mind had become accustomed to the thought of defeat. Only one desire consumed him—to destroy as many accursed Edomites as he could before he himself was slain. He had girded himself with three swords and carried a reinforced shield.

As he watched, he could see in a nearby street, directly below, a handful of stragglers being brought out of the dark under an escort of Roman soldiers. One carried a torch, and by its light Bar-Kokba could discern a figure expostulating with the centurion. The centurion pushed the man aside twice, three times, but he persisted. Bar-Kokba suddenly recognized Agrim, and at that moment the centurion drew his sword and split Agrim's head in two.

"May all Thy foes perish thus," whispered Bar-Kokba.

The battering-rams kept on pounding. Then came a crash and a Roman cheer—the wall had been breached. Bar-Kokba flew down the winding steps. Roman buglers were sounding the attack. He reached the breach. The blacksmith and Malanos were already there. A few wild-eyed women, carrying pots of burning tar, were mounting the steps to the wall. The shattering blows of the machine were still falling, as the breach was not large enough. Finally the wall collapsed.

Bar-Kokba shouted the old Biblical battle cry, "Who is for God—with me!" In response came the blasts of rams' horns. The surviving Heromavs cried, "The Lion lives!" "David, King of Israel, lives and endures!" roared the Thumbless.

Bar-Kokba plunged into the onrushing foe, the last defenders about him. From the wall boulders and burning tar came down on the Romans. Desperate men and women leaped down onto their enemies to take at least one Edomite to death with them. The air shook with yells and curses, the clashing of swords, the clanging of shields, the groans of the dying and, farther back in the courts and narrow streets, the mournful strains of prayer.

Bar-Kokba was near the breach, on the wall, outside, near the breach again. Nothing could stand before his unbridled fury. He had already broken two swords, and now he drew his third. His shield absorbed the enemy's blows. Elhanan went down. Malanos was being set upon. Bar-Kokba rushed to his aid. They fought back to back. Then he no longer felt Malanos' presence. He warded off an attacker and his eyes caught a huge Ruman, on the western side of the wall, who had thrown off several of the defenders. Bar-Kokba cut his way to the wall and mounted. The huge Roman was still there, doing his deadly work. Bar-Kokba came closer. Their swords clashed and broke. They grappled, and together they plunged down the steep slope. The battle went on.

Still clutching each other, Bar-Kokba and the Roman rolled down and down. A clump of bushes stopped their descent. Bruised and bleeding, they struggled on. Frightened lizards darted for cover to a nearby boulder, and a large serpent hurriedly coiled after them. Bar-Kokba's fingers closed on the Roman's throat. The Roman threshed about, his eyes staring out of his battered head. Then he lay limp, lifeless.

Slowly Bar-Kokba sat up, his back against the bushes. His body ached; his skin was torn; there was a gash in his head, and it pounded unbearably. High above he could hear shrieks of pain and horror. They were maddening. His people were dying and he was still alive, impotent.

He leaned forward in an effort to climb up. He dug his feet and fingers into the reluctantly yielding soil and began to crawl upward. His thoughts were in a jumble: Meredya, his son, Akiba, incoherent words of prayer and the burning sting of defeat. Like an ox at the slaughter, he emitted a roar. It was directed to Heaven. But only the echoes responded. Summoning his remaining strength, he attempted to raise himself but slipped back. A heavy weight was on his feet. They were being seized. He turned. A python, its sharp tongue quivering, its narrow eyes aglow with a greenish fire, was tightening its powerful coils about his legs. Bar-Kokba's fighting spirit was aroused. With a superhuman effort he twisted himself up and gripped the serpent's neck. Under the weight of his body, they went tumbling down the mountain, striking against its rocky ledges and bounding downward until they lay still in the ravine.

Day was dawning when Saturnius and a small patrol of his veterans passed by. For the final assault on Betar and the mopping-up of Southern Judea every available legionary had been mobilized. The news of the fall of Betar and of Bar-Kokba's disappearance was already known.

"Look at this," exclaimed one of the soldiers. The others looked, and shrank back in horror. A man and a large serpent, both dead, lay intertwined in a bloody heap.

Saturnius came close and bent down. He gasped. "By all the gods! The Copperhead! The Judean!"

It took him quite a while to find speech again. Then he said, "He straddled a lion and he lived; swords struck at him and he lived; he fought a Hercules and he lived. By Jupiter! If a god had not killed him, no one would have."

Saturnius paused, and then added respectfully, "Not a bad sort was this Judean. Remember? He let us go from Ludd with honor.

Come on, men, let us bury him. And not a word to anyone about it."

A small boat, with four rowers pulling at the oars while four others rested, slowly plied its way toward Alexandria. Its solitary sail was folded, for there was no breeze on the sun-flooded Mediterranean. The boat carried a small consignment of spices from Nitsa to a client in the Egyptian capital. There were also five passengers in the boat: Meredya and her son, Tamar, Elon and Asaph. The two men carried documents certifying to their connection with Nitsa's firm. The papers were necessary to satisfy the curiosity of the officers of the Roman fleet, still blockading the shores of the Holy Land. The rowers were Judeans, all tested servants of Nitsa.

The boat kept close to the shore—so close, in fact, that the passengers could clearly see the dunes and the plodding, almost endless lines of captives on the coastal highway. The boat, which now was midway between Askalon and Gaza, moved leisurely. The passengers kept their eyes fixed on the shackled, ragged, sun-blackened men and women trudging wearily toward Gaza, where they would be auctioned off at the slave mart or sold to arenas. They had been seized in all parts of the country, but principally in Southern Judea; few came from Betar, for few had survived there.

So terrible had been the carnage in Betar, it was said, that the blood of the victims had flowed through the Valley of Tears, in the dry bed of the stream Akor, to the Dead Sea. The passengers in the boat knew that; they also knew that the object of their quest, Bar-Kokba, had tracelessly disappeared. Their gaze searched for a proud and unyielding figure among the broken fighting men and women, now reduced to the status of domestic animals. At the Gaza mart, it was reliably said, a slave now rated lower than a horse.

The overseers, bending from their saddles, urged the captives on with their whips. Meredya could not endure the sight. She leaned back and shut her eyes. Tears slowly trickled down her cheeks.

"Gone is the Star of my people," she lamented, "gone is the Star. He came down to earth in man's flesh to fight for the Law of Heaven and the redemption of his people, but the earth swallowed his flesh. For too many are the ravenous beasts that roam the earth, and too few the men who truly care for the ways of God. O Lord, O Lord! He and my people stood alone, fought alone, fell alone; and now the remnants, men of courage and lovers of Thy ways, are dragged to shame and slaughter even as lowly beasts. O Lord, O Lord! My lacerated people cries out to Thee. Wilt Thou not respond? Will not Thy Law, O Lord, ever truly rule the world? Will redemption never come?"